Praise for *An*

"This book will leave you chang
crets and draws you into the days
War and the Great Depression. It astound you how the characters persevere while making difficult decisions amidst heartache and their determination to make it through the toughest of hard times."

—*RT Book Reviews*

"*Angel Sister* paints an inspirational portrait of forgiveness and grace in the midst of trial and hardship. . . . It reveals how forgiveness brings freedom, not so much for the one forgiven as for the one doing the forgiving. Two major strengths to Ann Gabhart's writing include her deeply textured characters and rich atmosphere. She moves the plot forward by weaving the past with the present. . . . There are many levels to this deftly written novel."

—Crosswalk.com

Praise for *Small Town Girl*

"The characters of Ann Gabhart's *Small Town Girl* pulled me into their lives and did not let me go. This love story, painted upon the canvas of a small Kentucky town struggling with WWII, is one of the most riveting historical romances I've ever read."

—**Serena B. Miller**, winner of the 2012 RITA award
for Inspirational Romance

"Gabhart writes wonderful, fast-paced stories with faith-driven, hardworking protagonists who find time for love amidst mistakes, misunderstandings, and miscommunications."

—*RT Book Reviews*

"A classic. Ann Gabhart pens an enduring tale from the very first line of *Small Town Girl*. Rosey Corner is a world you won't want to leave, rife with spiritual truths, rich romance, and memorable characters that linger long after!"

—**Laura Frantz**, author of *The Colonel's Lady* and *Love's Reckoning*

Love Comes Home

Books by Ann Gabhart

The Outsider

The Believer

The Seeker

The Blessed

The Gifted

Words Spoken True

Angel Sister

Small Town Girl

Love Comes Home

Christmas at Harmony Hill

The Heart of Hollyhill

Scent of Lilacs

Orchard of Hope

Summer of Joy

Love Comes Home

A Novel

Ann H. Gabhart

Revell
a division of Baker Publishing Group
Grand Rapids, Michigan

Published by Revell
a division of Baker Publishing Group
P.O. Box 6287, Grand Rapids, MI 49516-6287
www.revellbooks.com

Printed in the United States of America

Library of Congress Cataloging-in-Publication Data
Gabhart, Ann H., 1947–
Love comes home : a novel / Ann H. Gabhart.
pages cm
ISBN 978-0-8007-2185-5 (pbk.)
I. Title.
PS3607.A23L68 2014
813′.6—dc23 2014007013

Scripture used in this book, whether quoted or paraphrased by the characters, is taken from the King James Version of the Bible.

This book is a work of fiction. Names, characters, places, and incidents are the product of the author's imagination or are used fictitiously. Any resemblance to actual events, locales, or persons, living or dead, is coincidental.

Published in association with the Books & Such Literary Agency.

14 15 16 17 18 19 20 7 6 5 4 3 2 1

To the Hawkins sisters
whose wonderful stories and laughter
made my Rosey Corner stories come to life

1

The news was good. The news was wonderful. Kate Tanner grabbed her notebook and headed out of the newspaper building to join the people spilling out onto the Lexington, Kentucky, streets. Tommy yelled that she could get a better view from the upstairs window, but she wasn't worried about the best view. This wasn't just the chance for another story. Her feet wanted to dance in the streets too.

The boys were coming home! Japan had surrendered. The bombs, the terrible bombs, had finished the fighting. The war was over.

The instant she stepped out on the sidewalk, a stranger grabbed her, lifted her off her feet, and spun her around. He was smiling. She was smiling. He said something when he turned her loose, but she had no idea what as church bells and horns drowned out his words. He laughed and slung his hat up in the air with no thought of retrieving it before he ran on up the street.

Everywhere people waved handkerchiefs and papers in the air. Kate joined in with her notebook. Sal from the restaurant across the street grabbed her in a bear hug and knocked her notebook out of her hand. It didn't matter. She didn't need to take notes. Every second of this scene would be burned in her memory forever. The shouts and laughter. The boys shimmying up the lampposts who wouldn't have to go to war now. The girls sparkling at the thought of their sweethearts coming home. Sparkling like Kate.

She felt the crackle of Jay's last letter in her pocket. His words played through her mind. *I love you. I'll be coming home to Rosey Corner soon unless I have to ship out to the Pacific. Nobody's sure what's going to happen there.*

But now he could be sure. They could all be sure.

He was in Germany. Not fighting anymore. Blessedly not fighting since the Allied forces rolled through Berlin in May. Hitler was dead and the Germans defeated. The prison camps had been liberated. Mike, her sister's husband, was free after two years in a German stalag. Praise the Lord neither he nor Jay would have to go to the Pacific. The only place they had to come now was home. Home to Rosey Corner, Kentucky.

Kate wished one of the happy people pushing past her was Evie. Her sister would surely be dancing in the streets in Louisville where she worked. It would be even better if they were both in Rosey Corner with their other sisters. Lorena would be singing, her beautiful voice calling Jay and Mike home. Tori would be celebrating too, or trying to. She'd be happy for Evie and Kate. She would. Sincerely happy, but tears would be under her smile. Not all the boys would be coming home. Tori's Sammy would not.

Sadness stabbed through Kate. How many other wives and mothers watched the celebration with sorrow in their hearts? Those like Tori who had taken down their Service flag to cover the blue star with a gold one, showing the terrible price of the war? She shook away the thought. This wasn't the time to weep for the dead. It was time to rejoice that the dying was over.

Two girls she knew from the dime store grabbed Kate's hands to pull her on up the street. Not to get anywhere, but just because if they didn't move, they might explode from the joy. The boys were coming home!

2

When Graham Lindell burst through the door of Merritt's Store in Rosey Corner, Victoria Harper whirled around from stocking the shelves to see what was wrong. He'd lost his hat and his gray hair was poking out in every direction. Chaucer, his mottled tan and gray shepherd, was right on his heels, barking like he was chasing a bear. Out front, Mr. Henderson blasted his horn even though Tori's mother was right beside his car, ready to pump his gas.

Tori's little girl, Samantha, let out a wail when Graham rushed past her without so much as a glance.

"What in the world, Graham? Did one of the Redlegs hit a grand slam?" Tori stepped out from behind the counter to pick up Samantha, but she wouldn't be placated. In all her two years, she'd never had Graham completely ignore her. He was her best buddy.

"Way better than that, Victoria." He grabbed Samantha out of Tori's arms and swung her around, changing her tears to giggles in an instant. "It just came over the radio. The Japanese surrendered. The war's over."

Tori stared at him while the words sank in. The war was over. Good news for sure, but not soon enough for her and Samantha. For her husband, Sammy. She leaned back against the counter and burst into tears.

Graham stopped in mid-spin, and Samantha stared at her mother and stuck her fingers in her mouth. "Aww, Victoria, I reckon it's hard for you to feel happy, what with Sammy dying over there in Japan." He patted her shoulder, awkward in the face of her tears. Chaucer stopped barking and pushed his nose up against her leg.

"I'm happy." Tori swallowed hard and wiped her face with her apron, but the tears wouldn't stop. "Happy tears." She managed a smile, glad nobody else was in the store to see her falling apart. She'd gotten better. She really had. She hadn't shed tears in front of anybody for months now.

"Of course they are." Graham gave her shoulder another clumsy pat.

"They are." Tori took Samantha back from Graham and gave him a little shove toward the door. "Go on with you. I know you're dying to tell the rest of Rosey Corner."

Graham's smile came back. "I done told your daddy. He's headed down to the church to ring the bell."

"Everybody will think there's a fire."

"Maybe so, but then we'll tell them the good news." Graham threw his hands up in the air and Chaucer let out another volley of barks. "Don't you know your sisters are happy up in their big towns? And where's that Lorena? We need to tell her."

Another horn began honking out on the road and then the church bell was tolling. Lorena raced through the door, a smile all the way across her face. She was as tall as Tori now but beanpole skinny. People who didn't know Lorena had been adopted into the family were always saying how much she looked like Tori. It was their black hair, although Tori's was straight and Lorena's exploded in curls. Other than that, they didn't look much alike. Tori's eyes were green and Lorena's brown as buckeyes. Tori knew she wasn't hard to look at, but even in the midst of the awkwardness of being fourteen, Lorena could make people stop for a second look. She was that striking, especially when she was as happy as she was this moment.

She threw her arms around Tori and Samantha in a hug that had Samantha smiling again. Then Lorena grabbed both of Graham's hands and pulled him in a circle like a kid playing ring around the rosie. Chaucer danced around them, his tongue spilling out the side of his mouth in a goofy dog grin. Scout, Lorena's dog, jumped up on the screen door and whined in protest at being left outside with that other dog inside.

More horns started blowing and the church bell kept ringing. Tori could imagine her father's smile as he pulled the bell rope. He hated the war. Every bit of bad news from the battlefronts had weighed him down. In the spring, he'd caught a cold that lingered, and now here in August he still had a wheezy cough. Aunt Hattie blamed it on the mustard gas in the Great War, the one Daddy fought in before Tori was born and that people claimed would end all wars. They had been wrong about that. Very wrong.

"I wish Kate was here. And Evie. Don't you, Tori?" Lorena reached back to grab Tori's hand. "Come on. You have to dance with us. You have to be happy for them." Her smile lit up the store. "For me. For all of us."

Tori was glad she'd swallowed down her tears. Their traces

might still be on her cheeks and show in her red-rimmed eyes, but she wasn't weeping now. She was happy for Kate and Evie. Their husbands would come home to them. Maybe Kate would quit her job at the newspaper and come back to work here at the store.

That would suit Tori. She'd rather wave away sweat bees out in the garden picking beans than work at the store. But when Kate moved to Lexington, their mother needed help and Tori needed a job. Some days, though, Tori wanted to be sitting alone on the bank of Graham's pond watching her cork bob in the water. That wasn't exactly true. She didn't want to be alone. She wanted Sammy there beside her.

She pushed away the thought to keep the tears from leaking out again. She could keep smiling, especially with Samantha laughing out loud when Graham bumped against one of the loafer's chairs against the wall. Making a silly face at the little girl, he plopped down in the chair. Chaucer jumped up to lick him.

"He's no Poe," Graham groused, but he didn't push the dog away. Since Poe, his old hound, had died and he'd taken in the stray shepherd, he said that a lot. So much that they'd all started saying it when something didn't quite measure up to what they wanted. *It's no Poe.*

But this news did measure up. Definitely wonderful. Now Kate and Evie would have the chance to be mothers like her. Tori pulled loose from Lorena to hug Samantha closer.

She might be a widow at nineteen, but she had Samantha. She had her mother and father. She had her sisters. And her brothers-in-law were coming home. For that she could keep her smile bright and not let tears pop out again. At least not until tonight when she was alone in her bed.

When Mama opened the door, Scout slipped past her to add to the craziness. But Mama just laughed and kept laughing even when his long tail knocked some cracker boxes off the shelf. Tori set Samantha down beside Graham to grab the crackers before Scout got them. Scout would eat anything, wrapped or unwrapped.

"It'll be good to have the store stocked again." Tori's mother looked around at the scarcity of cans on the shelves. "Mr. Henderson out there thinks they'll lift the gasoline rationing right away."

"It wasn't gasoline in short supply anyway." Graham pushed Chaucer out of his lap but didn't stand up. "The government didn't want folks wearing out their tires. Not a bother for me. Never had no use for a car. Shoe leather works fine, and if your shoes wear out, you just figure a way to keep on wearing them." He held his foot up to show the hog rings holding the upper part of his shoe to the soles.

"You should have let Victor resole those for you." Victoria's mother shook her head at Graham, but she was smiling. "That's one reason he started working on shoes. So people wouldn't have to buy new ones and maybe rob a soldier of boots he needed."

"He remembered the foot rot in the Great War."

"Yes, yes he did." A frown flickered across Mama's face, but then her smile came back. "Just listen to him ring that bell. You can tell it's good news, can't you? No slow, sorrowful tolling."

"He's yanking that bell rope hard," Graham agreed. "Giving it some joy, for a truth."

As Mama tilted her head toward the sound of the bell, a shadow of concern crossed her face. "Victoria, you better go down there and see about your daddy. Make sure he's not overdoing it."

Mama always knew when Tori needed a few minutes alone. Tori reached for Samantha, but she had crawled over into Graham's lap and was petting Chaucer's nose. She didn't want to give up that treasured spot.

"Leave her," her mother said. "We'll watch her."

"Scout and I can go see about Daddy," Lorena volunteered. She had Scout's collar to keep him from knocking over anything else.

"No. You need to take Mrs. Jenkins her groceries. You'd better go on now. She might have heard the bell and be worried."

"Okay. I'll let her know the war's over," Lorena said. "She'll be happy. Maybe she'll tell me a story."

"You're the only person in Rosey Corner who knows what she's talking about," Tori said. Miss Jenkins was hard of hearing and was always thinking people said something different than what they actually said.

"I never know either. We just make it up as we go. As long as she's smiling, and she'll be smiling if I take her a few of those cinnamon candies." Lorena eyed the jar of candies on the counter. "They're her favorite."

"Not to mention yours." Mama's smile returned as she scooped a few pieces out of the jar into a paper bag. Then she put some in another bag for Tori. "In case all that rope pulling has brought on your father's cough. These sometimes help him."

"I won't be long," Tori said.

"Take your time," her mother said.

"No reason to hurry." Graham settled deeper in the chair with Samantha.

"No hurry," Samantha echoed his words.

She was talking more and more. Tori had to fight the urge to write every new word down the way she had all Samantha's firsts to save for Sammy before she got the telegram. *Missing in action. His ship torpedoed.* When the confirmation came that Sammy was in a Japanese prison camp, she'd thought that was good. He was alive. She prayed and prayed. He was tough. He'd make it. Mike was in a prison camp too in Germany. God would take care of them. He had to. But he hadn't. At least not Sammy.

Tears gathered again behind her eyes, and she turned toward the door before anybody could notice.

The August sun beat down so hot the asphalt was sticky underfoot. Scout started to follow her, but when Lorena came out with Mrs. Jenkins's groceries, he ran back to her. He was Lorena's dog, but that didn't keep Tori from feeling even more alone in the midst of the jubilation.

A man blew his horn and waved as his car passed her. Smiling. Happy. She had no idea who he was. Some women were out in their yards talking about the news, but not Mrs. Burgin. She stayed inside, peering out the window where a gold star hung for her son killed at Normandy. For a second, Tori considered calling out to her. But what could she say? Nothing that hadn't already been said a thousand times. Words couldn't bring her son home.

Out in front of the new mechanic's shop, a group of men shouted back and forth to one another to be heard over the clanging church bell. Clay Weber spotted Tori and peeled away from the others. And where a moment before she'd felt too alone after Scout deserted her, now she wanted to be alone.

It wasn't that she didn't like Clay. He was a nice enough

fellow. He and Sammy had been friends in school, but Clay had to drop out after his father died suddenly. His mother needed him to work the farm and keep food on the table for his younger sisters and brothers. Mrs. Weber was always saying how blessed she was to have such a good son. As it turned out, the farm kept Clay out of the army. He tried to enlist, but the government said his patriotic duty was to keep milking cows and raising corn. The country had to eat.

Tori wished Sammy had been a farmer.

She didn't slow her step, but Clay caught up with her easy enough.

"Need a lift somewhere, Victoria? My truck's just over there." He looked hopeful as he pointed back toward Henson's Garage. His broad hands were tan from hours in the sun.

"I can walk. It's not far." Tori kept her eyes on the road in front of her. "You can go on back and talk with the men."

"I'd rather talk to you."

She looked up at him. He had to be at least a half foot taller than her, and his blue cotton work shirt was stretched tight over his broad shoulders and muscular arms. A straw hat shaded his face, but it didn't hide the red spreading across his high cheekbones. She didn't know why he wasn't already married or at least promised. If only he was, so he wouldn't keep showing up in her shadow. He had to know she couldn't look at any man without seeing Sammy. It didn't matter that it had been almost a year since she'd gotten that final telegram. She and Sammy were supposed to be forever.

Tori blinked away the tears poking at her eyes and managed a polite smile. "I'm kind of in a hurry, but maybe we can talk some other time."

"I'd like that." Clay wasn't a man to give up easy. "How

about Sunday after church? I promised my little sisters we'd make ice cream. Mama's been saving our sugar rations." A bead of sweat ran down toward his eyebrow, but he paid it no notice. He looked completely too hopeful as he waited for her answer. His dark blue eyes made Tori remember lighter blue ones that had looked at her with that same kind of hope. Sammy's eyes.

She turned back toward the church and felt a wriggle of discomfort as she dashed his hope. "I'm sorry, but my sisters come home on Sundays and what with this news, I wouldn't want to miss seeing them."

"We could make the ice cream at your house."

She felt his eyes on her, but she didn't look at him. "No, no. That wouldn't be right. Your little sisters are looking forward to the ice cream."

"I guess you're right." Disappointment laced his words. "Maybe another time then." The hope was back in his voice.

She should stop and tell him straight out that no time was going to be right. Dash his hopes once and for all. But instead she kept walking. She wasn't sure if it was cowardice or niceness that stopped her words. She didn't want to hurt him. Wasn't she hurting enough for all of Rosey Corner?

Behind them more horns sounded as another car pulled in to Henson's Garage. When Clay glanced back that way, Tori made a graceful exit.

"It is great news." She made it sound as if she meant it. She did mean it. She looked back at the garage. "Look, there's Mr. Jamison. Will you tell him I'm glad his sons will be coming home from the Navy? I'd tell him myself, but Mother asked me to go down to the church and make sure Daddy's okay. He's been ringing the bell a long time."

"I could come help him."

"No." The word came out sharper than she intended, so she softened it a bit. "No, the bell's rung long enough already. Go talk to your friends."

"I am. Talking to a friend." He was like a dog shaking a stick. He just wouldn't give it up. "At least I hope we're friends."

Sometimes a girl had to be plain. "Sure, Clay, but I can't talk now."

"Another time then?" he asked again.

She was the one who gave in. "Another time." She started walking faster, leaving him on the road. She wished she could run the way she used to as a kid. Why was it that mothers weren't supposed to run? Her legs weren't old. Only her heart.

Her father had stopped ringing the bell by the time she got there. He was pale, his shirt soaked with sweat, but he was smiling as he came down the church steps. When he saw her face, his smile turned tender and he held his arms out to her. "Sometimes tears happen in the middle of the happiest moments."

3

The waiting was the hard part. The war was over. In Europe for months. In the Pacific for weeks. Over and finished. Yet here he was still in Germany with his gun slung over his shoulder, as natural and necessary as the boots on his feet. Still far from Rosey Corner. Far from Kate.

Jay Tanner sat on a pile of rubble that used to be a building. Maybe a house where people lived and were happy before war stole all that was normal from them.

Normal. After three years of killing, could there even be normal anymore? He wanted normal. The German citizens in this town wanted normal. The townspeople even now were trying to recapture normal by going about their business while they kept wary eyes on the soldiers.

From up on his post, he watched the people on the street, his camera in his hands, but he didn't lift it to look through the viewfinder. He only had a couple more shots left. A sick tremble went through him at the memory of the images captured on that film.

He pulled in a long breath and forced his thoughts away from the horror of the death camps. Instead, he fastened his eyes on an old man coming up the road toward him. The man stopped now and again to dig in the debris with his cane. He bent slowly and picked up something to drop down in the gunnysack he carried. Three women came out of a house that had escaped the shelling and walked past the old man. Their words of greeting drifted back to Jay. He still didn't know what the words meant, but they no longer sounded so strange.

The women moved on down the road with purpose in their steps. Perhaps to find food for their families. Here and there, children scrambled over the ruins of the buildings with no thought of how the town had looked before the bombs and mortar rounds smashed their country into submission.

Some of the younger ones wouldn't remember a time when there weren't bombs. A time when people didn't disappear in the night never to be seen again. Some of the last-stand soldiers in Berlin had looked almost as young as the kids playing in the street now. One terrified boy admitted to being barely fourteen. Fourteen. Jay's gun was pointed at the boy's chest when he gave his age. Relief swept through Jay yet again that he had held his fire. Shooting a child soldier would have done nothing except add one more nightmare to those already crowding his memories.

The old German shuffled a little nearer and slid his eyes over Jay as though he were no more interesting than a lamppost. The man didn't speak or smile, but he didn't shake his cane and curse Jay either. Jay wondered if the old man and the women walking down the road might not be as relieved as Jay to have the conflict over.

The townspeople here didn't look all that different from the folks back in Rosey Corner. Yet, the death camps were in their very backyards. They had to know their Jewish neighbors were disappearing. But then, they also knew those who went against the Nazis were taken out in the city square and shot. Or so one of the older German soldiers told Jay's sergeant after he eagerly surrendered to the Allied forces. He never wanted war. He never wanted Hitler, but uttering those words brought death to one's door.

Whether they knew what was happening during the war or not, the German people were being made to face the truth now. In the cities closest to the death camps, the citizens were forced to watch movie reels of what the Allied soldiers found when they liberated the camps. Images the same as Jay had taken for the Army. The sight of those starving men and women and the bodies pitched aside like so much refuse were burned into his memory. Some things once seen could never be forgotten.

"And you shouldn't forget them," his sergeant had told him. Sarge believed in God. He prayed. He told Jay that a man needed to keep in touch with his Lord.

Some of the men in the unit made fun of Sarge, but not Jay. He'd found the Lord in the Army and had been glad to have him marching alongside him ever since. The doubters said he was crazy to believe that. They liked to point out how this or that soldier had bought the farm with a Bible in his pocket and a prayer on his lips. Jay let their doubts slide off him. It was war. People died. But the death camps were different. Seeing that had Jay doubting everything.

The night before, Jay had given up on sleeping and gone outside to find Sergeant Crane leaned against the building with his Bible open in his lap.

Jay dropped down on the ground beside him. "Can you see to read?"

"Don't need to see to know what's there." Sarge smoothed down the Bible page.

"Do you think all the answers are there?"

Sarge glanced over at him. "What answers you looking for?"

Jay hesitated, worried Sarge wouldn't like his question.

"Spit it out, Tanner."

It seemed like a command, so Jay asked the question circling in his head. "Why did God allow evil like that? Like those camps."

"Man always wants to know why." Sarge scrubbed his hand across his day-old beard. "But evil's been in the world since Adam and Eve were thrown out of the garden. It's the way things are."

"He could stop it." Jay looked up at the stars, bright in the dark night. The same stars Kate might be looking at back home in Rosey Corner. What would she tell him about God and this? Then he knew he would never share the grisly scenes of the death camps with Kate. No need shoving those horrors into her mind. But Sarge had seen it too. He knew.

"He did," Sarge said after a long minute.

"He did what?" Jay looked over at him, but now Sarge was staring up at the night sky.

"Stop it. He used us and a few million others to stop it."

"And a few million died before we got it done."

"They did." Sarge turned his head toward Jay, his eyes glittering in the dark. "So they most certainly did." Then he breathed out a sigh and looked down. "Nothing I've found in my Bible says life here is meant to be easy. It's the next life where easy is the assignment. We did what had to be done down here."

That didn't exactly answer Jay's question, but he didn't ask more. Silence had fallen over them as they stared out into the night.

Now here in the broad daylight while keeping watch over the conquered town, he let his thoughts slide to Kate. His beautiful Kate. They'd gotten married in a rush with only a couple of months together before he boarded the ship for Europe. That was over three years ago. A lifetime in more ways than one. There'd been letters. Hers were full of love and happenings at home. His were stilted and short in comparison, but he couldn't write about where he was or what he was doing. Even with the fighting over, there were things he couldn't write. Things too horrible to put into words.

Jay glanced at the sun and stood up. He needed to get back to his unit. His sudden movement startled the old man. Jay waved to let him know he had no need to worry, but the man just kept staring at him. Without conscious thought, Jay pulled up his camera to take the old German's picture with the ruins of his town behind him.

As Jay turned the knob to advance the film, the man muttered something and started picking through the rubble again.

Jay dropped the camera into its case, brushed his black hair back from his forehead, and settled his helmet on his head again. The thing was hot, but a man had to protect his head.

He used to think a man had to protect his heart. That was before Kate and Rosey Corner. Before the Lord had finally got his attention. That could be because of Kate too. Kate with her sure faith nourished by the enduring faith of those around her. Aunt Hattie who could pray down miracles. Kate's mother who gently held them all together with her love and prayers. Mike preaching the gospel with never a trace of doubt. Lorena Birdsong's innocent trust. He smiled thinking about how he'd nicknamed Lorena "Birdie" when she first told him her name.

Birdie wrote him almost as often as Kate. Letters full of hometown news. She'd written when Poe, Graham's old dog, died. Some of the ink was smudged by her tears. Jay had touched those spots while tears welled up in his own eyes.

Wars could do funny things to a man. Harden him so much he didn't feel anything when guns started firing and men beside him fell. Then a letter came about an old dog dying and tears stabbed his eyes. It wasn't that he didn't feel sorrow for the men who fell, but a soldier had to keep marching. Keep firing. Defend his square of ground and push forward into the next square.

Sometimes nothing but dumb luck kept one man on his feet and sent another on to his eternal reward. Like poor Artie Bixler. Jay ran his fingers over the camera case that bounced against his chest as he headed back to camp. Artie, the unit's photographer, switched places with Jay on a German street because he wanted a better angle on his shot. Two minutes later, a sniper's bullet hit Artie in the head. He fell, cradling the camera, even as he died. So Jay had picked up Artie's camera and taken his place, seeing the war through the lens of the camera.

That was war. A matter of inches. A man stepped on a mine or didn't. He was in the way of shrapnel or dived into a foxhole before it hit. Many times Jay had been next door to death, but here he was, still breathing as he walked through the rubble of Germany with his mind on home.

Home. After his mother died when he was a kid, no place had felt like home until he got to Rosey Corner and met Kate Merritt. Kate Tanner now.

It seemed like a lifetime ago he'd kissed her goodbye and climbed the gangplank to go to war. In a matter of weeks, he would climb another gangplank to leave war behind. He could hardly wait. But under the eagerness to be back in Kate's arms, to have the welcome of her family at Rosey Corner, was a quiver of worry. He loved Kate. She loved him. But what did either of them know about being married? About being a family and raising kids? Kate wanted kids. She'd been disappointed she didn't get in the family way before he went overseas.

Her little sister had beat her on that. Tori had a baby eight months after her husband shipped out. Then Sammy had checked out for good in a Japanese prison camp.

The poor kid. Barely nineteen. So young it hurt to look at him. Like dozens of others Jay had met since then. Boys holding the fate of the world in their hands. Kids flying bombers. Jumping out of airplanes behind enemy lines. Charging pillboxes. Starving in prison camps. Dying to win the war.

Now the war was won. Those like Jay who'd made it through just had to wait for a spot on a ship to take them home. Home. Jay looked out past the buildings to the trees on the horizon that had survived the bombs. Trees much like those in Rosey Corner. Could that place possibly be as beautiful as he remembered? Soon now he'd walk back up that road. Kate would hold on to his arm. Birdie would run out for a hug. Mrs. Merritt would bake him a brown sugar pie. Maybe it could all be as good as he remembered.

4

Mike made it home first. The end of October. A much thinner Mike. His brown hair streaked with gray. Deep creases around his mouth and eyes that had nothing to do with smiles.

But he was smiling now. Very glad to be back in Evie's arms. Kate drove to Louisville to take Evie to meet the train. Evie had refused to let Kate teach her how to drive. Instead if Kate mentioned driving, Evie informed her that riding the bus supported the war effort. Evie had a way of turning on the guilt faucet, but Kate kept saving up her gas rations. A newspaper reporter needed a way to follow a story.

Taking her sister to meet her husband at the train station had "story" written all over it. Whether she ever wrote it or not. When Mike grabbed Evie in an embrace, Kate stepped back to give them some privacy. Happy reunions were happening all around her. Soon Jay would be the one climbing down from that train. Her heart skipped a few beats at the thought of his arms around her again. It had been so long that sometimes she wasn't sure if she remembered real embraces or only those in her dreams.

Mike got home on a Monday. Evie took a week off work for them to get caught up. On everything, she said with a blush. Tuesday afternoon she called Kate at the newspaper office to ask her to drive them to Rosey Corner on Wednesday. Mike was restless. The late October days were wasted in the city. He wanted to see the rest of the family. Kate heard the edge under Evie's words, so she dared her editor's ire by asking for another day off.

"I can't believe this old heap is still running," Mike said when she showed up at Evie's apartment. He'd hardly noticed the car on Monday. His eyes had been too full of Evie.

"It's got a few miles on it for sure." Kate ran her hand down the rusty gray fender. "But it gets me where I need to go."

"Jay will want a new one when he gets home," Mike said.

"Maybe," Kate said. "The guys at work think there'll be a rush on new cars. That they're sure to sell lots of car dealer ads."

"Everybody wants new everything," Evie put in. "We've had to do without so long. It's wonderful having silk stockings again." Evie lifted the hem of her skirt to admire her stockings.

"Yes, indeed." Mike eyed her legs a minute, then looked back at the car. "Can I drive? I haven't been behind the wheel since the Germans captured me."

Kate handed him the key and crawled in the backseat. She'd hoped they could talk on the long drive to Rosey Corner. She had a million questions about the war, but once out on the open road, Mike rolled down his window and asked Evie to do the same. He must have forgotten how Evie hated her hair blowing in her face. Kate expected her to tell him that, but instead she cranked down the window without a word.

The wind whipping through the windows made talking all but impossible. Mike didn't seem to care as he mashed down on the accelerator. Kate grabbed the armrest on the door and bit her lip to keep from telling him to slow down. They made it to Rosey Corner in record time.

When they pulled into the yard, Tori came out the door with Samantha riding on her hip. Kate blew out a breath of relief when she saw Tori smiling. Ever since Sammy died, Tori dissolved into tears over everything. She had a right, but Kate hadn't wanted tears to spoil Mike's homecoming. Kate's relief was short-lived. Instead of Tori breaking down, Mike climbed up the porch steps, took one look at Samantha, and tears started coursing down his cheeks.

Kate had never seen Mike cry, but his tears shouldn't have surprised her. Samantha, with her daddy's red hair and freckles, had to make Mike remember Sammy, a kid he watched grow up in the church. It didn't matter that Sammy had been gone over a year now. For Mike, it had to be like just showing up at the funeral.

Beside Mike, Evie looked bewildered, with tears brimming in her eyes too, whether for Sammy or Mike or herself, Kate couldn't be sure. Tears came easy to Evie. And to Tori too. But then Tori did the unexpected. She didn't cry as she handed Samantha to Mike. The child had seen so many tears in her two years that she wasn't a bit bothered by Mike's. She was more interested in the shiny buttons on his jacket.

"Button." She touched the button and flashed such a smile at Mike that he laughed.

He held Samantha closer. "Yes, indeed. Button." He rubbed his cheeks on his shoulders to wipe away his tears. "I can see you've inherited the Merritt girls' charm."

"Mike!" Lorena's long legs flashed as she raced across the yard, home from school, and practically leaped up the porch steps.

He stared at her. "Lorena?"

Kate had to smile at the look on his face. Lorena wasn't the little girl he'd last seen. Kate couldn't wait until Jay got home to see how his little "sister" had grown up. She'd sent him pictures, but pictures didn't do Lorena justice.

"Lonie." Samantha held her hands out toward Lorena.

Lorena's smile slid off her face as she took Samantha. "What's the matter? Why are you crying? Has somebody else died?" She looked from Mike to Kate. "I don't want anybody else to die."

"A man can shed a few tears when he comes home and meets his niece for the first time, can't he?" Mike swiped the last of his tears off his cheeks. "If you really are Lorena Birdsong, come here and give me a hug."

"It's me." Lorena's smile exploded back across her face. She handed Samantha to Tori and threw her arms around Mike. "Maybe I should ask if it's really you, Mike Champion."

"In the flesh." Mike pushed Lorena back to look her up and down. No tears now. "I can't believe how tall you are." He glanced around at the others. "I can believe how good it feels to be here on this front porch surrounded by you beautiful Merritt women." He reached for Evie's hand.

They were turning to go inside when Kate's mother and father came down the road, big smiles on their faces. Mama claimed she couldn't wait a minute longer to see if Mike was home. Some things were more important than selling another loaf of bread or gallon of gasoline. More hugs all around. More smiles. A long hand clasp with Daddy and a look exchanged that said more than words could.

The news that Mike was home swept through Rosey Corner and people started showing up to see him. Since the day was sunny, Mike stayed out on the porch to greet them. Graham came down with his new dog. Aunt Gertie and Uncle Wyatt drove down in their car.

Fern showed up without Aunt Hattie, whose rheumatism was acting up. Her steel gray hair, in desperate need of a comb, bushed out around her face, and she wore a man's faded flannel shirt under her bib overalls. While Fern's harsh edges had softened a bit the last few years, she still preferred the company of trees over people any day. So she wouldn't come up on the porch but said what she came to say from out in the yard. "Hattie prayed you home."

"I counted on her prayers. Thank her for me." Mike stepped over to the edge of the porch. "It's good to see you, Fern. You haven't changed a bit."

"Some changes don't show on the outside." Fern narrowed her eyes as she stared up at Mike. "But you know that."

Mike looked so somber Kate worried he might cry again. Evie reached toward his arm as though to pull him back from the edge of the porch. Back from Fern. But she let her hand hover in the air and didn't touch him.

"I do know," he said.

"Hattie will pray some more."

"Good. Aunt Hattie can pray down the power."

"Couldn't pray everybody home." Fern slid her eyes over to Tori, then turned without another word to leave.

A strange silence fell over the porch until Lorena rushed out of the house and down the steps after Fern. "Wait, Fern."

Fern stopped in a patch of sunlight halfway across the yard to let Lorena catch up with her. Kate wished for her camera, even though the picture wouldn't be one for the newspaper. But the sight of Lorena hugging Fern with the abandon of a child would have been worth the cost of the film. That Fern stepped into Lorena's embrace was one of those changes that couldn't be seen. For years, Fern hadn't bothered to love anybody until Lorena found a place in her heart. And Aunt Hattie prayed for her.

The odd feeling that Mike might want to follow Fern and head off by himself to get away from too much too soon disappeared as Fern went on out to the road. Lorena ran back up on the porch to let Kate know Mama needed help in the kitchen.

"You know Mama." Lorena made a face. "She has to feed everybody who shows up on our doorstep."

Evie stayed beside Mike on the swing until the deacons let out prayer meeting and showed up in force to welcome their former pastor home. In the kitchen, Evie watched impatiently as they fixed drinks for the men. The minute Lorena and Mama picked up the glasses to carry out to the porch, Evie grabbed Kate's arm and yanked her out the back door.

But once they were outside, Evie just stared at the chicken house at the end of the yard and didn't say anything. The sun had gone down and daylight was fading. Kate needed to start back to Lexington soon. She hoped Evie and Mike intended to stay the night in Rosey Corner, but that moment didn't seem the best time to ask their plans. Her sister was either about to blow up or break down in tears.

Whichever it was, better to get it over with. "Since I don't think you pulled me out here to see if the chickens had gone to roost, out with it before you explode."

Evie blew out an angry huff. "They're just out there taking turns praying. If we wanted to go to prayer meeting, we'd have gone up to the church."

"Those men have said a lot of prayers for Mike while he's been gone." Kate picked her words carefully, not sure why Evie was upset.

"Well, haven't we all?" Evie sounded ready to fly apart.

"Yes, of course we have, and now we're thankful those prayers were answered."

"I know." Evie shut her eyes and clamped her jaws together.

"They just want to see him with their own eyes. That's all. To know he's okay."

"That's all I want to know too." Evie's mouth trembled and a tear slid down her cheek.

Kate put her arm around Evie. "What's wrong, Evie?" She didn't know how Evie could be unhappy two days after Mike came home, but she obviously was.

More tears spilled out of her eyes as she looked at Kate. "He's not the same."

Kate fished her handkerchief out of her pocket. "Mama warned you to expect that. He's been through things we can't even imagine. The same as Daddy did when he was in the war."

"But Mike's not like Daddy." Evie snatched the handkerchief, but didn't put it to any good use. She stared at Kate. "Is he?"

"I don't think he'll turn to drink, if that's what you mean." Kate couldn't quite keep the irritation out of her voice.

Evie didn't notice. She looked a little like an abandoned

puppy. So Kate pulled in a breath and summoned up patience. "He'll be back to the guy you remember soon." With the tips of her fingers, she brushed away Evie's tears.

"How do you know?" Evie jerked away from her and gave her nose an angry swipe with the handkerchief. "How could you know? You don't know how it is."

"You're right. I don't. Jay's not home yet, but he will be soon. And he could be changed too."

"It won't be the same for you the way it is for me and Mike. You barely knew Jay before you married him. I doubt if you'll be able to tell if he's changed or not. But Mike . . ." Her voice trailed off.

Kate drew in another breath to stay calm. Evie was just being Evie who thought the world revolved around her. Besides, she could be right. Kate and Jay had only known each other a few months before they married and some of those months were pretty rocky. Nothing at all like Mike and Evie, who had dated for years with Mike doting on Evie the whole time.

Evie had no clue she'd said anything that might upset Kate as she went on. "Well, you know what I mean."

"No, I'm not sure I do."

Evie gave her a look as if she couldn't believe that. "You saw him crying."

"Men cry sometimes."

"But Mike's a preacher. He's not supposed to get all blue and depressed. Not once he's back home with me." Tears started down her cheeks again. "It wasn't supposed to be this way."

Kate didn't know whether to hug her or slap her. She settled for grabbing Evie's shoulders and giving her a little shake.

"You stop all this crying. Mike's home. He's the Mike you love. The Mike who loves you. That hasn't changed. Not one little bit. His homecoming might not be the fairy tale you were imagining, but it's good and it will get better every day."

Evie choked back her tears. "How do you know, Kate?"

"Because you are going to make it better. You are going to be sweet and understanding and loving."

"He says he doesn't know if he can preach again. That he doesn't know what the Lord wants him to do next." Evie wiped the tears off her cheeks, but her eyes were even more distraught. "What if he decides to be a missionary or something? I can't go to Africa, Kate. I can't."

"Good heavens, Evie. You sound like me, thinking up such crazy things."

"It's not crazy. God calls people to be missionaries all the time."

"Did Mike tell you God wants him to go into the mission field?" Kate asked.

"No, but what if he does?"

Kate shook her head at Evie. "Then you'll figure out something with the Lord's help. But maybe the Lord is just calling him to be a bus driver or something."

"A bus driver?" Evie's forehead wrinkled in a frown. "Whatever are you talking about?"

"Might be a good place to reach people. You have to admit, he had a great time driving us here."

Evie put her hand up to her head. "Absolutely ruined my hair." But the corners of her mouth twitched up.

"It just released the curls. You look great. You always look great." Kate put her arm around Evie. "Now, drag that smile back across your face. Mike will be missing you."

And he was. When they went back inside, Mike was in the kitchen, looking for Evie. "There's my girl."

Those words were no different than he might have said before the war, but Evie was right. Mike was different. They all were. Fern had told them. Some changes didn't show, but they were there all the same.

5

The week after Mike got home was filled with the kind of October days that were a gift to someone who liked to fish. On Thursday, Tori begged a day off from the store, packed a picnic, grabbed her pole, and headed to Graham's pond with Samantha. After Samantha wore herself out chasing butterflies, she fell asleep on a blanket in the shade. Tori could hear her soft breathing, a sound her mother's ear continually noted. And needed.

While her cork drifted undisturbed on the sparkling water, Tori raised her face toward the sun. Her skin didn't tan easily, but neither did it freckle. Samantha's would. She was that much like Sammy. Tori used to try to count the freckles across his nose and cheeks, but he couldn't sit still that long. She turned her mind away from that memory before tears spoiled the day. Better to think about Mike being home instead.

She hadn't expected Mike to cry, but who knew what to expect after a war? Tori hoped he could feel the sun in Louisville, but the narrow backyard of the house where Evie had an upstairs apartment was a drab place that wouldn't even grow crabgrass. The houses, piled in close together, blocked the sun. Evie said the yard didn't matter if the inside shined.

She did have a nice place with showroom furniture and color-coordinated pillows and drapes. Closed drapes, since in the city one couldn't leave windows uncovered for people to peep through. When Kate pointed out she was on the second floor, Evie bristled and reminded Kate there were such things as ladders. Sometimes, when those two were together, all Tori could do was stay back out of the way.

Kate's tiny apartment in Lexington above one of the downtown stores spilled right out on the street. No yard at all. Kate wasn't worried about how things looked outside or inside. A brick replaced the broken leg on her couch and a wobbly card table served as a place to grab her meals. She had salvaged a desk from the trash heap behind the newspaper building and put it back together with screws and glue.

That's all she needed, she told Tori. "It's not like I'm going to have a party or anything. I couldn't anyway. Not with only two plates and three glasses."

A dime store was right down the street where Kate could buy more dishes, but she said she'd buy things when Jay got home and they found a place to live. *When Jay gets home.* Kate was always saying that as though she needed the words in her ears to believe it.

Tori understood. She'd said the same. When Sammy gets home. And now he wasn't coming home. Sorrow pressed down on her so heavy she didn't even try to hook the fish when her cork bobbed.

"That might've been a whale." Graham came out of the trees. When he saw Samantha asleep, he snapped his fingers to keep Chaucer next to him as he settled down on the pond bank beside Tori.

"You need to teach me that trick for Samantha."

"Dog tricks and kid tricks might be some different." He stroked Chaucer's head and the dog's tail brushed back and forth on the ground. "This one's learned a few things, but he's no Poe."

Tori smiled and looked over her shoulder at Samantha, who hadn't so much as moved a toe. Tori stared back out at her cork. Her worm was probably gone, but she didn't pull in her line. "I'm surprised Chaucer doesn't growl whenever he hears you say Poe."

"No, no. He knows he's no Poe. Poor Chaucer here doesn't know the difference between a raccoon and a squirrel. Ready to chase anything that crosses his path." The dog lowered his ears and dropped his head down on his paws as though embarrassed by Graham's words.

"Do you miss hunting raccoons?"

"Some." Graham looked up at the clear sky. "On a night like this one's going to be, it's a fine thing to be out in the woods with a good dog to sniff out trails and tree a few coons."

"You could get another coonhound."

"I could." Graham plucked a grass stem. "But he wouldn't be no Poe either."

"I guess you're right. Some things can't be replaced." To keep from thinking about what she couldn't replace, she asked, "Where's your fishing pole?"

"You haven't been over here at the pond for a while, so I figured I'd give you first crack at the fish today." Graham leaned back on his elbows. "Besides, this old sun is making me too lazy to fish."

"Sammy used to say that." Tori kept her eyes on her cork. She was surprised when a smile lifted up her lips and no tears raced to her eyes at the memory. "But he wasn't really lazy. Just bored with not catching anything. Then he'd be throwing rocks in the water or making grass blades whistle." *Or kissing my neck*, she added silently.

"The boy had a surplus of energy. That's for sure."

"I miss him so much." Tori sighed.

"You're supposed to. That's the natural thing." Graham looked out at her line. "You'd best pull that in before it gets hung up over in that moss."

Tori reeled in her line. She was right. No worm. She dug through the dirt in her can for another one. "This is why Kate hates fishing. Worms."

"She don't have any fondness for them. That's for sure. Even Lorena can't change her thinking on that."

Tori cast her line back out in the pond. Silence fell over them as they watched the cork. The sun seemed to be dissolving her bones and it felt fine.

"It was good seeing Preacher Mike last week," Graham said after a while. "I thought maybe they'd be back Sunday what with Lorena singing at church. The girl was some disappointed."

"I know, but Evie had reservations at a fancy hotel. To celebrate Mike being home. You know Evie." Tori watched the soft ripples slide across the pond. "She likes things going according to plans. Her plans."

"Evangeline does like keeping her ducks in a row." Graham plucked another grass stem.

"Mike's not a duck." Tori glanced over at Graham.

"No, course not." Graham studied his grass stem. "But he's always wanted Evangeline to be happy."

"He joined the Army. That didn't make her happy." Tori checked her line. Still not the first tug on her hook. The one she let get away might be her only bite. "Actually she didn't seem all that happy last week when she came home."

"So you think she might have a happiness problem." Graham stuck the stem in his mouth.

"Kate says Evie was worried about Mike being restless when she thought he should be happy at home with her."

"Sounds like happiness problems going around. But could be Mike just needed to see some Rosey Corner trees." Graham spit out a piece of the grass. "That car Wyatt found for him should help. The boy looked happy as a kid at Christmastime when they took off for Louisville Thursday."

"I'm thinking about getting a car." She kept her eyes on the pond.

"Are you now?"

"Kate says she'll teach me to drive after Jay gets home. She thinks she'll have more time then."

"She quitting at the paper?" Graham sounded surprised.

"Sort of. Two of the men who worked there are due back from the Army. Kate's pretty sure they'll give her job to one of them. She's hoping to work until Christmas."

Christmas. Tori hoped she could dig up some Christmas spirit for Samantha this year. Last year every bit of her joy had been smothered from knowing Sammy would never be with her at Christmas again.

"She won't like giving up that camera, but it'll be good to have her back home in Rosey Corner."

"It won't be the same." She glanced over at him almost as if hoping he'd tell her she was wrong.

But he didn't. "Nothing ever is. Just look at you, still a kid to me but with a baby of your own." Graham smiled over at Samantha. "Things do have a way of changing."

"Everything's changed for me." Tori fastened her eyes on her cork again. "With Sammy gone."

"That's one of those hard changes. Sammy gone." He reached over and gave her arm a little pat.

"Now you're going to tell me life goes on." She couldn't keep a hint of irritation out of her voice. She'd heard that over and over in the last year.

"Nope, those words weren't in my head at all." He moved his hand from her arm to Chaucer's head. The dog's tail thumped against the ground. "But it does. The sun keeps coming up. The little ones keep growing and us old folks get older."

"You're not that old."

"Not that young either." Graham blew out a breath. "But I don't have any happiness problem. Here with the sun on my shoulders, two pretty girls for company, and an old dog at my feet. Ahh, I know a happy moment when I feel one." He looked over at her. "Happy will come visit you again too. Sammy would want that for you."

"I know." That was another thing people kept telling her. *Sammy wouldn't want you crying all the time.* Even Sammy's mother told her that.

A breeze lifted her line and she reeled it in a bit. When Graham stayed silent, she glanced over to see if he'd dozed off like Samantha, but he was staring up at the red oak leaves above their heads.

"The leaves will all be gone soon," she said.

"Till next year. That's the way of nature. To everything there is a season."

"Ecclesiastes."

"Yep. The words of the preacher, the son of David," Graham said.

"I'd just as soon skip over winter." Tori looked back out at the water.

"But the ground gets thirsty for the snow. Besides, little Samantha will be big enough to like snow this year. You can teach her to make snow angels." He smiled over at Tori and then looked back up at the tree.

"If I don't, Lorena will. I'd better get Mama to order her some boots."

"I was up at the store awhile ago. That Clay Weber stopped by." Graham kept his eyes on the tree. "He asked after you. Seemed sorry you weren't there to wait on him."

"Sammy and Clay were friends." Relief whispered through her that she hadn't had to find a way to say no to whatever Clay would have asked her to do.

"The boy had a right hard time after his daddy died."

"He didn't have to go the Army."

Graham switched his gaze from the tree to Tori. "That wasn't his choice. He got in line with the other boys."

"I know." Tori stared out at the pond until the water shimmered. Sammy used to tell her if they stared like that long enough, they might see a fish jump out of the water and stick its tongue out at them. She kept her eyes on the pond. "Do fish have tongues?"

"I reckon they have fish tongues, but nothing to compare with us or Chaucer here. Never had one lick me or give me the raspberry." Graham threw away his grass stem and sat up straight. "Hook that one nibbling on your bait and we'll see."

The little fish, barely big as her hand, had something that

passed for a tongue, but nothing it could ever stick out at her. She worked the barb out of its mouth and let it slide back into the pond where it flashed toward the deeper water. She wouldn't be catching that one again anytime soon.

She stared at the spot where the fish disappeared. "It wasn't supposed to be this way, Graham."

"There's more fish in this old pond, Victoria girl. Some you can catch with hardly any bait at all. Good fish."

Samantha picked that moment to open her eyes. When she saw Graham, she let out a squeal and scrambled to her feet. Chaucer jumped up to lick her face. Graham called him back, but Samantha giggled and reached for the dog.

Tori didn't bother baiting her hook again. Fishing was over for the day. That was all right. She really didn't care whether she caught another fish right now anyway.

6

Jay felt a hundred pounds lighter when he climbed down off the ship in New York after the long voyage home. His number had finally come up to be transported home. Red Cross volunteers lined the dock in the cold December wind to welcome him and the other soldiers home with coffee and doughnuts. It didn't matter that the coffee wasn't exactly hot anymore. It was coffee served to him in America by an American woman that he could drink with his feet back on American soil. At last.

Not exactly home yet, but a lot closer than he'd been for a long time. A few men kissed the ground when they got off the ship, but Jay wanted to wait until he was on real home ground. Rosey Corner ground.

Rosey Corner. A smile curled up inside Jay at the thought of walking down that road again. Home. So what if he'd only lived in Rosey Corner a few months and never owned any kind of house there. Before Pearl Harbor and the Army, he'd just borrowed a bed from Graham Lindell. Then after he married Kate and they went back to Rosey Corner until he had to ship out, they stayed with her aunt Gertie.

Home was more than a house. It was a place in a person's heart. A place to belong. A place he'd been hunting since he was a kid.

He and Kate hadn't had much privacy sleeping in Gertie's front parlor, but Kate had an apartment now in Lexington. As soon as he had his discharge papers in hand, he looked forward to a little privacy with her there. His insides went soft at the thought of her in his arms.

But he'd be glad to have his feet on Rosey Corner ground again too. To see Birdie running to greet him with Scout chasing after her. He could hardly believe the long-legged girl in the pictures Kate sent him was his Birdie. A kid could change a lot from ten to fourteen. He wondered if she'd think she was too old to hug him now. He hoped not. He wanted to do a bunch of hugging when he got back to Rosey Corner to see Kate's family. His family now.

A funny feeling, thinking about having a family. He'd left behind his own family a long time back. Then just when he was ready to embrace a new family in Rosey Corner, the war tore him away from them. He spent some lonely nights huddled down in cold foxholes, not sure he'd see the sun come up, wondering if the Lord had something against him having family. Seemed like things kept separating him from the people he loved. But he wasn't the only soldier far from home.

Not so far anymore. Just a few more days until he'd hold his release from the Army. They sent him to a discharge center in Virginia where they counted up his service months and the times he'd seen action. He could have gotten points for kids, but he was just as glad that hadn't happened yet for him and Kate. He needed to get used to being married first. He had no doubt Kate would be a wonderful mother, but he did have some doubts about the kind of father he might be. His own father lacked plenty in that department.

The Wednesday before Christmas, he finally had his discharge papers in hand and a train ticket to Lexington. Home for Christmas. The train didn't leave until the next morning, but he saw no need to rent a room for the night. After the places he'd slept during the war, the depot was practically a luxury hotel.

During a slow time between trains, the ticket agent struck up a conversation with Jay. "How about I get you on an earlier train? My son's waiting for transport from the Pacific and I wouldn't want him to have to cool his heels at a train station on the way home." He studied Jay's ticket, then ran his finger down the train schedule. "Let's see. Lexington." He glanced up at Jay. "You got somebody waiting for you there?"

"My wife." Saying that sent a thrill through him.

"No kids, huh?"

"Not yet. We were only married a few weeks before I went overseas."

The man looked up and winked. "One of those whirlwind romances, eh?"

"I guess you could say that." Loving Kate had made him feel like he was in the middle of a whirlwind often enough.

"Well, let's get you home to that anxious bride of yours." The man found Jay a new ticket. A little farther in miles since the train went to Cincinnati, then back to Lexington, but with an earlier departure time.

He should have slept on the train, but he couldn't. He kept picturing how Kate would look when he surprised her by getting to Lexington hours earlier than she expected. Happy, excited, bursting with life. That's how she looked when they exchanged vows in Georgia with her father standing up with her and a nurse from the infirmary standing up with him. Backwards maybe in the best man and bridesmaid way, but it worked for them. He had a feeling that was going to be their way. Maybe not always by the book, but a way that would suit them.

On the ship home, in spite of the cold, he'd spent time up on the deck, looking toward the west. Toward Kate and his future. He wasn't going to be afraid of it. He'd been afraid enough the last few years. And not just during the war. Before that, he'd been afraid to allow anybody close to him. Afraid they'd let him down. Even more afraid he'd let them down.

The same bit of Scripture that had circled in his head then as he stared out at the cold ocean waters ran through his head again in time with the train wheels. *Perfect love casteth out fear.* Kate quoted that verse to him back when he'd been so timid about revealing his heart to her. It took some searching, but he had finally found and marked the verse in the pocket Testament he carried through the war. First John 4:18. But the love John was talking about was the Lord's perfect love.

Jay was far from perfect. Fear lurked around a lot of corners for him. Kept him alive a few times when something raised the hairs on the back of his neck.

That kind of fear could be a soldier's friend. Keep him from doing reckless stuff to get himself killed. "You've seen it happen," Sarge had told him. "A soldier not keeping his head down. Running into fire like he thinks he's wearing tank armor."

"Sometimes that's fear too," Jay said. "Crazy fear. The get-it-over-with fear because you can't stand it another second."

They'd been keeping their heads down as they ate their rations back behind the lines. The artillery was a constant rumble in their ears, but it wasn't their turn to face it yet. Instead they kept their ears tuned for enemy planes, ready to dive for cover.

"I've seen it happen," Sarge admitted as he spooned out the last bite of his K rations. It didn't matter about the taste. A soldier ate what he was given. "Just don't let it happen to you. I'm expecting you to have my back when we move on up. And don't stop to take some fool picture and get your head blown off like Archie."

"It's my duty now to take pictures."

"Not when you're getting shot at." Sarge gave him a hard look. As two of the older men in the unit, they'd been through a lot together. "Not when I'm getting shot at."

"Yes, sir." Jay saluted. "Gun first. Camera second."

Sarge let out a sigh and pitched his empty can to the side. "A man can get killed either way."

"Do you get scared, Sarge?" Sarge was so tough, Jay never thought about him being afraid.

"What do I look like to you, Tanner? Some kind of machine?" Sarge glared at Jay. "I'd be a fool not to be scared when bullets start flying or we have to step our way through a minefield." He tipped his canteen up for a drink and wiped his mouth on his sleeve. "A man tells you he's not scared, you give him a wide berth. He'll get you killed straight out."

"All kinds of ways to be afraid." Jay chewed on one of the hard biscuits in his rations and thought about Rosey Corner food. A man missed real food. And a woman's arms around him. He looked over at Sarge. "You've been married a long time, haven't you, Sarge?"

Sarge let out a snort that was half laugh. "You sure are jumping around today, Tanner. You thinking of home?"

"Who isn't?" Jay said.

"You aren't lying there. Me and the old lady, we've been married since I was twenty. Going on fifteen years now." He narrowed his eyes on Jay before he went on. "What's the matter? You get a bad letter from the wife?"

"No, no, Kate's great. Busy. Full of what we'll do when I get home." Jay finished off the last of his rations.

"You not wanting to do what she's wanting to do?"

"It's not that."

"What you got stuck in your craw then, Tanner?" Sarge sounded impatient.

"It's just thinking about being married." Jay rubbed his hands off on his pants."We weren't together but a few weeks after we tied the knot and now it's been years."

"You get a pile of letters every mail call."

"Yeah, but that's just words on paper." Jay stared off down the road where the artillery boomed. The noise didn't seem to matter any more than a train rattling past. It ought to matter. Somebody was probably dying.

Sarge leaned over and stared him in the face. "You're sounding like you're scared of being married?"

With a self-conscious grin, Jay dropped his head down to stare at the ground. "Maybe I am."

"You're an idiot, Tanner. A certifiable idiot." Sarge grabbed his pack and gun. "Come on, soldier. Time to go down the road and see if we can get ourselves killed. I figure the two of us are on borrowed time already."

Without another word, Jay got up. He didn't know what it was about Sarge that had him always talking about things that might be better kept inside. Sarge was right. He was an idiot.

The other men in the unit were falling in behind them when Sarge looked over at Jay with a sideways grin. "Idiot or not, you've got a pretty good handle on what being married can be. It's God's own truth that a good woman can put a scare into a man if he don't do right. You just make sure you do right for that girl and you'll be fine."

The screech of the train brakes jerked Jay back to the present. As he climbed down from the train, he looked around at the crowded platform. No way would Kate be there, but she'd be in his arms soon.

Perfect love casteth out fear. The verse ran through his head again as he walked away from the train station. He might not be perfect, but he did love Kate. And she was only a few blocks away. His heart started pounding. Not with fear, but anticipation. He picked up his pace, hating the very air that held him back and kept him away from her.

He found the newspaper building easy enough. He stared at it, wishing she'd look out and see him. He thought about throwing something up at a window. Like Romeo getting Juliet's attention. But he had no idea which window.

Instead he went inside to the front desk where a girl with sausage curls was on the phone. She hung up and smiled at him. "Can I help you, sir?"

"I hope so. I've got this story. A big story." He flashed a smile back at her and color bloomed in her cheeks. Maybe he hadn't lost all his charm in the Army. But he wasn't interested in charming her. He had another girl on his mind.

"I'll call someone down to talk to you." She reached for the phone again.

"I'm not giving my story to anybody but this woman reporter

who works here." He pretended to think a minute. "Kate something."

"Tanner?" she suggested.

A little thrill inched through him. Kate Tanner. His wife. "That's the one. Nobody but her. I've read her stuff. Trust me, it's a story she'll want to write."

7

"It's almost quitting time." Kate couldn't believe Francine was calling her with something like this. Not today when she knew Jay would be home soon.

Kate looked at the clock on the wall. In two hours and eight minutes. Kate's heart gave a little jump at the thought. She shut her eyes and pulled up Jay's face. The years hadn't dimmed his memory. He won't be the same, she reminded herself. War changed people. She didn't want to be like Evie and expect nothing to be different. But Kate couldn't think about Mike and Evie right now. Tonight was her night.

Francine broke into her thoughts. "I know, but he says it's a big story."

"What kind of story?" In spite of herself, that itch started up inside her. To be first to break a story. She grabbed a pencil to scribble down the date, 12-20-45, and checked the clock again for the exact time. 4:45 p.m. Writing the time broke the spell. She couldn't write the story. She had a hundred things to do before Jay's train came in.

"I don't know. He won't say."

Kate cut her off. "Look, Francine, I'll get Tommy to come

down." It didn't matter how big the story was. She wasn't going to write it. She wasn't even going to stay until quitting time. With the telephone pinned against her ear, she covered her typewriter and dropped her pencil into the drawer.

"He says he won't give the story to anybody but you. He asked for you."

"He asked for me?" Kate frowned. Who would ask for her? She tried to remember how long it had been since a story had carried her byline. Gus Black, the editor, didn't think news stories needed bylines. "Are you sure?"

She grabbed her purse out of the drawer and shrugged on her coat as she listened to Francine say she was very sure.

"I don't care. He'll just have to tell his story to Tommy," Kate said.

She heard the mumble of the man's voice telling Francine something. No doubt that he had the story of the century. She didn't care if he did. She wasn't staying late today.

Francine's voice came back over the line. "I think you should talk to this guy, Kate." She lowered her voice. "I know I'd be ready to listen to his story if I was the reporter."

"Good-looking guy, huh?" Francine didn't have a fellow, but she wanted to.

"He's wearing a uniform."

"A soldier?" Again she heard the deeper tones of a man's voice. Even though Kate couldn't make out any words, a tremble started up in her.

Francine's smile was easy to hear in her voice. "He says to tell you that maybe his story isn't right for a big-city newspaper after all. Maybe he needs to go find a Rosey Corner reporter. One who likes to dance."

Kate dropped the phone and took off for the stairs.

"Whoa, Kate. Where's the fire?" Tommy yelled after her.

"In my heart."

Her heart was on fire. She fought her way down the steps that were holding her back from Jay. It had to be Jay. Earlier than she expected. But never too early.

She'd planned to put on her fanciest dress, pin up her hair, and look her best when she met the train. But what difference did any of that make? Not when, if she could only move faster, he might be right in front of her eyes. Now!

She swept around a corner and bumped into Wilma, Gus Black's secretary. The jostle knocked the file folder out of the woman's hands. Papers scattered all over the floor.

"My word, Kate. Slow down." She frowned and grabbed Kate's arm.

"Can't. Big story." Kate jerked away from her. "Sorry. Really." The door was in sight at the end of the corridor. Jay was on the other side of that door. She knew he was.

"Something I can let Gus know about when I tell him why his letters have footprints on them? So he can get the big headline type ready?" Wilma called after Kate with a good measure of sarcasm.

"The biggest," Kate said over her shoulder. "Jay's here."

Wilma's frown disappeared. "Then why are you moving so slow? Get out there, girl, and chase that headline." Her laugh followed Kate down the hallway.

Kate pulled open the door, and across the lobby beside Francine's desk, a soldier turned toward her. Her soldier. A smile, the smile she knew so well, lit up his face. He took a step toward her as she practically flew across the floor and into his arms.

Kissing must be something a person didn't forget how

to do. Like riding a bicycle. Three long years since the last kiss, but their lips hadn't forgotten. A warm feeling soaked through Kate until she thought she might simply melt in Jay's arms. But she wanted to see him too, to let her eyes feast on his face. She wanted his voice in her ears.

She was so wrapped up in the joy of Jay's arms around her that it was a minute before she heard the applause. Kate pulled back from Jay to look around. Francine was jumping up and down, clapping like a kid. Wilma joined in from the doorway behind Kate. Some guys from upstairs had paused on their way out the door to add their applause. Even a man and woman she'd never seen were cheering them on. They must have come in off the street to pick up a paper.

Jay kept his eyes on Kate. "I think they want an encore."

"Definitely."

Another kiss and then he lifted her up and spun her around. Happiness sparked off them to light up the room.

"I knew the promise of a big story would get you down here fast." He set her back on her feet and stared down into her eyes. "Are you ready to go take some notes?"

"Ready," she whispered. "Very ready. I've wanted to follow up on this story for a long time."

"So, where's your notebook?" His eyes were teasing her. The same Jay. The Jay she loved.

"Who needs a notebook? These notes will be written on my heart."

Jay stared down into her eyes. "You are so beautiful."

She felt beautiful with his eyes caressing her. Everything around them was forgotten as they stood there, wrapped in love.

"I love you, Jay Tanner." She remembered how hard it had

been for her to admit that before they married, but now the words bubbled out of her with ease.

"Let's get out of here, Mrs. Tanner. We've got a story to chase." Jay kept one arm around her as he picked up his duffel bag.

They waved as they went out the door, and more applause followed them out on the street.

Right on cue, a few snowflakes drifted down. Once before the war, they had danced in snow much like this, so now the snow seemed to be falling just for them.

"Do you hear the music?" Jay dropped his bag and reached for her hand.

"Oh yes. I hear it."

He pulled her close and with fat snowflakes falling around them, they danced as if they owned the sidewalk. Snow caught in their hair and melted on their cheeks.

A kid ran up with Jay's duffel bag to break the spell over them.

Jay laughed, tossed the boy a nickel, and grabbed Kate's hand. "Let's go home."

Kate led the way down the street. Home, what a beautiful word. In all the time she'd lived in her apartment, she'd never once thought of it as home, only a place to sleep. But now with Jay climbing the stairs behind her, home awaited. And the music played on.

8

Something woke Jay. It didn't take much. A man slept light on a battlefield. He started up and reached for his gun. Instead of hard metal, his hand touched soft hair on the pillow beside him. He wasn't on a battlefield or even in a barracks. He was home. With Kate.

His heart slowed as he pulled in a deep breath and let the memories of war slide back into that black wasteland in his head where he willed them to stay. His fingers played through Kate's hair as he stared down at her sleeping face. She had the blanket pulled up to her chin, gripping it for all she was worth. Once asleep, she didn't share covers. He remembered that from their brief weeks together before he shipped out.

He smiled. As long as she shared everything else the way she had tonight. He folded his arms across his chest to keep from touching her face. He didn't want to wake her. It was enough to feast his eyes on her lying there.

His homecoming had been everything he'd dreamed it would be. They belonged together. So what if they'd had to dodge a few obstacles in their path of love before they realized that. They did realize it now. The years apart didn't matter. Her letters had let him get to know her in ways he might not have if they'd sat across the table from one another every morning.

He doubted she'd be able to say the same. Even if he had been as fluent with his pen, his letters couldn't be like hers. The censors hadn't let him say what he was doing or even where he was. All he could do was tell her how much he loved her and dreamed of home.

That was all he could tell her now. No need dragging the war back to America with him. He wanted to leave it over there. All of it.

A shaft of moonlight through the window fell on Kate's face, and he wished for his camera to capture the sight of her there to keep forever. Then, in spite of his best efforts, the memories of the images he had caught forever on film for the Army poked him. Things too horrible to believe true, except the camera didn't lie.

He swung his legs over the side of the bed. He needed to move. Funny how he still felt strange without his gun slung over his shoulder and the camera around his neck. Both had been part of him for so long. When he stood up, he glanced back at Kate, wishing her eyes would open, but her breath whispered in and out, her sleep undisturbed by his movement.

Jay pulled on his pants and went to peer out the window at the street below, quiet in the deep of night. His bare feet made no sound on the wooden floor. Quiet was good, but he wasn't used to it. Perhaps what had wakened him was the very quiet instead of a noise. He'd get used to it. Back in Rosey Corner, quiet was a nightly occurrence. Moonlight and quiet and Kate.

With his hands in his pockets, he leaned against the facing

of the tall window and took in the spare furnishings of the room. He hadn't noticed much but Kate and how she felt in his arms when he'd first bounded up the stairs behind her. Later they sat at the rickety card table and finished off every bit of food she had. That wasn't much. A few apples. Crackers. Cheese. Some beans and peaches they ate straight from the can. She'd intended to stock up before his train came in, even planned to pick up a pie at the restaurant down the street. But all that was forgotten when he showed up early. Even then as they downed the food, he could barely tear his eyes away from her. Nothing else mattered. Not the food. Not the place. Not the hour of the day. Just her.

But now with her sleeping, he blocked out the leftover dregs of war by checking out her place. A lot of bare space. Nothing on the walls. No curtains. Obviously not somewhere she planned to stay long. The tiny kitchen barely had room for a two burner stove and a half-size refrigerator. The bathroom was even smaller, but the essential equipment was squeezed into it. The rest was one big room, bedroom and sitting room combined. Not that Kate had much in the way of sitting furniture. A couple of folding chairs, a wooden chair in front of a desk piled with books and papers. The bed, just a rail frame with mattress, dominated the room.

That was his Kate. No frills necessary. She was too busy chasing after life to care about frills in her surroundings. Books were her decorations. Plenty of those filled a bookcase fashioned out of bricks and unpainted planks. That was the first thing he'd noticed about her house in Rosey Corner. The books. And family.

Now, because of her, he had family. She was his family. Could be that even tonight they had made a baby. She wanted a baby. She told him he wanted a baby, but he wasn't as sure about that. He wasn't sure about anything except how very much he loved Kate Merritt Tanner and how glad he was to be her husband. The rest he'd figure out with time. The job. The place to live. Whether he had what it took to be a decent father.

Her eyes flickered open and she snaked a hand out from under the blanket toward his side of the bed. When he wasn't there, she bolted up off her pillow. "Jay?"

"I'm here," he said.

She rubbed the sleep out of her eyes. "Are you all right?"

"As right as right can be." He stayed where he was by the window. "Just admiring the beauty in the moonlight."

A smile played across her face. "I knew you were a charmer the first time I met you."

"No fooling Kate Merritt. Best I remember, you were determined to not let me charm you."

"I was. Very determined."

"Of course, you were in love with Mike."

She laughed. "The fantasies of youth. I had no idea what real love was then."

"Do you now?"

"I'm learning," she said. "How about you? Do you?"

"Maybe once you learn, you can teach me."

"I've got an idea." She held her arms out to him. "Maybe you can help me with my homework."

Together in the bare little apartment with the street noises drifting up to them, Friday and Saturday passed in a breathless rush. They talked. They laughed. They bumped elbows in the tiny kitchen, cooking eggs and bacon. They ate apples and cheese in bed while reading aloud to one another. They shopped for Christmas presents to take to Rosey Corner and gave a man selling Christmas trees fifty cents for a skinny cedar tree.

"Wait until Graham hears we paid good money for a cedar tree." Kate laughed as they propped the tree up in the window. "We'll never hear the last of it."

"But it smells like Christmas, doesn't it?" Jay shook one of the branches to release some of the fragrance, and a shower of needles fell. "Might need a little water."

"And a few thicker branches." Kate stood back and studied the tree through narrowed eyes. "I'm not sure we got our money's worth."

"Four bits? Sure, we did," Jay said. "Our first Christmas tree. Cheap at any price."

They decked out the tree with a string of lights and shiny red balls. Kate popped popcorn and sat down with a needle and thread. Jay lay on the bed and watched as she tediously strung the popped kernels together. After fifteen minutes, two stuck fingers, and only about a foot of popcorn garland to show for her efforts, he got up and stuffed a handful of the popcorn in his mouth.

"Hey, you're eating the decorations." Kate laughed and reached for the bowl.

He grabbed it first. "The tree doesn't need popcorn." He held his hand out to her. "But I've always wanted to eat popcorn in bed by the light of a Christmas tree while the most beautiful girl in the world tells me what she wants for Christmas."

Kate stuck the needle into the spool of thread and took his hand. "Popcorn in bed. Mama would tell us we might have mice in bed with us too after that."

"I've slept with worse." He pulled her close. "But never with better than my gorgeous wife. Now what is it you want to find under the tree on Christmas morning?" Jay kept the ring he'd bought in Virginia secret in his pocket, glad he'd gotten something for her then, because now he couldn't bear to let Kate out of his sight long enough to shop.

"You," Kate whispered. "Only you."

"But you've already got me."

"Sometimes Christmas comes early."

Jay pulled the string on the light in the kitchen to turn it off. Outside the streetlights kept darkness at bay while inside the red lights on the Christmas tree cast a rosy glow over the room. "It does indeed, Mrs. Tanner. It does indeed."

Sunday morning they got up early to drive to Rosey Corner in time for church. As much as he wanted to have his feet on Rosey Corner ground again, Jay regretted the end of their private time together. For two days they'd been totally wrapped up in one another. Now they were going to let others in. Life would be poking them with decisions to be made about what next.

Even sliding behind the wheel of his old car and wrapping his hands around the familiar steering wheel changed things. It felt good, but it made him realize how long he'd been gone. The fenders were rusty and the motor smoked a little when he pushed on the gas. "I wasn't sure the old heap would still be running."

"All the old heaps had to keep running since they weren't making any new cars." Kate ran her hand along the dash. "But they will now."

"So that's what you want for Christmas? A new car?"

"Shh." Kate put her finger to her lips. "She might hear you. Sonny at the garage back home says he doesn't know how she keeps running. He's worked on her a few times when she got contrary."

"Gone from horseshoeing to car repair in Rosey Corner. Who would have thought it?" Jay pulled out onto the road.

"Not Dad. He loved shaping iron, but he doesn't fire up the forge these days. No reason to."

"Right. You wrote he was shoeing people now." Jay smiled over at her but she didn't smile back. She was staring out at the road. "Is he all right?"

"He has this awful cough. He gets winded just walking home from the shop."

Jay reached over to squeeze her hand. "He'll feel better in the spring."

"It's a long time until spring."

"I feel like it's spring now with you beside me." He looked over at her.

That made her smile. "Maybe you'd better watch the road instead."

"If I have to." He squeezed her hand again before putting it back on the steering wheel. "But what about Aunt Hattie? Doesn't she have a magic elixir to fix him up?"

"She needs a magic elixir herself. Her rheumatism is working on her." Kate sighed.

"How old is she now?"

"She turned eighty this year."

"Fern still living with her or has she gone back to the woods?"

"Fern's changed like everybody else. You'll see. Mama likes

to say everything changes except the Lord. And Daddy says war changes everybody."

"You think it's changed me?" Jay tightened his hands on the steering wheel, not sure how she'd answer. But whatever she said, there wasn't any doubt the war had changed him.

"Of course. You're even more handsome than you were when you left." She scooted across the seat to kiss his cheek. "How about me? How have I changed?"

"Let's see." He looked at her out of the corner of his eyes. "You wear your skirts shorter, your lipstick brighter, your hair longer. Can't say that you cook any better."

She whacked his arm. "I can cook."

"Popcorn, maybe." He put his arm around her. He could drive with one hand fine out on the open road until time to shift gears. "But other than that, you haven't changed a bit from the girl I fell in love with at my best friend's wedding."

"You didn't fall in love with me that day."

"Sure, I did. Don't you remember I asked you to elope? And don't you remember wanting to take me up on it?"

"In your dreams."

"That we can agree on. You've always been in my dreams."

Kate leaned her head on his shoulder. "I wish we could just keep driving forever."

"You don't want to go home?" Her words surprised him.

"I do. Yes, of course I do, but I'm not sure I'm ready to share you. Everybody will want to talk to you and I'll have to help Mama in the kitchen."

"We can turn around and go back to Lexington." He could wait to put his feet on Rosey Corner ground. It wouldn't go anywhere.

"No, no. Lorena is too excited about you coming home.

And I'm sure Mama was up early this morning baking you a brown sugar pie."

"I dreamed about those pies. Your mother is an angel." Jay licked his lips. "Oh wait, that's what Birdie says you are. Her angel sister."

"She might not be so ready to call me that today after I've kept you to myself since Thursday. I'm surprised she didn't find a way to get to Lexington to see you. She probably would have if Mama had let her. She thinks you hung the moon."

"It will be fun to see her. To see all your family."

"Your family too." Kate poked a finger at his chest.

"My family too." The words made him smile.

Kate checked her watch. "We're late. We'll have to go straight to the church."

"Mike preaching again?"

"No." A frown chased across Kate's face. "Mike's not preaching right now."

"Mike not preaching?" Now it was Jay's turn to frown. "You're kidding me. That's all he's ever wanted to do."

"Yeah, well, I don't know. Aunt Hattie says he must have got tested in the war and the test isn't over."

"Is it ever?"

"Maybe not." Kate let out a long breath. "Evie says he likes his job at the bank in Louisville and she still has her job with that lawyer firm. They bought a car and they're looking at houses."

"In Louisville?" When Kate nodded, he added, "No houses in Rosey Corner?"

"I don't know. Do you want there to be?"

"I've been wanting to be in Rosey Corner for a long time."

"Three long years."

He didn't contradict her, but he'd dreamed of belonging in a place like Rosey Corner most of his life. A place with family.

Kate sat up straighter to peer out the window when they got close to Rosey Corner. She pointed out a new house or two, but nothing seemed changed much to Jay as he turned down toward the church. The parking area looked full, so he parked alongside the road. Church attendance obviously wasn't slacking any.

"They'll be singing already." Kate slid out of the car, took his hand, and hurried toward the church. "I hope Lorena and Mama saved us a seat."

A tall, long-legged girl exploded out the front door. The strains of a hymn spilled out with her.

"Tanner," Birdie yelled and ran across the yard toward him just the way she always had when he showed up at the Merritt house.

Kate laughed as he caught Birdie up and swung her around as though she were still the ten-year-old he remembered. And she was. Only taller. His little sister of the heart.

9

Kate thought her heart was already filled to bursting with love for Jay after the two days in their little honeymoon cocoon, but now seeing him with Lorena, her heart swelled even more. He was going to be such a wonderful father.

Oh dear Lord, please. The prayer whispered through her head. Her hand slipped down to her middle. The Lord had answered so many of her prayers, and now he'd brought Jay home to her. The same Jay. Well, if not exactly the same, then still the man she loved. The man who loved her.

There was something almost magical about how time apart couldn't change love. Aunt Hattie's voice was in Kate's head. *Katherine Reece, you is always overthinking ever'thing. Leave a few things up to the Lord. And accept the plenty of blessings he rains down on you.*

She was in a garden of plenty here in the chill December air with Lorena's laughter in her ears and Jay filling her eyes and heart. It was like beginning a story. So many possibilities. So many ways the story could go. Their story. First, they would have to think about jobs and a place to live. Her apartment wouldn't do for a family. They needed a house. A yard with a picket fence. A dog and some cats. Hens scratching in the backyard. And a cow.

She smiled at the thought of Jay milking. She didn't know why. He'd grown up on a farm. Had done farm work before he went to the service. But he was so different from the farm boys around Rosey Corner. So different than any boy she'd ever known. Different could be good. No, not could be good. Was good. Was very good.

Jay set Lorena down on the ground and stepped back to give her the once-over. "Where's Birdie? What have you done with my little sister?"

She threw her arms out wide. "Here I am. Right here."

"Can't be. That girl was only this tall." Jay held his hand up about the middle of his chest. "And look at you. Taller than Kate. You have to be hiding the real Birdie somewhere." Jay peered around behind her.

"No, it's me." Lorena hit her chest with her fingers, happiness leaking out of every inch of her. "Just taller. Aunt Hattie says I'm like a sunflower reaching for the sun. But I don't want to reach any higher. I already look like some kind of goofy giraffe."

"Giraffes' necks are longer. Lots longer." Jay didn't crack a smile. "So that won't work. Remains to be seen about the goofy."

"You're the one who's goofy." Lorena smacked his arm.

"Could be. Love can make a guy pretty goofy." He grinned over at Kate and then back at Lorena. "I'm surprised a dozen goofy boys aren't following you around."

"Silly." Lorena giggled. "They can't. They're all in church."

"So if not for the preacher keeping them in their pews, they'd be out here making eyes at you."

"I'd chase them away. I don't like boys." A blush rose up in Lorena's cheeks to give lie to her words.

"But that doesn't keep them from liking you." Jay put his arm around Lorena's shoulders and reached for Kate's hand. "Besides, not all guys are bad. You just let me check them over first and you'll be fine."

"You and Daddy. Kate too." Lorena rolled her eyes. "Even Graham. If it's up to you all, I'll never have a boyfriend."

Kate laughed. "I thought you just got through saying you didn't like boys."

"Well, that doesn't mean I might not like them someday." Lorena lifted her chin a little. "When I get older."

"Older is good." Kate kissed Lorena's cheek. "But right now, we'd better go inside before Mama comes looking for us."

"She told me I could wait at the door for you. They'll stop church when we go in anyway. We waited awhile for you, but then the deacons said Reverend Winston better get started so we could get out by dinnertime." Lorena looked over at Jay. "He's not like Mike used to be. If Mike didn't quit on the dot of twelve, Evie would give the signal to cut it short." Lorena slashed her finger across her throat. "But if Reverend Winston hasn't said all he wants to say by twelve, well, we just have to sit there until he's finished."

"Maybe his wife doesn't have a watch," Jay said.

"Then we need to take up a special offering to buy her one."

"Be nice, Lorena." Kate tried to look stern, but the corners of her mouth twitched up.

"That would be nice! For all of us. We could give it to her for Christmas," Lorena insisted.

Jay laughed as he turned Lorena toward the church door. "I've missed you, Birdie. You know how to make a guy laugh."

"What's funny about Reverend Winston preaching till your legs go numb from sitting on a hard pew?"

"A little preaching might be a good thing today," Jay said. "Let's go get some religion."

"Sounds like somebody needs it," Kate said, but she didn't hide her smile this time. It was a day for smiling.

Lorena was right. When they went inside, everybody stopped singing to welcome Jay home. It had been that way each time one of the boys came back to church after the war. As Reverend Winston said, after everybody finally settled back into the pews, there were all different ways to worship. Celebrating victory with a church family was one of the best ways. Then he surprised everybody by cutting his sermon short at five minutes after twelve.

It was good to belong. Jay remembered being at Kate's house on a Thanksgiving Day before the war and wanting to have a permanent place at their table. To be part of the family.

He'd never wanted to be part of his aunt's family. Maybe because they didn't want him. He was nothing more than an obligation and a burden. Love or kindness hadn't entered into the arrangement. On either side.

Here in Rosey Corner, he'd found love and not only from Kate. Birdie had wrapped her love around him and pulled him into the family even when Kate was trying to hold him away. This family embraced more than those with the same name. Even Birdie didn't have the same last name. None of them really knew why she'd been abandoned on the church steps. Since it was during the Depression, everybody assumed her parents were desperate with no way to care for her.

That's what Kate told Birdie. That had to be easier to live with than thinking they simply wanted to be rid of her the way Jay's father had wanted to be rid of him. If a person didn't know for sure, why not go with the better story? It didn't matter that no one had ever come looking for Birdie. Could be neither of her parents had survived the Depression. Or could be they didn't want to spoil her happiness here at Rosey Corner. Could be lots of things.

She hadn't forgotten them. Kate said Birdie still spoke her name every night before she went to sleep. Lorena Birdsong. So while she was part of Kate's family here in Rosey Corner, his family now too, much of the truth of Birdie's past lurked below the surface of her memory. To keep from forgetting completely, she said her name time and again.

Jay had done that while he was under fire overseas. Whispered his name so the Lord wouldn't forget him. He knew the Lord didn't forget. The Bible told him that. Perhaps he said it more so he would remember. *Jay Tanner, married to Kate Merritt Tanner, with a home and family waiting in Rosey Corner.*

When he had been most afraid, when the rain had soaked him to the skin and the foxhole filled with water, when the man next to him, who had just told him about his family, was hit by shrapnel, that's when Jay whispered those words. Someday he would be home. In heaven or Rosey Corner. At times, the two had seemed very near the same in his mind.

Now his prayers had been answered. His feet were on home ground at last in Rosey Corner with Kate by his side and family all around him. It was every bit as good as he'd imagined.

Not that things were all the same. While he might like to

live in that bubble of memory where everybody was fine, he had eyes to see. Just as Birdie had gone from a little girl to an emerging young lady, everybody else had changed too. Some showed it more than others. Kate's mother had hardly aged a bit, but Kate was right about her father and his cough. It wasn't a simple cold. Still, his handclasp was firm and his welcome true.

Graham hadn't been at church, but he came down off the porch to meet them when they drove up to the house. A shepherd dog trailed behind him. Graham didn't look right without Poe, his coonhound, beside him.

"It's about time you got home." A big smile spread across Graham's face that was a reflection of Jay's own. Graham stuck out his hand.

"You always did see things pretty straight." Jay grabbed Graham's hand and pulled him close for a hug. "You and that Mrs. Henderson who was sweet on you tie the knot yet?"

"What are you talking about?" Graham stepped back from Jay with a little shudder. "Being in the Army must have addled your brain. I painted her house. That's all."

Jay cleared his throat. "Who painted her house?"

"I did." Graham's smile came back. "Well, I did have some help from this drifter who happened through Rosey Corner. But I never had no intention of moving inside that house. No sirree. Chaucer and me, we like our independence."

Jay gave the dog a closer look. Its mottled grayish-tan fur looked like it might have been spattered with white paint at one of Graham's painting jobs. One ear cocked up while the other one drooped, and it held up a stiff back leg. "I've seen better looking dogs, but then Poe couldn't win any beauty contests either."

Graham frowned. "You must've forgot what Poe looked like. He was a fine figure of a dog. This one, poor thing." Graham ran his fingers across the white streak on the dog's head and its tail flapped back and forth as it rolled up its lips to give Graham a toothy grin. "He's no Poe, but I gotta admit, he is a dog." The dog leaned against Graham's leg.

"That he is." Jay looked around. "But where's Scout?"

Birdie whistled and shouted Scout's name. When she spotted the dog racing across the field toward them, she grinned at Jay. "Watch out, Tanner. Here he comes."

"Don't let him tear your stockings, Lorena," Kate warned before she gave Graham a peck on the cheek and hurried up the porch steps to protect her good clothes from the dog's paws.

Seeing Kate there by the post brought back such a flood of memories Jay had to fight the urge to go take her in his arms. That was where she had waited for him while they were dancing toward love. Then the dog was all over him, jumping up and yapping.

"Whoa." Jay laughed and pushed him down. "Now that's a welcome."

"I think he remembers you," Birdie said.

"Dogs never forget," Graham added. "They're like elephants."

Scout quivered with excitement as Jay patted him. "Who was it that decided elephants don't forget?" Jay asked Graham.

"I don't know, but they should've said dogs." Graham kept his hand on top of Chaucer's head.

"Come on. We can talk about dogs and elephants inside. It's freezing out here." Kate held her hand out toward him.

"Mama probably needs help with dinner. Mike and Evie will be here soon, and who knows how many more."

"True enough," Graham said. "Fern said Hattie might even walk down here to set her eyes on Jay."

"We could go get her," Kate offered.

"Now you know Hattie don't like riding in those machines unless it's an emergency." Graham gave the car a wary look. He obviously hadn't changed his opinion of cars either.

"It is an emergency." Birdie grabbed Jay's hand. "I thought Kate was never going to let you come home."

"I'm here now." Jay followed her up the porch steps where Kate waited, her very presence intoxicating. "Home."

He remembered the very planks of the porch under his feet, the feel of the Rosey Corner air on his skin, the smell of home. Dogs weren't the only ones who didn't forget. Home.

10

Tori was disgusted with herself. She simply couldn't keep crying when everybody else was smiling. But when Jay lifted Samantha high above his head to make her giggle, tears filled Tori's eyes. It looked so natural. So right. That was what Sammy should be doing. But Sammy never would.

"Again," Samantha demanded when Jay brought her down out of the air.

The child didn't shy away from anybody. Mama said it was from being at the store all the time. Perhaps, but more than that, she was so like Sammy. He'd never known a stranger either. In every letter home, he'd told her about a new friend. Men from all across the nation. He probably even tried to make friends with his guards in that Japanese prison camp. The men who had killed him.

She would not cry. She would smile. For Jay and Kate. For her mother and father who worried about her. For Samantha. Especially for Samantha.

A few weeks ago, Aunt Hattie had told her to look to Jesus for smiles. "That don't mean you won't have troubles. Every soul is burdened down with troubles from time to time." Aunt Love knew about troubles. After all, she'd lost her son in the first war. "But the good Lord is right there helping you carry that load. That's how you can pull up those smiles for yo' little one even when you're feelin' sorrowful. And for yo'self. A body has to keep on smilin' for yo'self same as others, else the dark can overtake you. You's way too young to not look for the sunlight of the morrow."

With Aunt Hattie's words in her ears, Tori could believe the morrow would be better. But then the dark of sorrow would overtake her again. She hoped Aunt Hattie would come for dinner. That way Tori would have to smile to keep Aunt Hattie from preaching at her. The old woman was getting decrepit, but Fern would walk her down if Aunt Hattie wanted to come. Aunt Hattie had taken Fern in when she didn't have anywhere else to go.

Tori didn't know what would happen to Fern if Aunt Hattie moved on up to heaven the way she said she was ready to do. Fern had let the dark overtake her for years before Lorena brought light back into the woman's life with a little simple trust.

For some reason, Lorena hadn't been afraid of Fern. Tori had never understood why. Tori was terrified of the woman back then. Any time Fern stepped out of the shadow of the trees, Tori was up on her toes ready to run or slipping behind Kate to hide. She wasn't afraid of her now, only afraid of becoming like her. Fern had lost her love when she was young. Not in a war the way Tori had lost Sammy, but in an accident.

Tori didn't know the whole story. Nobody would talk about it, saying some things were better not remembered. That's the way they thought she was with Sammy, but it wasn't true. She wanted Sammy's name in her ears.

That was why it was especially good when Jay held Samantha out in front of him and said, "Look at that hair. And are those freckles sprouting on your nose? You're your daddy made over." He pulled Samantha close to kiss her nose and make her giggle again. Then he looked over her head at Tori. "Sammy would have been so proud of her."

Behind him, Kate frowned a little. Tori knew she was thinking that at any minute, Tori would dissolve in tears at the mention of Sammy. A few tears did spill out of her eyes and streak down her cheeks, but they weren't bad tears. In fact, she had no problem smiling through them as she said, "I like to think he is. That he watches over her from heaven."

At least she thought that when she wasn't angry with him for being in heaven instead of right there in Rosey Corner with her. Sometimes she was even mad at the Lord. That was wrong. She knew that, but the anger lurked in the bottom of her mind like a snake under a rock that slithered out from time to time to check the weather. Why hadn't the Lord put his hand over Sammy and protected him the way Tori had so earnestly prayed he would? Others had been protected. She'd read their stories in the papers. Miracle escapes from death.

Why would the Lord do a miracle for them and not for Sammy? She couldn't understand it and she couldn't ask anybody about it. Not even Aunt Hattie. Some things couldn't be spoken out loud. She shouldn't even be thinking such things.

Jay looked at her as the others around them got too quiet. It had been that way ever since she got the news that Sammy was dead. Everybody tiptoed around her like she might fall apart at the first loud noise. But Jay must not have known that. He handed Samantha off to Lorena and stepped toward Tori.

"You're right, Tori. You are so right." He put his arms around her. "When Kate wrote me about Sammy, I didn't want to believe it. He was just a kid. After that, every time I saw another kid get it, I'd be thinking of Sammy and you all over again."

She leaned against him the way she sometimes leaned on her father and swallowed the lump in her throat. "You never saw him while you were in the Army, did you?"

"No. But I saw plenty of boys like him. They looked like they ought to be shooting paper wads in school, but instead there they were, storming the beaches. Flying bombers and coasting back to base on fumes. In tanks crawling across the battlefields."

"And dying." Tori's voice was flat. Everybody else in the room was forgotten. Everybody but Samantha. She could never forget her even for a second.

"Too many did. But they did save the world. For us." He looked back at Samantha, who watched them with big eyes. "For her."

"How do we know it won't just happen again when she grows up?" That made her mad too. Why couldn't the first war, the war her father fought in, have been enough?

A shudder went through Jay. "God forbid."

She'd never seen him look so grim. The Jay she remembered was always smiling and trying to make people laugh. But that was before the war. "I'm sorry. Don't let me spoil your homecoming."

"Don't worry, Tori." His smile bounced back. "Nothing

could do that. It's good to be home. To see you. To see all of you."

Kate stepped up beside Jay to kiss Tori's cheek. That was enough to summon up Tori's tears again. So she was glad when Mike's car pulled up outside to divert attention from her.

Lorena peered out the window. "Mike and Evie are here."

"I thought they'd be at church," Jay said.

"They've found a church in Shelby County," Kate said. "Halfway between here and Louisville. Evie says the church is three times bigger than ours and that you should see the collection plates when the deacons carry them back to the front. Spilling over with bills. And not all ones, either."

Jay laughed. "What's she doing? Campaigning for Mike to take over the pulpit there?"

"She might like that, but remember, I told you Mike's not preaching right now." Kate lowered her voice as though afraid Mike could hear her outside. "He's not sure he'll ever take a church again."

Jay looked surprised, but he didn't say anything. Tori had been surprised too when Mike came home. He wasn't the same Mike who'd always had a ready answer or prayer for problems before he went to war. She missed that Mike. They all missed that Mike. Evie most of all. But at least he came home. That was what Tori wanted to tell Evie. But she didn't.

Evie's smile looked forced when she came in the door. Her hat was new and perfectly matched her charcoal suit. Jay and Mike shook hands and clapped each other on the back. Two who came home. Then Fern helped Aunt Hattie up the steps and all the hugs started over. Mama came in from the kitchen to make sure they all stayed to eat.

Lorena still had Samantha, so Tori told Mama she'd finish putting dinner on the table as she slipped past her out to the kitchen. They'd closed in the old back porch when they piped water to the house from the well and put in plugs for the stove and refrigerator. The new kitchen was smaller than the old one that now held the big dining table for when everybody was home, but it was cozy with room for a small table and chairs.

Tori liked to cook. Not as much as she liked to fish, but in the winter, the fish didn't bite. In the kitchen, she could take a recipe and put all the ingredients together and make something turn out right, the way it was supposed to. Even better, nobody seemed to mind when she went off by herself to cook.

People were always trying to keep her from being by herself. Especially that Clay Weber. He would not give up asking her to do things. Every week, sometimes twice a week, it was something different. A movie. A trip to the library in Edgeville to get his little sisters and Samantha picture books. Did her mother need help unloading the stock at the store since Daddy wasn't feeling well? Roller-skating. There was a new rink in Frankfort and didn't he remember that she used to like to roller-skate? She didn't know how many times she was going to have to say no before the man got the message.

Just that morning at church, he'd found her in a back pew trying to keep Samantha quiet while the older ladies went over their Sunday school lesson in the front of the sanctuary. He sat down beside her without even asking, and what could she say? The pew didn't belong to her. Then he offered Samantha a sucker, not asking if that was okay either. Of course the child wanted a sucker, but if Tori had wanted her to have a sucker, she'd have given her one. Sticky hands and Sunday dresses didn't go together, but Clay didn't appear to know that.

"Suckers used to keep my sisters quiet in church when they were little," he whispered with a glance up at the Sunday school ladies.

Mrs. Jamison and Mrs. Wilson let their eyes wander from Miss Sadie talking about how Mary had pondered in her heart things like the shepherds coming to see her baby. It was obvious from the looks on the two women's faces what they were pondering about Clay and Tori.

Samantha reached for Clay and Tori let him take her. It would serve him right to get sticky sucker juice on his suit. But he was ready for that too with his handkerchief out to wipe Samantha's hands without her making the first complaint.

He waited until the bell rang to signal the end of Sunday school to ask, "Would it be all right if I bring the girls by your house later today? Mama helped Lillie and Mary make Samantha a rag doll. It's not store-bought, but Mama is pretty good with a needle."

"I've seen your mother's dolls. They're wonderful, but the girls should keep the doll for themselves." Mary was only seven and Lillie nine, not too old for dolls.

"No, they wanted to make something for Samantha. They think she's the cutest kid ever."

Tori wanted to tell him he shouldn't use his little sisters to get his way, but maybe she judged him wrong. The girls did really like playing with Samantha. And what could it hurt to let them give Samantha a present?

Now here in the kitchen, she stirred sugar into the applesauce and wished she'd said no. Clay would show up at the house and everybody would think she wanted him there. It wasn't that she didn't want him there. She didn't care whether he came or not. She simply didn't care.

Tori looked out the kitchen window over the new sink to where some hens scratched in the dirt. Maybe Graham's pond wouldn't be frozen over. She could go pretend to fish. But she couldn't take Samantha. It was too cold.

She sighed. She couldn't escape. She didn't truly want to disappear on a Sunday afternoon. Sundays meant family.

She didn't want to escape family. She just wanted to be that girl she was before the telegram came. A girl who cared.

11

They gathered around the dinner table, laughing and talking. Everybody except Evie. Kate didn't know what was wrong with her, but something was. Evie picked at her food with her preacher's wife smile pasted on. Whatever her problem was, it could wait. Jay deserved the spotlight today. Not Evie and whatever crisis she was deciding to have.

That could be anything from a bad week at work to Mike forgetting to pick up something at the grocery. Evie said that happened a lot. She claimed Mike's mind was always somewhere else. Like he and God were having this deep conversation they weren't letting Evie in on.

If Mike was upset with Evie's bad mood, he didn't show it. He seemed the same to Kate. Careful to hold Evie's chair at the table and then Mama's too. He was quiet, but while that wasn't like the old Mike—the Mike before the war—it was like the Mike who'd come home from Germany. Daddy said Mike needed time. Mama said he needed prayer. Evie said he needed to figure out things and do it soon. Evie had never been long on patience.

Kate did her best to ignore Evie and just enjoy Jay at home and her family crowded around the table. Family that included Aunt Hattie and Graham and even Fern, though she'd refused to stay and eat today.

She missed Fern there. Kate could hardly believe she'd thought that, but somehow Lorena had pulled Fern into the family. That didn't mean the woman wanted to be at the table with them. Too many people made her nervous, but she'd passed up a great meal. Mama must have gotten up before daylight to cook.

When it was time for dessert, Mama sat a whole brown sugar pie in front of Jay. "I thought maybe you would want to slice your own piece." She handed him the knife.

Jay smiled at Mama. "Nadine, I want you to know I dreamed about this pie. Whenever things would get bad over there, I'd think about eating another piece of your pie and keep my head down."

"What about thinking about us?" Lorena said.

"Sure, I did that too." Jay winked at her. "I'd think about all those pieces of my pie you were eating."

"You told me to." Lorena insisted.

"So I did, but I do have to admit I'm happy to see you aren't fat as a pig from eating all that pie."

"Hey." She tried to frown, but a smile pushed it off her face. "From now on, eat your own pie."

"That I can do." Jay studied the pie a minute, then sliced right through the middle of it. He slid one of the halves out on his plate. "There, that'll probably do me right now."

When everybody laughed, Jay looked around the table. "You think I'm kidding? Well, you're wrong." He attacked the pie with his fork. "Umm, even better than I remembered."

"Mercy sakes," Aunt Hattie said. "Don't know that I ever saw a boy like pie so much, 'cepting maybe my Bo. He did love my raisin pie. You remember Bo? He didn't make it home from that first war, you know." She looked across the table at Jay.

Down at the end of the table, Evie let out a heavy sigh. Kate spoke up quickly to keep Aunt Hattie from noticing. "We didn't get to know him, Aunt Hattie, but we wish we could have."

"Us old ones remember, Hattie." Graham said. "And those raisin pies too. They were fine."

"Better than fine," Kate's father added.

"I don't know what's the matter with me." Aunt Hattie shook her head. "Course you babies here don't remember. You weren't even born then. My old head loses track of the years from time to time. Hard to think about being eighty and that it's been nigh on forty years since Bo went on ahead of me to heaven."

"You think he's eating raisin pie in heaven?" Jay asked her between mouthfuls of brown sugar pie.

"He might have to wait till I'm up there for that to happen." Aunt Hattie's laugh made her wrinkles dance. "You just keep on enjoyin' that pie down here, son, and we'll enjoy a little of it with you. If I know Nadine, she made plenty."

"I did," Mama said. "Lorena, get the other pie out of the pie safe."

"Somebody can have my piece," Evie said. "I never cared all that much for brown sugar pies anyway."

Since when, Kate wanted to ask, but she kept her mouth shut. Some stews were better left simmering instead of stirred up.

"Birdie can have it. Now that she's not getting my piece." Jay took another bite and closed his eyes as he chewed.

"I think your pie is about to make the boy float up in the air." Kate's father reached for his slice.

"I am being transported." Jay took another bite. "I knew this place was the closest thing to heaven the first time I came here. Beautiful women. Divine food. Books everywhere." He glanced over at Mike. "Wedding music. All thanks to you, buddy."

"The Lord works in mysterious ways his wonders to perform." Mike smiled almost like old times as he dug into his pie.

With pie still on his plate, Jay groaned and pushed away from the table. "Don't throw any of that away. I'll eat the rest later, but my poor stomach's not used to such good food. Got to break it in slowly."

"Could be you should have taken a smaller slice," Graham told him.

"When somebody offers you a slice of heaven, you grab hold of as much of it as you can." Jay reached for Kate's hand and then Lorena's. "And you hang on."

"Can't argue with that," Graham said.

"Heaven don't come down ev'ry day," Aunt Hattie said.

"Not unless you live in Rosey Corner," Jay said.

Kate leaned over and kissed his cheek. It was good to have Jay home. He had a way of making everybody smile, even Tori. Everybody except Evie, who had stopped faking good humor and held her head in her hand. Mike stroked her arm and glanced down the table toward Kate as though asking for help. Kate pretended not to notice. She would not let Evie's dramatics spoil this day.

Samantha picked that moment to spill her glass. Tori jumped up to mop up the water. Daddy moved his chair back and started coughing.

Aunt Hattie frowned over at him. "Is he taking that tonic I made up for him, Nadine?"

"He's taking it, Aunt Hattie." Mama rubbed his back. "He's getting better."

Daddy held up his hand and stood up. "I am," he choked out. "Better."

That had to be wishful thinking. Or maybe just wishful talking. The cough didn't sound better as he pulled out his handkerchief and made his way into the other room. Her mother stared after him with a worried frown, then pushed a smile back across her face as she asked, "More pie, anybody?"

"We're stuffed, Nadine. Couldn't hold another bite," Graham said.

Kate pulled her hand away from Jay's with regret. She wanted to be touching him all the time. "You go visit with Aunt Hattie and the men, Mama. We'll do the dishes."

Mama took off her apron and handed it to Kate. When Samantha reached her hands up to her, she picked her up out of the high chair. "Her dress is wet, Victoria."

"I'll change her." Lorena jumped up to take the little girl. Then she slid her eyes back to Kate. "Unless you need me to help with the dishes."

Kate laughed. "You go hang out with Jay, Lorena. After all, I get to take him home with me."

"But you're coming back Christmas morning, aren't you? Or you could all just stay." Hope lit up Lorena's face. "Tomorrow's Christmas Eve. We could go caroling and come home and drink hot chocolate while Daddy reads the Christmas story to us. Christmas morning we can have pancakes and cinnamon rolls and play Santa Claus for Samantha. You can't miss that."

"Sounds like more heaven coming down." Jay smiled at Lorena. "But let's get out of here now before Kate changes her mind and gives us KP duty."

"I wish I could do the dishes." Aunt Hattie pushed up from the table. "It ain't a good thing to get so feeble a body can't do a piddlin' thing. Seems to be time to move on up when that happens."

"No, no, Aunt Hattie. You have to make Victor his tonics." Mama helped Aunt Hattie through the door to the sitting room. Daddy had finally stopped coughing and was opening the stove top to load it with more coal.

"I can do that for him if he'll wait," Jay said.

"It's better to let him." Mama looked over her shoulder at Jay. "This cough has been hard on him, but it's like Aunt Hattie said. Nobody wants to feel helpless."

Mike stayed beside Evie after the others were out of the room. He looked a little helpless himself as he asked, "Are you all right, honey?"

"I'm just peachy." Evie shook his hand off and stood up. She snatched up her plate and stacked it on his with a clatter. "Go." She made a sweeping motion with her hands. "Do your man talking things."

He looked so troubled Kate wanted to give him a hug, but it wasn't her hug he wanted. Tori raised her eyebrows with an unspoken question when she moved past Kate to put up the leftover pie. Kate shrugged. She didn't have any answers, but she was going to. Just as soon as Mike went in the other room.

Kate picked up some glasses and headed toward the kitchen, but that didn't keep her from hearing Mike and Evie.

"Do you want to go home?" Mike said.

"Who said anything about going home?" Evie's voice had

an edge in it. "I've got to help wash these dishes. Probably ruin my new suit, but who cares? The dishes must be done. Food on the table. Food off the table. Clean dishes. Dirty dishes. Over and over."

"I love you, Evangeline." Mike sounded weary as if he had no hope his words mattered to Evie.

Kate turned in time to see Evie jerk back when Mike touched her cheek. He dropped his hand and shut his eyes a moment. Maybe praying for patience. It was obvious he needed it as Evie kept glaring at him until he turned away from her and followed the others out to the sitting room.

Kate broke the silence that fell over the room. "Have you lost your mind, Evie? Whatever in the world is wrong with you?"

"Wrong? What could possibly be wrong in this heaven-on-earth place?" She snatched up the plates and stomped toward the kitchen to set them on the counter by the sink. A fork bounced to the floor. When she started to lean over to pick it up, the color drained from her face. Grabbing the edge of the counter, she stood very still for a few seconds, then ran for the back door with her hand over her mouth.

Kate and Tori followed her out. Evie held onto the porch post and heaved out everything she'd just eaten.

"I think we can be pretty sure what's wrong with her now." Tori smiled as she pulled a handkerchief out of her pocket to hand Evie.

Evie wiped off her mouth. She was trembling as she stared down at her skirt. "Did I get any on my suit?"

"Don't worry about your suit." Kate wrapped her arms around her and turned her toward the door. "You're freezing. Let's get you inside."

"But you don't understand. I just bought this suit. Last week. And now I'm not going to be able to wear it and I'm going to lose my job and I'm not ready. I'm just not ready." She looked at Kate and Tori and burst into tears.

"Maybe I should go get Mama," Tori said as they guided Evie back into the kitchen.

Evie clutched Tori's arm and kept her voice low. "No. I don't want anybody to know."

"Why not?" Kate eased her down into a chair. "Mama will be excited."

Tori dipped the edge of a dish towel in the dishwater to wash Evie's face. "And it's not something you can keep secret for long. Especially when the morning sickness hits."

"It's not morning," Evie wailed.

"Morning can sometimes last all day with this," Tori said.

"Don't tell me that. I can't stand thinking that."

"You'll forget all about it when the baby comes." Tori knelt down beside Evie's chair, took her hands, and looked directly in her face. "It will all be worth it then."

"I'm not like you, Tori." Evie stared at her, anything but convinced. "I'm not ready."

"I am," Kate said. "I so want this to be me in a few months."

"I wish it was you now."

Kate smiled. "It can't happen quite that quickly."

"That's what you think. A person forgets to take precautions one time and the next thing you know you're heaving out your insides." Evie rubbed the towel across her face and smeared her makeup. "I'll bet you're not even taking precautions."

"Why should I? I can't wait to be a mother."

"But what about Jay? Does he want to be a father?"

"Why wouldn't he?" Kate frowned. "Isn't Mike happy about the baby?"

When Evie didn't say anything, Kate said, "You haven't told him, have you?"

"Don't look at me like that." Evie glared at Kate and then slid her eyes over to Tori. "You don't understand. Nobody understands."

12

Tori fought the urge to give Evie a good shake. What was the matter with her? Her husband had come home from the war. She was being blessed with a baby. Tori knew what a blessing that was. She had Samantha. And here Evie was acting as if it was the end of the world instead of the beginning of life.

Tori stood up and went to the sink. Somebody had to wash the dishes. Evie wouldn't listen to her anyway. Kate could handle it. Not that Evie would listen to Kate either. She obviously wanted to feel sorry for herself. Tori poured a capful of soap into the dishpan and stirred her hand around in the water to make suds.

"You're right there. I don't understand," Kate said. "Mike loves you and you're making him miserable."

"I'm making him miserable? What about me?" If a person could shout in a whisper, that was what Evie was doing.

Kate didn't answer right away. Tori kept her eyes on the glasses in the dishpan, but she didn't have any trouble imagining Kate with her hands on her hips glaring at Evie, ready to explode. How many arguments had Tori sat on the sidelines and watched between the two of them? Tori didn't like arguing. When they were all home and shared a bedroom, she had often covered her ears and hummed a tune to block out their fussing.

They had argued about everything from when to blow out the lamp to who had the softest pillow. She thought about humming now, but instead she set the last glass in the drainer and dumped the silverware in the water. She could rattle that if things got too heated behind her.

She was surprised to hear Kate's soft voice. "I'm sorry, Evie. Tell me what's wrong. Let us help you."

"You already know what's wrong." Evie sounded near tears again. "I'm going to have a baby and we don't have a house yet. We were supposed to have a house before I got in the family way. Worse, the firm won't let me keep working after I start to show. They have a policy against it. But you know that Mike's job doesn't pay all that much. I thought he'd start preaching again. A lot of churches have parsonages. The bigger churches."

Tori looked over her shoulder at them. Kate had pulled one of the kitchen chairs over in front of Evie to hold her hands. In spite of herself, Tori felt a little sorry for Evie too. And for Mike who wasn't the Mike who'd once led their church with such confident belief.

"Do you think he wants a church?" Kate asked.

"How would I know? He won't talk about it at all. Not since he came back. But you remember how he always said the Lord called him to be a preacher. That he knew from the time he was a kid the Lord wanted him to preach. The Lord wouldn't change his mind about that." Evie leaned toward Kate. "Would he?"

"I don't know," Kate said. "That's something Mike will have to figure out, but either way it might work out all right for you. You never really wanted to be a preacher's wife."

"But don't you see?" Evie sounded distraught. "Maybe that's what's wrong. Maybe I've messed everything up for him."

Tori dried her hands on the tea towel and came over to put her hands on Evie's shoulders. There were times to be irritated with her sister and other times to show her love.

"No, Evie. That's not what happened. The war happened. Things we can't even imagine happened." Kate shook Evie's hands a little. "It's not you. It's the war."

"But Jay seems the same. He was over there too."

"He's only been home a few days, and he's so happy to be here right now that the shadows are pushed back." Kate hesitated before she went on. "But they're there. Every night he's been up in the wee hours of the morning. Not able to sleep. Fighting demons like Daddy did."

"Does he tell you about it?"

"No, but I know. None of us are the same as we were four years ago. The war robbed us of those years together. Robbed Tori of Sammy." Kate looked up at Tori. "Things can't be the way they were before."

"But I want them to be."

Those words echoed in Tori's head. Her wants were just as futile as Evie's.

Kate's voice took on a harder edge. "We don't always get our wants."

"But we were so happy before."

"You still love him, don't you?" When Evie nodded, Kate

went on. "Then you'll be happy again. You just have to give him some time and pray about it."

"What about the house?"

Tori tightened her hands on Evie's shoulders. She wouldn't shake her. Instead she would try to remember how it felt to be newly expectant. Ready to cry at the drop of a hat. She leaned down and brushed the top of Evie's head with her lips. "Babies don't need a new house. They just need love."

"I'm sorry, Tori." Evie gave her a tearful look. "I must sound awful to you. Here you are still living with Mama and Daddy."

"Where Samantha is surrounded with love. Too much sometimes. It'll be good for her to have a cousin to get some of the spoiling. Maybe more than one cousin." Tori smiled at Kate.

"Oh, I'm hoping," Kate said. "And you'll have your own place someday, Tori. You will."

"Of course you will. Mama said this boy at church is sweet on you. A Weber boy. I can't remember which one he is. Is he good-looking?" Evie pushed at the waves in her hair and touched her cheeks. "Did I ruin my makeup?"

Tori bit her lip. Sometimes it took more patience to deal with Evie than with Samantha. Way more.

Kate shot Tori a sympathetic look. "Looks aren't everything, Evie. You know that. But your makeup could use a little repair."

"I need a mirror." Evie dabbed her cheeks with the dish towel. "And looks might not be everything, but they certainly matter. You don't want to sit at the breakfast table every morning the rest of your life staring across it at a face that makes you cringe."

"You're impossible." Kate stood up and got another dish towel out of the drawer to dry the glasses.

"I just want a mirror. I don't know why that's impossible." Evie stayed in her chair. "And to know if Tori thinks this guy is somebody she wouldn't mind looking at across the breakfast table."

Tori drew in a breath and turned back to the sink to wash the knives and forks. She hoped Kate would speak up for her, but she didn't. Tori rattled the utensils in the rinse water before she lifted them out to the drainer. She didn't have to answer. Some things were better ignored. She washed one plate and then another.

"Well?" Evie said.

"Kate's right. You are impossible." She set the plate in the drainer and turned to get another stack of plates to put in the water. The soapsuds were dying out. "Clay's a nice guy, but nobody I plan to look at across the breakfast table unless he talks Mama into making him pancakes. I don't think he's tried that yet."

"But I hear he's tried nearly everything else." Kate peered over at her, obviously wondering whether Tori was entertaining ideas about Clay too.

They would all get the wrong idea when Clay showed up at the door with his little sisters. Maybe she would go fishing and leave Samantha with Lorena. She'd be fine and Tori would be fine alone out by the pond even if the wind was cold. She had a coat. That would be better than everybody thinking she was warming up to the idea of Clay Weber across the breakfast table from her.

She was relieved when their mother came in the kitchen

to get the attention away from her. "What's taking you girls so long with the dishes?"

"We had a little delay," Kate said. "Evie's not feeling so good. But we're almost finished now. Just the pans left."

Tori set the last of the dessert plates in the drainer and attacked the mashed potato pan. She listened to see what Evie would say, but as usual, Mama was way ahead of them.

"So did you tell your sisters you're going to be a mother?"

They all three stared at her. "I haven't told anybody. Not even you."

Mama touched Evie's cheek. "You're my daughter, Evangeline. I know you."

"Why didn't you tell me you knew?"

"It's your announcement to make. Yours and Mike's."

When Evie didn't say anything, Kate spoke up. "Mike doesn't know yet."

"You haven't told him?" Mama's smile didn't disappear, but now it was tinged with sadness. "Why not?"

Whenever Tori had seen that disappointed smile directed toward her, she'd ducked her head and felt ashamed. But Evie stared straight at Mama while fresh tears spilled down her cheeks. That had always been Evie's answer to trouble. Tears. But then who was Tori to talk about somebody crying when her own tears were plentiful?

Beside her, Kate was chewing on her lip to keep from answering for Evie. That was Kate. Tackling everything headfirst. No tears. Just fight. Tori turned back to the sink to finish scrubbing the potato pan. What was her answer to trouble? Blocking her ears? Going fishing? Wishing it away?

Some things couldn't be wished away. Not babies on the way. And not people dying.

Behind her, Evie said, "I'm not ready, Mama. We haven't even got a house and Mike is . . ." She hesitated. "Well, I don't know what Mike is, but he's not ready either."

Tori placed the clean pan in the drainer and turned to get the last skillet off the stove. Her mother was rubbing her fingertips across her forehead as if she had a headache. A headache named Evie.

"Oh, Evangeline, sometimes you purposely put on blinders." She pulled in a breath and leaned her face down right in front of Evie's. "You may not be exactly ready right now and that's fine. The good Lord gives you time while the baby grows inside you to get ready. But you have to let Mike get ready too."

"But what if he's not happy?"

"What makes you think he won't be happy?" When she didn't answer right away, Mama went on. "Because you're not happy?"

Evie dashed away her tears with an impatient hand when she saw they weren't working on Mama. She lifted her chin with a bit of defiance. "He says he's not happy if I'm not happy."

Mama gave Evie that little shake Tori had wanted to give her earlier. "Then it could be time you got happy. For him. For your baby. For you."

Evie looked almost shocked that Mama was speaking to her so firmly. It wasn't something that happened often. Mama usually guided with a gentle hand and words.

"Were you happy when you found out you were expecting me?" Evie asked.

Mama's face softened. "Oh, my darling daughter, happy

doesn't even begin to describe how I felt. I was ecstatic. I loved you long before you were forming inside me. I loved the promise of you. All of you." Mama looked up at Tori and Kate. "From the first moment I knew I was carrying one of you, I felt blessed. Mightily blessed."

"And Daddy? Was he happy too?" Evie asked in a little girl voice.

"From the very first, you belonged in his heart. Mike will be the same. He's wrestling with what the Lord wants from him right now, like Jacob did in the Old Testament, but he'll find his way. The Lord knows his heart." Mama kissed Evie's forehead. "You know his heart. He will make a wonderful father. You will make a wonderful mother."

"Do you really think so?" Evie asked.

"I really do," Mama said. "I'll help. Your sisters will help. Victoria knows how it is."

"But she says you can be sick like this all day long." Evie moaned. "I thought it was called morning sickness."

Mama laughed. "Unfortunately, some mornings are long. But you'll get through it. With crackers and careful eating."

"Ugh, I don't even want to think about food right now. Or getting fat. I just know I'm going to get big as a barn." Evie looked ready to cry again.

"Maybe you'll have twins," Kate said with a wicked grin.

"Or a ten-pound baby. Samantha weighed seven pounds, you know," Tori added.

"Girls, stop trying to scare your sister," Mama said, but she was smiling too. "Come on now, the boys are getting worried about what you could be up to. Hiding out in the kitchen so long. And Aunt Hattie's ready to go home. That's what I came back here to tell you. Jay's taking her home in the car since it's so cold out there. He thought you might want to ride along, Kate."

Tori dumped the dishwater down the drain. Running water made everything so much easier.

Then Lorena rushed into the kitchen. "Tori, Clay Weber's here with his little sisters. They've brought Samantha a gift, but she's taking a nap. She'll be cranky if we wake her up."

Tori felt their eyes on her, wondering. She was wondering too. Wondering why in the world she'd told Clay Weber it was okay to come by. She draped the dishrag very precisely over the sink edge and looked out the window toward the trees across the field. Graham's pond was on the other side of those trees. Ice would be forming around the edges of the water against the banks.

She could be like Fern and walk out the back door and wander alone through the trees. Or she could remember that she had a family who loved her. She could remember that her little girl needed friends. She could remember it was almost Christmas and a time of giving. She couldn't deny that pleasure of giving to Clay's little sisters, no matter his ulterior motives.

She pushed a smile across her face and turned to Lorena. "We can wake her up in a few minutes, but I guess we'd better go say hello first. Clay said his mother helped Lillie and Mary make a doll for Samantha."

Mama helped her out. "Samantha will love it. Mrs. Weber makes wonderful dolls."

Evie jumped up, being sick apparently forgotten. "Great. I can't wait to see him." She shot Tori a grin. "I mean the doll."

Kate put her arm around Tori to follow the others out of the kitchen. “Pay no attention to her. You just do what you want.” she whispered.

“Sometimes that’s not possible.” Sometimes it was just too cold to go fishing.

13

Clay Weber tugged on the starched collar of his Sunday shirt to loosen it a bit as he stood inside Victoria's door with Mary and Lillie pressed against him on both sides. He made himself smile as he looked around at the people in the room. Victoria's father, Graham Lindell, Pastor Mike, and Kate's husband just home from the war. For the life of him, he couldn't remember the man's name and they'd just welcomed him home at church that morning. Victoria's little sister, Lorena, sat on a stool right beside the man.

Clay slid his eyes over to Aunt Hattie leaning forward in her rocker to give him the eye. They were all giving him the eye. They knew exactly why he was there and were probably thinking it was hopeless. That he was hopeless. Clay swallowed and wished he'd taken off his confounded tie. At least then he might be able to breathe.

Mr. Merritt was friendly, inviting them in. Smiling at the girls. Mr. Merritt was always friendly. But it wasn't Mr. Merritt Clay wanted to be friendly. Victoria was nowhere in sight. What did he expect? For her to be watching out the window for him? Hardly. He'd been surprised she'd agreed to let them come. Of course, it was because of the girls and their gift for Samantha.

When he thought about it, he couldn't believe he was shameless enough to use the girls and Victoria's baby, but sometimes it was better not to think too much. Just do whatever a person wanted to do. And he wanted to find a way to get Victoria to like him. No, more than like him. He wanted her to fall in love with him. That's what he wanted, but he'd settle for the liking him.

He'd been in love with Victoria for years. He hadn't ever let it show. Sammy was his friend and Sammy loved Victoria. Clay wouldn't have tried to butt into that even if Victoria had given any sign she might be looking for a fellow besides Sammy. She never had. All through school, the two of them were together every minute they could be together. Sammy and Victoria. Everybody knew they'd get married. Clay knew it too. He was glad for his buddy. Sad for himself, but glad for his friend.

One thing about Clay, he looked at things straight on. He'd had to do that ever since his father died. At sixteen, Clay was the oldest of the six kids he left behind. Aaron was four years younger than Clay. Then came Joseph, Lillie, and Mary. His mother was only six months along with Willie when Clay's father grabbed his chest while they were out planting corn. He never heard Clay trying to call him back.

His mother cried when Clay told her he was quitting school, but that was the only way they could keep the farm going. The only way the other kids could stay in school. A man did what a man had to do. Even if he was only sixteen.

Sometimes choices were made for a man. Like the war. He'd wanted to join up when Sammy did. All the men in Rosey

Corner were enlisting. It was the thing to do. But Uncle Sam said he had to keep milking cows and planting corn. The nation had to be fed.

After Sammy and Victoria got married, Clay blocked thoughts of her from his mind. He even stopped going to church, making the excuse that he had more cows so he couldn't get the milking done in time. But the truth was, he didn't want to see Victoria and be reminded of what could never be. After a while, he started driving down the road to see Paulette Browning, who was more than happy to climb in his truck and go to the movies on Saturday nights. Victoria might still visit his dreams, but in the daylight, he moved on with his life.

Then news came that Sammy had died in a Japanese prison camp. Clay didn't feel the first bit of happiness about that. His heart was broken for Sammy and for Victoria. At the same time, he quit going to Paulette's house and bided his time. For nearly a year, he watched Victoria from afar, letting her grieve, but she was too young to live her whole life as a widow. She needed a husband. Her little girl needed a father. Clay saw no reason he couldn't fill both of those needs. When Victoria was ready.

The trouble was, when he did start letting her know he was interested, she showed no sign of being ready to do anything with him. While he was ready enough for both of them, it took two to make a couple. Right now, standing in Victoria's sitting room, he was feeling very much alone in spite of the girls plastered against him. Mary had always been a little shy, but he had no idea why Lillie was acting so backward.

"Come on in, girls. Ain't none of these menfolk gonna

bite." Aunt Hattie waved them into the room. "Step on over here and show me what you've brung little Samantha."

Clay nudged Lillie, and she took Mary's hand to lead her across the room to Aunt Hattie. Clay had wanted them to move, but now he wished them back. His excuse for being there.

"Pull that chair out and sit down, Clay." Mr. Merritt pointed to a straight chair over in the corner.

Clay stayed where he was. "No, we don't want to break in on your family time. The girls just brought Samantha a gift." It wasn't a lie, but it wasn't the whole truth either. He didn't want to break in on their family time. He wanted to be part of their family time. His heart was galloping along like he'd just split a load of hard oak wood. Where was Victoria?

"Samantha's taking a nap," Lorena spoke up.

"Oh." Clay should have thought of nap time. It wasn't like he hadn't been around kids all his life. They took naps even on a Sunday. "I guess we can come back later." They couldn't. Not today. He had to milk in a couple of hours.

"No need in that." Mr. Merritt smiled over at the girls, who were looking disappointed. "That baby never sleeps long. I know she'll be tickled to see you and even happier to see whatever you've got in that package."

Lillie cradled the box wrapped in red tissue paper. They'd been more excited about this present than the presents his mother had wrapped for them. Mother too. He had never told her how much he loved Victoria, but she knew. Mothers didn't have to be told things like that in words.

"You're wearing my neck out looking up at you, boy," Graham Lindell said. "Take your coat off and sit down."

Lorena jumped up from beside the man who'd just come home from overseas to take his and the girls' coats. Tanner. Jay Tanner. That was his name. A rush of relief went through him that he remembered the name. He had black hair like Victoria's and Lorena's. More like Lorena's since it was curly. But he wasn't their brother, so that wasn't why they all had black hair, and Lorena was adopted into the family too.

Why was he thinking about the man's hair? Maybe because the guy was so good-looking. He'd probably never had one problem getting girls to like him.

A few girls had liked Clay too, even if he wasn't the best-looking guy in Rosey Corner. He wasn't exactly hard to look at. At least that was what Paulette told him. Clay never worried much about how he looked. At least not until lately when he started hoping Victoria would see something in him worth liking.

He was relieved when Pastor Mike asked him how his mother was getting along. Then Clay asked Pastor Mike how he liked Louisville. Over on the other side of the room the girls were telling Aunt Hattie about the doll they'd brought Samantha. Small talk. He could handle small talk as long as they stuck to things like the farm and the Christmas tree in front of the window.

The girls stared at the lights sparkling on the tree. They had decorated a tree at home, but the electric lines hadn't made it out to the farm yet.

When Mary reached toward one of the blue glass balls, Clay stopped her. "Don't touch it, Mary. It might break." She jerked her hand back and ducked her head.

"Wouldn't be the first thing that ever got broken around here," Mr. Merritt said. "That dog of Lorena's can wag his tail and knock off more in a second than you could in an hour, Mary."

"That's why he's outside," Lorena said. "We were running out of decorations."

"You let your dog in the house?" Lillie sounded even more awestruck by that than by the lights on the tree. "Mama would never let us bring our dog inside."

Jay Tanner spoke up. "But your dog is a farm dog. He wouldn't even want to be in the house. Scout, he's a town dog."

"That's right," Graham agreed. "Lot of difference between town dogs and country dogs."

Clay looked toward the back of the house. He could hear women talking. They must be in the kitchen. The way things were going he might have to head home without even a glimpse of Victoria. It was already going on three o'clock, and they had a half-hour ride home. If he didn't have any trouble on the road. One of the truck's tires had been going flat a lot lately.

Mr. Merritt must have seen him check the clock on the mantel behind the stove. "I guess it won't be long till milking time."

"Well, it's easier to get them up before dark."

"Night comes early on a winter day," Aunt Hattie said. "Wherever are those girls? I sent Nadine back there to tell them I needed to go on home. I'm like those old cows. Better in the barn before dark."

"You live in a barn?" Mary stared at Aunt Hattie with big eyes. Clay could almost see her thinking that if dogs lived in houses, then people might live in barns.

When everybody laughed, Mary raced across the room

to hide her face against Clay's chest. He pulled her up in his lap and whispered in her ear, "They aren't laughing at you." But he was wondering if they weren't all laughing at him. Lillie came over to rub Mary's back. She took care of her little sister.

"Now, don't you mind them, sweet child. My words were confusin' to you, but I was just meaning I wanted to get to my house 'fore darkness fell." Aunt Hattie rocked forward to get out of her chair. "Lorena, get those girls out of the kitchen and tell them more company's come calling."

Mr. Merritt started up to help the old lady, but the Tanner man beat him to it. He looked comfortable there in the Merritt sitting room like he'd only been gone a few days instead of a few years. He belonged. Clay mashed down on the envy rising up inside him. He didn't want that man's spot. He wanted his own spot. But that spot could only be given by Victoria.

Then the sisters and Mrs. Merritt were coming in the room. The sister with the pretty red hair, Evangeline, the one married to Pastor Mike, was in front with her mother. Clay hadn't gone to their wedding. That wasn't long after his father died and his mother hadn't felt up to a wedding. But he'd heard it was some affair.

Mrs. Merritt smiled at him and her eyes softened on Mary who had gotten nerve enough to raise her head up off his chest. But Evangeline stared at him like he was a frog just coming up out of the pond mud for air in the springtime. His tie felt too tight again.

Then Victoria was there, looking none too happy to see him in spite of her polite smile. The other sister, Kate, was beside her. Something about the way they stood close together made him think of how Lillie had rushed across the room to Mary. Protecting her. But Victoria didn't need protection from him.

For the hundredth time he thought he shouldn't have come. But he was getting to see Victoria's beautiful face. She told him he could come. He was in her house whether he felt like the odd man out or not.

"They brung little Samantha something fine," Aunt Hattie said.

Right on cue, the little girl cried out from somewhere in the house. Victoria turned toward the sound, but Lorena rushed in front of her. "I'll get her."

Lillie picked up their present, and Mary climbed down out of Clay's lap. Clay stood up, all too aware of everyone studying him and wondering about his intentions. Maybe he should just say right out loud that he wanted to court Victoria. He smiled a little at himself. He didn't need to say anything. They all already knew. Even Victoria.

When Lorena brought Samantha into the room, the child wasn't bothered at all by the people looking at her. A big smile spread across her face that looked just like Sammy's. Everybody liked Sammy. He was that kind of guy. He didn't stew in his own juices and worry until his heart was ready to jump out of his chest. But then he knew Victoria loved him. He didn't have to work to find ways to win her favor.

Clay wanted to believe Sammy would be glad to have Clay so ready to step into his shoes and take care of his family. Clay knew how to take care of little girls. He knew how to work. He wanted to know how to love.

Lillie dropped to her knees and held the present out. "We've got something for you, Samantha," she said in a singsong voice.

"Lil Lil." Samantha ran toward Lillie.

"It's from me too," Mary said.

Everybody had their eyes on the little girls. Everybody but Clay. He looked straight at Victoria, drinking in the sight of her. She was so beautiful his insides ached. He loved the way her dark hair rested lightly on her shoulders. He rubbed the tips of his fingers against his thumbs and wondered if it felt as silky as it looked.

"Merry Christmas," Lillie and Mary said when Samantha pulled the doll out of the box. They'd practiced saying that together on the drive over.

The doll had red yarn for hair and eyes stitched with green thread to match Samantha's. They'd even dyed a few freckles on the doll's face. Then they'd dressed it in a yellow checked dress and black cloth shoes. His mother was a wizard with her needle.

"Mine!" Samantha hugged the doll against her chest.

Everybody laughed, even Victoria. She looked over at Clay with a smile that looked real. "Thank you. It's so sweet of Lillie and Mary to give Samantha such a nice present. And please thank your mother too."

"I will." Clay evermore would. That smile would be the best Christmas gift he could get except another one to go on top of it.

When Samantha ran around the room to show everyone the doll, Lillie and Mary laughed out loud.

Aunt Hattie broke up the fun. "Snow's a-coming. I feel it in my bones, so's I better get on home."

"It's been awhile since I've wanted to see snow clouds, but a white Christmas sounds fine." Jay Tanner smiled across the room at his wife. "Kate and I like to dance in the snow."

"We do." Kate left Victoria's side and went across the room to Tanner like filings drawn to a magnet. "And I think it's time for a new dance."

Clay wouldn't have been a bit surprised if they had started dancing right then and there. He looked back at Victoria and wished he was handsome and slick like Tanner, but he was just a clumsy old farm boy.

"Dance alls yo' want." Aunt Hattie nudged Kate's leg with her cane. "After you take me home."

"We've got to go too," Clay said. The clouds would make nightfall come even earlier and he had to get the cows. The girls looked at him with pouty frowns, but they knew better than to argue.

After a rush of goodbyes and another smile from Victoria, more polite than warm this time, they were out the door and back in the truck.

At least he did have the one good smile to carry home with him. Christmas didn't come every day. He'd have to think up something new to get her to step closer to him in the New Year. He might not be able to dance. He might not be the handsomest guy in the room. But he knew how to stick to something and get it done if it was worth doing.

Working a farm taught a man that. Every year that a man plowed a field, more rocks rose up out of the dirt to be hauled away. Weeds kept sprouting no matter how many calluses a man got plying his hoe. Horses went lame. Machinery broke down. Cows went dry and hawks swooped out of the sky to steal the chickens. The ground didn't give up its yield without a man watering it with plenty of sweat. But just because something was hard didn't mean it wasn't worth doing.

Clay wasn't about to give up. He gripped the steering wheel

and drove through the snow falling so thick now he had to turn on the windshield wipers. He pulled up the memory of Victoria's smile and wondered how it would be to dance with her in the snow. That would probably never happen. He wasn't the dancing type, but he could make Samantha a sled.

Maybe he could talk Victoria into riding out to the farm with him to sled down some hills. They had plenty of hills on the farm. He thought about sitting on a sled with Victoria in front of him, sharing something fun. It could happen, he thought. As long as he didn't give up.

Lillie interrupted his thoughts. "Clay, what did that woman mean when she said that?"

"Which one?" Clay frowned trying to figure out what Lillie was talking about.

"The one that has red hair like Samantha."

"I don't know. Did she say something to you?"

"She wasn't talking to me. She was talking to Samantha's mama."

"Well, if she wasn't talking to you, then maybe you shouldn't have been listening." Clay mashed down on his curiosity. "It's not nice to eavesdrop. You know that."

"I didn't aim to, but I couldn't keep from hearing her when we were leaving."

"Okay. What did she say?" Clay wasn't sure he should ask, but whatever she'd heard was worrying Lillie. It was his job as big brother to listen.

"That you wouldn't be so hard to look at across the breakfast table," Lillie said. "Are you going to have breakfast with them?"

Clay was glad the light was dim in the truck as he kept his eyes on the road. It wouldn't do for Lillie to notice the color rising in his face. "What makes you think she was talking about me? She didn't say my name, did she?"

"No, but she was talking about you, wasn't she?"

Clay blew out a breath. "Well, I'm not going to be eating breakfast there anytime soon, so maybe she was, but more likely she wasn't."

"I wish I could eat breakfast there," Mary spoke up. "I bet they have pancakes every morning."

Clay reached over and rubbed Mary's head. "Tell you what. I'll ask Mama to cook pancakes Christmas morning."

"And we don't have to worry about our dog stealing them off our plates or knocking stuff off our Christmas tree," Lillie said.

The girls giggled and started talking about other things a dog might do to make a mess in a house.

That left Clay to wonder about what Lillie had heard Evangeline say, because Lillie was right. She had surely been talking about him.

14

On Christmas morning Kate woke before dawn, not wanting to miss a minute of her first Christmas with Jay. They had never celebrated Christmas together. That first Christmas after they met in 1941 was not only a dark time for the country, but a dark time for Kate too. Jay had enlisted in the Army the week after Pearl Harbor and was gone from Rosey Corner, but more than miles had separated them then.

They were married before the next Christmas, but an ocean apart. Letters had flown back and forth. Love written in words, but her arms felt extra empty at Christmastime. Each year she prayed that by the next Christmas the war would be over and the boys would be home. She prayed for the war to be over every day, but somehow praying it at Christmas made it special.

After all, Christmas was when the greatest gift was sent down to mankind. The angels even announced it by saying, "Glory to God in the highest, and on earth peace, good will toward men." So what better time to pray for peace? Now at last, that prayer had been answered, and after three

Christmases apart, Mr. and Mrs. Jay Tanner were going to have the best Christmas ever.

She planned to be awake before Jay, to have his present under the tree and the coffee perking. She should have known better. Jay was the one who woke at the slightest noise. So when she opened her eyes, the lights were already shining on their little tree and Jay's smile was waiting for her.

"Merry Christmas, Mrs. Tanner." He brushed the hair back from her face.

She'd gotten used to the name while he was in the Army, but it was different coming from his lips. Lips that he touched to hers.

She sat up and rubbed the sleep out of her eyes. "And Merry Christmas to you too, Mr. Tanner." She reached for his hand. "Do you remember when we first met and I called you that?"

"And ordered Birdie to call me Mr. Tanner too. I do indeed. So what do you want to call me now?"

"My love." Kate scooted over to lean her head against his chest. She loved hearing his heart beating steadily under her ear. She had prayed for that heart to make it through the war still beating. "Ever my love. I'm so glad you're home."

"Not as glad as I am to be here." His arms tightened around her. "Do you think Santa Claus visited us last night?"

She raised her head to peer at the tree. The floor under it was bare with not a present in sight. Her gift for him was in hiding under the bed. No present waited there for her either, but she didn't care. His voice in her ears was enough.

"Doesn't look like it." She smiled up at him. "Did you believe in Santa Claus when you were a kid?"

"Nope. Not after my mother died. Never saw the first bit of

evidence to support any jolly old elf at Christmastime." He was quiet a few seconds before he went on. "I didn't believe in anything then."

"How about now?" She ran her fingers over his hands. Strong hands that she loved touching her. Hands that would help her raise their children.

"Still got plenty of doubts about that old guy in red, but then again, I did see him down at the dime store yesterday. So I could be wrong."

Kate laughed. "That poor guy needs a new beard. Even Samantha would know he was a fake."

"The magic of belief covers up a lot of fake beards."

"But the magic of Christmas isn't Santa Claus. It's love." Kate pulled his hand up to her mouth and kissed his fingers.

"Do you remember when you quoted that Scripture verse to me? About perfect love casting out fear. I never forgot that."

Kate cringed a little at his words, remembering. "I shouldn't have. The only love that's perfect is the Lord's."

"And so we find Christmas. Perfect love in a manger."

A little shiver went up Kate's spine. She'd never really known this Jay. This man who believed enough to talk about the Lord with her. "Daddy will be reading the Christmas story this morning."

Jay rubbed his cheek against her hair. "Do you wish you were there?"

She shut her eyes and thought about her father sitting in his chair with the Bible on his knees, but barely looking at it as he recited the verses. This was the first year she wouldn't be with her family as Christmas morning dawned. "A little. In some ways, but in a more important way I want to be here with you. Wherever we are together is home now."

"We could have slept on the floor in front of the tree at your house."

"We could have, but instead we slept by our own Christmas tree. A new family needs new traditions."

"If waking up with you and watching the lights on a Christmas tree are traditions, I'm all for that." Jay kissed the top of her head.

"And think. Next year we could have a baby to enjoy the lights. Samantha loved the Christmas lights from the very first." It was the new prayer of her heart. Oh dear Lord, please, a baby to make their family complete.

"Don't be in such a hurry, Kate." Jay's arms stiffened a bit around her. "Can't we just enjoy the moment?"

"This moment here, I am enjoying very much." She twisted around to kiss his chin. He hadn't shaved yet and his beard was scratchy against her lips.

His arms tightened around her again. "A fine moment to enjoy."

She leaned against him, matching her breathing to his. "But I like thinking about the future too. What we'll be doing in six months or six years or sixty years."

"Sixty years! I'll be ninety in sixty years." Jay laughed.

"Then maybe we'd better not wait that long to have children."

His chin rubbed back and forth across her hair as he shook his head. "My Kate. Graham warned me from the very start you were a girl who thought you could fix things, but he wasn't sure you could fix me."

"You were never broken."

"Oh, but I was, but then I came to Rosey Corner and found you."

"If any fixing was done, it was done by the Lord. Not me." She didn't like him talking about being broken. "Aunt Hattie's always telling me to leave some things up to the Lord. I guess that's what I need to do about starting a family."

"Aunt Hattie is a wise woman. Let's enjoy this Christmas before we start thinking ahead to next Christmas."

"Evie's in the family way." The words slipped out. Kate hadn't meant to tell him that until she was sure Evie had told Mike about the baby.

"Having a family isn't a competition, Kate." He shifted behind her as though the headboard was suddenly too hard against his back.

"Sisters always compete."

"Then Tori's already won that competition."

"So she has, and a good thing. Samantha kept Tori from falling apart after she got the news about Sammy. She and Sammy were such sweethearts." Kate brushed away a tear. "You could really think about them together in sixty years and going strong."

"No sad thoughts allowed here. We're living in the moment, remember." Jay pushed her away and swung his feet over the side of the bed. "And right now's the moment to see if Santa Claus showed up last night."

"Santa must have missed our tree." Kate got up and pretended to be hunting under the bed for her slippers but instead pulled out the package she'd hidden there. "Oh wait, here's something he must have dropped. I think it's for you."

He laughed as he tore the paper off the camera she'd bought him.

"Do you like it? One of the guys at the paper helped me pick it out."

"It's great." Jay ran his hand over the camera, then pointed it toward her as he looked through the viewfinder. "Is it loaded?"

"Don't you dare take my picture. Not until I comb my hair." She grabbed a pillow and held it up in front of her face.

"I like your hair messed." He pulled the pillow away to kiss her.

She was ready for more kisses, but instead he jumped up and went to the tree. "Hey, I think I found something." He pulled a small box out of the branches. "Maybe Santa didn't forget you after all." With a big smile, he handed it to her.

Her breath caught in her throat as she flipped open the velvet-covered box. A diamond ring glittered against the black lining. "Oh, Jay, it's beautiful." She looked up at him, her heart swelling with love.

"A beautiful ring for a beautiful girl." He took the ring and slipped it on her finger. It was a perfect fit. "When I saw this, I had to get it for you. See the way it catches light?" He held her hand up so the diamond reflected the glow of the Christmas lights. "That's the first thing I noticed about you. How your eyes seemed to capture the light and explode with life. I wanted to be part of that life."

"You are my life." She slipped her arms around his neck. "I love you so much."

He wrapped his arms around her. "Do you hear the music?"

"Oh yes," Kate said.

"Can I have this dance?" His eyes burned into hers.

"This dance and every dance forever more."

When they were first falling in love, they danced to the music of the trees in Lindell Woods and then in the snow. Now their love wrapped them in joy as they glided across the floor to the sparkle of the Christmas lights. A prayer of thanksgiving rose inside Kate for this Christmas with Jay and all the Christmases to come.

By the time they finally made it to Rosey Corner, breakfast was long over, but a plate of her mother's cinnamon rolls waited for them on the table. Even if they'd been all gone, Kate wouldn't have missed the morning's dance for all the breakfast rolls in the world.

Still, it was good to be home in Rosey Corner with Jay, who was as happy to be there as she was. Between bites of his cinnamon roll, he teased Lorena about peering out the window every five minutes to watch for Evie and Mike. Mama said they couldn't open presents until they came.

Lorena might be fourteen, but she still acted like a kid at Christmas. She would love the locket with a bird etched on the front of it that Jay had for her. He'd found them both the perfect gifts. The diamond on Kate's hand caught the light, and its glitter made her feel so loved.

Across the room, Samantha giggled at the story Kate's father was reading to her. A warm feeling swept through Kate at the thought that next year Daddy might be holding her baby. Samantha clutched the doll the Weber children had brought her on Sunday. Tori said she rarely put it down. The edge in Tori's voice warned Kate not to ask about Clay Weber. Not today on Christmas when Tori would miss Sammy so much. But after the first of the year, it might be time to encourage Tori to think about her future.

What had Jay said? That Kate needed to enjoy the moment and not be forever looking ahead and trying to fix things. He was right. This was a Christmas to enjoy with the family around the Christmas tree. Her mother and Tori were on the couch, Mama for once not in the kitchen cooking. Graham was in the straight chair close to the stove with Chaucer at his feet, but Aunt Hattie's rocker was empty.

Not long after Kate and Jay got there, Fern stopped by to tell them Aunt Hattie wasn't about to set one foot outside with snow covering the ground. Aunt Hattie hadn't lived eighty years without having more sense than to dare fate by walking around on snow and ice.

They tried to get Fern to come inside, but she stood in the door and let the cold air sweep into the room while she delivered Aunt Hattie's message. But she smiled as much as she ever smiled when Lorena promised to bring her and Aunt Hattie Christmas dinner and their presents later.

Fern let her eyes fall on Jay. "Bring him with you. Hattie likes him."

"Kate can come too," Lorena said.

"If she has to." Fern tilted her head to peer at Kate from under the cap she wore. "But don't be bringing that picture box with you."

Graham spoke up from across the room. "Fern, you need to go on if you're going. You're letting all their heat out."

"Merry Christmas to you too, Brother." With that, she turned on her heel and stomped off the porch.

"Bye, Fern," Lorena called after her, but the woman didn't look around. Perhaps she didn't hear her with the ear flaps pulled down on her fur cap.

"Same old Fern," Jay said.

"Not really," Kate said. "The old Fern would have never come up on the porch."

"Hattie's changed her," Graham said.

Kate didn't contradict him, but she knew who had really

changed Fern. Lorena. She had changed all of them. Even Jay.

"Can't we just go ahead and open one present?" Lorena begged Mama now. "Mike and Evie might not even come. You said you weren't sure because of the snow."

"I think they'll be here," Mama said.

"But it's already past twelve. Everybody will want to eat again in a little while and then we'll have to put off presents even longer." Lorena looked at the gifts under the tree with longing.

"The longer you wait for something, the better it can be, Birdie." Jay got up off the floor where he'd been leaning back against Kate's armchair. "And unless Mike's changed more than I think, he'll be here for your Mama's fruitcake or whatever she spent all of yesterday cooking."

"Applesauce cake with caramel icing, but who cares about cake?" Lorena stuck her lip out in a pout.

"Lorena."

Kate had heard that same warning in Mama's voice plenty of times herself when she was younger.

Jay laughed. "I know a girl who needs something to do. Get your boots on, Birdie. It's snowman-building time." Jay poked Kate's knee. "You too."

"Go." Samantha reached her hands toward Jay.

"Okay, kiddo, come on. And your mama too." He looked toward Graham. "How about you?"

"I'll watch out the window." Graham scooted his chair a little closer to the stove.

An hour later, a snow family with sticks for arms were lined up in front of the porch. Lorena had fixed the sticks to touch like they were holding hands. After Tori took Samantha inside to warm up, a snowball fight broke out. So when Mike and Evie got there, Jay barely waited until Mike was out of the car before he hit him square on the shoulder.

"Don't you dare throw one of those at me," Evie yelled at Kate, making the temptation impossible to resist. But her aim was bad and the snowball hit the side of the car.

Mike laughed, scooped up some snow, and sprinted after Jay. Lorena shrieked and joined in the chase. Scout barked and ran circles around them.

Evie put her hands on her hips and yelled, "Good heavens, Mike. Stop acting like a child and help me into the house."

"Oh, let him have a little fun." Kate went over to Evie.

"But he's got to bring in our packages."

"He'll get them in a minute. Come on, I'll help you inside if you need help."

"You can't be too careful when you're in my condition. Mike should know that." Evie looked ready to spill a few tears. The girl could cry at the drop of a hat or a snowball.

"So you told him."

"I told him."

"He's happy?"

"Jubilant." Evie threw her hand out to point at him. "Look at him."

"And you? How are you?"

"Just peachy. Never mind that I may throw up any second and my waistband is already too tight."

"So a ray of sunshine as ever." Kate reached to take her arm, but Evie knocked her hand away.

"Your glove is wet. How long have you been out here acting like a kid?"

"I don't know. A while. We were just playing around until you got here."

"Playing around." Evie gave her that big-sister look Kate hated. "Don't you think it's about time you grew up?"

Evie didn't wait for an answer, but stomped toward the porch, keeping to the rock walk that had been cleared of snow.

"Not if I have to be like you," Kate muttered under her breath. She shook herself a little. It was Christmas. Jay was home. Presents waited under the tree and hot cider on the stove. Jay and Mike were still running around in the yard like two boys escaped from the schoolhouse. Lorena wasn't with them now. Instead she was by the snowmen. She'd insisted they make a father, a mother, and two kids.

A moment ago Christmas joy exploded out of her, but now she looked almost sad.

"Are you freezing, baby?" Kate flexed her hands inside her gloves. "I can't feel my fingers. Or my toes."

"Me either." Lorena pushed a smile out on her face, but it slid away like the snow blowing off the roof.

"What's the matter? Christmas too long in coming?" Kate put her arm around Lorena.

"No, my mother, not Mama, but my mommy from before, she told me that Christmas always comes. It doesn't matter whether there are presents or not. She said Christmas is in a person's heart."

"Your mommy was right." Kate tightened her arm around Lorena. She couldn't remember the last time Lorena had talked about her birth parents, although she continued to say her name every night the way her mother had told her to.

Lorena sighed, and her breath hung in the air before the wind whisked it away. "I can't remember what she looked like." She ran her gloved fingers over the snow mother's face. Bits of coal made the eyes and mouth, and a twig was the nose. Lorena had found pebbles to make her a necklace.

She looked up at Kate. "I didn't want to forget what she looked like. Or Kenton or Daddy. I was always a little afraid of Daddy. He wasn't like Daddy now. But I shouldn't forget what he looked like, should I?"

Kate sent up a silent prayer for wisdom. "You haven't forgotten them. They're all right there where your mommy told you Christmas lived." Kate touched Lorena's coat over her heart. "They'll always be there."

"But why didn't they come back for me the way Mommy promised?"

The girl's words stabbed Kate. Hadn't Lorena been happy all these years with their family? "I don't know. Maybe they couldn't. Maybe they still will. Maybe they knew we couldn't bear to lose you after you became part of our family."

Lorena's eyes flew wide open as she spun around to look at Kate. "You wouldn't lose me. Never. You're my forever sister."

"I am that." Kate blinked away tears that were not completely from the chilly wind blowing.

Lorena was taller than Kate, not a child anymore, but Kate saw the little girl she'd found abandoned on the church steps almost ten years ago. Beautiful then in her threadbare dress, bare feet, and tangled hair. Beautiful now with her black curls escaping her sock hat, her cheeks red from the cold, and those deep brown eyes begging Kate to understand.

"But if you had a brother and another mother and father, wouldn't you want to know them?"

Kate met her eyes. She did understand. "Yes. Yes, I would."

Behind them, a car door slammed and Mike started for

the house with a sack of gifts. Jay ran up behind them with Scout on his heels. "What's going on over here? I thought somebody wanted to open Christmas presents."

Lorena's smile came back full force as Jay grabbed their hands and pulled them toward the porch. But Kate noted her quick look back at the snow family. Maybe it was time to use her reporter skills to ferret out some information about the Birdsong family. Then again, Aunt Hattie said some pots were better not stirred.

15

Tori pulled her wool scarf tighter around her head as she walked toward the store. The wind spit snowy ice in her face. February had to be the longest month of the year. It didn't matter if the calendar did count fewer days. Those days stretched out and mocked them by piling more freezing weather down on the winter weary. Now and again, the sun appeared, but not with any warmth before the clouds blew back in, darker than ever, to dash hope of an early spring.

She'd caught a cold. She always had a cold in February. Her nose was rubbed raw from constant wiping, and she and her father had kept up a duet of coughing all through the night. Daddy's cough was no better in spite of trips to the doctor and Aunt Hattie's potions.

"Spring will be here soon," he told Mama when she worried over him. "Warm weather is the best cure."

But the sound of his coughs hung a pall over the house and made February even darker. This very morning he looked so tired at breakfast that Mama talked him into not going to his shop until later. Mama told Tori to stay home too and keep Samantha in out of the weather, but Tori couldn't stay home every day. It was her job to help her mother at the store even if she hated waiting on people and listening to their complaints about every livelong thing from the price of coffee to the bananas being too ripe. Or not ripe enough. Still it was her job. A job she needed. She was an adult. An adult with a child. So she left Samantha with her father and headed to the store.

At least it was her job now. Kate was moving back to Rosey Corner. She and Jay had found a house to rent. Jay got a job at the feed store over in Edgeville where he'd worked before the war. Kate had lost her job at the newspaper. Kate said she didn't care, but Tori wasn't sure she meant it.

Once Kate was back in Rosey Corner, she could work at the store again. "And give you more time with Samantha," she'd told Tori. Trying to help. That was Kate. Always trying to make things right. She knew Tori hated working at the store. But what would Tori do instead?

She'd asked Kate that. "If I don't work at the store, what am I going to do?"

"I don't know. Why do you have to do something? Can't you just be a mama?"

"That's the problem. I am a mother. A single mother. I can't expect Mama and Daddy to take care of me forever."

"Are you tired of living here?" Kate had looked around the bedroom where they were changing clothes after church on Sunday.

"I don't know that I'd say tired, exactly." Tori peeled off her good dress and reached for a skirt and sweater. Lorena had already grabbed up Samantha and headed back out to the stove where Jay and Daddy were talking. Pans rattling meant Mama was finishing up dinner.

Evie and Mike weren't coming. They hadn't been home on Sunday but twice since Christmas. Evie claimed there were just so many times a day a person could upchuck, and riding all the way to Rosey Corner from Louisville put that number over the top.

It was chilly back in the bedroom they had once all shared and that Tori and Samantha still shared with Lorena. Even though the house was small, the stove in the sitting room couldn't put out enough heat to warm every corner when winter winds pushed at the walls. This time of the year they missed the old woodstove in the kitchen. A shiny electric range had replaced it, but unless they left the oven on with the door open, that stove didn't do much to keep a person warm on a cold winter day.

"Do you wish you had your own house?" Kate didn't wait for an answer. "But of course you do."

Tori wasn't sure whether she did or didn't. It might be nice to have a house, but what would she do without her parents helping her with Samantha? "I don't know. Samantha and I might be lonely rattling around in a house by ourselves."

"Maybe you could move into one of Aunt Hattie's spare bedrooms."

"And live with Fern giving me those stares?" Tori shuddered at the thought. "No, thank you. Samantha doesn't need that. And neither do I."

Kate laughed. "Fern's not so bad."

"Would you want to look at her every morning at breakfast?" She was sorry for the words as soon as they were out. They echoed back to that Sunday before Christmas when Evie had asked if Clay Weber was someone she could look at across the breakfast table.

"Maybe not." Kate hung her suit up on a hanger hooked to the back of the bedroom door. She smoothed out the skirt for a long moment. "I see Samantha is still carrying around that doll the Weber girls gave her. Mrs. Weber should sell those dolls."

"I think she does." Tori slid off her stockings and pulled on wool socks. She hated being cold. She rolled her stockings into a ball and kept her eyes away from Kate. She knew what Kate wanted to ask, but it was a question she didn't want to answer.

"I didn't know that. I could have taken some to Lexington and sold them for her."

"That would have been nice." Tori kept her voice carefully neutral. Mrs. Weber was a wizard with her needle, but Tori didn't want to talk about her. She didn't want to talk about any of the Weber family, especially the one Kate was edging toward talking about.

"I remember when Mr. Weber died. So hard for Mrs. Weber to lose her husband with all those children and one on the way."

"You don't have to tell me how hard it is to lose a husband." Tori's voice sounded tight even to her own ears as her insides clenched like a fist. Why couldn't people just leave her alone? If she wanted to grieve for Sammy the rest of her life, what was wrong with that? It was her life. She shoved her stockings down into the toes of her Sunday shoes and put them in the bottom of the wardrobe. She could feel Kate watching her.

"I know." Kate hesitated. "Maybe if you talked with her it would help you. It sometimes helps to talk to people who have experienced the same troubles you have."

Tori took her time getting her everyday shoes out of the wardrobe. She had the feeling Kate had more to say and she wasn't sure she wanted to hear it. One thing was certain. She wasn't going to go to Clay Weber's house to talk to his mother. Seeing him at the store was trial enough.

That wasn't exactly fair. Clay had brought Samantha the cutest sled. He'd fashioned the wooden part himself and asked Tori's father to make the runners. Samantha had been thrilled. Daddy had been thrilled. Tori's challenge was finding a way to thank Clay without encouraging him. And to keep everybody else from deciding what was best for her.

She couldn't keep staring at her shoes forever. Besides, that didn't keep Kate from saying what she was thinking anyway. "Why don't you let him take you to the movies? It would be good for you to get out."

Tori pulled on her shoes. Without looking up, she said, "I don't want to encourage Clay, Kate. He wants more than I can give."

"Going to the movies doesn't mean you're getting married or anything."

"But don't you see? That might be what Clay thinks. I have the feeling that's what he wants."

"Well, tell him you're not ready for that. If you're not." There was a question in Kate's words.

"I'm not," Tori looked up at Kate to make sure she knew she meant what she said.

Kate didn't quite hide her sigh as she pulled on her sweater. "Then tell him you just want to be friends. Buddies. Somebody to get out with and do something different. You can't go fishing in February."

"I don't need a buddy," Tori said firmly as she stood up.

"I've got sisters. And you can go fishing in February if you want to. You just won't catch anything."

"Except a cold, and you've already caught that. And some sisters don't like to go fishing any month of the year."

"But Lorena likes to fish. And then there's Graham."

"Okay." Kate hugged Tori's shoulders. "I'll let you pick your own buddies. But don't slam the door too fast on Clay. He seems quite smitten with you. As he should be. You're smart and beautiful. Even with that poor red nose."

Right on cue, Tori had started sneezing. It was one time she had welcomed the need to blow her nose. Anything to stop Kate from talking about Clay Weber. Once she moved back to Rosey Corner, Tori would simply have to tell her to mind her own business.

Now Tori hurried past the gas pumps and into the store out of the wind. The warmth rushed out to meet her when she opened the door. They'd put in a furnace that kept the store warm, but they still kept a fire in the potbelly stove in the back corner where some of the folks liked to gather and catch up on the news. That's where Clay Weber sometimes stood and watched her while she waited on customers. At times she could almost hear him thinking up new things to ask her to do.

But nobody was there now. Not even Graham. Her mother looked up from her account books to smile at Tori. "Go warm up."

Tori held her hands out toward the stove, letting the heat embrace her. She was glad nobody else was in the store. Mondays were always slow, but they could count on Graham coming by. Then at noon, the men from over at the garage generally showed up for sandwiches and sodas. Clay was sometimes with them since he was friends with the owner.

He didn't usually buy anything to eat, but more often than not, he'd buy some penny candy for his little sisters and then give Samantha a piece. Even when he didn't buy the candy, Samantha still reached her little hands up to him. He looked comfortable as anything carrying her around the store, talking with her as though he understood her every jabbered word. He'd miss Samantha if he came in today.

But when she thought about it, Clay hadn't been to the store for a while. She frowned and tried to remember how long. Not that it mattered. The bad weather could be keeping him away from Rosey Corner. Or maybe Clay had simply gotten the message. Finally. Maybe he was visiting Paulette again. Paulette had been dating a boy from Frankfort, but she made no secret of the fact she wouldn't mind Clay pulling up to her house again.

That would be good. Good for all of them. But then all day long, Tori looked up every time the bell over the door jingled, wondering if it would be Clay coming in.

When the day passed without him showing up, a little finger of disappointment wiggled awake inside her. No, not disappointment, she told herself quickly. Worry. That was all it was. While she'd been pushing him away, they had been friends since school days. A person should be worried about a friend when he didn't show up in his usual places.

At closing time, Tori cleaned out the onion bin and then went into the small water closet to wash her hands. When her eyes caught on her reflection in the mirror over the sink, she hooked her hair back behind her ears. It could be she should try to curl her hair. Maybe powder her nose.

What was she thinking? She stared at her face in the mirror. "Victoria Gale Harper, you have got to be out of your mind," she whispered.

She jerked the string to turn off the light, glad for the dark that wrapped around her before she opened the door back out into the store. It made no difference how she looked. No difference at all. Or whether Clay Weber showed up at the store. She didn't care. Not at all. That funny feeling in her stomach was simply because she hadn't eaten anything since breakfast.

16

Who would have thought she'd be excited about losing her breakfast? More than excited. Jubilant. If Kate didn't feel so shaky, she would be tap dancing on the little back porch. It was proof her prayers had been answered. She was going to be a mother.

The late March day was full of sunshine. The whole world looked bright from the yellow jonquils bursting into bloom along the side of the yard to the flash of a bluebird's wings as it flew by. Perhaps looking for love. Love she had already found. Gloriously found.

The song they sang at the beginning of Sunday services bubbled up in her mind. "Praise God from whom all blessings flow."

She did praise him. And thank him. She leaned against the porch post and put her hands on her flat belly. Soon it would be swelling with the blessing of a baby. She'd been almost holding her breath for a couple of weeks now. Hoping, but not sure. She hadn't shared the hope with anyone. Not Jay. Not her mother. She wanted to be sure first.

They all knew what she was hoping. They knew how

much she wanted to be a mother. But nobody seemed to be in as much a hurry as she was. Jay wanted to just enjoy being home, being with her. Her mother was wrapped up in guiding Evie along her rocky path toward motherhood. Evie had finally gotten through the morning sickness, but now she was distraught over the loss of her waistline. And the loss of her job.

"What does a person do sitting at home all day long?" she had complained last Sunday. "Twiddle her thumbs?"

"If she wants to," Kate told her. "Or you could take up knitting or sewing. Maybe make the baby a quilt."

"Quilt? Me?" Evie sank down in one of the kitchen chairs. They were cleaning up after dinner and as usual Kate was doing all the work. Tori was rocking a very cranky Samantha, who was teething. Jay and Lorena left with a plate of food for Aunt Hattie. Kate wished she'd gone with them, but then Mama would have thought she had to do the cleanup. Her mother rarely sat down. She deserved a few minutes of Sunday afternoon peace. So here Kate was. Stuck with her hands in dishwater and her ears full of Evie's whining.

"Well, then read some books."

"You're saying what you'd like to do. I guess what you can do now that you're not working." Evie shifted in the chair and held out her feet to stare at them. "Even my feet are fat."

Kate looked down at Evie's fashionable black pumps. "It's not permanent, you know."

"But I just bought these shoes. I thought at least I wouldn't outgrow shoes and now they're killing my feet."

"If they hurt your feet, take them off."

"You always act like everything is so simple." Evie stomped

her shoes down flat on the floor. "But it isn't. Lots of things aren't simple at all."

One thing was more than simple—how Evie could drive her crazy. Kate counted to five and turned back to the sink. Washing dishes, now that was simple. Glasses first, then plates.

"Yeah, I guess you're right." If she wanted to keep things simple, agreeing with Evie was generally the way to go. No need to fuss about things that didn't matter, although they'd done plenty of that in their time. But they weren't little girls anymore.

It worked. Evie quit worrying about her feet. "I thought you were going to work at the store."

"Not right now. I decided to try writing some freelance stuff."

"What kind of stuff?" Evie didn't sound all that interested.

Kate concentrated on washing a plate and rinsing it. She had dreams of writing stories for magazines, maybe even writing a book, but she wasn't ready to tell Evie that. Evie might say something to shoot down her dreams. Not on purpose, but just being Evie.

"Oh, I don't know." Kate carefully placed the plate in the drainer. "The editor at the *Herald* said he might consider something with a human interest angle. And the Edgeville paper wants me to submit some ideas to them. Besides, Tori didn't want to give up the job at the store."

"Really? I'm surprised. She's never liked working there. You remember how she would rather haul in the coal and cook supper than be at the store."

"I know, but now she has Samantha. She feels like she needs to work."

"What she needs to do is get married again. You know Tori never wanted to be anything except a wife and mother. Unlike us."

"I want to be a wife and a mother." Kate set the last plate in the drainer and began washing the utensils. She hated washing the knives and forks. So many of them.

"But that's not all. You've always wanted more. We both do."

"More. More what?"

Evie pushed up from the chair. She wasn't that big yet—only six months along—but she already acted as if she weighed a ton. What on earth would she do two months from now? Kate remembered Tori's final month of carrying Samantha when just moving was difficult for her and they had to help her up off the couch. But Tori was so slim, the baby weight had been extra heavy on her.

That wouldn't be true with Evie. Mama said she was carrying well. But everybody got big. That was part of it. Big and beautiful. Expectant mothers were always beautiful. Mike certainly thought so. He was more like the old Mike, the Mike before the war, as he tried to do everything and anything to please Evie. But nothing pleased Evie right now. Mama made excuses for her. She said being in the family way made people moody. Kate had to bite her tongue to keep from saying that Evie had always been moody.

Evie picked up a dish towel to dry the plates. "You don't have to act like you don't know what I mean, Kate. You liked working at the paper and seeing your pieces in print. Doing something yourself. Good gracious, you've been trying to fix the world for years."

"Maybe." Kate dumped a handful of spoons in the drainer.

On to the forks. “So I want to fix the world. What’s the more you want, Evie?”

“I like typing up letters. I know how to keep things organized in an office so work can get done.” She gave Kate a look as if daring her to doubt the importance of that. “And I’m good at it. Very good at it. Mr. Winters said he’d never had a secretary half as good as me.”

“That didn’t keep him from letting you go as soon as he found out you were expecting.”

“Policy. He couldn’t go against company policy.” Evie leaned against the cabinet and didn’t pick up another plate to dry. She stared out the window. “Do you think it would be awful if I went back to work after the baby comes?”

“What would you do with the baby?” Kate looked over at her in surprise.

“There are such things as babysitters. I met a woman at the grocery store who says she loves taking care of babies.”

“Oh.” Kate didn’t trust herself to say more. She couldn’t believe Evie was thinking about turning her baby over to some stranger in Louisville who wasn’t even family.

“You do think it’s awful. So does Mike.” Evie sighed. “But what’s wrong with a woman having a career? Tell me that.”

“Babies need their mommies. You’ll feel different once you have the baby and hold him.”

“Not him. Her.”

“How can you know that?” Kate looked at her with curiosity.

“I know I don’t know the first thing about little boys. Maybe I can figure out a baby girl, and a girl will be so much more fun to dress.” She dried the spoons and carefully stacked them in the utensil tray in the drawer.

Kate laughed. "You'll have a boy and you'll love him so much you won't let any of us hold him. You'll have a conniption fit when Tori tries to take him fishing the way she does Samantha, because you won't trust anybody else to watch him as well as you do. You'll nearly spoil him to death, but thank goodness, a little sister will come along before you completely ruin him."

Evie rolled her eyes at Kate. "You are out of your mind. It's going to be awhile before I try this again. You'll change your tune about how wonderful it is when you start looking like you swallowed a watermelon seed." Evie made a face. "That's what crazy old Graham told me the last time I came home."

Kate smiled as she washed the knives. "That's a seed I want to swallow."

She hadn't told Evie about her suspicions of maybe already having that seed growing inside her. She wanted to be sure.

And now as she leaned against her porch post, she looked to the west, toward Louisville. Her child and Evie's child would grow up together. Playing here in Rosey Corner. Exploring Lindell Woods together. Letting Aunt Tori bait their hooks. Perhaps fussing like sisters. Maybe being terrified of Fern appearing out of the gloaming the way Kate and her sisters were as kids.

In fact, at that very moment she spotted Fern across the field behind the house. On her way to the woods. The woman had to wander, perhaps searching for her more. Could it be that every person always wanted more the way Evie said she and Kate did? Even Tori, in spite of Evie saying all she wanted to be was a wife and mother. That could be her more right now. She needed more to happen to be a wife again.

Kate stared out at the field. Fern climbed over the fence

and disappeared into the trees. Fern needed her solitude. Tori seemed to need that solitude now too. She slipped off to Graham's pond every time the sun warmed the day the slightest bit. While Kate hated to think about it, she had to wonder if Tori wanted to shut out the world the way Fern did.

Clay Weber was in love with Tori. The man's longing for Tori was almost palpable, but she would barely give him the time of day. Samantha loved him and ran to him with her arms stretched up every time she saw him. That seemed to make Tori want to push him out of her path even more. He was a good man. A perfect solution to Tori's need for more, but love couldn't be orchestrated. Kate sighed.

Evie was right about her. She did want to fix the world and make everybody happy. Especially her sisters. She wanted Evie to embrace becoming a mother. She would. Already Kate could see a different look on Evie's face when the baby moved inside her. Kate was so ready to feel that quickening of life. A smile slid across her face. That would be worth tossing a few breakfasts.

Since she was thinking on fixing the world, what else could she want? Tori to fall in love again. Not to forget Sammy, but to open her heart to new love. Then there was Lorena. Her little sister was growing up. Soon she might have her own heartaches. Perhaps she already did. Kate remembered the snow family they made at Christmas. Lorena was right. No matter how much she loved her family now, she couldn't block out her first family.

Lorena treasured the memory of her mother's love and her promise to someday come back for her. That was why she said her name every night. *My name is Lorena Birdsong.*

Her name was her connection to the mother whose memory was fading in Lorena's mind.

Kate leaned her head against the porch post. She'd been glad when the snow family melted away after Christmas. Lorena's eyes were too sad when she looked at the shrinking mounds of snow.

Right now, Lorena would be at school in Edgeville. Fourteen. Beautiful without trying. With a natural voice that got stronger the more she sang. A church in Edgeville had asked Lorena to sing at their services a few Sundays ago. Kate and Jay had taken her.

Lorena sang all the time at their church, but seeing how her voice reached out and grabbed the attention of a congregation that wasn't all family and friends opened Kate's eyes to the passion Lorena had for singing.

Jay had felt it too. On the drive back to Rosey Corner, he said, "Wow, Birdie. Someday I'll get to say 'I knew her when.'"

"When what?" Birdie said, although it was obvious she knew what he meant.

"When you were just a curly headed little kid who sang at her sister's wedding."

"I didn't sing at your wedding," Lorena said.

"But you did at Evie's. You and Kate both. Remember? That sweetheart song." Jay reached over to squeeze Kate's hand. "Made me want to have a sweetheart."

Lorena burst out singing right there in the car. Then they were all singing, even Jay, though he was a little off pitch. That made Lorena laugh and lean her head on Kate's shoulder. She was happy with them. She was. And she'd be ecstatic when Kate told her about the baby.

First Kate had to tell Jay. Tonight. She'd make a pie to

celebrate her news. It didn't matter that the very thought of pie made her queasy again. Jay would like the pie. She wanted him to be happy too. She wanted him to be as happy about the baby as she was. He would be. Of course, he would be.

But when she opened the refrigerator to see if she had enough milk for the pie, her stomach flipped and she had to run back out on the porch. Some things were better about being in the family way than others.

17

"Are you sure?" Jay asked Kate.

When he had gotten home from work, candles were on the table. Already lit. More telling, she had a glow brighter than the candles. Something was definitely up.

After she sliced the pie, she reached across the table and took his hand. Even before she said anything, her news was plain on her face. He was going to be a father. And though he was expecting them, the words still slammed him right in the chest and made it hard to breathe for a few seconds.

"I'm sure," she said.

He managed to whisper, "A baby."

Kate giggled like a little girl, happiness bubbling up out of her. "You're happy, aren't you?" She looked at him, her heart in her eyes.

"How could I be anything else?" His pie forgotten, Jay kissed her, then put his hand on her flat belly. Inside her, his baby was growing. A baby she already loved. It didn't matter that there was nothing there to feel. Soon there would be. Soon he'd be a father.

"I'm so glad you're happy."

Her words poked him. He tried to ignore the tremble in his fingers as he gently smoothed down her hair. "Did you think I wouldn't be?"

She looked up at him. "You did keep telling me not to be in such a hurry. To live in the moment."

"The moments have been good. Very good."

"I know. That's why I thought maybe you didn't want the moment to change."

"Why would you think that?" He kissed her forehead and wished she'd been satisfied with his embrace and kiss. But that wouldn't be Kate. She wanted to examine every word sometimes as if looking for worms under rocks.

"I love you, Jay, with all my heart. I believe we were meant to be together, but there's a lot I don't know about you."

"And that I don't know about you, but what I do know, I love." Jay tapped her nose with his finger. He wasn't ready to pick up the rocks of his past. Maybe someday, but not now with the news of his baby on the way fresh in his ears. He tried to ease away from her questions. "But we'll have years and years together to find out all those things."

"You already know everything there is to know about me. It's all here in Rosey Corner. Family, friends, places I love." She touched his cheek. "But you? You never talk about your family. You don't talk about the war."

"Some things are better forgotten."

"But can you forget?"

"Not everything. Not every day. But right now, this moment, I can. A very happy moment." He held her close and kissed her hair. He did love this woman so very much.

He was happy. He really was. The trouble was he was also

terrified. Absolutely terrified he wouldn't be a good father. He thought of Sarge. Married with two kids. He tried to think about him at home in Michigan. Out of uniform. Going to work. Loving his kids. Doing what had to be done. Jay could do the same.

Kate breathed out a long sigh. "Do you hear music?"

He smiled with not the slightest tremble in his heart. This part of loving Kate had ever been easy. "I'll always hear the music with you." He held up his hand. She took it and they waltzed around the kitchen.

Kate laughed when they bumped into a chair. "We need a bigger kitchen."

"Or a bigger dance floor." He led her out the kitchen door into the backyard. The sun had already headed down to the other side of the world, leaving a rosy afterglow to mark its passing. The twilight air wrapped around them like a well-worn cloak while a chorus of tree frogs added to the music of their hearts. He'd dreamed of dancing with Kate like this as he huddled in foxholes. Dreams and prayers.

"Good that you haven't forgotten how to dance." Fern's voice stopped the music.

"Fern like the plant." Jay looked around at her. He had no idea how long she'd been there by the fence.

Enough light remained for him to catch the woman's near smile as she inclined her head in acknowledgment of the memory of the first time she'd appeared out of the shadows to poke him with her words. "Jay like the bird."

Jay kept his arms around Kate. The evening air was cool and he wanted to protect her from the chill. And from Fern.

"Yes, Fern." Kate's voice was soft. "You told us about the music. Do you remember?"

"You think I'm a doddery old fool who can't remember what happened yesterday?" Fern snorted.

"I thought maybe you wouldn't think it important enough to remember." Kate stiffened against Jay. Bracing for the battle she and Fern always seemed to have when they talked.

Jay tried to head it off. "Good to see you haven't forgotten how to sneak up on people, Fern." He'd make the woman battle him this time, but instead she surprised him by making a sound that could have been a laugh.

"I don't sneak," she said. "People just don't use their eyes. Or ears."

"But you do," Jay said.

"Remember Fern like the plant. Ferns grow in the shade. They don't make noise even when the wind is blowing. Little things hide under them. They tell no secrets."

"Secrets? Do you know secrets?" Jay narrowed his eyes to see her better, but the day was losing its battle with night. He couldn't tell what was behind her words.

"Fern knows everything," Kate said.

"Not everything, but enough." Fern stared at Kate a moment before she turned away.

"Goodbye, Fern like the plant," he called after her.

She looked back over her shoulder at them. He couldn't see her face, but he could hear her plain enough. "Better keep on dancing before the baby bump gets big and keeps you apart."

Kate pulled away from Jay to run after her. The woman's words obviously surprised her. "How did you know?"

Jay followed Kate to the fence.

Fern kept walking, but again there was that sound that passed for her laugh. "You said I know everything."

"You saw me." Kate looked at Jay to explain. "Fern was

passing by in the field this morning when I lost my breakfast out on the porch."

"So that explains that." Jay put his arms around her again. She was shivering.

"I use my eyes." Fern stopped then to look back at them. "I see that little sister too. Not the one that likes me, but the other one. The one that's afraid. See her fishing."

"Tori likes to fish," Kate said.

"Too much. Could end up like me. Packing a fishing pole instead of a hatchet." She held up the little ax she used to chop down cedars.

"No." Kate spoke the word too loudly.

Jay tightened his arms around her. Her trembles now weren't completely because of the night air.

Kate's voice softened as she added, "She has Samantha."

"But something could happen. Something can always happen." Fern turned away from them to head on toward Rosey Corner.

"Good things too." Kate seemed to push the words through the night after Fern.

This time Fern gave no sign of hearing.

Kate shivered against Jay again. He rubbed his hands up and down her upper arms to warm her. "That's just Fern. She forgot how to be happy a long time ago."

"I know."

"But you haven't. We haven't." He pushed cheer into his voice. The woman's words had cast a pall over him too, because he knew it was true. Things did happen.

Kate turned toward the house. "What if she's right? About Tori. Lately she seems to want to get away from us all."

"Maybe because you keep pushing that Weber guy at her."

Kate looked up at him as they went back into the kitchen. The candles, still burning on the table, cast flickering shadows on the wall. “He’s a nice guy. Samantha likes him.”

“It’s not Samantha he needs to like him.” Jay shut the door behind them and reached for the pull string on the overhead bulb. The light glared brightly after the soft darkness outside and candlelight inside.

Kate blew out the candles. “I like him. Mama and Daddy like him. He won Lorena over with that sled he made for Samantha. Even Scout likes him.”

“Scout likes everybody, but the name you didn’t say is the one that matters. Can he get Tori to like him?”

“I don’t know. He keeps trying.” Kate sighed as she began to clear off the table. “I just don’t know. She won’t talk about it. Fern’s right. She goes fishing.”

“You could go with her.” Jay sat back down at the table to eat the last few bites of his pie. “Keep her company.”

“You know I hate to fish. Squishing worms on hooks and getting fishy smell all over your hands.” She shuddered and shoved her untouched piece of pie toward him as if even the thought of fishing had turned her stomach. Then she got a funny look on her face. “You did know that, didn’t you?”

“Nope, I don’t think the subject has ever come up.” He dug his fork into the pie. “See, there’s something I didn’t know about you.”

“I don’t know if you like to fish either.”

“I went with Mike some when we were kids.”

“I did know Mike liked to fish. He used to go with Tori and Lorena on Saturday afternoons before the war. He talked Evie into going with him a few times too.”

“I’m guessing that was a disaster.”

"You might think so, but actually Evie sort of likes to fish." She looked up from putting the leftovers into smaller bowls to fit in the refrigerator.

"You Merritt girls are full of surprises. Have you told them? The sisters?"

She shook her head. "Not even Mama. Nobody knows but you."

"You're forgetting Fern."

"I'm trying. I'm definitely trying." The sparkle came back into her eyes. "I can't believe she saw me heaving up my breakfast this morning and figured out I was expecting."

"A lucky guess. She likes to keep you off balance. It's a game with her."

"A game." Kate carried the plates to the sink. "Funny to think about Fern playing a game, but you're right. She does like to aggravate me, but then she tells me things I need to hear sometimes too. Things she sees that I don't want to see. Or I'm too blind to see."

"What things are you talking about?" Jay forked in the last of the pie.

"Lots of things. She used to warn me about maybe ending up like her too."

"Never." Jay looked up, surprised. "I can't imagine you hiding out in the woods and popping out of shadows to scare the fainthearted."

"When you put it that way, it sounds sort of fun." Kate laughed, but then her smile leaked away. "But she's right about Tori." Kate tightened her lips as she stared at the dark window over the sink.

"Uh-oh." Jay cupped his hands around his mouth and

pretended to yell. "Look out, Tori. Sister Kate is ready to come to the rescue."

Kate balled up the dishrag and threw it at him. "You're the one who just got through telling me to go fishing with her."

He got up and exchanged the dishrag for a dish towel. "Tori will figure things out. Right now she's sad, but she'll be okay."

"If something doesn't happen." Kate sounded worried.

"Don't borrow trouble, Kate. Remember, we're living in the moment. A moment that's good, with nothing happening except the dishes getting done and bedtime coming."

"And a baby on the way." Kate smiled over at him, as beautiful as he'd ever seen her, even in the harsh overhead light.

Later, as they lay in bed with her head resting on his shoulder, she asked him again, "Are you happy? Really happy?"

"I told you I was happy about the baby, Kate." He rubbed his cheek against her head. "Very happy."

"Not just about the baby. But being married and living here in Rosey Corner? With your job and everything?"

Jay didn't let himself hesitate. "You make me happy, Kate." And there was no reason for him to hesitate. She did make him happy.

She snuggled closer to him, her body relaxed and content there beside him. "But the other things. Are you happy about them?"

"Do you want me to make a list, Kate?"

"That might be good," she murmured.

"Let me count the ways." He held up his fingers and began counting them off. "Alive. Home from the war. A job. A beautiful wife who makes pies almost as good as her mother's." She roused enough from her sleepiness to laugh at that and try to poke him. He caught her hand and kept going. "A baby on the way. Rosey Corner as my address. Fern like the plant to tell me what's going on. Birdie to make me laugh. Scout to make me happy we don't have a dog."

"Scout's not that bad." She laughed again the way he'd intended. Then she was sleeping in his arms. He looked down at her peaceful face in the dim moonlight sneaking through the window and his heart swelled.

A baby. Mothering would be easy for Kate. As natural as the sun coming up in the morning. But would he be able to pull off being a father? And how about all the bills? He didn't mind the work at the feed store, but the pay wasn't great. They just squeaked by now.

He knew other men home from the war who were going to college on the GI Bill. He hated school when he was a kid, but he wasn't a kid anymore. College sounded like a good thing now and a path to a better job. Plus, Kate once told him she dreamed about going to college. With the GI Bill paying his way, he'd been thinking of ways both of them could go. He hadn't mentioned that to Kate. He wanted to plan it all out and surprise her. But a baby changed everything.

He slid his arm out from under her head and slipped out of bed. He couldn't lay still. He had to be moving. Standing. Watching. A man had to be ready. Not so long ago, he'd been on a battlefield, with artillery exploding in his ears. He'd known what to be ready for then, but now he wasn't sure. As much as he hated to think it, Fern was right. Something could happen. Even so, a man couldn't always be peering around the next corner, worrying about what was to come. Live in the moment. That's what he'd told Kate. That's what he needed to do. He wasn't going to be afraid of the future.

Perfect love casteth out all fear. That verse came to mind as it had so many times during the war. He moved quietly through the house to the back porch. The spring air, cool against his skin, smelled damp with the promise of things growing. Above him, the sky glittered with thousands of stars. It was good to stand in the dark without a helmet. Without a gun. With no boom of artillery pounding in the distance.

He was glad to leave the war behind, but he couldn't forget it. He blocked it out during the day. He didn't think about it. He didn't talk about it. He sometimes didn't flinch now when somebody at the feed store dropped something with a clatter or when a truck backfired. Noise was part of life and all booms didn't presage death. But at night, the war had a way of sneaking back.

Kate's father warned Mike and him to expect that. Mr. Merritt knew. In spite of all the years since he'd been over there, he said he still had nightmares about the mud in the trenches of that First World War. "Some nights the mud tries to swallow me. Those nights I wake up not able to breathe. But it's not the mud. It's this muck in my lungs." He coughed and hit his fist against his chest.

They had been sitting around the stove in the front room a few weeks after Jay got home. The noise of the women finishing up dinner had floated out to them. Ordinary sounds. Birdie's laugh. Samantha's little-girl squeal. Dishes rattling. A pan top clanging. Wonderful sounds Jay wanted to plant in his head to cover up the memories of war. Mike must have felt the same.

"But I don't want to remember." Mike's face was creased with lines of sorrow. "The dying. The hunger. The fear." He looked over at Jay. "You know how it was. You might have even had it worse."

"It was all worst. Except getting to know your brothers." He hadn't had to explain. They both knew what it meant to be part of a fighting unit with men ready to die for one another. And in that moment, they felt the bond among themselves. They knew what it was like to go to war.

But he was home now. He gazed at the stars and felt gratitude for that rise within him. He'd made it through the war. Done unimaginable things as a soldier. Being a father had to be easy compared to that. One day at a time. That was how it was in the Army. That was how the Lord said life was supposed to be. One day at a time.

He told Kate to live in the moment. He needed to take his own advice. And the moment was good and got better when the door opened behind him and he heard the whisper of Kate's bare feet coming across the porch.

She put her arms around his waist and leaned her head against his back. "Trouble sleeping?"

"Haven't tried yet. Just out here checking the stars."

"They're bright tonight." She leaned around him to peer up at the sky without loosening her arms around his waist. After a moment, she asked, "You okay?"

He turned in her arms to embrace her. "Better than okay. Always better than okay with you around."

He wouldn't worry about months from now when the baby would be there between them. October, she'd said. He had time. They had time. Time. That was the one thing the war had taught him. To treasure time.

18

Tori didn't know why everybody was so worried about her. She always had fishing fever once spring chased winter away. So on a Saturday late in April when the sun felt more like June, it was only natural for her to wish she was at Graham's pond instead of stuck at the store.

They'd had a rush all morning the way they generally did on Saturdays, but by two o'clock, most everybody had headed home to get ready for Sunday or maybe to plant the corn seed they'd bought. Or to go fishing. Business was so slow that her mother told Tori to take the rest of the day off.

"Call a friend and go to a movie since you don't have Samantha tonight," Mama said.

Tori managed to keep smiling. Samantha was spending the night with Sammy's mother. Her very first night away from Tori. Mrs. Harper had started keeping Samantha for a few hours nearly every weekday morning. She doted on the child and wanted to help Tori out, she said.

It was a help. At the store, Samantha was forever getting into things while Tori waited on customers or stocked the shelves. Besides, it was good for Samantha to be with Sammy's family, but that didn't keep Tori from feeling lost without her. Not being able to see her and know for sure she was okay made Tori's throat so tight she could barely swallow.

"But what if Samantha cries and won't go to bed?" she said. "They might have to bring her home."

"Don't be such a worrywart. Christine Harper raised four boys. I think she can get one little girl to bed." Mama smiled. "You made her so happy letting Samantha spend the night. And Samantha too. She loves her Mama and Papa Harper. She'll be fine."

"I know." Tori couldn't keep the tremble of threatening tears from showing up in her voice. "But will I be fine?"

"Oh, my sweet and lovely Victoria. You will be fine. You are fine already." Mama hugged her close for a moment. They both knew she was talking about more than Tori missing Samantha, but she pretended that was what she'd meant as she went on. "That first night away from your little one is hard, but babies grow up. So very fast. One minute you're nursing them, the next you're watching them nurse their own babies. At least I still have Lorena for a little while longer."

"And you have me."

"I do, and you'll always be my baby. But you will find your wings to fly away again. In time." She stepped back from Tori and cupped her cheek with her hand. "I want that for my girls. It's such a joy to see you becoming mothers. First you, and now Evangeline and Kate. That's the way the good Lord intended things to be."

She did her best not to stiffen at her mother's words. People always talked about things happening according to God's will. She'd grown up believing the Lord was watching over her. That if she did what she was supposed to, he'd shower blessings down on her. Ask and it shall be given. But then she'd asked and it hadn't been given. Sammy had been taken.

Her mother stroked her cheek. "I'm praying for you, sweetheart. Do you want to know what I pray for you?"

Tori wasn't sure she did, but she nodded anyway. Her mother expected her to listen.

"I pray you'll stop being angry at God."

"I'm not mad at God." Tori's denial was instinctive. A person wasn't supposed to get mad at God.

But her mother simply gave her another hug before she pushed her toward the door with a little sigh. "Go on. Get your fishing pole. I know you'd rather do that than go to the movies, and who knows? A pond bank might be a good place to feel God's love. To think about the plans the Lord has for you."

Plans? She had no plans, she thought as she walked down the road toward home. Except to go fishing. Maybe that was what the Lord planned for her too. The Bible talked a lot about fishing. Some of the disciples were fishermen. Maybe with nets instead of poles and hooks, but fishing was fishing.

Everybody thought Tori went fishing too much. Her mother and father. Kate. Well, not everybody. Not Evie. She was too wrapped up in being in the family way to notice anything Tori did. Jubilant one minute. Distraught the next. Fishing would do Evie good, and she might even go if the weather was perfect.

Evie wasn't like Kate. Before the war, she enjoyed fishing as long as Mike was along to bait her hook and take the fish off her line if she happened to catch something. Tori had never asked Sammy to do that for her. Never. She could handle her own bait and fish.

When she reached the house, Tori didn't go inside. There was no need. Her father was still at his shop, and Kate had borrowed Uncle Wyatt's car to take Lorena to audition for a radio program. Lorena was so excited, she'd been spinning in circles all week. Her little sister could very well be famous one day. She was already in demand at churches in the area.

Her mother's words about the Lord's plans fit Lorena better than they did her. He'd blessed Lorena with a beautiful voice and the desire to share that gift with others. But he'd let the war smash Tori's plans for her life. Now she didn't want to think about her future.

She had plans for Samantha's future, but for herself she just took each day as it came. The Bible said to think on the day and not store up for a future a person might not have. Futures weren't guaranteed. How well she knew that.

She let out a long breath and headed toward the barn for her bait bucket. Samantha had helped her dig for worms after the rain last week, squealing with delight each time she managed to grab one out of the dirt. But she was too young to sit quietly and enjoy the finer moments of fishing. Tori's mother was right. It was a good place to think, but even more, it could be a place not to think all that much about anything except the breeze in her face and the rippling rings on the pond when a fish kissed the surface of the water.

At the pond, she settled in her favorite spot, baited her hook, and cast her line in the water. Inch by inch her body relaxed in the sunshine. The pond was peaceful. Birds flew between the trees, building nests and chirping at one another. Buzzards circled high in the sky, floating in and out of sight on the air currents. A couple of rabbits popped out of the bushes. They paid her scant notice as they hopped on about their business.

The word "Look!" jumped to her tongue and made Tori miss Samantha that much more. She liked pointing things out to her. Tori pulled in a deep breath and thought about Samantha making cookies with her grandmother or sitting with her on the porch swing while her grandmother told her things her father did when he was little.

Mama Harper liked planting memories of Sammy in his child's head. A good thing, since Samantha would have no actual memory of him on her own. She didn't miss him. She didn't realize her father was missing. Yet. But someday she'd ask about Sammy. Tori had copied every word he'd written in his letters about Samantha in a composition book to give her when that happened. Between the two of them, Tori and Sammy's mother, they'd make sure Samantha knew her father.

What she might tell her ran through Tori's head. *Your daddy was funny. His smile was just like yours. He had a hard time sitting still. He wanted to help everybody he met. He loved us. He didn't want to leave us.*

When she heard somebody coming through the trees toward the pond, she smiled and kept her eyes on the water. It would be Graham and his dog. It wouldn't be Fern. Not making that much noise. Tori rarely saw Fern in the woods or here at the pond, but Tori didn't have to see her to know she was often there. She just had to feel the odd tingle across the back of her neck.

It used to scare Tori and make her want to shout at Fern to stop watching her. A few times, she had yelled at the woman, but if indeed Fern was back in the trees, she never came out where Tori could see her.

These days Tori didn't let it bother her. If she got the feeling Fern was there, she simply rubbed the back of her neck and shrugged it off. In some ways it made fishing by herself at the pond easier. Any different noise, she blamed on Fern and kept fishing.

She kept fishing now, setting her hook when her cork bobbed, and waited for Graham to come out of the trees. Graham was such a part of the woods and pond that she expected him to show up whenever she was fishing. She liked hearing him talk in those muted tones that had a way of blending into the day.

She reeled in her line. The fish was a keeper if she could catch some more to go with it. She was putting it on her stringer when someone spoke behind her.

"Hello, Victoria."

It wasn't Graham. She was so surprised she dropped the fish and it slid back into the water.

"Clay." She whirled around and stumbled over her fishing pole on the ground.

He reached a hand out to steady her. "I didn't mean to startle you. I thought you'd hear me coming."

"I did, but I figured it was Graham." Tori stepped back from him a little too quickly and stumbled again. Her foot slid down into the mud at the pond edge and she threw out her arms to catch her balance.

"Watch out." Clay dropped his cane pole and grabbed her before she fell backward into the water.

His arm was strong around her and she caught the fresh scent of soap as she leaned against him in order to jerk her foot free. She started to pull away from him then, but it seemed wiser to get back on solid ground before they both ended up in the pond. He kept his arm around her as she climbed the bank. Her heart hammered inside her chest. Only from the surprise of seeing him there and then almost falling. It had nothing to do with his arm around her.

"Thank you," she said politely, stepping away from him. "I'm not usually so clumsy. I haven't fallen in the pond since I was fifteen."

She was sorry for that memory as soon as her words summoned it up. She and Sammy had both fallen in the pond that summer day. But being clumsy had nothing to do with it. The hot day and Sammy pushing her in had everything to do with it. When he reached a hand to help her out, she'd jerked him in too. They had laughed until their sides hurt.

"My fault," Clay said. "I should have hollered at you when I came out of the trees."

"What are you doing here?" The question was out before she could stop it, but even to her own ears it sounded rude. It wasn't even a question that needed asking. They both knew why he was there.

His smile dimmed, but stayed on his face. "Graham told me the fish were biting and I could come catch a mess."

"Oh." Tori picked up her fishing pole. Wait until she saw Graham. She knew what he was up to. He was playing Cupid again the way he'd done with Kate and Jay. While that had worked out fine for them, she didn't need anybody matchmaking for her. She had half a mind to just pick up her stuff and go find Graham right then to make sure he knew that. But the sun was shining, and the fish were still in the pond instead of on her stringer.

"He didn't think you would mind sharing the pond bank." Clay began unwinding the line from around his cane pole.

"I didn't know you liked to fish." Tori kept her eyes on her bait bucket as she dug out a worm.

"I used to go some with my father before he died." Clay had the line loose, but he didn't pick up the hook to bait it. Instead he stared out at the pond as if he'd awakened some memory he was sorry he'd disturbed. Then he shook himself a little. "I don't have much time for fishing these days. Too busy on the farm."

Tori cast her line out into the pond, then looked over at Clay. His jaw was tight as though he had his teeth clamped together. Not mad. More sad as he stared at the hook.

"And it hurt too much when you went." She knew how that felt. Even now after more than a year she sometimes felt Sammy's loss more acutely at the pond. At the same time, she couldn't give up fishing. Not and keep her sanity. With Samantha, she made new memories, new times to remember here at the pond. "That would have gotten better after a few times."

"I guess so. But I never was very good at fishing anyway."

"Anybody can be good at fishing. If you have the right bait and throw your line in where the fish are." She looked over at him. He still hadn't baited his hook. "Did you even bring any bait?"

He smiled sheepishly. "I knew I forgot something."

The laugh that bubbled out of her as she handed him her bait bucket was a surprise, but it felt good.

"Thanks. I'll dig you some worms in the barn lot to pay you back." He pushed a worm on his hook and then stepped away from her to flip his line in the water.

For a while, they fished in silence. The plop of their corks hitting the water and the birds singing gave a lazy summer feel to the day. At the same time, the air seemed to carry a little extra charge. Clay wasn't holding a cane pole for the love of fishing. He'd chased her to Graham's pond, and not because he wanted fish for supper. She watched her cork for the slightest wiggle. Better to think about that than how Clay kept looking over at her. She sensed he wanted to say something but hesitated, unsure of his words.

She felt a little unsure too as she remembered his arm around her when he helped her up the bank. It had been good to lean on somebody. Sometimes she got so tired of being alone. She almost smiled at her thought. She was actually very rarely alone, surrounded by family at the house and people at the store. But the alone she was feeling was a different kind of loneliness. Everything came in twos. The rabbits earlier. The buzzards floating above her. The birds building nests. Pairs. Adam and Eve. Abraham and Sarah. Mary and Joseph.

She stared out at the pond, wishing for a nibble to give her something to do besides think about the man beside her on the pond bank. He was so sweet with his little sisters at the store or church. She'd never seen him say a cross word to them. Ever. He worked hard to take care of his family. A man who wanted to make her part of that family. That was why he was here fishing.

She didn't know whether she wished he would just come out with whatever he was trying to work up the nerve to say or that he would keep quiet. It was pleasant to fish in companionable silence. She was glad he was there. That made her so unsettled that she moved back from the pond and began reeling in her line. Maybe everybody was right. She was fishing too much.

"Did you catch something?" Clay asked.

"No. I don't think the fish are biting today." She caught her hook in one of the eyelets and tightened the line. "Guess I'll head home."

"Oh." He stared at his line. "They don't seem to be biting for me either."

"I think you lost your bait awhile ago. The little fish can nibble the worms off without grabbing the hook." She picked up the bait bucket and held it out toward him. "You want to keep some of the worms?"

"No, guess I'll give it up too." He pulled in his line and wound it around the pole.

Tori looked toward the sun sinking in the west. "I suppose it is almost milking time."

"I don't have to milk tonight. My brother's taking care of the cows. So I could go fishing, you know."

"I see."

He looked out toward the pond and then back at Tori to push out his next words. "How about, since the fish aren't biting, that we go to the movies?" His cheeks were red. Maybe from the sun. Maybe from what he'd asked.

She hesitated. For just a second, she thought about sitting in a dark movie theater beside the man looking at her with hope evident in his eyes. Yes was on the tip of her tongue, but she bit back the word. The fact she was even thinking about saying yes made her want to get up on her toes and run the way she used to when she saw Fern. Not because she was frightened of Clay, but because she was frightened of what she was feeling.

She lowered her eyes away from his face. She couldn't look at him. "It's nice of you to ask." She did her best to hide the quiver in her voice. "But I'd best go home."

He blew out a long breath of air. Then with a hint of challenge, he asked, "Why?"

His question surprised her. She had to have turned him down a hundred times. Maybe more. Each time his smile had faded and his shoulders slumped, but he'd not asked why.

She stared at the ground and wondered what to tell him. That she was afraid? That she wasn't ready for the feeling his touch had awakened inside her. Nothing like how she'd felt with Sammy. Sammy had been like an extension of herself, a part of her for almost as long as she could remember. But when Clay put his arm around her, it had felt strangely different. And not at all bad.

She hadn't yet figured out what to say when he stepped closer to her. "We're friends, aren't we?" He waited for her to nod. "A friend can tell another friend the truth."

"If she knows it." Tori spoke barely over a whisper.

"You know it. You're just afraid of it."

She changed his words. "I'm not afraid of you."

"I would hope not. I would do anything for you, Victoria. Anything to make you happy." He gingerly put his finger under her chin and lifted her face up to look in her eyes.

"Anything?" Tori's heart was pounding.

"Anything."

"Then go away."

He looked as if she'd slapped him with her words. He dropped his hand away from her chin. "Is that what you really want?" His voice was rough with feeling.

"Yes." Tori made herself keep looking at his face. "It's not time."

"Will it ever be time?" He sounded as lost and lonely as she had felt earlier.

She wasn't sure he expected an answer, but she gave him one. "I don't know." She hesitated a second, then went on. "Maybe not."

He let out another burst of air as if she'd punched him hard in the stomach. He looked away at the pond and blinked a few times before he settled his eyes on her again. "Sammy was my friend. You know that. But he's not coming back. I wish he was, but he's not."

A spark of anger flamed inside her. "Don't you think I know that?"

"I guess you do." He reached toward her again, but stayed his hand without touching her. "If you ever need anything, remember we're friends."

Without waiting for her to say more, he picked up his pole and walked away. She stared at where he disappeared into the trees. He was gone. Just the way she'd asked. She was glad. That was what she wanted, wasn't it?

The tears surprised her. She sank down on the ground, leaned her head on her knees, and sobbed like a broken-hearted child. She'd cried buckets for Sammy, but she wasn't seeing Sammy now. She was seeing the sad goodbye in Clay's eyes. He wouldn't be back.

19

A tree limb smacked Clay in the face. He was walking blindly paying no attention to anything, just needing to get away from the pain of Victoria's words. Why had he told her he would do whatever she wanted? He knew she didn't want the same thing he wanted. He should have stepped back and kept hope for another day. Instead he had the same as bared his chest and invited her to rip out his heart.

She wasn't cruel. She hadn't enjoyed hurting him. She'd looked as unhappy as he was feeling. It was his fault. He messed things up by pushing her too fast.

He was fooled by how well things started out between them at the pond, in spite of his misgivings when Graham Lindell told him he should go fishing there Saturday afternoon. The man hadn't mentioned Victoria, but some things didn't have to be said out loud. Everybody in Rosey Corner knew Victoria was at Graham's pond whenever she had time off from the store.

When he told Graham he hadn't been fishing for years, Graham said it didn't matter whether a man was practiced at fishing or not. That a determined man kept baiting his hook and throwing out his line. It was plain he wasn't only talking about catching fish. So even though Clay worried that Sammy's ghost would be there on the bank of Graham's pond beside Victoria, he got his old cane pole and found his way through the trees to the pond. A man couldn't fight a ghost. Not that he wanted to. He didn't want to take Sammy's place in Victoria's heart. He wanted his own place there.

When she'd laughed and offered him a worm out of her bait bucket, hope took wing in his heart that at last she was ready to give him that chance. It was good to stand on the pond bank with her so close he caught the scent of whatever soap she used to wash her hair. A flowery smell. Her dark hair was beautiful in the sunlight. Her profile lovely. He sneaked look after look at her while she kept her eyes on her cork floating on the surface of the green pond water that was so like the green of her eyes. She knew he was looking at her, but she pretended not to.

For months she had pretended not to know how he felt about her. Perhaps he'd been doing some pretending too. A blackberry briar grabbed his pants. He shoved it aside, almost glad when the thorn ripped into his thumb and brought blood. He was bleeding inside. He might as well bleed on the outside too.

He stuck his thumb in his mouth to suck away the blood and stopped walking. No need in crashing through the trees with no idea of direction. It was best to take stock of where he was. He wasn't worried about being lost. His sense of direction was true, at least when it came to north and south. In matters of the heart, he was lost before he started.

In front of him, the trees reached toward the sky, their

trunks so big it would surely take a man all day to saw through them. Not that a man would want to fell them. At least not this man. He walked under the first tree in front of him, an oak, and stared up at the emerging leaves far above his head. They weren't all oaks. Some yellow poplars were mixed in among the oaks, and here and there a maple had elbowed out space to grow.

He'd heard people talk about the old-growth trees in Lindell Woods, but he'd never seen them. The oak's bark felt familiar to his touch. He didn't cut oaks for firewood unless a tree was downed in a storm, and even then, it took seasoning to burn it for heat. Locust and ash made better firewood. Clay knelt to dig through the thick layer of leaves to the rich loamy soil under the trees. The dirt was damp and cool in his hand.

He raised it up to his nose and sniffed it. His father used to do that. He told Clay a man could tell a lot about whether dirt would grow anything by how it smelled and how it felt in his hand.

Clay made a fist and squeezed the dirt into a ball. It felt right, but good dirt wasn't enough. Nothing would grow here except maybe mushrooms. The trees would drink in all the moisture and their thick canopy of leaves would keep away the sun. A farmer knew that. Just as he knew poor ground and rocks didn't yield good crops.

Even so, a man had to work with the land the Lord gave him. Rocks could be hauled away, poor ground changed with fertilizer. A man plowed away from the tree line or cut down the trees. But sometimes even after all that work, it wasn't enough. The crops still failed. Then a man had to change his crop or find a new field. One with better dirt and fewer rocks. One that welcomed the sunshine and rain.

He stared at the dirt in his hand. He wasn't a man to give up easy, but a man was a fool to keep plowing a field that wouldn't yield a crop. He slung the dirt ball against one of the trees and watched it break apart and shower down on the leaves.

She wasn't ever going to make room for him in her heart. She wasn't even willing to let him love her. He leaned his forehead against the tree and shut his eyes, unable to block out the echo of her words. *Go away.* His heart felt like that clod of dirt slamming against the tree trunk. Breaking into a thousand pieces.

Above his head, a bird chirped the same note over and over. Tree frogs tuned up for night too, but Clay stayed crouched there, waiting to know what to do next. In the past, each time Victoria had said no, he had a next. A new thing to try. But not this time.

He sat back on his heels and looked up at the tree towering over him. Majestic. Strong. Not bothered by the passing troubles of life. Clay remembered when the fire had swept through Lindell Woods some years back, and how happy Victoria and Sammy had been that these trees were spared.

The trees made him feel small. The same kind of small he felt looking up at the stars on a dark winter night. Who was he that God would be mindful of his troubles? And yet the Bible said he was.

"Dear God, help me," Clay whispered. "I love her so much."

You told her you'd do anything to make her happy and she said go away. Did you mean what you said? The words slid through his head. Not the Lord speaking comfort to him, but his own voice taunting him.

"I don't want to give her up."

You can't give up what you've never had. She doesn't want you to love her.

He wanted to argue with the words in his head, but it did little good to hide from the truth. He bent his head and let out a long breath. She said it wasn't time. That it might never be time. How plain did he need to hear her say she didn't want him?

He was beaten. It was time to accept that truth. He didn't want it to be true, but he was beaten. Slowly he stood up and looked back in the direction of the pond. The sinking sun would be reflecting the dying embers of day onto the water.

"Go back."

With his heart in his throat, Clay jerked up his head. Listening with every inch of his being, he held his breath and studied the trees. Nothing moved. He couldn't hear the slightest rustle in the carpet of leaves. The bird must have flown to another tree. The only noises were the frogs and a squirrel far overhead chattering at him. Clay let out his breath. He had surely imagined those words. The desire of his heart must have been so strong that it sounded in his ears. *Go back.*

But she would be gone now. Even if she wasn't, she wouldn't welcome the sight of him coming back to disturb her peace.

Peace. He could pray for that. Contentment with his lot in life. Acceptance of what he couldn't change. The Lord would honor those prayers.

"That wasn't you telling me to go back, was it, Lord?"

Clay stared up at the faraway glimpse of blue through the canopy of new leaves. The blue was fading. Night was falling. He'd best find his truck before dark or he might be wandering around among these trees until morning. But just in case it was the Lord speaking to him, he kept his eyes on that little spot of blue and said, "If that was you, Lord, can you maybe say it again? So I can be sure."

He waited, hardly daring to breathe. A profound silence pounded against his ears. The squirrel stopped fussing and the frogs paused their evening song as if they too were listening. No sound but the pounding of his heart in his ears.

At last he let out his breath. How desperate could a man get? Hearing things and then expecting the Lord to speak to him. Not only in his heart, but right out loud. That might happen to men the Lord called to preach, but not to a man whose struggle was getting a woman to look favorably on him.

Sunday school stories of Abraham's servant finding a wife for Isaac and Ruth gleaning wheat in Boaz's field popped into his mind. The Lord had lent a hand to those matches, but that was back in Bible days. It wasn't about to happen for him, even if people did say good matches were written in the stars. His name wouldn't be written up there with Victoria's. That would be Sammy's. Clay's name must have been on a falling star.

He shook away the silly thought, picked up his cane pole, and turned to the south. Without looking back even once at the grand trees, he headed out of the woods, his eyes on the path ahead of him. It was time to look ahead, not back. Time to move on.

Strangely enough, a song began running through his head. The hymn they'd sung last week in church. "Trust and Obey." That didn't mean anything. Sometimes a song just got stuck in a man's head.

At the edge of the woods, Clay sat in his truck and wondered again what next. He couldn't go home. Not yet. His mother would take one look at his face and feel his unhappiness. She had enough troubles of her own. She didn't need to take on his. He started up the motor and turned the truck toward Edgeville. He'd go on to the movies. He could sit in the dark and not worry once about smiling. By the time he got home, everybody would be in bed, and come morning, he'd find a way to smile again.

He parked behind the theater and walked to the front to buy his ticket. He felt conspicuous by himself. Everybody else was coupled up or in a group. Who went to a movie by themselves on a Saturday night?

"Clay." Paulette peeled away from a group of girls to come over to where he was in line to get his ticket.

"Hi there, Paulette." It had been more than a year since they'd gone out. Somebody told him she had a boyfriend in Frankfort now. "You heard whether the movie's any good?"

"Wilma says it's not bad. Good for a few laughs."

"Just what I need then. A few laughs."

She peered at him, perhaps hearing something in his voice, but he pushed a smile across his face.

"Been awhile since I've seen you. How's things going with you and Victoria?"

That was the trouble with a little community like Rosey Corner. Nothing stayed secret long. Clay let his eyes drift to the movie poster. *Go back*. The words flashed through his mind again. He could have sworn he heard them, but that was crazy. He looked back at Paulette. She was a nice girl. Attractive enough. Not beautiful like Victoria. She didn't make his heart pound, but they'd had some fun together.

"I guess they're not," he finally answered her. No need to pretend different. People would notice when he stopped hanging around the store. He'd still have to go to the store, but he'd just be in and out. Or maybe he'd give Lillie a list and just wait outside. No sense torturing himself by looking at what he could never have. Better to do as she asked and disappear from her life. That might not be easy in Rosey Corner, but a farmer had a lot to do in the spring. He didn't have time for many trips to the store or anywhere else.

"Good." Paulette hooked her hand through his elbow and leaned against him.

Her hair brushed his cheek and he caught the scent of her shampoo. A lemony odor so different from Victoria's. But Victoria would never be clinging to his arm. "I heard you've been keeping company with a guy from Frankfort."

"From time to time." She gave an offhand wave.

"He here with you tonight?" Clay looked around for an unattached man.

"He's not much for love stories." She peeked up at him through her lashes. "How about you? You like love stories?"

"I guess so. I'm buying a ticket." Clay shoved the money through the window at the kid working the booth.

"You are." She held his arm a little bit tighter.

"I can buy yours too." He reached in his pocket for more money.

"Thanks anyway." She held up her ticket. "But tell you what. You can get it next time."

Next time. He'd been wondering what next. Maybe this was it. Stop being a fool and move on. "I'll save up. For the next time a love story comes around."

"They happen all the time." When he looked over at her, she added, "In the movies."

"Not in real life?" He was sorry for the words the minute he said them.

"Sure, they do." She smiled. "But those happily-ever-after storybook endings happen fast in the movies. It sometimes takes a little longer in real life."

"Happily ever after sounds good," he agreed. But could a splintered heart find that?

"It does. Very good. Come on." She tugged on his arm. "Sit with me and my girlfriends. You know most of them already. Wilma. Josephine. Betty. It's no fun going to a movie by yourself."

So he sat in the dark theater next to a girl who made no secret of liking him. Paulette kept her hand on his arm or her shoulder against his the whole movie through as they watched the hero get the girl. In the movies, the hero always got the girl. A shame it didn't happen that way outside the movie theater. Then again, nobody would look at him and think hero. At least not the girl he wanted to think that.

Go back. The words haunted his thoughts. What would have happened if he'd heeded those words that sounded in his ears from nowhere? Nothing, that's what. Victoria would have been long gone, and he'd have simply ended up at the pond by himself with a longer walk back to his truck. That would have made him late to the movies, and Paulette and her friends would have already been inside.

He stared at the screen, hardly noticing what the actors were doing. *Go back.* Maybe he should have gone back to make sure she was all right. What if she had needed a hero?

In the movie, the cameras zoomed in on the hero kissing the girl. If only Clay was a hero. Then he might get the girl in the end too. Paulette leaned close to him and grabbed his hand. Maybe he could get the girl. Just not the girl he wanted.

20

Do you think people might be able to hear the radio program in other places too? Not just Kentucky," Lorena asked.

"Maybe. What places are you thinking about?" Kate glanced over at Lorena. They were on the way home from Louisville after Lorena auditioned for *Songs of Tomorrow*, a radio program that featured young singers. The producers had recorded her song and told her she'd be on their next broadcast. They loved Lorena's singing.

"Oh, I don't know." Lorena tried to sound casual, but Kate knew her too well. "Some of the bigger towns. Maybe Chicago or New York City."

"Chicago maybe. Cincinnati. I doubt New York City." Kate reached over to touch Lorena's arm. "But who knows? Someday you might be singing in New York City for thousands of people on the Arthur Godfrey show. Wouldn't that be something?" Arthur Godfrey always had singers on his morning show.

"That show plays all across the country, doesn't it?"

"It does. My famous little sister." Kate smiled at Lorena

and then quickly fastened her eyes back on the road. She wasn't used to driving Uncle Wyatt's car. It didn't rattle and bounce along like Jay's old car, but she was very anxious to get it parked back in Rosey Corner without doing any damage to it. She straightened in the plush seat and tried to find a more comfortable position. Her back was aching.

She needed to ask Aunt Hattie if she was supposed to feel this way. Tired and achy with odd pains stabbing her from time to time. The doctor in Edgeville said everything was normal. He'd smiled at her complaints and told her a little discomfort was to be expected. She knew that. She'd expected the nausea. Her mother had warned her about the fatigue. What she hadn't expected was the back pain. At least not yet. She was barely showing. It couldn't be from extra weight. Still, a little backache wasn't anything she couldn't stand. She certainly wasn't going to be like Evie and do nothing but talk about how miserable she was.

Kate wasn't miserable. She was too happy to worry about a few pains now or in the coming months. Evie said she might change her mind when she got so big she could barely waddle around. Mama had laughed and told Evie she'd hardly gotten to the waddle stage. She had two months to go and to just wait.

Evie had stared down at her bulging form and burst into tears. "I can't get any bigger," she wailed. "My skin can only stretch so far."

"You look beautiful, sweetheart," Mama told her. "It's a blessing to carry a child. And it won't be long until you'll be carrying him or her in your arms."

"Her." Evie's mouth tightened in a determined line. "I'm having a girl. Kate can have the boy. She can handle anything."

A baby boy. Kate smiled at the thought. A boy for Jay would be nice. Jay was saying all the right things, but sometimes she caught a worried look on his face when she talked about when the baby came. And there were all the nights she awoke to find him gone from the bed.

The war, he said. Bad dreams. She had no doubt that was true. Hadn't she seen her father struggle with the same? Jay wouldn't talk about the war. A couple of nights ago when she found him on the back porch in the wee hours of the morning, she told him she'd read the accounts sent in to the papers. Things that were never published because the editors deemed the stories too harsh for their readers. She was strong. He could share the burden of his war memories if it would help him sleep better.

"You help me sleep better." He put his arm around her and kissed her cheek. "It's that I got used to waking up at the slightest noise. It will get better."

"Oh no." She turned toward him and laughed. "Babies are notoriously noisy at night."

"That will be a good noise," he'd said, but in the light that drifted out from the kitchen window, she had caught the worried shadow that slipped across his face.

"I can't imagine being famous." Lorena brought Kate back to the present. "Like Judy Garland with everybody knowing your name."

"Lorena Birdsong." Kate let the name roll off her tongue. "Your name even sounds like a song. People might think you made it up."

"Do you think I did?" Lorena's voice was too quiet.

Kate frowned. "Did what?"

"Made up my name."

"Why would you even think that?" Kate dared another look over at Lorena, who was staring down at her lap.

"I don't know. You said it sounded like something made up."

"But it wasn't. You know that. Your mother wrote your name and birthday on a piece of paper and gave it to you. You still have it, don't you?"

"In my Bible." Lorena hesitated before going on. "But maybe she made it up."

"Why would she do that?" Kate gripped the steering wheel and wished she wasn't driving so she could get a better look at Lorena's face.

"I don't know," Lorena mumbled, fingering the clasp on her pocketbook.

"All right, out with it. What's going on?"

"Nothing really."

"Nothing, huh. You just wowed a radio show producer and next week you'll hear yourself singing on the radio and instead of being on top of the world, you look like you lost your last friend. Are you having boy troubles?" Kate didn't think that was the problem, but she hoped that might get Lorena talking.

"Boys don't like me. I'm too tall." Lorena sighed.

"Fourteen-year-old boys haven't got sense enough to come in out of the rain. Give them a couple of years and they'll all be lining up for a smile from you."

"Yeah, right."

"Absolutely right. Jay's already planning out strategies to make sure only boys he approves get a chance to knock on your door."

"He is not." Lorena giggled.

"You wait and see. He'll be down there guarding the door. He says Daddy obviously isn't careful enough or he'd have never slipped up and let him come courting me."

"I'm glad he did come courting you."

Kate smiled, but kept her eyes on the road. "Thanks to you and Graham. You both championed him from the beginning."

Lorena began fiddling with her purse again. "But once the baby comes, Tanner will be too busy to worry about me." She clicked her purse open and closed. "You will be too."

"Oh, baby." Even though the road was curvy in front of them, Kate dared to take a hand off the steering wheel to squeeze Lorena's arm. "You can't be worried about that. I love you. I've loved you since the first moment I saw you on the church steps. You moved right into my heart that very day."

"But your baby will belong there now. You might forget about me."

"Don't be silly. You're my sister. Sisters are forever."

When Lorena didn't say anything, Kate watched for a place to pull off the road. She needed to look her in the eyes, but there was nothing but more curves winding toward Rosey Corner. So she kept driving. "Okay, what are you thinking?"

When Lorena finally answered, her voice was almost too low for Kate to hear. "Mothers are supposed to be forever too."

"Yes." What else could Kate say? Mothers were forever. Right now with her baby only beginning to form within her, she'd do anything to keep him or her safe. "Yes, they are."

"Then why didn't my mother come back for me the way she promised?" Lorena looked over at Kate, needing an answer. An answer Kate didn't have.

"Maybe she couldn't."

"Or maybe she forgot about me." Lorena stared back down at her purse.

"Maybe she forgot where she left you and wasn't able to find her way back."

"How could you forget a name like Rosey Corner?" Lorena sounded angry. "How could she forget me?"

"I don't think she did." Kate prayed the Lord would give her the right words. "You know how you always say your name every night before you go to bed?"

"Because she told me to. She said she'd hear me wherever she was." Lorena's voice cracked. "But maybe she just told me that."

"No, she meant every word. And I believe she does hear the echo of your name in her heart each and every time you say it. I can't say why she couldn't come back, but I do believe she prayed you'd find a new family who would love you just as much as she does. And we do. You'll always belong with us."

"I know. I want to belong with you." Lorena sighed. "But lately it feels like there's a hole inside me that's all dark and empty. I have no idea what might fit there, but I know something needs to." She looked over at Kate. "That's why I wondered about the radio show. Wherever my mother is, she might listen to the radio, and if she hears my name on the *Songs of Tomorrow* show, she might remember promising to come back for me."

"That's a lot of ifs, but I suppose it could happen. She might find you." Kate couldn't quite keep the tremble out of her voice. She'd worried for years that Lorena's parents would come back for her. She wanted Lorena to be happy, but she didn't want to lose her.

This time Lorena reached over to Kate. A tentative, feathery touch like the brush of a paintbrush on her arm. That's the way her mother said the baby's first movements might feel inside her when she was a little farther along. She was looking so forward to that quickening movement.

"Forever sisters, remember?" Lorena said.

A straight stretch in the road was coming up, so Kate captured Lorena's hand and pulled it up to kiss her fingers. "Forever. And I'm expecting plenty of help from Aunt Lorena with little Jay or Jayleen."

"Jayleen?" Lorena laughed. "You can't do that to her."

"Maybe not. If I have a girl, maybe I'll name her after Jay's mother."

"What was her name?"

Kate stared out at the road. "I don't know. He told me she died when he was a boy, but I don't think he ever said her given name."

"Maybe he doesn't know what it was."

"I'm sure he does. I just didn't ask."

"I don't."

"You don't what?"

"Know my mother's name. My brother's name was Kenton, but I don't know what my mother's or father's names were. I should, don't you think?" She glanced over at Kate and then back down at her purse. "I was five. You should remember things when you're five."

"Nobody remembers everything from when they were that young. And maybe you never heard their names. She was Mommy to you. Do you remember telling me about her that day?" They hadn't talked about this for years.

"I remember everything about that day. Mommy waving at me until she was out of sight. How scared I was sitting on that step. You coming around the corner of the church, sparkling just the way I thought an angel would."

"I wasn't sparkling," Kate smiled. "The morning sun must have played a trick on your eyes."

"You sparkled to me. I knew Jesus sent you especially to help me." Lorena hesitated a moment. "I still know it. But that doesn't keep me from wanting to know about my first family." She twisted in the seat to look over at Kate. "You and Tanner could help me find them."

"You sound like you've given this a lot of thought."

"Some," Lorena admitted. "She should have put her name on the paper too. So I'd know. Wouldn't that be what you would do?"

Kate couldn't imagine ever deserting her baby. Even now with the baby so very small, she wanted to protect him with every ounce of her being. But Lorena's mother had set her out on the church steps and left her there. What could make a mother do that? Kate chose her words carefully. "It's hard to say what I would do if I was that desperate."

"Desperate." Lorena let out a long sigh. "That's what I've always wanted to believe. Mommy cried when she left me. But maybe they just didn't want me. Maybe my daddy didn't. They kept Kenton."

"You said he was sick. Remember?" Kate's heart hurt for Lorena. Some sorrows never went away. "You said that was why they kept him."

"I know. He was too sick to wake up to tell me goodbye. I wanted him to wake up. Mommy let me kiss his cheek before I got out of the car and he still didn't wake up. I shook him a little, but Mommy made me stop. Since he was so sick. I wanted to be sick so they wouldn't leave me."

"But the Lord made a different way for you." Kate was glad to see the house up ahead. Her mother might have wiser words for Lorena. "And we needed you too. You made things better in our family."

"I wish I could make things better for Tori now. She goes out on the porch in the middle of the night sometimes. Even when it's cold."

"I used to do that. It's a good place to think."

"Did you cry?" Lorena asked.

"Not much. I was always too busy thinking up ways to make things come out the way I wanted them to."

"Tori can't do that."

"No, she can't." Kate pulled the car into the driveway and switched off the key. "But Tori's tougher than she looks. She'll be okay. With us sisters helping her."

"Am I tough?" Lorena asked.

"Tough enough to be one of the Merritt sisters." Kate leaned across the seat to hug her. "Even if your name is Lorena Birdsong."

"Daddy says there aren't any Merritt girls left. Tori is a Harper. Evie, a Champion, and you're Kate Tanner."

"He can't get rid of us that easy." Kate laughed. "Getting married didn't stop us from being the Merritt sisters. All of us. You too. Now, come on. Mama has come out on the porch, so she must need to tell me something before I take Uncle Wyatt's car home. We'll have to make him those oatmeal cookies he likes so well to thank him for letting us use it."

"Yeah." Lorena pushed open her door and slid out of the car. "Are we late? Mama looks worried."

"I told her I didn't know when we'd be back. She's probably just anxious to hear how your audition went." Kate got out and put her hands on her hips to stretch her back. The dull throb wouldn't quit. She'd ask Aunt Hattie about it tomorrow. Aunt Hattie probably knew more about babies than that Edgeville doctor ever would, but she'd been the one who told Kate to go to him.

She'd been sitting in her rocking chair by the window the day Kate went to tell her about the baby. "I'm getting old, chile. Much as I'd like to walk you through havin' this sweet baby of yours, I don't have the strength to catch babies no more." She put her wrinkled hand on Kate's cheek. "But I'm gonna ask the good Lord to put off me moving up to heaven so's I can hold your little one. He's bound to be something, coming from you and that Jay Tanner boy. Have I ever tol' you how much your boy puts me in mind of my Bo?"

Kate smiled, remembering her words, but then her smile disappeared as Lorena rushed across the yard toward their mother. "What's wrong, Mama?"

Kate ignored the pain in her back and followed her because Lorena was right. Mama was worried about something. Kate looked past her to see if she could see Daddy. Maybe his cough was worse and he needed to go to the doctor. Or something was wrong with Samantha. Or Evie. Worries poked her from all sides.

She shook herself a little. No need in worrying until she knew what was wrong. And no need then either. Then it would be time for praying or fixing things.

"I'm glad you're here." Mama came down in the yard to meet them. "Your father is putting on his shoes to go look for Victoria."

"Where is she?" Kate asked. "Graham's pond?"

"Where else? But she never stays this late. Never." Mama

looked to the western sky where the sun had already slipped out of sight, leaving a burst of red behind.

"She doesn't," Lorena echoed.

"Is Samantha with her?" Kate asked.

"No, Sammy's mother has her overnight. Victoria is probably just taking advantage of that to fish a little longer, but it's almost dark. And I don't know. I have the feeling something's wrong. I wanted to go see about her, but your father insisted he could go. But it'll make his cough worse."

They could hear him coughing through the open door.

"I'll go," Kate said.

New worry lines traced across her mother's face. "Are you sure you're up to that? You don't want to overdo."

"Walking is not overdoing. I walk all the time." Kate leaned over and kissed her cheek.

"I'll go with you," Lorena said.

Kate looked at her in the Sunday clothes she'd worn for the audition. "You can't go walking in the woods in those shoes. You'll end up ruining them and have to go barefoot to church tomorrow."

Lorena looked down at her black patent leather shoes. "I'll run change."

"No need. Just stay here and tell Mama about being on the radio. I know the path Tori takes to the pond. I'll probably meet her coming out and we'll be back before you can get the supper table set."

21

Walking along the path to the pond brought back memories of the times Tori begged Kate to go fishing with her when she was a kid. Kate let Tori catch the fish while she sat on the bank and dreamed up stories or talked to Graham, who had a way of appearing out of the trees whenever they were at the pond. Kate didn't fish.

The thought of fish smell and worms made her stomach lurch. She took a deep breath and brought to mind the fragrance of the blooms on her mother's lilac bush. She didn't need to start heaving. It was hard enough just walking. She was so tired and the pain in her back kept poking at her. But nobody said being in the family way was easy. At least not for everybody.

The thing was, she had expected it to be easy. She wasn't Evie. She was strong. Healthy. She thought she'd sail through the months until she was holding her baby. But easy journey or not, she could handle it. Throughout time, millions of other women had done the same.

When she walked under the old trees, she stopped and looked up at their branches reaching toward the sky. A prayer of thanksgiving rose within her for these trees, the solid, forever heart of Lindell Woods. She ran her hand over the bark of one of the oaks. Here in this spot, she and Jay had shared their first kiss and danced to the music of their hearts. That night had been the beginning, even though it was far from easy coasting for them after that.

The Lord didn't promise easy coasting. He promised to stay with those who loved him, whatever the ride. Or walk.

Kate pushed away from the oak. She didn't have time for woolgathering. Light was fading fast under the trees.

When she finally reached the pond, she found Tori on the bank, staring out at the water. Her fishing pole on the ground next to her had the line reeled in.

She looked around when Kate came out of the trees and then turned her face back toward the pond that reflected the pinkish orange of the sky. She made no attempt to get up. She didn't even say hello. Scout, who had been leaning against her shoulder, jumped up at the sight of Kate. His tail flapped slowly back and forth, as though he knew the mood was too somber for his usual jubilant greeting.

"Hey, Scout, how's things?" Kate gave his ears a tousle and sat down by Tori. As if relieved Kate had taken over for him, Scout waded into the pond to lap up a drink. Tori had been crying, even though no tears were sliding down her cheeks now. She still didn't say anything.

After a couple of minutes, Kate broke the silence. "The pond looks pretty."

"I suppose." Tori kept her eyes on the water.

"Did you catch anything?"

"One, but it got away. Wasn't very big anyway."

"Maybe it's too early. Graham says the fish have to warm

up enough to get hungry for worms. Or could be Scout scared them away."

"He just found me a little while ago. Must have been out in the woods hunting." Tori sighed. "Didn't matter. I didn't care if I caught anything or not."

"I guess not, since you don't have your line in the water." Kate let her eyes go to the fishing pole.

"Or my hook baited." Tori looked around at Kate then. "Do you think I should bait my hook?"

Kate had the feeling they weren't talking about fishing anymore, but she wasn't sure exactly what they were talking about. "Maybe. If you want to, but not tonight. We need to head home. Mama's worried about you."

"Mama worries too much." Tori turned her eyes back to the pond. The pink had faded from the sky and the water was going dark. "If I want to sit out here all night, what difference does it make? Samantha's with Sammy's mother. Nobody needs me."

"Mama and Daddy need you. I need you. Lorena needs you."

"You love me. You don't need me."

"I need you to be happier." Kate wished she had grabbed her sweater out of the car. With the sun gone, the air was cool.

"Happy. Are you happy, Kate?" Tori shivered, and Kate scooted closer to put her arm around her.

"You know I am. I so want to be a mother like you."

"Like me." Tori let out a long sigh. "Have you always been happy, Kate?"

"Not always," Kate admitted. "Once when I was about Lorena's age now, I was so unhappy that I sat on this very pond bank and told Daddy I didn't believe in God."

Tori whipped her head around to stare at Kate. "But you didn't mean it."

"I thought I did when I said it. I was that unhappy with what was happening, and I was sure if God really loved me the way everybody always said he did, then he would have stopped the bad things from happening. I was very young."

"But you figured things out."

"Not everything by any means, but I did figure out the Lord was right there hurting with me even while I was saying I didn't believe in him. He never once turned his back on me even when I turned my back on him."

"Mama thinks I'm mad at God. She told me she was going to pray that I would let go of my anger. But I'm not mad at anybody. Certainly not God." Tori stared back toward the pond. "Even if he did take Sammy."

"Is that why you've been crying?" Kate gently brushed a strand of Tori's black hair out of her face. "Were you and the Lord talking about Sammy?"

"No." The word came out so harsh that Scout forgot about the frogs at the pond's edge and slunk back to Tori. She ignored him and stood up. "We better head home. It'll be dark under the trees."

"Right." Questions circled in Kate's head, but she bit her lip and kept quiet. She got to her feet and then had to grab hold of Tori as the world spun around.

"Are you all right?" Tori put her arm around Kate's waist.

Kate forced out a little laugh. "I'm fine. I just stood up too fast. This being in the family way takes some getting used to."

"You shouldn't have walked over here after me."

"I'm fine, Tori. Really."

"Really?" Tori frowned at Kate, probing her words and

her face. "You look like you're not so sure about that. What's wrong?"

"You mean besides my sister forgetting to come home?"

"Don't try to change the subject. What's wrong?"

Kate blew out her breath. "Nothing's wrong except the thought of worms and fish is making me queasy and my back hurts some. Didn't your back hurt while you were carrying Samantha?"

"Not until the last couple of months. What does the doctor say?"

"That things hurt when you're going to have a baby. And sometimes you throw up."

Tori smiled. "No doubt about that one. And sometimes you feel like crying like Evie."

"Evie has always cried about everything."

"Well, now she has reason." Tori picked up her fishing pole and bait bucket. "But who am I to talk about somebody crying?"

"You have reason too." Kate eyed the bait bucket. "I can carry the fishing pole, but no worms."

"Worms won't hurt you." Tori laughed. It was a good sound. "But I carried them over here. I can carry them back."

"Just keep them away from my nose."

"You do look a little pale." Tori peered over at her. "I can leave the bait bucket and help you."

"Help me how? Carry me?" Kate smiled. She did wish she could sit back down and rest awhile, but they needed to go home before Daddy came searching for them both.

"You could lean on me, Kate. You don't always have to be the strong one."

"I'm all right, Tori. Really." Kate pushed assurance into

her voice. She was all right. She was. "It's just been a long day, but Lorena did great. She's going to be on the radio."

"I knew she would be. I guess she's excited."

"Very." Kate hesitated, but Tori was Lorena's sister too. Sisters needed to share worries. "She hopes her mother will hear her and come see her."

"Oh." Tori rested her fishing pole on her shoulder and began walking without saying any more.

Kate dodged the end of it and followed her. That was Tori's way. She had to think about things. She didn't just blurt out whatever she was thinking the way Kate sometimes did.

"Did you know she'd been wondering more about her family?" Kate asked.

"I knew something was bothering her. I guess now that she's older, it's natural for her to wonder about her family." Tori looked back at Kate. "That doesn't mean she doesn't love us."

"That sounds like something Mama would say."

"You mean instead of something your little sister would say?" Tori shook her head a little. "I grew up, Kate. And Lorena is growing up too. You have to let her make her own decisions."

"But what if they do hear her on the radio and come back for her? She might go away." Just saying the words squeezed Kate's heart. She couldn't imagine Lorena not part of their family. "I don't want that to happen."

"Neither do I, but we do want her to be happy."

"I want all my sisters to be happy."

Tori's shoulders sagged a little. "You can't make happy endings for everybody, Kate."

"Maybe not," Kate admitted. "But how about happy

beginnings?" When Tori just kept walking without saying anything, Kate went on. "Happy moments? You have those, don't you? Times when you have to smile in spite of everything? When Samantha hugs your neck?"

"Or a certain sister chases me down at the pond," Tori said. "I smile. A lot."

"But you cry too."

"So? You should be used to that by now." Tori's words sounded stiff.

"I don't think that's something I can get used to." Kate wasn't sure she should push her for more, but at the same time, she had the feeling Tori wanted her to ask. "You want to talk about it?"

"If I do, yours will be the first ear I bend."

Kate gave up then. She couldn't force Tori to talk. She couldn't force Lorena to not be curious about her family. She couldn't make her back stop hurting. She couldn't cure her father's cough. But she could pray. Even if she didn't know what was making Tori feel so sad today, the Lord did. He knew about Lorena and Daddy too. He could fix things a lot better than Kate could. She looked up and sent her prayer winging upward, then tacked on an extra thought. *But if you do need me to do anything, I'm right here.*

With the light rapidly fading, Kate had to concentrate on not tripping on the roots and rocks. It wouldn't be good to fall. Women in the family way had to be careful about things like that, didn't they?

By the time they came to the edge of the woods, twilight was giving way to night. Scout pushed past Kate to run on ahead. "Scout's ready to be home for his supper." She tried to hide that she was out of breath. She had no idea expecting a baby could make somebody get so winded. Maybe she should have been more understanding of Evie's complaints.

"Home." Tori stopped in the path. "That's where I said I had to be."

"Had to be?" Kate moved up beside her, but Tori didn't look at her.

"I could be at the movies." Her voice carried a mixture of defiance and disappointment.

"Oh?"

"Graham told Clay I was fishing."

"So, is Graham in trouble?"

"I think I'm the one in trouble." Tori stared down at the ground.

Kate touched Tori's arm. "Why? You're not at the movies."

Tori was quiet as the night sounds wrapped around them. The tree frogs. A cow bawling for her calf. A screech owl. Scout barking. When Tori finally spoke, her voice was so soft Kate had to hold her breath to hear her. "But I think I might want to be."

"And so?" Kate said.

"And so that scares me to death."

Kate dodged the bait bucket to put her arm around Tori. She was too slim. "It will get easier. Next time."

"There won't be a next time."

"Of course there will. Clay's been asking you somewhere twice a week for months."

Tori let out a sigh and moistened her lips. "But I told him to go away. He said he would do anything to make me happy and I told him to go away."

"And he did." Kate was beginning to understand.

"He did." Tori drew in a ragged breath.

Kate hugged Tori closer. "I'm sorry."

"I shouldn't have told you this. You're already worried about Lorena and now I'm heaping this on you too when you need to just think about yourself right now."

"Don't be silly. I'm your sister. Sisters are for leaning on. And for telling you that tomorrow is another day." She looked up then to see Jay coming across the field toward them. "I told Jay to go away once."

"I remember. You were afraid of loving him."

"I don't know that I'd say afraid exactly," Kate said.

"Then what would you say? Terrified?"

Kate smiled. "That might be more like it. I was terrified that I'd never see him again."

"So you went after him."

"I did."

"I don't think I can do that. I don't even know if I want to do that." Tori sighed. "Loving Sammy was so easy. I'll never stop loving Sammy."

"Nobody wants you to forget Sammy. He was such a great kid, always wanting everybody to be happy. You remember how he used to drive Evie crazy by doing handstands whenever she started griping about something."

"He thought that would make her smile. He never could understand why it didn't, so he just kept trying." Tori laughed. "You're right. That was Sammy. Do you remember how he'd bring me fistfuls of dandelions if I was in a bad mood?"

"And now Samantha picks you dandelions."

Tori blinked a few times. "I miss her."

"She'll be back tomorrow."

"Tomorrow. Everybody is always telling me things will be better tomorrow." Tori looked over at Kate. In the fading light her features were soft, but it was easy to see the sad yearning there. "But will tomorrow ever come?"

"I think so. Don't you think we have to think so? And tomorrow when it does come, you can look at the first dandelion you see and think about Sammy. He would want you to be happy. You know he would."

"Clay won't be back."

Kate searched for the right words. "Then, he might not be the right one. But on some tomorrow, there will be a right one. You're nineteen, Tori. Love will come visit you again and your heart will expand and make room without shoving out any of the loves already there."

Jay was almost near enough to hear when Tori asked, "Is that what you'd do if you lost Jay?"

"I don't know, Tori. Nobody can know for sure what she'd do until she walks that path. It's a path I don't want to walk any more than you did, but it was a fear I did live with all through the war. Now I'm thankful he's here and that we can start a family. But if he hadn't come home—" Kate's voice caught a little and she started over. "If he hadn't come home, I hope, in time, I would have been able to welcome love again if the Lord gave me that chance."

"In time," Tori echoed.

Kate thought she might have said more, but Jay called to them. "Hey, girls, what's going on?" He looked around. "You planning to pitch a tent here and spend the night? I've got to tell you it's no fair to go play in the woods without me."

"We were just coming to get you," Tori said.

"Forget that. I had enough sleeping on the ground to last a lifetime." Jay laughed.

Kate tried to say something, but talking about what she

might do if he was lost to her had put a lump in her throat. Instead she rushed to hug him as though she hadn't seen him for weeks instead of just hours. He smelled of cow feed and dust from the feed store, but she didn't care. She would have hugged him right then if he'd been covered with mud. It felt so good to belong there against him.

Tori set down her fishing gear and was right behind her, trying to wrap her arms around them both.

"What's the matter, girls? Something scare you?" Jay pulled Tori into their embrace. "Never fear, I'll protect you from those creepy Lindell Woods shadows."

"We're not afraid of the dark. We're just glad to see you." Kate found her voice. "Very glad."

"We are," Tori said.

"Well, I'm glad to see you too, because if you aren't afraid of those creepy shadows, I am. I thought I might have to wander around in there, getting lost looking for the two of you."

"We wouldn't get lost in Lindell Woods," Tori said.

"Even in the dark?" Jay said.

"Even in the dark," Kate said. "But if we did, Fern would find us."

"Now you're trying to scare me," Tori said.

"And me," Jay added.

"Fern's not scary," Kate said.

"In the dark?" Jay raised his eyebrows at her.

Kate laughed. "Okay, maybe a little, in the dark."

Jay turned them toward the house. "So were you out there playing hide and seek with Fern?"

"I went fishing." Tori pulled away from him to pick up her pole and bait bucket. "I don't know why everybody got all excited about that. I go fishing all the time."

"In the dark?" Jay kept his arm around Kate as they waited for Tori to catch up.

Kate leaned against him, glad for his strength. She was so very tired.

"Twilight's the best time to catch fish," Tori said.

"Then where are they? All these fish. I don't see supper on your stringer." Jay looked around.

"Some twilights are better than other twilights. All fishermen know that."

"Some twilights are better for sister talk," Kate added.

"Sister talk. This guy knows better than to mess with that. But if we don't get on back to the house, we're all going to get some mother talk."

22

Tori pretended all was fine through supper. No, not pretended. All was fine. Other than missing Samantha so much that her insides ached. The little girl always settled down in Tori's lap after supper and the sweet warmth of the child's body had a way of soaking through Tori to make the day's worries slide into the background. Tonight instead, the worries gathered on the edge of her thoughts like dark thunderclouds.

Worry clouds were bothering her mother too. Tori hadn't wanted to worry her mother, but after she sent Clay away, time hadn't seemed to matter. She cried until she had no tears left and then stared at the pond. At every rustle of brush, she held her breath and wondered what she would do if he came back out of the trees. But he didn't. She should have baited her hook and started fishing again. That would have made more sense than sitting there like a turtle afraid to stick its head out of its shell to move on.

Back at the house, after she stashed her fishing pole and bait bucket in the barn, Tori had dipped water out of the rain barrel to wash away every last trace of tears. She didn't want her mother to know she'd been crying. She'd already told Kate too much.

When Tori went in the back door, her mother turned from the stove to give her a hard look.

Tori rushed out her apology. "I'm sorry, Mama, but I didn't think you'd be worried about me. You knew I was fishing."

"You never stay this late."

"But I didn't have Samantha tonight." Tori met her mother's eyes and added gently, "I'm not a little girl anymore, Mama. I can take care of myself."

"I know." Mama breathed out a sigh. "But you've got to realize you'll always be my little girl no matter how old you get. The way you feel about Samantha, that's how I feel about you." She put her hand on Tori's cheek. "Age doesn't matter."

"But you have to let your children grow up."

"You don't let them. They just do." Mama smiled. "And that's what you want, but that doesn't mean you stop worrying."

"You don't have to worry about me when I'm at Graham's pond."

"Was he there today?" She turned to stir the soup bubbling on the stove.

"Not today. Wasn't he at the store?" Tori went to the sink to wash her hands with soap.

"He came in for a soft drink right after you left, but then he headed over to Buddy's. More man talk over there, I suppose."

"With all that banging and clanging I don't know how they hear any talk."

"Mechanic work is noisy. Then so was shoeing horses when your father used to do that. But I always loved the ring of his hammer on iron." Mama looked toward the sitting room.

"Me too." The pinging rhythm of her father's strikes on the glowing metal played through Tori's memory. "I used to beg to go to his shop to watch him shape horseshoes. Or even better, those pokers with the fancy handles. Did he keep any of them?"

"No, he gave them all to the scrap metal drives during the war. Your aunt Gertie kept hers even though your father told her it was unpatriotic, but Gertie didn't pay any attention to him. She said the president wouldn't expect them to poke their fires with sticks." Mama smiled. "Not that she ever poked a fire with that poker. It's been hanging next to the door in her kitchen for years."

"Daddy misses blacksmithing, doesn't he?"

Her mother sighed and stirred the soup again. "Some, but he can't swing the hammer anymore. His shoulder gets stiff. And there's his cough." Right on cue from the front room, they heard him cough. Mama raised her head up and stayed frozen until all was quiet again.

"I hope he gets better soon."

"He will," Mama said. "Of course, he will. But there's not much call for blacksmithing now. He doesn't like repairing shoes as much as shaping iron, but as he'd be the first to tell you, everything changes. A wise person faces those changes straight on. With the Lord's help."

Tori sneaked a look at her mother to see if she was pointing her words at her, but Mama had turned away from her to take up the cornbread. Whether she meant her words for Tori or not, they burrowed down in Tori's head. *Everything changes.* As much as Tori wanted to hold on to the past, it was gone. Clay's words echoed in her thoughts. *Sammy's gone.*

As if her mother heard her thinking about Clay, she said,

"Clay was asking after you at the store today. He brought a little nightgown his mother made for Samantha's doll."

"Samantha will like that." Tori kept her voice level as she got plates out of the cabinet. "Do I need to set places for Kate and Jay?"

"I told them we had plenty, but Kate was tired. I shouldn't have let her go after you." Mama looked worried again. "She's not having an easy start with this baby."

"I know, and I figured she would. Kate always handles everything all right."

"Babies are different."

"Did you have easy times with us?" Tori got an ice tray out of the refrigerator.

"You came hard, but Aunt Hattie and I got you here with lots of prayer. We didn't lose you." Mama smiled over at Tori as she dished up the soup.

"You did lose one baby, didn't you?" Tori lifted the handle to break loose the ice in the tray and began filling the glasses.

Mama's smile disappeared. "The first one. My only boy. Your grandfather Merritt was disappointed I never had another boy."

"Were you? Or Daddy?"

"Not at all. You girls were each a blessing and then Lorena on top of that. What more could we have wanted?"

"Where is Lorena?" Tori looked around.

"Feeding the cats. If I know our little songbird, she's out there singing to them."

"Kate says she's going to be on the radio."

"She's so excited she's about to jump out of her skin." Mama laughed. "I'm pretty excited too. Our little girl on the radio."

"She's not so little anymore."

Mama made a face at Tori. "Don't try to make my last baby grow up too fast. She needs a mother watching after her awhile longer."

But which mother, Tori wondered later as she listened to Lorena tell every detail of the audition. Tori watched her talking about being nervous and how Kate calmed her down. Even with her everyday clothes on now and her hair caught back in an untidy ponytail, she was remarkably pretty. The brown of her eyes seemed to go a mile deep. The surface was warm and happy, but underneath there was more.

That was true with everybody. Everything wasn't on the surface. Tori slid her eyes over to Mama. How would she feel if Lorena's family did come back for her? She'd be sad. They'd all be sad with Lorena's chair empty at the family table.

Mama patted Lorena's hand when Lorena worried about how she would sound on the radio. "You'll sound great. Your father and I are so very proud of you."

It was easy to see the love in Mama's eyes. The same kind of love she had for Tori. The same kind of love Tori had for Samantha. Perhaps the same kind of love that Lorena's first mother had for her. But if she had that love, then how could she desert her here in Rosey Corner?

Some questions couldn't be answered by guessing. Perhaps that was why Lorena wanted to find her mother. So she could know the answers. Then again, it could be the answers wouldn't be good answers.

Tori watched them, missing Samantha more each second. Nothing short of death could keep her away from Samantha for years.

Later, when they got ready for bed, they tiptoed through

their nightly routines even though Samantha wasn't in her little rollaway bed.

"I miss Samantha." Lorena climbed into her bed and fluffed her pillow. "Do you think she's all right?"

"She's probably having a great time." Tori did believe that. If she didn't, she'd be walking the two miles to Sammy's parents' house, no matter how dark the night.

"But you're not."

"She's all I have." Tori sat on the edge of her bed and picked her Bible up off the bedside table. For years, she'd read a chapter every night, but lately the Scriptures just lay flat on the page and didn't speak to her. It wasn't the Bible. It wasn't the Lord. It was her. She was the flat, out-of-sorts problem. With Samantha around, she could hide from it, but without her there, everything hurt.

"You have us," Lorena said very softly.

"I know." Tori looked at Lorena on the other side of the room. "I didn't mean to sound like you didn't matter to me. You do. Very much. I don't know what I would do without Mama and Daddy and you to help me with Samantha."

"But sometimes you need more."

"What makes you so smart?" Tori smiled over at her. "Kids aren't supposed to be so wise."

"I listened to you and Kate." Lorena was smiling now too. "And Mama and Aunt Hattie and Graham and Fern."

"How about Jay and Mike and Daddy?"

"Them too."

Tori stood up, picked up the Bible, and went to sit on Lorena's bed. "Are you needing more too, Lorena? More than us?"

Lorena scooted up to lean against the wooden headboard

on her bed. She stared at her hands a moment before she answered. "I don't know. It's just that sometimes now when I say my name at night, it sounds so very lonely." She looked up at Tori and went on quickly. "I mean I'm not lonely. Gosh, who could be lonely here in Rosey Corner? It's just my name that feels lonely. I guess that sounds silly."

"I understand lonely," Tori said.

"I wish Kate was here."

"I'm glad she's not. I'm glad she's beginning her life with Jay and has a baby on the way."

"I'm glad for that too, but I miss her stories. You remember how she used to tell me stories at night."

"Oh yes. The room danced with princes and princesses and all sorts of characters."

"But you know the story I liked best?"

"The story of you. The ones about finding you. The first time on the church steps and the other time in Fern's cedar palace."

"And how she loved me." Lorena folded her cover back and forth. "But now she'll be a mommy. You changed when you got to be a mommy."

"I didn't stop loving you, Lorena. I just couldn't be a kid any longer and play paper dolls with you."

"I know. I'm not a kid anymore either."

"No, you're not." Tori leaned over to kiss Lorena's cheek. "But love doesn't stop because you get older, and it doesn't go away just because you have new people to love. It just expands. Kate could never stop loving you. Never."

Lorena pointed to the Bible. "Read something out loud tonight. Please."

"What?"

"I don't know. Whatever you see first."

"Okay." Tori held the Bible up sideways and stuck her thumb into the pages to make it open to the New Testament. Her eyes fell on a verse in the middle of the page. Philippians 4:7. "And the peace of God, which passeth all understanding, shall keep your hearts and mind through Christ Jesus."

"That's in one of the first songs I learned here at church. I've got the joy down in my heart. I thought I'd never be able to sing that verse about the peace that passeth understanding down in my heart. Do you remember?"

"How could I forget? It started you on your path to radio singer. And now you can teach Samantha."

"She's already singing the joy, joy, joy part."

"Except she can't say the *j* sound." Tori smiled.

"Jesus knows what she's saying. That's the thing, isn't it?" Lorena looked up at Tori. "Jesus always hears us. So my name shouldn't feel lonely with him listening."

"Maybe it won't feel lonely tonight." Tori closed her Bible but held her place with her finger. She wanted to read more of the chapter. "It's late. Better say your name and go to sleep."

"My name is Lorena Birdsong." Lorena spoke in a clear voice as she covered her heart with her hands. "Your turn, Tori."

Tori smiled. It had been awhile since she'd added her name to Lorena's at night. "My name is Victoria Gale Merritt Harper."

"That's a lot longer name than mine, and just think. When you get married again someday, you'll add another one." Lorena said the last like it was a given that Tori would get married again someday. "Let's say Samantha's name too. Just for fun."

So they held hands and said in unison, "Samantha Gale Harper." The name sounded sweet in Tori's ears.

With her nighttime ritual out of the way, Lorena slid under the covers and was asleep almost before Tori climbed into her own bed. Tori had been that way once. Young enough to bounce between worries without losing sleep.

She read the whole chapter in Philippians. Her eyes dwelt on the thirteenth verse. *I can do all things through Christ which strengtheneth me.* But what all things did she want to do?

Tori turned off the light and listened to Lorena's even breathing while some of their words slipped back through her mind. *Love doesn't stop . . . It just expands . . . When you get married again . . .*

"Oh, Sammy, what should I do?" she whispered. "Should I take back what I said to Clay?"

She stared into the dark air as the questions swirled in her head. She didn't get any answers. But at the same time, that peace that passed understanding seemed to fall down on her after a while. The answers would come, and when they did she'd have the strength to face them. She could talk to Clay again. "Go away" didn't have to be the last words between them. Not if she didn't want them to be. With that thought settling in her mind, she fell asleep.

The next morning, she brushed her hair until it gleamed. She picked her best clothes instead of whatever she grabbed first the way she usually did. Then she hurried on to church ahead of her parents and Lorena. She wanted to be there when Samantha got there. She was tired of having empty arms.

Samantha was happy as could be with Sammy's mother when they got to church. Tori grabbed her for a hug, but then

Samantha pushed her away to go play with the other kids in the churchyard.

Mama Harper gave Tori a quick kiss on the cheek and hurried on in for Sunday school. Tori started across the yard to get Samantha, but one of the older girls had already picked her up. Samantha giggled with delight as the girl carried her inside.

Tori hesitated by the side of the church when she spotted Clay coming up the steps onto the sidewalk. Her heart did a funny flip. What in the world could she say to him? Perhaps it was just as well his eyes were on the church door and he didn't notice her there in the shadows. Or maybe he did see her and was only doing what she'd asked.

She took a step toward him, searching for the right words to say, but then it didn't matter. Paulette Browning hurried across the yard to tuck her hand under Clay's elbow. An ownership touch. They walked into the church together.

23

Grab a chair and sit awhile." Aunt Hattie was settled in a metal lawn chair in her backyard. "The sun might freckle your face, but it feels good to these old bones. I don't never recall you worryin' overmuch about freckles anyhows. Now that Evangeline, we'd be havin' to move to the shade."

Kate pulled a chair off the porch over next to Aunt Hattie's. "You're right about Evie. Trouble is, she can get freckles in the shade."

"Freckle spots goes with red hair."

"I have a few freckles and my hair's regular old brown." Kate flipped her hair and made a little face.

"Not one thing wrong with brown. A fine color for hair. But I do have to admit the three of you girls is the most different I ever saw in natural-born sisters."

"Right. The two beauties on either end of the plain sister."

"I ain't never seen much plain about you, Katherine Reece. You's pretty enough on the outside. You don't believe me, just ask that boy you married. I've seen him lookin' at you. But even better than them outer looks that fade with time, you got the kind of beauty that matters most in this life. That inside kind that shines right out of your eyes and lands on the folks you is with."

"Thank you, Aunt Hattie. You know how to make me feel pretty."

"You is or you ain't. The good Lord does the making, but he did give me eyes for seeing." She leaned forward in her chair. "Where is that Jay? It's Sunday, I'm pretty sure. I forget the day some through the week, but I always remember the Lord's Day. So how come he didn't come with you when he knows this old woman likes restin' her eyes on him? You two aren't fussing, are you?"

"No, everything's fine."

Aunt Hattie settled back in her chair and folded her hands in her lap. She'd always been a little woman, and now age had shrunk her even more until it seemed her wrinkles might swallow her whole. Her hair was a gray cloud of fuzz around her face, but in that face, her dark brown eyes were as sharp as ever.

"That's good to hear. Married folks spatting ain't something I want to hear about. He likin' the idea of being a daddy?"

"He's glad," Kate said a little too quickly. "Of course, he's glad."

Aunt Hattie bent her head and looked at Kate through her eyebrows. "Ain't no need you tryin' to hide your worries from me, child. I done been reading your face too many years. Out with it."

Kate sighed. "I don't know, Aunt Hattie. I think he's worried he won't know how to be a good father because he didn't have a loving father. When he was a kid, his father dumped him on an aunt and uncle who didn't want him either."

"You send him on around here to me. I'll point out Victor to him. Wasn't never a man who loved his babies more than Victor."

"Daddy had troubles too after the war."

"That he did." Aunt Hattie inclined her head a little. "But weren't never no trouble about lovin' his girls."

"I know Daddy loved us. Even when he was struggling through the hard times."

"Your boy ain't havin' that kind of hard times, is he?"

"No. Well, not the drinking, but he has bad dreams like Daddy did. Things from the war. He won't talk about it."

"War's a terrible thing. Stole my Bo from me." A tear trickled out of the corner of her eye down through her wrinkles. She didn't brush it away. "I still miss that boy. But it won't be long till I see him in paradise."

Kate put her hand on Aunt Hattie's arm. "I'm not ready for you to move up to heaven yet."

"It's not you that has to get ready, child." Aunt Hattie's smile set her wrinkles to dancing. Then her smile faded. "I'm thinkin' you won't never be ready to tell me goodbye. I ain't wantin' to say goodbye to you neither. But goodbyes, they come. For young and old. And I'm feeling the goodbye coming on."

"But we still need you. Evie's baby will be here soon, and if ever anybody needed some sensible advice, it's her."

"That's God's own truth." Aunt Hattie chuckled, a hoarse sound that ended in a cough. "But you know that girl hasn't never listened to me. Nadine will bring her along. Your mama knows a heap about mothering. More than this old woman."

"But you've delivered hundreds of babies here in Rosey Corner."

"The Lord did bless me with good hands for catching babies back when doctors were scarcer than hen's teeth around here. Rejoiced and praised the Lord ever' time one of those sweet babies pulled in that first breath. A miracle each and ever' time." Aunt Hattie shook her head again. "But birthing and mothering ain't the same."

"The birthing has to come first."

Aunt Hattie must have heard something in Kate's voice because she narrowed her eyes on her. "You's lookin' a mite pale around the eyes. How far along did you tell me you were?"

"About three months."

"That town doctor give you a delivering time?"

"October."

"A good month for birthing babies. Gives them time to get strong before the cold sets in."

"I want my baby to be strong," Kate said.

"Course you do. And he has ever' chance of being that way with you as his mama." Aunt Hattie took her hand. "What's worrying you, child?"

"I'm not sure. I don't want to be like Evie and complain about every little thing when I know some discomfort goes along with being in the family way."

Kate looked down at Aunt Hattie's hand on hers. The woman's fingers were bent with arthritis and her skin felt paper thin. From the time Kate could remember, when she really wanted to know something, she came to Aunt Hattie for answers. Aunt Hattie didn't jig around the truth. But now for some reason, Kate was tiptoeing around her worries.

"Your sister looked to be carrying fine last I saw her, but Evangeline never was one to handle bumps without wailing about it some. Between Nadine and that sweet Preacher Mike working to make the world pleasin' for her, she never got no practice on gettin' tough. Like you has. You never took to babying. Even when you was a little child. You was always ready to go out there and meet the world head on."

"I'm not feeling so tough right now."

"How is you feeling?" Aunt Hattie's eyes bored into Kate. When Kate didn't say anything right away, she gave her hand a shake. "I ain't never known you to sashay so around what you's wantin' to say. This is your old Aunt Hattie. You can tell me anything. You knows that."

Kate swallowed hard. She'd come to Aunt Hattie for advice, but now she didn't want to give voice to her fears. At last she said, "I'm just so tired and my back hurts."

"What kind of hurt?" Aunt Hattie had on her doctor face.

"I don't know."

Aunt Hattie swept her words away with an impatient hand. "A little passing pain? A lifted-something-heavy pain? Does it ease up when you lays yo'self down and then worsens when you stand up?"

"Not a little pain. More a gripping pain. Laying down doesn't help much."

"Pressing down on you?" Aunt Hattie's face lost every hint of smile when Kate nodded. "You showing any issue?"

"A little spotting," Kate admitted. Her heart had frozen inside her when she first saw that in her underwear.

"You call your doctor?" Aunt Hattie asked.

"He said unless it got worse, it wasn't anything to worry about and I could just wait until my appointment next week. He didn't sound concerned."

"He's right. Such is not uncommon in the early months," Aunt Hattie said. "By itself not reason to worry, but I don't like that your back's aching. I never knew you to complain about a backache even at those times of month. Stand up here and let me do some probing."

Aunt Hattie ran her fingers up and down Kate's spine. In spite of the arthritis, her fingers were still strong pushing against the tops of Kate's hip bones. "Any spot I'm touching hurt more than others?"

"No, it's more a cramping type of pain all across my lower back."

"Could be you pulled a muscle," Aunt Hattie said, but she didn't sound as if she believed it. "Turn toward me and let me touch that baby."

"Should we go inside?"

"Ain't no need. Nobody's gonna see us out here in the backyard, 'cepting maybe Fern if she's around. Just lift out your skirt a little so I can slide my hands up over your belly to see how big you're getting."

Kate did as she said. She felt comforted by the feel of Aunt Hattie's hands sliding over her tummy. If there was anything wrong, Aunt Hattie could tell her how to fix it.

"Ain't much of a baby bump," Aunt Hattie murmured.

"But that's normal this early, isn't it?"

"Mamas carry babies in a hundred different ways. Some show on day five. Others not till month five."

Aunt Hattie frowned and scooted forward in her chair. She pulled Kate close to put her ear against her middle. When Kate started to say something, she shushed her and told her to hold her breath. Kate was beginning to feel light-headed when Aunt Hattie said, "You's can breathe now."

"Did you hear the baby?" Kate asked.

"My ears ain't what they used to be and even when my

hearing was strong, I couldn't always pick up a heartbeat. According to where the little fellow was inside his mama. But the doctors don't need good ears nowadays. They got instruments to beat out the best ears. And the baby is small. Right now the sweet thing will have fingers and toes, but not be big as your hand."

For some reason, Kate felt abandoned when Aunt Hattie pulled her hands away from her belly and sat back. "But he is okay, isn't he?"

Aunt Hattie hesitated for a bare second. Then she let out a whisper of breath. "I ain't never knowingly lied to you and there ain't no need in me starting now. I'm some worried about what you're telling me. Perhaps with cause. Perhaps not. I'm hopin' not. Sometimes worries bedevil us for no reason."

"You're not making me feel better." Kate sank back down in her chair. "What should I do?"

"Might be that you should go on home and lay yourself down for a while. Don't get up 'cepting when you has to relieve yo'self."

"You mean for the rest of today?"

"For today and tomorrow and as long as you needs to so's you can give this baby a chance."

"You're telling me to stay in bed all day?" Kate stared at Aunt Hattie, not sure she understood her right.

"That's what I'm tellin' you."

"I can't do that. Who'll do the housework? The cooking?"

"That boy of yours can fix his own eats and yours too for a few days. And houses don't have to be cleaned ever' day. Dirt don't go nowhere. It sits right there and waits till you is able to chase it away. If something has to be done, Lorena or Victoria will run right over to help you. Sisters is good that way."

"But I'm the one who helps them."

"You has always wanted to hold everybody in your hands and be the strong one." Aunt Hattie shook her head a little. "But there is times when each and ever' one of us has to realize how weak we really are. That's when a body learns to lean on the strength of the Lord. Compared to him, we is all weak as kittens."

"I don't want to be weak." Kate's voice was barely above a whisper. "Not when it comes to carrying my baby."

Aunt Hattie gripped Kate's hands. "The Lord will give you strength."

Tears edged up into Kate's eyes. "But my baby is going to be all right, isn't he?"

"We is going to pray hard for this baby, and put him into the Lord's hands. There's no righter place to be."

Kate wanted promises and Aunt Hattie was only offering prayers. Still, Aunt Hattie's prayers were powerful. "Will you pray for me, for him?"

"You know I will, child. Day and night."

"I mean now." Kate swallowed back her tears. She wasn't weak. She wouldn't lose this baby. She wouldn't. She stood up and cradled the slight swell of the baby with her hands.

"Come closer." Aunt Hattie put her hands over top of Kate's. Then without closing her eyes, she looked up and began talking to the Lord. "Dear Lord, we knows you are watching over us. That you has loved us from the moment you began knitting us together in our mothers' wombs. You is knitting this little child now in this mama's womb and we ask that you give him ever'thing he needs to make the long journey to life. Give this mother strength for the days ahead and shower down your love on her the way you has all the livelong days of her life. We send these petitions to you, Lord, knowing you is in control." Aunt Hattie suddenly bowed her head and her voice softened. "But your will, not ours, Lord, for you knows best. Amen and amen."

Each step Kate took on the way back to her house from Aunt Hattie's felt like a betrayal of the baby inside her. It wasn't far. She could walk it in ten minutes, but maybe that was too far for this baby. Maybe going to get Tori at Graham's pond the day before had been too far. Or driving Lorena to Louisville or standing around the audition area all day. Could be she shouldn't have gone to church that morning. Or stood and washed dishes after dinner. The worries made the pain in her back worse with every step.

The house was empty when she got there. She knew it would be. Jay had taken Lorena to sing at a church in Frankfort. Kate told them to go without her because she had to finish a piece for the Edgeville paper. It wasn't a lie. She had promised to send the editor something.

Kate stared at her notebook on the kitchen table. Their dirty breakfast dishes were stacked in the sink. She felt guilty turning her back on them, but dishes could wait.

The bedroom shades shut out the late afternoon sunshine. She had at least straightened the covers on their bed, but Jay's clothes from the day before were piled on the chair in the corner. She carried them to the hamper in the closet. She'd have to get up early tomorrow to do the laundry and get her article finished before the mail ran.

The pain shooting through her back reminded her of Aunt Hattie's orders to stay in bed. Aunt Hattie knew a lot about babies, but she was getting old. Her ideas were from years ago. She could be wrong. She had to be wrong. Kate couldn't lie in bed all day long. She couldn't.

Kate never got sick. Never. She wasn't like Evie who complained about every twinge or Tori who was sickly as a child. But Tori had carried Samantha without one problem and now Evie was well along and doing fine. Nobody was telling her to lie down.

Kate caught sight of her reflection in the dresser mirror. She didn't like what she saw. Worried eyes. A waistline that showed not the first sign of expanding for a baby. Too pale cheeks. She told herself it was just the dusky light. Pale didn't matter that much anyway. But she'd lie down today so she could tell Aunt Hattie she'd done what she said.

She slipped off her shoes and lay down on top the covers. No sense in getting all the way into the bed. Not yet. She pulled Jay's pillow over to hug close to her. Jay would be worried about her when he got home and found her in bed. He'd want to know what was wrong. What could she tell him?

That she was tired. That would be enough. No sense worrying him. By morning everything would be fine. She wasn't weak. She wasn't.

24

Some of the church people came over to welcome Jay and Birdie before the service started. Jay kept his smile firmly in place as he shook their hands, but he felt a little out of place without Kate beside him to be the one on the front line of the greetings. She was good at making sure everything was organized for Birdie to sing. Since they'd moved back to Rosey Corner, they'd taken Birdie somewhere to sing nearly every weekend.

The kid had a gift. He smiled over at Birdie beside him in a pew toward the back of the church. If Kate had been there, they'd have been on the third row, but Jay liked being closer to the door. He managed to cover it up when Kate was with him, but he felt easier having a quick way out, even if he wasn't planning on leaving until the service was over.

Birdie didn't care where they sat, but she did seem a little antsy without Kate to buoy her confidence. As people filed in to fill the other pews, she twisted her bracelet around her arm and jiggled her leg up and down. He finally touched her knee to stop her when the pew started shaking.

He leaned close to her ear to ask, "What's the matter?"

"I'm singing a new song," she whispered back. "What if I forget the words?"

"Not likely. You sang it about five hundred times on the way over here." Jay lowered his voice more. "I know the words and I never heard it before today."

"Then maybe you should sing it." A smile jerked up one side of her lips.

"Well, if you want me to."

She put a hand over her mouth to keep the giggle in her eyes from finding its way out.

"Don't be silly, Tanner. You can't sing."

"But you can," he told her as the organist crashed out some gathering notes. Then a woman with tightly coifed gray hair added piano notes to the organ music. She was supposed to play for Birdie. That was how they'd been doing the church visits. Birdie sang out of the hymnbook and hoped somebody at the church would be willing to play the songs for her. If not, Birdie sang without accompaniment. Jay liked her singing best that way, her voice pure and unhindered.

The congregation stood for the opening hymn. Jay mouthed the words. Birdie was right. He wasn't much of a singer.

His roundabout pep talk must have been enough. As soon as the song leader spoke Birdie's name, she popped up and headed toward the front without the slightest sign of nerves. She was like Kate that way. Ready to embrace opportunity and seize whatever life had to offer.

He wanted to think he was the same, but most of his life, he'd had his fists up, ready to sock life in the nose instead of embracing it. With cause. Life had a way of blindsiding him. But that was before Kate. Everything was different in Rosey Corner. Life was good there.

Birdie launched into her first song. "Just a Closer Walk with Thee." That's what Aunt Hattie would tell him made being in Rosey Corner good. Made everything good. Opening his heart up to the Lord. Sometimes Jay was still surprised the Lord had hunted him up. Aunt Hattie would say that wasn't true either. She'd say the Lord was there with him all along. It just took Jay awhile to open his eyes and see him. Aunt Hattie could outpreach most anybody.

Not that he didn't agree with her. He did. He didn't know how he would have made it through the war without the Lord. Even so, often as not, he felt closer to the Lord while he was running the corn grinding machine at the feed store than he did in churches like the one he was in this night.

Kate couldn't understand that. Being in a church pew every Sunday was important to her. Even necessary. A worry wriggled awake in him. It wasn't normal for Kate not to want to come with them. Wanting to had nothing to do with it, she'd insisted. She needed to get the article done for the Edgeville paper. She'd promised. But Kate never wrote on Sundays.

She wasn't feeling good. He could see that on her face, but she kept saying she was fine. Putting up a front. That was Kate too. The one who made everything fine. She did make things fine for him, but he hadn't been able to keep his worry about being a father completely hidden. Kate knew him too well. So to keep him from worrying more, she pretended to be all right when he could see she wasn't.

They were both doing too much pretending. Losing that closeness he'd so treasured when he first got home. Now for whatever reason, they seemed to be stepping back into their own shadowy corners where neither one of them was willing to reveal what they were thinking. That needed to change. He wanted that to change. He was glad Kate was strong, but he wanted her to lean on him when she needed to. He wanted to put his arms around her and be a good husband. A good father.

He stared at the men in front of him. Family men. Some maybe home from the war like him. But comfortable there in the Lord's house with their children beside them. Next year that could be him and Kate with a baby between them. Not between them. Tying them even tighter into a family. He was ready for that. He really was, but at the same time he needed time to get used to families and churches. Things were so different from the war days.

A man in the Army didn't get much chance to sit in church pews. Jay's best churchlike times had been under the stars, talking to Sarge about the Bible. Sarge knew his Bible. He didn't have to open it to tell the men in their unit what it said. He had verse after verse hidden in his heart so no enemy could ever steal the Word of God from him.

There were good times to be had at church too, if Jay could keep his mind from straying from whatever the preacher had to say. When that happened, when he stopped hearing the preacher and started hearing the echo of artillery instead, that's when he needed to be moving and not a sitting duck for memories of blood and dying. He shut out those thoughts now and concentrated on Birdie singing. With a panicked look, she stuck the word "mountain" in where mountain didn't fit, but then the right words came back to her.

She let her eyes slide over him. A person could maybe get teary and sing, but not laugh and do any good singing. As she usually did at revival meetings, she sang "Amazing Grace" last. Every eye in the church was on Birdie as her voice wrapped around them. Even the babies were quiet. Jay had heard her sing that song dozens of times, but it never failed to put chills down his back. He sent up a thankful prayer for the grace he'd been granted and the love he'd been given. For Kate. For Birdie. For living through the war and making it home to Rosey Corner.

At the end of the services, the preacher extended the invitation hymn through five extra verses. Then, most every person there wanted to tell Birdie how much they enjoyed her songs, so it was full dark by the time they got on the road home. Birdie was keyed up the way she always was after singing.

"Did I sound all right?" Birdie didn't wait for him to answer. "Don't just say what you think I want to hear. Tell me what you really thought. Did the people like it?"

"You heard them. They thought you were great."

"But what do you say?" Birdie pushed him for an answer.

Jay glanced over at her. "You know I think you're great. You give me the holy shivers when you sing."

"Even when I sing the wrong word?" She made a face and put her hand to her head. "I can't believe I did that. Didn't you want to laugh out loud?"

"Seeing as how that bunch seemed pretty straightlaced, I decided I'd better hang on to my solemn look." Jay grinned at her.

"I know, but I almost got tickled."

She laughed now. An easy sound that warmed Jay's heart. She'd changed so much while he was in the Army. Grown nearly as tall as him and become a young woman. He'd been afraid she wouldn't feel the same about him as she had when she was ten, but they were still buddies.

He laughed with her. "Nothing wrong with laughing in church. I'm thinking the Lord probably laughs at us plenty when he looks down on us at church."

"That's what Mike's always saying too. Or he used to before the war." Birdie sighed, her laughter gone. "Do you think he'll ever be like he used to be?"

"Mike had a hard time in that German prison camp. War can test a man's faith."

"But you found faith."

Jay gripped the steering wheel. What he believed still sometimes seemed too raw and fresh to put into words, but he wanted to be able to talk about it to Birdie. "That started with you and Kate here in Rosey Corner before I went off to the war. And believe it or not, Graham. He has a way of setting a man's thinking straight. That doesn't mean I didn't have plenty of testing times during the war. But I didn't get captured. I stayed free to keep fighting."

Birdie reached across the seat to give his arm a butterfly touch. "I prayed for you every night, Tanner. Right after I said my name."

"I felt those prayers, Birdie. Mike knew you were praying for him too. I'm sure the whole church was praying for Mike, but everything has always been sort of easy for Mike. A good family. Knowing what the Lord intended for him early on. Falling in love with Evangeline. Your church here thinking he was the best preacher they ever had."

"He was the best. I don't know anybody who didn't like Mike." Birdie hurried to change her words. "Everybody still likes Mike. Do you think he'll start preaching again?"

"I don't know. Maybe. He's talking about it again some."

He'd talked about it to Jay last Sunday. The day was sunny,

so they'd walked out to lean on the fence and watch Mr. Merritt's two cows in the pasture.

Mike broke the silence between them. "Evangeline wants me to get a church."

"Why?" Jay asked. "The Lord been talking to her?"

"You don't have to sound like you don't think that possible. He talked to you, didn't he?"

"Yeah, nobody was more surprised about that than me." Jay looked over at Mike. "So is that what happened? She get a sign from the Lord to prod you back onto the preaching road?"

Mike stared back out at the field and let out a long sigh. "Just the sign coming in with all our bills. With her having to quit her job, things are a little tight. If I had a church along with my job, that would bring in extra money for the baby and all."

"Babies don't need a lot."

"That's what I thought before Evangeline let me know different. You'll see when Kate starts talking about fixing up a nursery."

Jay didn't say anything. They both knew that while Kate and Evie were sisters, they weren't much alike. Somebody from the church would loan Kate a cradle and baby blankets and she'd be fine with that. Not Evie. She wanted everything to look like the pictures in the magazines. "Preaching isn't the only kind of extra job you could get."

"I know, but it's not just the money. She thinks I'd be happier if I'm preaching." Mike kept his eyes straight ahead. "She needs me to be happier with the baby coming."

"You're happy about that, aren't you?"

"I am. I dreamed about getting home and having a family

while I was in Gulag 5. It was all that kept me sane at times. How about you? Did you feel that way too?"

"I wanted to come home for sure."

"And now here you are settled down with a baby on the way." Mike smiled over at Jay. "Funny how things work out. Us being best buddies and marrying sisters and now both of us about to be dads."

"Yeah, funny." Jay kept his smile on. It wasn't the time to talk about his worries about being a dad. It was time to help his friend figure out how to be happier again. "Do you want to preach again, Mike?"

"I loved preaching. You know that, Jay." He gazed up at the clouds drifting across the sky as if searching among them for the right words. "It was good to share the gospel with my church family and be part of their lives in good times and bad."

"Then why aren't you preaching now?"

Mike stared down at the ground. "I don't know."

"Do you still believe?"

Mike whipped his head around toward Jay. "Of course, I believe. Nothing could ever change that."

"Okay, so what's the problem?"

Mike looked back out at the field. When he finally spoke again, his voice was so low Jay had to strain to make out his words. "I was afraid, Jay. I didn't have enough faith. A man of God shouldn't have a spirit of fear."

"You reading the same Bible I am?" Jay didn't give him time to answer. "Because in my Bible, people get scared all the time."

"Daniel didn't. Or Shadrach, Meshach, and Abednego. Or David when he faced Goliath."

Jay couldn't argue about that. Staring at sure death in a fiery furnace or going up against a giant with nothing but a slingshot was more than he could imagine doing without trembling no matter how much he believed. He had charged into enemy fire, but he couldn't say it was without fear. He ran his hand over the weathered wood fence rail and said the only thing that came to mind. "You didn't have a slingshot."

"I could have made one."

"It wouldn't have been much good against machine guns."

"David's brothers didn't think a slingshot would be much good against giants with eight-foot swords."

"But it never says he wasn't afraid."

"It doesn't say he was," Mike said. "What it does say is that David trusted the Lord."

"Yeah, but that didn't mean his heart wasn't jumping up in his throat when Goliath was stomping down toward him. But even if it wasn't, even if he wasn't afraid, there are plenty of others in the Bible who were." Jay picked at a piece of cedar bark on the fence post while he tried to remember his Bible stories. "What about Elijah running to hide in a cave right after he brought fire down from heaven? Or Moses cowering in front of that burning bush telling God he had the wrong man? Or Peter saying he never knew Jesus? What about those? Afraid in the presence of miracles the likes of which we'll never see."

"But they went on and did what God had for them to do."

"Exactly." Jay peeled the bark off the post and pitched it into the field.

Mike laughed. "I can't believe we're talking Bible and you're the one trying to convince me instead of the other way around."

"Things change."

Those words echoed in his head now as Birdie brought him back to the present by saying, "Mama says he'll never come back to preach at our church."

"She could be right." He pulled out the same words he'd told Mike. They were just as true for Birdie as for Mike. "Things change. People the most of all."

"You haven't changed."

"That's where you're wrong. Way wrong. I'm as changed as can be. From a loner to a man with family on every side. Here coming home from church with my little sister." Jay stared out at the road. "You can't imagine how different that is to how I was before I came to Rosey Corner."

"And now you're going to be a daddy."

"I am." Jay kept his eyes on the road and made his hands relax on the steering wheel. He could do this. Men became fathers all the time. But was that the same as being a daddy?

"You have a sister, don't you?" Birdie asked.

Her question caught him off guard. "I'm surrounded by sisters. You, Tori, Evie. When you marry a Merritt girl, you are gifted with sisters. But I do have one favorite sister." He glanced over at Birdie. "Since she was the first sister to really like me."

She covered her mouth to hide her pleased smile. "You were funny."

"Funny, huh? That's me. Jay like the bird good for a million laughs."

"That's what Fern calls you. See, she thinks you're funny too."

"I didn't think Fern thought anything was funny."

"She laughs." When Jay shot her a look, she added, "It's

just that her laugh is so rusty, hardly anybody knows she's laughing."

"Maybe she needs a bottle of laughing oil."

"See, if she heard you say that, she'd laugh. Fern's not like everybody thinks she is. She really loves us."

"You anyway."

"And Kate," Birdie said. "Kate doesn't think so, but she does."

Birdie was quiet then as they rode along the dark road. Jay pretended he had to focus on driving and hoped she wouldn't remember he hadn't answered her question about his sister. He didn't like thinking about Amanda Faye. It brought out too much guilt. Not that he had any reason to feel guilty. As far as he knew, Amanda was fine. She'd be—he had to stop and think about that—twenty-five. Probably married with kids. She'd been a sweet kid of around eight when he last saw her. She had other brothers. Those his father and stepmother had after they shipped Jay off to his aunt's house. Amanda wouldn't have missed him being around at all.

But Birdie wasn't one to be sidetracked when she wanted to know something. She was like a bulldog shaking whatever was hiding what she wanted to know until it fell out. Another thing she'd learned from Kate.

"That sister," she said. "The one you had before you came to Rosey Corner. You should go see her."

"It's been a long time, Birdie. I figure she's forgotten all about me. And it's better that way."

"She wouldn't forget you. She probably wonders about you all the time, no matter how many years it's been." Birdie paused a moment before she pushed out her next words all in a rush. "I wonder about my brother. Not you. But the brother in my first family."

"Yeah, you told me about him once. He was a couple years older than you, wasn't he?"

"He'd be sixteen now. Old enough to drive."

Jay quit trying to steer her away from whatever she wanted to say. Instead he reached for it. "What was his name? Do you remember?"

"How could I forget my brother's name?" Birdie sounded a little incensed at his question.

"Hey, I'm sorry." Jay lifted his hands off the wheel in a quick gesture of surrender. "I was just asking."

"Kenton. Kenton Birdsong."

"Could he sing like you?"

"Maybe. We sang in the car before he got sick." Birdie sighed. "I can't remember his face. All I can remember is him being so sick and not waking up when I had to get out and not go on with them."

"That must have been tough."

"Mommy said she'd come back for me, but I don't think she will now." Birdie fiddled with the clasp on the purse in her lap. "I think I'll have to go find her."

"Not by yourself," Jay said quickly. "At least until you get out of school."

"Right. That's what Mama says too. It's sort of weird asking Mama about finding my mother. Since Mama is my mother now."

"And she loves you. We all love you."

"My mother before loved me too. And so did Kenton."

Jay noticed she didn't mention her father, so he didn't either. "I'm sure they did."

"Kate said she'd help me find them. Someday."

"How was she going to do that?"

"I don't know." Birdie sighed again and clicked her purse open and shut a few times. "I thought maybe she'd told you."

"Things have been a little hectic lately."

"Right. With the baby and all. My mama was expecting too. So that might mean I have another brother too. Or a sister."

"I guess so."

"Kate's worried I'll leave Rosey Corner if my mother hears me on the radio and remembers she promised to come back for me."

"Oh." Jay didn't like to think about Birdie being gone from Rosey Corner any more than Kate did. "Would you?"

Birdie raised her head, but she didn't look at Jay. Instead she stared out the windshield. They were almost to her house. "Not forever. I'd always come home to Rosey Corner."

"It's a good place to call home." Jay pulled in the driveway. The porch light was on and through the window he could see Kate's mother and father in the sitting room, waiting for Lorena to get home.

She gave him a hug, then was out of the car, running for the steps. Scout raced out to greet her and she laughed as she danced away from him to keep the dog from messing up her Sunday dress.

He waited until she was inside before he backed up and headed home. Kate had left a light on for him, but she was already in bed. Before he turned out the light, he stood a moment and watched her sleeping. He could barely keep from touching her face, but he didn't want to wake her. She'd been so tired that day. Because she was carrying his baby. His heart swelled inside his chest. He loved her so much, and he would love their baby.

She woke when he crawled into bed and turned into his embrace, murmuring a hello. Yes, indeed. Rosey Corner was a good place to call home.

25

Clay Weber didn't have a good start to his Monday. His shoestring broke when he laced up his shoes. The bossy cow kicked over a half full pail of milk and then swished her tail in his face. Twice. When he got corn for the hogs, the mice were having a party in the corncrib. He'd have to find a black snake to put a stop to that nonsense before nothing was left but cobs.

At breakfast, he snapped at Mary when she asked if he'd given the doll dress to Victoria. Big tears welled up in Mary's eyes. He was sorry at once and hugged the little girl, but that didn't make it all right. Mary had nothing to do with Victoria telling him to go away.

His mother shooed the girls off to get their schoolbooks. Aaron blew the horn on the old jalopy Clay had helped him buy. He wanted his brothers and sisters to have a way to school. Aaron would graduate this year, the first high school graduate in the family. Clay would have been the first if things had been different, but they weren't. They were what they were, and he'd never have that rolled-up piece of paper that was the ticket to a better life. Instead he'd keep wrestling a living out of the ground for his mother and the kids.

Maybe that was why Victoria told him to go away. He wasn't smart enough for her.

He stared down at his eggs and bacon and biscuit smeared with blackberry jam. All products of his or his mother's hands. Thankful, that's what he should be. He had a good family. A farm to work. Enough schooling to get by. He tried to push thankful to the front of his thinking, but it didn't work. Grouchy was what he was. Not a bit thankful.

He moved his eggs around with his fork as he listened to Aaron's car going down the lane. The boy needed to patch that muffler.

His mother came back in the kitchen and told Willie to stop playing with his food and eat. She looked ready to tell Clay the same, but instead she poured a cup of coffee and sat down across from him. "Something bothering you, son?"

"No, ma'am. Just didn't sleep so well."

"I see." She took a sip of coffee and gave Willie another look that at last got the little boy to spoon some oatmeal into his mouth.

Willie was a dreamer. Being the last and a child who never laid eyes on his father had made them all spoil him too much. Maybe Clay should talk to his mother about giving the boy some regular chores. At five, he could feed the chickens or gather sticks for kindling.

Willie would be easier to talk about than Victoria. Her words telling him to go away had sounded in his head over and over the night before. Then when he did drift off to sleep, he dreamed she was looking at him with longing eyes. That was a dream he might have wanted to keep on dreaming, but something jerked him awake. Reality, he supposed. He lay there in bed and stared up at the dark, trying to replace Victoria's face in his dream with Paulette's. Paulette was the one looking at him with longing. Not Victoria. That was what would make sense, and hadn't everybody always said that Clay had good sense?

He looked at things straight on. Wasn't much use imagining things were different than they were. The ground on their rocky farm was so hard a man could spill blood on it and still not grow a decent potato. But even more than the farm, he knew the man who stared back at him from the mirror every morning was only a farm boy without much to offer any girl except a lifetime of work like his mother had.

It didn't much matter that his mother claimed she would never have chosen a different path than marrying his father. That didn't have anything to do with the choices Victoria was ready to make. He was lucky to have any girl wanting him to come around. So he should be glad Paulette was ready to grab his arm and sit with him at church on Sunday.

He hadn't wanted to go to church, but he couldn't come up with a reasonable excuse to stay home. Besides, he had nursed this tiny hope Victoria might take back her words. After all, for a while there on the pond bank, she'd almost seemed glad he was there. He'd even had his arms around her for a few seconds when she stumbled toward the water's edge.

All the way to church, he thought up what he could say to her. *Victoria, I know what you said, but we've been friends a long time. We don't want to throw that away. Can't we just keep talking now and again? Won't you let me hang on to a shred of hope?*

But he didn't get a chance to say any of that. Paulette

captured him as soon as he set foot on the front walk. He did see Victoria come in the church, but he could hardly get up from beside Paulette and go talk to her then. Even if that was what he wanted to do. The very sight of her pulled at him. He'd have gone down on his knees right there in front of the whole church and begged her to change her mind about him if he thought that would make a difference. But he figured a scene like that would make her even more eager for him to disappear from her life.

He did speak to her after the services, but she kept her eyes down, barely looking at him or at Paulette either before she eased away from them. Minutes later, she grabbed Samantha and headed down the road toward her house, even though her parents were still talking in the churchyard. If only he'd had a reason to walk with her. If only Paulette hadn't been hanging on to his arm, chattering about the movie they'd seen.

"The fishing trip didn't go well then?" his mother asked now.

"The fish weren't biting." Clay finished off his eggs even though they were cold and about as appetizing as Willie's oatmeal. He hoped she'd see him chewing and let it drop. They both knew she wasn't talking about catching fish anyway.

"Maybe you should give it another try," his mother said.

His mother had aged a lot in the last five years. Hard years after Clay's father died. She and his father had been like two halves of the same person. A softer, gentler side and a harsh, honest side. Mother and father. Now she had to be both sides and it was wearing on her. Deep lines traced around her eyes. She was always working. In fact, it was uncommon for her to sit like this with her coffee. Generally she just took a sip now and again while starting in on her chores.

But today she studied him across the table, her hands wrapped around her cup. Willie scraped the last bite out of his bowl, gave their mother a smile, and headed outside to check on the kittens under the porch.

"Maybe you should give him some chores to do," Clay said.

His mother's face softened as the little boy ran past the kitchen window. "Let him play. He'll have plenty of time for working later."

"You're babying him too much." Even to his ears, he sounded grouchy again.

She reached across the table and laid a work roughened hand over his. "He helps me in the garden."

"That's play for him."

"Working in the dirt isn't a bad thing to enjoy, son. You liked the planting when you were his age too." Her eyes on him were concerned. "I'm sorry we couldn't baby you longer."

"I never wanted to be babied."

"No, no you didn't. Your father used to call you his little man. Do you remember that?"

Clay nodded, not sure he could trust his voice with that memory pushing at him. He'd followed his father out to the fields when he was younger than Willie.

His mother patted his hand and sat back. She took another drink of coffee. "I saw you sitting with Paulette yesterday at church. You two back together?"

"Maybe."

"She seemed all smiles," his mother said mildly.

"Yeah. She was at the movies with some friends Saturday night and she asked me to sit with them."

"I see." His mother ran her finger around the rim of her cup.

Clay wanted to get up and go on out to hitch the horse to the plow, but his mother wasn't sitting at the table for no reason. She had something to say and she hadn't said it yet. While he wasn't sure he wanted to hear it, she was his mother. He owed her a listen, even as he hoped she'd have second thoughts and get up to go about her work and let him go about his.

That wasn't to be. "I'm guessing Victoria wasn't one of those friends."

"No." Clay drained the last of his coffee from his cup. Anything to keep his eyes away from his mother. She had enough troubles without taking on his heartache. And that was what he had. Words weren't going to make it better. Time maybe, or so people said. Time hadn't seemed to make Victoria's heart stop hurting for Sammy.

Clay pushed back from the table and stood up. Whatever she wanted to say would have to wait for another time. "I've got to get that back field plowed before the rain comes."

She caught his arm as he moved past her. He had to stop, but he kept his eyes on the door.

"You're young, Clay. Only twenty-two. Don't settle for less than love."

Clay shut his eyes and pulled in a breath. The kitchen was so quiet he could hear the clock on the mantel in the front room ticking past the seconds. Finally he opened his eyes and looked at his mother. "I can love Paulette."

"Can you?" she asked, but she didn't expect an answer. She dropped her hand away from his arm and began scraping up the breakfast dishes.

He was glad to be out of the house. Glad to have something to do with his hands as he lifted the yoke down off the barn wall. Ace stood still, resigned to another day of pulling the plow. Some of the farmers around them were getting tractors, but Ace and Clay were still a good team that could get the work done without worrying about buying gasoline.

Then again, maybe it would be good to need gasoline. Only one place to buy that in Rosey Corner. He could almost see Victoria coming out to the pumps, the wind blowing back her dark hair. A smile on her face. For him. That part was nothing but fanciful imagination.

With a sigh, he leaned his forehead against Ace's neck and answered his mother. "Maybe I can't." He'd have to tell Paulette. He couldn't lead her on when he was in love with another woman. It didn't matter whether that other woman loved him back or not. It wasn't fair to Paulette to settle for less than love.

The last person Tori wanted to see Monday morning was Graham Lindell, but Graham would be at the store. He came into the store every morning for a banana or a chocolate bar. So unless she played sick and stayed home, she was going to see him. She was too old to play sick, but she did feel Samantha's forehead. The child didn't feel the least bit warm. Tori was glad Samantha wasn't sick, but that didn't keep her feet from dragging as she took the little girl's hand and headed toward the store.

Her mother and father always went to the store to open up and be there to sell gasoline to the people on their way to work in Frankfort. Tori stayed at the house to get Samantha up and ready for their day at the store. Once she got there, her father went on to his shoe repair shop. Sometimes Tori wished she could trade with him. Learn to fix shoes and let him wait on the customers.

Kate would have taken Tori's place at the store after she moved back to Rosey Corner, but Tori hadn't figured out what else she could do. Maybe be a secretary like Evie. She could type. She'd learned on Kate's typewriter. She could find a ride to Frankfort where the jobs were, and Mrs. Harper would keep Samantha. But Tori wanted to be the one Samantha ran to when she bumped her head or found a pretty rock. She didn't want to just hear about it when she came in from work. Then again, she'd never planned to be a widow.

Graham was in one of the loafer's chairs with Chaucer stretched out at his feet when they got to the store. Chaucer's tail thumped the floor when Samantha ran to Graham. That was good. It would delay the questions about whether she caught any fish on Saturday. Graham hadn't been at church on Sunday, so he wouldn't know how his matchmaking plans had gone awry. He hadn't seen Paulette hanging on to Clay's arm like they belonged together.

And why did that make Tori's stomach hurt? It was what she wanted. What she'd told Clay would make her happy. He'd looked happy enough with Paulette. She shook her head a little to get thoughts of Clay out of her mind, but it didn't work. The more she tried not to think about him, the more she did. But it was only because she'd been so rude to him. That was all. It wasn't like she was part of a fairy tale with a happy-ever-after ending. Sammy was her happy ever after. An ending that had happened all too soon.

She had dreamed about Sammy. That wasn't unusual, but somehow this dream was different. In this dream, he seemed like he was standing right in front of her. When she reached toward him, he held up his hand to keep her from touching him. Then they'd been at the pond. She hooked such a big fish, it bent her pole almost double. Beside her, Sammy laughed and told her to make sure not to let it get away. When she finally reeled in the fish and held it up, Sammy backed away from her out onto the pond. His smile was bright, almost glowing, as he floated over the water and up into the air. She screamed at him to come back, but he only waved and called to her to not let the fish get away.

She must have cried out, because Lorena crawled in the bed beside her and stroked her head as though comforting Samantha. Tori pretended to be asleep. She was too unsettled by the dream to talk about it. It probably hadn't meant a thing. Just something that stuck in her head after she let the fish she'd caught get away Saturday.

When Lorena went back to her bed, Tori opened her eyes to stare at the dark air and wish for the morning light. Or failing that, Samantha to awaken and need to be held.

Now at the store, Graham raised his eyebrows at Tori overtop of Samantha's head, but he was too busy entertaining the little girl with some crazy story to ask Tori anything. Good, Tori thought as she went behind the counter to ring up Mrs. Williamson's groceries. But then the store emptied out.

Tori's mother picked up a basket of groceries to deliver to Aunt Hattie's. "I'd let you go, Victoria, but I'm worried about Aunt Hattie. I want to see how she's doing."

"Fern said she was poorly." Graham spoke up. "Said she guessed she'd stay out of the woods and watch after her today."

"She must be bad if Fern's staying out of the woods." Mama frowned as she headed toward the door.

Samantha clambered down from Graham's lap and caught up with her grandmother. "Wanna go." Chaucer wagged his tail and followed her, but Graham called him back.

Mama and Samantha both looked at Tori. "It might make Aunt Hattie feel better to see her," Mama said.

"Be good." Tori gave in, although that meant she wouldn't have the little girl as a buffer between her and Graham's questions.

"Be good," Samantha echoed and flashed Tori the smile so like Sammy's. "Go with Mama Nadie."

The little girl didn't look back as she went out the door, setting the bell above it to tinkling. Tori watched them through the window. Her mother had Samantha's hand clasped in hers as they walked up the road.

When they were out of sight, Tori picked up the broom. "I'd better go sweep around the gas pumps."

"Here. Let me do it." Graham clambered to his feet and reached for the broom. "Be good for me to get some exercise."

"No, I can." Tori didn't turn loose of the broom.

He kept hold of the broom handle too. "You appear to be a mite upset with me, Victoria."

She started to deny it, but what good would that do? She let go of the broom and turned to face him squarely. "I don't need you matchmaking for me."

Graham didn't seem the least bothered by her words. "So he came."

"He came."

"Catch any fish?" Graham leaned on the broom and Chaucer, seeing that his master didn't seem in any hurry to move, plopped down and heaved out a contented breath.

"No," Tori said flatly, but then she was remembering her

dream. Maybe she should tell Graham about it. She was irritated at him, but he did know how to listen. She shook away the thought. The dream hadn't meant anything. Certainly nothing to do with Clay Weber.

"He's a good boy, Victoria. And neck deep in love with you."

"Didn't show that yesterday at church. If he was liking anybody, it was Paulette Browning."

Graham looked a little surprised, but then he said, "Liking her maybe. Might even settle for her if you don't give him no encouragement, but that would be a shame. For the both of them." He narrowed his eyes on Tori. "For you too."

Tori stared at him. Graham had been part of her life since she could remember. A part of their family even if they claimed no actual kinship. He was somebody she could count on to be on her side. Somebody who would tell her the truth. Was he telling her the truth now? But what did he know about love? He was an old bachelor who'd never shown the slightest interest in changing that in all the years she'd known him.

He smiled, reading her thoughts. "You're wondering what I know about love?"

She didn't deny it. "The thought was crossing my mind."

"Well, Victoria, truth is, not enough. Not nearly enough." He sounded so sad that Chaucer got up and pushed his head against Graham's leg. Then without saying more, Graham went out the door.

She watched him sweep around the gas pumps. Tears popped up in her eyes, but she didn't know if she was crying for him or for herself. She was glad when the bell over the door jangled and a customer came in. She'd have to find a way to give Graham a hug later. Would she need to apologize to everyone before the week was over?

She turned to help Mrs. Riley find what she needed. But she was seeing Clay's face at the pond after she told him to go away. She wasn't sure she'd get a chance to make that apology because he'd done what she asked. Gone away.

Couldn't a girl change her mind? But changing her mind didn't mean she could unsay her words. Not if those words had sent Clay back to Paulette. The best thing she could do was wipe all thoughts of Clay out of her mind. Concentrate on Samantha. And on figuring out a job she could do that she liked better than waiting on customers who couldn't decide between brown beans or white beans and poked fingernails in the apples to see if they were ripe.

"Let me sack up some of these apples for you," Tori said in her sweetest voice to try to save some of the apples from Mrs. Riley's fingernail probes.

26

Monday morning Kate wanted to get up the way she always did to send Jay off to work, but she remembered Aunt Hattie's advice and stayed in bed.

"Do you think you can fry your own eggs this morning? I'm not feeling so hot." She watched him pull on his shirt.

"Sure thing." He sat down on the edge of the bed beside her and stroked her arm. "Anything I can get you?"

"A glass of water would be great." She did seem to be extra thirsty.

He was back in a flash with a glass of ice water and some crackers. He knew the crackers helped settle her stomach when she had morning sickness. He didn't know it wasn't morning sickness gripping her now.

She pushed her pillow against the headboard to sit up and sip the water. Even that worried her, but Aunt Hattie couldn't have meant she had to stay flat on her back. Surely she could sit up. And she'd already been up to the bathroom. The pain in her back hurt worse when she was on her feet, but that was just because she'd been lying down so long, wasn't it?

"I'm sorry," she said as he took the glass from her and sat it on the bedside table.

"About what?" He didn't wait for her to answer. "Not getting my breakfast? I didn't marry you for your cooking."

"Then why?" Kate played along.

"Your mother's brown sugar pie. Don't you remember?" He gave her hair a playful tousle.

"Then maybe you should have married her."

"Your father wasn't in favor of that idea."

"Lucky for me."

"I'm the lucky one here. Never forget that." He laid his hand on her cheek for a moment before he turned away to pull on his shoes. "And it has nothing to do with you getting up to cook me breakfast. I'm a big boy. I can take care of myself." He turned back to give her a kiss. "And you too. But right now I'm late. I'll just grab an apple on the way out."

"I love you." She made herself not cling to him.

They had already talked about Lorena's singing the night before and laughed about her messing up her words. The morning had seemed like most others except she hadn't gone to the kitchen to start the coffee.

He put his hand over hers. "Are you all right, Kate?"

That was when she should have told him. No. She wasn't all right. She was scared about the pains. She was scared about the way Aunt Hattie looked at her after she'd prayed that last line. *But your will, not ours, Lord, for you knows best*. Kate knew she should pray the same thing, but she only wanted one answer to her prayer. And she was terrified that wasn't the answer she was going to get. Speaking her fears aloud would make it too real. Maybe if she rested a few days, then she'd be strong enough to make it all okay.

So instead of being honest and leaning on him, she made excuses. "I'm just tired. Being in the family way is not as easy as I thought. I figured anything Evie could do, I could do twice as easy. Guess not, but I'm fine. Really."

She had thought that about Evie. And now look at Evie waddling around weeks from delivering her baby and Kate here in bed. Aunt Hattie had to be wrong about this being necessary. She had to be.

"You're better than fine." He put his hand over her barely rounded tummy. "He's going to be better than fine too."

"He?" She pushed a smile out on her face. "He could be a she."

"We both know he's going to be a he, don't we?"

She laughed, forgetting her worries for a moment. "Do you want a boy that much? Little girls dote on their daddies, you know."

"Maybe we'll have one of each. That way we won't have to choose."

"Twins. I don't think so. I'd be bigger if that was so." She managed to keep her smile, but the worry crowded up in her again. She should be bigger already with just one baby forming there.

He sat up and looked her directly in the face. "I don't care which we have. As long as you're okay."

"And the baby," Kate whispered.

"And the baby," he agreed. "But right now I'm just thinking about you. I want you to feel better. You stay right there in bed all day if you need to."

"I will. You better get going. You'll be late."

"Right." He looked at the clock and stood up. "Or if you want me to, I'll go up to the store and call the boss.

Take you to the doctor." They didn't have a phone here at the house yet.

"I've got an appointment tomorrow. Uncle Wyatt is loaning me his car."

"You can tell him never mind. I'll take off tomorrow and drive you to the doctor."

"If you want to."

"I do." He looked down at her and hesitated again. "Maybe I should get Birdie to come stay with you today."

"She's already on the way to school. She rides with the Baxter boy."

"She's not getting struck on him, is she?" Jay frowned.

"I don't think so, but she'll get struck on some boy someday. I did." She grabbed his hand and kissed it. "On you."

"Not when you were fourteen."

Kate laughed. "When I was fourteen, I would have probably told you to get lost unless you were good at playing ball or catching frogs."

"We'd have been okay. I was a world champion frog catcher when I was a kid." Jay leaned down to kiss her head. "You take care of my girl and boy today."

When she gave him a puzzled look, he pointed at her middle. "The twins." Then he grabbed his jacket and was gone.

He didn't go out to the kitchen to grab anything to eat, and Kate felt guilty all over again for not getting up. Her mother always got up and fixed breakfast. Always.

Maybe not when she was expecting, a little voice whispered in Kate's head. Three babies. And the one she'd lost. The first one while Kate's father was in France fighting World War I. Kate slid back down in the bed and pulled the cover over her head. She didn't want to think about that. Not today.

Instead she'd think about Jay warming up to the idea of being a father. Talking about twins. She smiled a little and pushed the cover off her head. Another reason she couldn't tell him her worries. But was that really right? Her smile slid away as she stared up at the ceiling and tried to ignore the pain in her back.

Why didn't she tell him how bad she was feeling and how scared she was? Why didn't she at least tell him to stop by the store and let her mother know she wasn't feeling well? Her mother would check on her no matter how busy the store was.

She might need somebody to check on her. She might need her mother. Or Aunt Hattie, but Aunt Hattie couldn't walk down to see her. She looked as weak as Kate had ever seen her yesterday, but not too weak to pray for Kate's baby. Aunt Hattie's prayers were powerful. *But your will, not ours, Lord, for you knows best.*

"Dear Lord, please." The longing in her heart reached toward the Lord.

Once, when she was Lorena's age, she'd been so angry at God that she turned her back on him, but the Lord hadn't turned his back on her. He'd simply waited until she came to her senses and opened her heart to him again.

Since then, Kate thought her faith couldn't be shaken, but perhaps she'd been coasting along thinking that because she hadn't been challenged with hard times. She hadn't had to read a telegram from the War Department the way Tori had about Sammy. Tori was going through a valley even now as she searched for answers to why her fervent prayers hadn't brought Sammy home. Aunt Hattie would tell her, and had, that everybody had dark valleys to walk through. That wasn't the Lord's doing. It was just the way of the world.

"But please, Lord." Kate closed her eyes. More words weren't necessary. The Lord knew what she wanted.

Trust him. He knows best. Aunt Hattie's voice sounded in Kate's head almost as if she were standing beside the bed.

Kate woke a little after noon, feeling better. She sat up and ate a few crackers and drained the water glass. Then she had to get up for the bathroom. Since she was feeling better, she washed her face, combed her hair, and got dressed. It just seemed what she ought to do. Kate Tanner didn't stay in her nightgown all day long. She could lie on the couch the same as the bed. Aunt Hattie hadn't said she couldn't use her eyes to read. Plus there was still that article for the newspaper to finish up.

Graham showed up just as she was settling on the couch with extra pillows and some cheese and crackers. Mothers-to-be had to eat whether they felt like it or not.

When Graham asked why she was lounging around, she told him the truth. "Aunt Hattie said I should lie down for a while."

Graham's face went from teasing to worried in an instant. "Something wrong?" he asked as he sat down in the chair closest to the couch.

Then she wasn't quite as truthful. "My back's been hurting some and Aunt Hattie told me it might be a good idea to take it easy. She knows a lot about babies coming."

"You're right there. She used to be the nearest thing to a doctor Rosey Corner had and a comfort to a woman carrying a child." His frown got a little tighter. "But Hattie's why I came by. Thought I ought to let you know she's not doing good."

"She looked tired yesterday, but not that bad." Kate raised up off her pillow, worry poking her now.

"I don't know about yesterday, but Fern says she's laying abed today. Not wanting to eat. Barely awake enough to pray."

Kate remembered her prayers that morning and the ones circling in her head even now about her baby. Prayers she'd thought Aunt Hattie would be saying too, and now Aunt Hattie needed prayers for herself.

"I could take her to the doctor." Kate sat up.

Graham waved her back down. "She wouldn't be happy about that if she told you to rest. Besides, a doctor can't do anything for what's ailing Hattie. Age. You know yourself she's been ready to go for months now. Eager even."

"I'm not ready for her to go." Kate stared toward the window. She couldn't lose Aunt Hattie today.

"And she may not go just yet. Just because she's ready don't mean the good Lord's ready for her. She's had these sinking spells before and come out of them."

"But one of these days she might not." Kate looked back at Graham, wanting him to tell her this wouldn't be that day.

Graham blew out a breath of air and leaned forward, elbows on his knees. "One of these days she won't. That's true for us all."

"Do you think we all have our time already set when we're born?" Kate sank back on her pillows.

"That question's too hard for this old man to answer." Graham stared down at his hands. "But the good Lord knows all the answers. And with Hattie, he might be thinking she's more than earned her rest. That he needs her good sense up there with him."

"Young people die too. Even babies sometimes." Her heart felt heavy at the thought. "There are a lot of babies' graves in the cemetery at church."

"You're right about that." Graham looked up at her. "Fevers of all sorts had a way of carrying off the little ones in the earlier days."

"And then there are wars. Sammy would still be with us if not for the war."

"Sammy and a lot of others." Graham rubbed his hands up and down his thighs as he considered her words. "Hattie would be a better one for you to ask this. Or Mike. I ain't no preacher."

"But what do you think? You've always told me what you think about things."

"Maybe so, but you used to ask easy questions about how many leaves were on the maple tree in your yard or if toad frogs really could give you warts. Your questions have gotten some harder over the years." He smiled at her.

"But you still know the answers." He'd been her best buddy since the day she could toddle after him. The same way Samantha loved him now. He was a favored uncle, best friend, and grandfather all rolled into one. A man who would run through fire for her. Who had, in a way, picked her husband by giving Jay a place to stay in Rosey Corner. Who would answer her questions whether they made any sense or not.

He pulled in another deep breath and blew it out slowly. "Okay, the way I see it, even if the good Lord does know our ending day, he might not have picked it. He set the world in motion and then us folks down here shook it up a little. I'm thinking the Lord would be just as happy if we didn't get into wars or have fevers and accidents that steal some of the seven-score years the Bible allots to folks." Graham peered over at her. "That make any sense to you?"

"You always make sense to me," Kate said.

"All right, so that's my answer. But you know the rules," Graham said, harking back to when Kate was a little girl. "You asked a hard question. Now you've got to ask an easy one."

When Graham's dog whined and scratched at the door to make sure Graham hadn't forgotten him out on the porch, Kate had her question. "I've got one. Do dogs go to heaven?"

"Whew! That is an easy one." He made a pretense of wiping sweat off his forehead. "Course they do. What would heaven be for me if old Poe wasn't up there waiting? I figure he's got us a spot picked out on the bank of a pond where the fish are biting and the coons come down out of the trees to play." Graham stood up.

When Kate started to get up too, he held his hand out to stop her. "I know where the door is. You don't have to show me. You rest like Hattie told you to."

"All right." Kate dropped back down on the pillows. "Thanks for letting me know about Aunt Hattie. I'll be praying." For Aunt Hattie and for herself. Her hand drifted down to touch her belly.

Graham stopped before he got to the door. "You need me to send your mama down here to see about you?"

"No, I'm feeling better. Really. I'm going to the doctor tomorrow. I'll stop by the store on the way home to let her know what he says."

When Graham still looked worried, Kate added, "Jay will be home in a little while. It's already after two."

"Is it that late? Well then, I guess it's about time for Chaucer and me to take a nap." When he opened the door, the dog slipped through it to lean against Graham. Graham put a hand on the dog's head. "It promises to be a nice night, and while old Chaucer here's no Poe, he don't mind sitting with me in the woods on a good night to see what we can hear."

"Sounds fun," Kate said.

"You get to feeling better, you can go with us sometime." Graham smiled over at her. "Later on, when you get that young'un here, you can bring him too. He'll need a proper introduction to the woods the way you got when you were a little tyke. You were wanting to go with me before you could climb the fences."

"I had you to help me over them."

"You might have to help me these days." Graham chuckled and pointed Chaucer out the door.

He was getting older. Age had rounded his shoulders a bit, but his step was still lively as he went outside. He had plenty more nights to enjoy the woods. After she fluffed her pillow, she lay back and shut her eyes, letting the memory of Poe baying as he chased after raccoons play through her mind.

She had so many memories of Lindell Woods. Some bad, like the terrible fire there years ago. Some wonderful, like dancing with Jay under the old growth trees when they were falling in love. It would be good to walk in the woods with her son and make new memories.

With those peaceful thoughts she drifted off to sleep, after sending up a prayer for Aunt Hattie.

A gripping pain jerked her awake and stole her breath.

27

Kate sat up and gasped. The cramp wasn't only in her back now but instead was a giant fist grabbing her belly. Could she have eaten something that was working on her? But all she'd eaten since she came home from Aunt Hattie's was crackers and cheese. It couldn't be that, but something was wrong. Very wrong.

It wasn't until she was in the bathroom and saw the blood that she knew. She was losing the baby. No vague fears of it maybe happening. This was real. She hadn't been strong enough to protect her baby. Her head started spinning and dark edges pushed in on the sides of her vision.

This couldn't be normal. Not this much blood, but she didn't really know. She hadn't asked Aunt Hattie what would happen if she did lose the baby. She hadn't wanted to need the answer to that.

She struggled up from the commode. She had to have help. Why had she told Graham not to bother her mother? She grasped the edge of the sink as the pain gripped her again. What was it she and Graham had said? Everybody had a time to die. Whether appointed or not.

Her heart pounded in her ears and her stomach went queasy on top of the gripping pain. Kate stared at her pale face in the mirror and spoke out loud. "It is not your time." The pain got stronger as though defying her words. She shut her eyes and leaned against the wall next to the sink. "Please, Lord," she whispered. "Please, let it not be my time."

Time. She had no idea how long she'd slept after Graham left. Jay could be on the way home and then it might be an hour before he came. How long could a person bleed without losing consciousness?

"Jay, please come home." Her words were swallowed up in the silence. If only she knew what time it was. She breathed out another prayer. "Lord, let it be time for him to come home."

She folded a towel to staunch the blood. Maybe if she could make it to the couch, lie back down, then she'd be all right until he came. She could do that. She could. She took one step and the room went black except for the sharp image of the doorknob in front of her. She reached for it. But her knees buckled and she sank to the floor and curled up in a ball. The linoleum was cool against her cheek. All she could do was hope Jay came in time. Or her mother. Or anyone.

She was drifting in a fuzzy world of pain when she heard the door. "Jay." She pushed the word out with all the force she could muster, but it was little more than a hoarse whisper.

No answer came from the front room. Instead the movements sounded unsure, almost furtive. Definitely not Jay. He always burst in from work ready to use up the rest of the day. But it was someone.

"Help me." This time her voice was stronger.

"Where are you?" The voice was familiar but somehow not right. Low with an uneasy edge.

"In here." Kate tried to sit up, but she was too weak. "Please."

Fern was the last person she expected to step into the bathroom, towering over Kate. The woman didn't have on her usual overalls, but somehow she looked even odder in a flowery dress that hung off her shoulders without touching her body anywhere else. Her steel gray hair was yanked back from her face and held there with a red kerchief. As she stared down at Kate, fear mixed with panic crossed the woman's face. Kate had never seen Fern look afraid. It was plain she wanted to turn and walk away. Kate didn't blame her. She wanted to get up and walk away from it too, but she couldn't.

"I lost the baby. He's gone." The words ripped through Kate's heart. "Gone."

"Hattie said you would. She prayed for you."

"It didn't help. I prayed too, but I still lost him."

"She didn't pray for the baby. Prayed for you." Fern's voice was harsh as she finally let go of the door and stepped closer to Kate. "Hattie sent me."

Katie looked up at her and the room started spinning. "Why?"

"An angel told her you needed help."

"You should have told Mama."

"Didn't think of that." Fern's face looked set as she crouched down beside Kate. "Never put much stock in angel messages, but for Hattie, I said I'd come. Hattie's sinking." Fern's rough fingers pushed down on Kate's wrist for her pulse. "You're sinking too."

"I prayed, Fern." Kate grabbed Fern's arm. The room was

going black, but maybe if she stared at Fern's face she could keep from passing out. She didn't want to faint. She needed to do something. "I prayed for Aunt Hattie. I prayed for my baby. But he's still gone."

Fern made a noise Kate wasn't sure was disgust or sympathy. "Prayer don't change what can't be changed."

"Then why pray?"

"To endure what has to be endured."

"Can't stand it." Kate gasped as a new pain struck her. When the pain eased a bit, she asked, "Am I going to die, Fern? Like my baby?"

Fern pushed her arm under Kate's shoulder and raised her head a little. "Don't know. Hattie's angel didn't tell her that."

"Angels." Kate shut her eyes. "Lorena thought I was an angel. Do you remember that?" She was drifting away from the pain now. Away from everything.

"I remember." She lifted Kate up. That brought the pain back.

"But I wasn't."

"You were her angel."

Kate stared at Fern's face as things came back into focus. Weathered skin splotched from too much sun and wind. Eyes forever sad. Lips not smiling. Lips that rarely smiled. "Are you my angel?"

Fern snorted as she lifted Kate up. "Been called lots of things, but never angel."

"My angel," Kate murmured, trying to get her legs under her. She could feel life pouring out of her. "Tell Jay I loved him."

"Tell him yourself. I hear his car."

"Jay," Kate whispered, but then the darkness won.

The front door was wide open. It wasn't that warm, Jay thought as he pulled in the driveway. But Kate could be letting smoke out after burning their supper. It wouldn't be the first time. She'd put something on the stove and then start writing. He needed to buy her a timer.

That could be it, but worry that something was amiss had the hairs up on the back of his neck as he pulled into the driveway. He'd been home for months and out of the fighting longer than that, but his nerves stayed on edge.

The empty open door wasn't right. Kate should be standing in it, ready to greet him with a sheepish grin about having tuna sandwiches for supper again. Then he had left her in bed that morning. Not normal either. He should have insisted on taking her to the doctor.

He ran across the yard and up the steps into the house. The smell hit him. A smell he knew but didn't expect to confront in his own house. Blood. Death. He had to be having a flashback to the war. He stopped and took a deep breath.

Someone yelled from deeper in the house. Not Kate's voice, but a voice he knew. Fern. He had to be wrong. Fern wouldn't come inside their house even if a thunderstorm was raging.

"Jay Tanner." The name was almost a bark, definitely an order. Something like Sarge would have said it, but not Sarge. Fern. Inside his house. Beyond the front room. Where was Kate? His heart hammered inside his chest as he moved toward the sound of Fern's voice like he was approaching battle.

"Kate?"

"In here." Fern again. Not Kate.

He stepped to the door and froze. The sight of the blood

threw him back to that fresh-faced kid stepping on the mine in front of him and Jay carrying his blood forward to the battle the kid would no longer have to fight. Then Artie had bled out on his shoes minutes after changing places with Jay on that street in Germany. Blood draining out of men in every battle. Dying men.

But this was Kate's blood. "Is she . . . ?" He couldn't say the word as his heart did a funny stutter. She looked so limp as Fern held her.

"She lost the baby."

A wave of sadness swept through him. "Oh, Kate." He knelt down to run his hand across her cheek.

"No time for that." Fern frowned at him. "She's sinking. Fast."

Jay reached under Kate and picked her up. She groaned and stiffened in his arms. "I don't know what to do."

"Hospital. Only thing." Fern pointed toward the door.

"All right. I'll get her mother."

"No time. Lay her in the backseat. Hattie said to put her feet up." Fern grabbed an armful of towels. "Go."

Jay looked around. "Hattie's here?"

"No. Hattie's dying." Fern said without emotion. "Sent me."

"Dying?" Jay felt shell-shocked, but thankful to feel Kate's breath against his cheek.

"Too much dying." Fern shoved him toward the door. "Go! The girl would be sad if you let Kate die."

"She won't die." Jay held her tighter as he went out the front door. Then he looked back at Fern. "Will she?"

"Maybe. Maybe not. Keep the maybe not in your head. Hattie was praying."

"You said Hattie was dying."

"Don't mean she can't pray on the way up. She was talking to angels." Fern opened the car door. "Do what Hattie said."

He placed Kate as gently as he could in the car, but even so, he bumped her against the back of the seat. She groaned and opened her eyes. "Jay?"

"I'm here, darling. We're going to the hospital."

Tears rolled down her cheeks. "I lost the baby."

"I know." He brushed away her tears as his own eyes flooded.

Fern grabbed his arm and jerked him back. "Go." She pointed toward the driver's seat as she pushed a pile of towels under Kate's knees with surprising gentleness.

Jay slid under the steering wheel and looked back at Fern. He couldn't be sure, but it looked like tears on her weathered cheek. "Tell her mother."

She nodded. "Drive fast. The girl and me, we want Kate breathing."

Mashing the gas pedal to the floor, he drove like a mad man. He yanked the rearview mirror down where he could see Kate in the backseat, not caring what was on the road behind him. Only about who was in the car with him. He couldn't lose Kate. He couldn't.

At the hospital, the nurses and doctors rushed out to get Kate. He tried to stay with her, but they pushed him back, told him go fill out papers. What good did papers do?

"I've got to see her," he told the woman at the desk after he answered her questions.

The woman looked kind, but she wouldn't let him through the doors to Kate. "The doctors are treating her. They'll come for you when you can see her. Right now you have to let them do their job."

"You don't understand. She needs me with her," Jay pleaded.

"I'm sorry, Mr. Tanner." She sounded sympathetic. "But you'll have to wait until they send for you. Until then, you can be assured they are doing everything possible for her."

When he just kept staring at her, she touched his hand. "Please have a seat. And if you're a praying man, perhaps that will help you bear the wait."

What could he do except what she said? He had his head in his hands, praying without words, when Kate's parents and Birdie came in. Mr. Merritt's breathing was ragged after their hurry.

"How is she?" Kate's mother demanded.

"I don't know. They took her back and say I have to wait here." Panic formed a knot in his chest.

Birdie put her arms around him. "She'll be all right, Tanner. She will."

"Of course she will." Mr. Merritt had caught his breath, but his voice still sounded wheezy. "Kate's strong."

Jay stared over Birdie's head at Kate's mother and father. "She lost the baby."

"We know." Mrs. Merritt's eyes sorrowed with him.

"Did Aunt Hattie tell you?"

Suddenly Birdie was sobbing against his shoulder and Mrs. Merritt's lips went white as she pressed them together and blinked back tears.

"Fern told us. Aunt Hattie—" Mr. Merritt had to swallow before he could go on. "Aunt Hattie passed on this afternoon. While Fern was with Kate."

They held hands then and ignored everybody around them as Kate's mother looked up at the ceiling and prayed like Aunt

Hattie would have if she'd been there. "Lord, we're here. Missing our dear Aunt Hattie but we know you're welcoming her home and that she's running to meet her Bo. Down here, we beg for your mercy. Watch over our Kate. Give the doctors skill in treating her. Give us power in praying for her as we wait. If it be your will—" Mrs. Merritt's voice weakened a little on those words. She cleared her throat and repeated them. "If it be your will, and we pray fervently that it will be, please heal her body and her spirit. Amen."

Birdie echoed her amen. Then she said, "Aunt Hattie would have called her Katherine Reece."

Mrs. Merritt smiled through her sadness. "She would."

"Can we say Kate's name?" Birdie said. "All of us together? The way I say mine?"

"If it would make you feel better." Mr. Merritt looked at Jay. "Is that all right, son?"

Son. How long had it been since anyone had called him son? And now that son he'd begun to imagine, had begun to love in his heart, would never have the chance to call him father this side of heaven.

He moistened his lips but was unable to push words past the lump in his throat. Mr. Merritt grasped his shoulder and Mrs. Merritt took his hand while Birdie leaned against him. They waited for him to find his voice.

He shut his eyes. Kate was there in his mind. Kate was always there in his mind. He took a breath and opened his eyes to look at Birdie. "Ready?" he asked.

She nodded.

He started and they joined in, voices strong as they pushed Kate's name out into the air. "Her name is Katherine Reece Merritt Tanner."

The woman behind the desk looked up at them, as did the few people scattered around the waiting area. Jay didn't care. He wanted Kate's name in the air. He wanted it lifted up like a prayer.

Their prayers must have had wings or perhaps Aunt Hattie grabbed them on her way to heaven and laid them right at the feet of the Lord. The nurses came for Jay. The bleeding had been slowed. Kate was going to be all right, but she'd have to stay at the hospital. The doctor wanted to monitor her condition.

She was pale but awake when the nurses finally allowed them to go to her. Jay stood by her head and held her hand while the others offered words of comfort. They didn't tell her about Aunt Hattie. Mrs. Merritt thought it best to wait until Kate was stronger.

It wasn't until Kate's parents and Lorena left that the room got too quiet. Words seemed useless.

A nurse came, poked and prodded on Kate, and smiled at him. She told him the chair wasn't very comfortable, but she'd bring him a pillow if he wanted to stay. The other bed in the room nearer the hallway was unoccupied, but the nurse closed the curtains with a swish of metal on metal anyway. "In case we have to bring a patient in here later, this will give you a little privacy."

After the nurse was gone, Kate said, "You don't have to stay. They say I'll be fine."

"I'm not leaving." He tightened his hold on her hand. "You're here. I'm here."

A tear slid out of her left eye and down her cheek. "I lost the baby."

He leaned down to kiss away the tear. "I know."

"I wasn't strong enough to protect him." More tears spilled over and she choked a little on her next words. "I'm sorry."

"Shh, you're the strongest person I know."

"Not strong enough." She pulled her hand free from his and turned away from him as sobs shook her body.

Nothing had ever hurt him as much as hearing her cry like that. He untied his shoes and kicked them off. Then he crawled in the narrow bed with her and put his arms around her. "I love you, Kate. Don't shut me out. Please."

She twisted in his arms back toward him, and his tears mixed with hers.

28

Tori and Lorena rode up in the elevator to the second floor of the hospital. Tori had never been in an elevator before. While it seemed totally foolish to step into it for one flight of stairs, neither she nor Lorena knew where the stairs were and the elevator was right there in front of them. So it was equally foolish to refuse to step into the closet-sized space, even though she felt robbed of air when the doors closed behind them.

It was all Tori could do not to pant, but Lorena wasn't bothered at all. She chattered on about the program that was supposed to play her song that night as she clutched the radio Uncle Wyatt had loaned them to bring to Kate.

Aunt Gertie and Uncle Wyatt were in the lobby waiting, since Kate could only have two visitors at a time. Tori hoped that meant two besides Jay. Her mother said Jay hadn't left Kate's bedside, not even to get something to eat. Tori had ham sandwiches for him in her bag.

Mama and Daddy had visited the hospital that morning to help Jay tell Kate about Aunt Hattie, but she already knew. Jay hadn't told her. He hadn't had to. Kate just knew. She and Aunt

Hattie had always had a special connection, but then Fern had told her Aunt Hattie was bad. Sinking, that was what Fern had said. But perhaps a better word was rising. Aunt Hattie would have shot right up to heaven. Tori blinked back tears thinking about Aunt Hattie's son, Bo, running out to meet her. And Sammy too. Aunt Hattie could tell him all about Samantha.

"I'm so glad Uncle Wyatt had this extra radio." Lorena grabbed the plug that wouldn't stay twined around the radio. "I hope the nurses won't mind Kate listening. Surely they won't care, will they?"

"I don't see why they would, but I don't know. I've never been in a hospital. Dr. Fielding came to the house when Samantha was born."

"But you didn't have trouble like Kate."

"No, I didn't." Tori thought of Samantha no doubt playing happily with Mama Harper and her heart hurt for Kate.

"Mama told me sometimes things like this just happen. She lost her first baby while Daddy was overseas during the war. She said she was sad for a long time and that Kate would be too." Lorena was talking too fast. "She said I'd have to understand if Kate didn't seem the same."

The elevator stopped and so did Lorena's words as she stared at the door waiting for it to swoosh open. The girl looked worried.

"She'll still be Kate," Tori said softly.

"But she looked so sick. You don't think she's going to die, do you? I don't think I could stand it if that happened."

"You can stand more than you think." Tori touched Lorena's shoulder as the elevator door finally opened. Didn't she know that for a truth? "But Kate will be fine. She just needs time to recover, that's all."

"You didn't see her last night." Lorena kept her voice low as they stepped out into the corridor. "Her face was white as the sheets and she could barely lift up her hand."

"She lost a lot of blood."

"I know. Mama says we all should give Fern a hug for going to see about Kate."

Tori couldn't keep from smiling. "I think we'd better just let you hug Fern. We all start hugging Fern, she'd go off in the woods and not come back for weeks. She's not exactly huggable."

A smile burst out on Lorena's face too. "You're right." But then the smile was gone as quickly as it came. "I don't know what Fern will do without Aunt Hattie."

Tori breathed out a little sigh. "I don't either, but one worry at a time. Right now, Kate. Fern won't have to move out of Grandfather Merritt's house right away."

"But will she stay there without Aunt Hattie?"

"That's something we have to leave up to Fern." Tori looked over at Lorena. "And remember, one worry at a time."

"Right. Kate first." Lorena shifted the radio in her arms. "Do you think the radio will pick up in here?"

"One worry at a time," Tori said again. "Better worry about finding room 206 now."

"That's no trouble. I know where it is."

Tori followed Lorena down the hallway. She needed to heed her own advice. One worry at a time. She needed to think about Kate and how they were all going to miss Aunt Hattie's prayers and common sense. She was the same as a mother to Tori's father and a grandmother who didn't put up with foolishness from Tori or her sisters.

"Mothering love that allows for anythin' ain't the right

kind of love," she'd told Tori time and again about making Samantha mind. "Your little one needs to know what you is expecting of her."

When Tori countered with how young Samantha was, Aunt Hattie had narrowed her eyes on Tori. "Ain't never too young to learn right from wrong."

Right from wrong. Aunt Hattie had a clear-eyed view of that. Sunday, Tori had thought about talking to Aunt Hattie about Clay, but time had run out. One worry at a time. Then Aunt Hattie's voice whispered through her thoughts. *Ain't never no use a-worrying. Praying, that's what you's need to be doing.*

But prayers sometimes just floated away into the dark nowhere and weren't answered. If Aunt Hattie heard her saying that, she'd give Tori a real talking to. *Prayers aren't like being in a candy store where you's can pick out your answer like choosin' your favorite sweets. Prayer gets you through when you's thinkin' there is no way through.*

Dear Aunt Hattie. Grandmother, aunt, preacher, teacher all tied up in one. Tori was going to miss her. That was enough to grieve along with sorrow over Kate's lost baby. She had no need to even think about Clay Weber. What had happened was for the best. She told him to go away and he had. She shouldn't be bothered in the least by Paulette hanging on his arm at church. She had no reason to think about how safe she'd felt when Clay caught her in his arms when she stumbled at the pond. No reason at all.

But she did think about it. In the last couple of days, it stole into her thoughts at odd moments. His arms had felt much different from Sammy's arms. Without doubt, a man and not a boy. She and Sammy were so very young when they chose one another. Children still and not much beyond that when they said their wedding vows. They barely had time to play at being married before Sammy went to war. He would have come home a man. The war would have forced him to grow up just as it had her. But together, they'd never gone much past being two kids promising love forever. *In sickness and health, till death do us part*.

Death had parted them. She'd never stop loving Sammy. She wouldn't. But when Clay had caught her in his arms for that moment, something had shifted inside her. She'd realized she could like the feel of another man's arms. That thought had scared her. That fear had chased Clay right into another woman's arms.

One worry at a time, she reminded herself yet again as they went into Kate's hospital room. An older woman looked up at them from the first bed, but the curtain was pulled around the second bed, hiding Kate from view. If they were in the right room.

"Come on in." The woman raised up in her bed and spoke as though inviting them into her living room.

"We're looking for Kate . . . ," Tori started.

"Well, of course you are. You don't look a thing like her, but I'm guessing you must be the sisters she told me about. Three of you with one well along in the family way." The woman peered at them as she adjusted her hospital gown on her shoulders. "It's easy enough to see that's not either of you. I don't think I was ever that slim, and while I might look in the family way now, if I was it would be a miracle to rival Sarah. Or maybe Mary, since no man would be involved." She laughed then, her hands against her chest.

She was on the heavy side with gray hair mussed from

being in bed. Tori stared at her, at a loss for words, but the woman didn't notice.

"Kate, dear, you have company." The woman looked at the curtain, then back at Tori and Lorena. "They've been sleeping most of the day. Poor dears. But I'm wide awake if you'd like to talk a few minutes while they're waking up." She beamed a smile toward them.

"I'm awake, Miss Myrtle." Jay stepped out from behind the curtain. "But thank you for making the girls feel welcome." He winked at Lorena and Tori. "Miss Myrtle had some chest pains last night, so the nursing home sent her here to check out her ticker. Seems to be ticking just fine now."

"Like a fine watch. But you know doctors. Once they get hold of you they won't turn you loose until they stick you with so many needles you feel like a pincushion. But I am meeting all sorts of delightful people. Like dear Kate and Jay here. And now you pretty sisters. One of you with curls and one without. And so tall." Myrtle smiled. "I love visitors. But don't let me keep you. I know you're visiting your sister and not me."

Lorena hesitated at the woman's bed. "You don't have sisters to come see you?"

"No, dear. My sisters are long gone. I had four, and three brothers, but I'm the only one left now."

"But you have other visitors, don't you?" Lorena looked sad.

"I'm sure the preacher will come by to pray over me when he hears I'm here. He's the nicest young man." The old lady's smile faded a little. "But I'm fine whether I have visitors or not. Fine as can be. Well, as fine as an old woman can be with everybody poking on her."

Lorena shoved the radio over to Tori and stepped up beside the woman's bed. "Kate won't mind if we visit a minute first. Do you like singing? I'm going to be on the radio tonight."

"On the radio. Well, my goodness. What's your name, dearie?"

"Lorena Birdsong." Lorena always had a lilt to her voice when she said her name.

"Birdsong. That's a name you don't hear every day." She gave Lorena a closer look.

"I've never met anybody who has ever heard it."

"Is that a fact?" Miss Myrtle frowned. "You know, seems I may have some time or other, but my memory isn't what it used to be."

"What's your name?" Lorena asked her.

"Now that I haven't forgotten." The old lady smiled again. "Myrtle Shumaker."

"I'm glad to meet you, Miss Myrtle, and this is my sister, Victoria." Lorena pointed toward Tori. "She's glad to meet you too. Aren't you, Tori?"

Tori smiled and waved.

"Our aunt Gertie will be up here in a little bit. You two might have a lot to talk about, so I'll tell her to visit with you a few minutes too." Lorena leaned down to give the woman a hug.

"Well, mercy sakes." Miss Myrtle grabbed Lorena's hand and held it in both hers. "I'm feeling blessed beyond measure. I've been praying about being lonely down there at the nursing home. Can't get around visiting people like I used to. My knees are giving out, you know. But could be the Lord, he gave my heart a little jerk just so I could come down here and meet you nice people." She looked straight at Tori then.

"You know good things can come out of bad. All things worketh for good to those who love the Lord."

Tori stared at the woman. She didn't look a thing like Aunt Hattie. Her voice didn't sound a thing like Aunt Hattie's. But it was almost like the woman was gone and Aunt Hattie was sitting there in the bed, pointing those words straight at Tori.

"But what about the bad things? Does he make the bad things happen first?" She wished the questions back as soon as they spilled out of her mouth. What was the matter with her? Asking for answers from a woman she'd never met before. Myrtle Shumaker was not Aunt Hattie no matter how Tori's mind was playing tricks on her.

The room went absolutely quiet. Tori wasn't sure if it was because they were embarrassed for her or if they too wanted the answers.

The woman kept her eyes on Tori as if she'd forgotten everybody else in the room, even Lorena whose hand she still held. "I'm no preacher, dearie. Some things that happen I won't ever understand, but I'm thinking I'm not meant to understand everything the Lord does. His ways are not man's ways."

"You're right." Tori tried to gloss over her questions and bring ease back into the room, but the woman wasn't through.

"It's good to be right, but better to be sure. I do know one thing. Whenever I've had to walk through a valley of hardship, the good Lord's shadow was right beside me on my journey. With me every step. Blessing me in the midst of trouble."

"That's good." Again Tori tried to escape a conversation she should have never started with Kate on the other side of the curtain, grieving over the lost promise of her child. Tori was there to comfort her, not beg answers from a stranger.

"Yes indeed." The woman gave Lorena's hand a shake and then let go at last. She smoothed down the cover over her stomach. "Better than good. And if the Lord will do it for old Myrtle Shumaker, he'll do it for you and this sweet child here and dear Kate and Jay there." The woman pointed toward the curtain.

"You sound like Aunt Hattie." Lorena stepped away from the woman's bed.

"I thought you said Aunt Gertie."

"Oh, that's another aunt." Lorena laughed at the puzzled look on Miss Myrtle's face. "How about I call you Aunt Myrtle?" That made the woman smile and forget about questions that couldn't be answered. "I've got to go find a place to plug Kate's radio in. Remember to listen tonight."

"I will," Miss Myrtle said. "Birdsong. I don't know why that name keeps tickling my brain."

"Mine gets tickled at it sometimes too, Miss Myrtle." Jay motioned toward them. "But come on, you two. Kate's awake."

He put his arm around Lorena and lowered his voice. "That was sweet, Birdie. Miss Myrtle will be telling everybody about you after she goes back to the nursing home."

"Wait until she hears my song. Then she'll really have something to talk about." A smile sneaked out on Lorena's face that she covered with her hand as though not sure she should be smiling in the face of Kate's sorrow.

Jay looked sad too. Weary and beaten down. Tori didn't know what to say to him. Then she realized no words could make the sorrow disappear. Didn't she know that from when she lost Sammy? People talked and prayed for her and wanted to make things better, but that couldn't happen. The words had hovered meaningless over her head and the prayers had seemed to comfort those praying more than Tori. But that was all right. They were grieving too, just as she was grieving for Kate's lost baby now.

She handed Jay the radio. "Uncle Wyatt loaned it to us in case Kate had to stay tonight. Mama said she didn't know when she'd get to come home."

"Tomorrow." Kate spoke up from her bed. "For Aunt Hattie's funeral."

She looked pale the way Lorena had warned. Tori turned to her and words deserted her. But sometimes words weren't necessary between sisters. Tori took one hand and Lorena clung to the other. Tori leaned her forehead down on top of Kate's head and the only words that mattered whispered out into Kate's ears. "I'm sorry."

A prayer silently wound through Tori's mind then. She couldn't remember the last time a prayer had felt so natural to her. Not stilted or resentful or begging for a change that couldn't come. This prayer accepted and asked only for comfort for this sister she loved so much. Perhaps it wasn't one worry at a time after all. Perhaps Aunt Hattie was right. One prayer at a time.

29

Kate scarcely dared breathe after Lorena's voice started coming out of the radio. She didn't want to miss a single note.

At home, Lorena would be biting her bottom lip and leaning toward the radio, her eyes wide as she listened. Her voice on the air. Kate squeezed Jay's hands. He was focused on the radio too, almost as though he could see Lorena singing inside it.

Then the song was over and Randy Harris, the host of the *Songs of Tomorrow Show*, was speaking again. "That was the lovely Lorena Birdsong. Remember that name. Lorena Birdsong. That girl is loaded down with talent. I'd better hurry and get her back here on *Songs of Tomorrow*, because unless I miss my guess, disc jockeys will be spinning her records soon."

"That ought to make her happy," Jay said when the program broke for an advertisement.

"Happy, I guess. Mama and Daddy will have to grab hold of her to keep her from floating off the ground." Kate smiled.

Her first real smile since she talked to Aunt Hattie on Sunday. Could that be only two days ago?

Her smile faded. How could so much change so quickly? Happiness sliding away without a backward look. The doctor told her the miscarriage was simply a correction of nature, a pregnancy not meant to be. She wasn't to let it distress her. She was young and should be able to get with child again as soon as her body healed.

Beside her bed that morning, the doctor had pushed his glasses up closer to his face and studied her chart. He said she would need to take things easy for a few weeks. Not lift anything heavy. Eat iron-rich foods to build up her blood. Before he left, he told her the vast majority of women who lost a pregnancy went on to have healthy babies with no difficulties.

The nurses said the same as they fussed over her, reassuring her she'd be right back in a year or so to birth a new baby the way the doctor promised.

She didn't want to talk about babies in the future. She wanted to talk about the baby she'd lost. Surely it was only right to give him life in her mind especially since he'd never know life in her arms. But everybody acted like the baby had never been. Even Jay seemed hesitant to mention their lost baby out loud, as though worried it would plunge her deeper into the despair hovering around her.

And now Aunt Hattie, the one person she could have depended on to look her in the eye and talk about this baby she lost instead of dancing around what had happened, she was gone too. It hadn't really sunk in that she'd never see Aunt Hattie again. Never feel her hand touching her cheek or hear her say Katherine Reece, followed by words of correction or encouragement. Never have her prayers filling the air around her.

Kate kept thinking she would at least hear her voice in her head the way she had so many times while Aunt Hattie was alive. She always seemed to know what the little woman would be ready to tell her about whatever was happening. But nothing was there. Kate felt so empty. So terribly empty.

That smile on her face for Lorena's song felt good, even if only for a moment. Then the commercial was over and the host introduced another young singer.

When the boy's song started, Miss Myrtle spoke up from her bed. "Well, I do declare. That doesn't sound near so good as your little sister did. They should have let that sweet girl sing more than one song."

"They do plan to have her back. Mr. Harris said so when we were there on Saturday." The day Kate had been on her feet all day. The day she'd walked into the woods to get Tori. Would things have been different if she'd talked to Aunt Hattie earlier and not done all that? How could she have lost this baby she wanted so badly? How could she?

Everybody had come to see her. Her mother and father. Tori and Lorena. Aunt Gertie and Uncle Wyatt. The only one who hadn't come was Evie. Evie with her rounded stomach and her swollen feet. Evie who hadn't been ready for a baby but was having one anyway and Kate who had been desperately ready and now had nothing.

So very empty. She wanted to ask Jay if he felt the same, but she stopped herself. He hadn't been carrying the baby. He hadn't been the one to lose him.

That first night after they'd put her in this bed, she'd drifted in and out of awareness, but every time she opened her eyes

Jay was there. She wanted him there, and at the same time she couldn't bear to see him. She wanted to shut out everyone, even him, and curl up in solitary sorrow, but he refused to let that happen. She could still feel the loving comfort of him cradling her body next to his after he climbed into bed with her. When a nurse had come into the room during the night, Kate braced for the nurse's outrage at Jay in bed with Kate.

But Jay raised his head and simply said, "I need to hold her."

Kate opened one eye enough to make out the nurse's features in the light from the hallway. The same woman had been in earlier, a plain woman in her middle years who looked worn down with taking care of people.

"I have to check her vital signs," the woman insisted.

Kate couldn't remember her name, but Jay did. He kept his voice soft, friendly. "Glenda, I can vouch for her pulse being steady and her breathing easy. If you know that, there's no reason to jerk awake someone who has suffered what my Kate has suffered."

Kate eased her eye shut and pretended sleep. She could feel the nurse hesitating. Jay had always been a charmer. She wanted him to charm the nurse. She wanted him to keep holding her.

The nurse summoned up her sternest voice. "It's against the rules for you to be in bed with her, sir."

"Yes, ma'am. I'm sure it is. But I spent more than three years marching across Africa and Europe to make sure we hung on to the freedom to break those rules when they need breaking. Most of the time they're good rules and you're right to insist on folks following them. But tonight that rule needs breaking. We just lost our baby and I need to hold her." His arms tightened around Kate. "She needs me to hold her."

Silence then. The nurse was obviously studying what to say or do next.

"Please, Glenda."

"Oh, very well." She pulled the curtain all the way around the end of the bed to hide them from view. "But you'd better be out of there before the morning nurse comes on duty. Nurse Cox is nobody to mess with. She's liable to chase you clear out of the hospital and you can be sure I'll swear I stated the rules to you quite plainly."

"As you did," Jay said.

"As I did," the nurse said. "Ring the bell if there's any change in her pulse or your wife feels too warm. Anything that doesn't seem right, anything at all, you call me."

That's when Kate had wanted to raise up and point out how the wrong thing had already happened. Instead she stayed cuddled against Jay, letting him be strong for both of them. And the first night passed.

Morning hadn't brought any change to the truth that her baby was lost. Jay's baby too. With the daylight, she knew Aunt Hattie had passed over as well. She didn't know how she knew. She just knew. Maybe it was the emptiness. If Jay hadn't been beside her, perhaps she would have thought him gone too.

Kate had thought she was strong. She didn't cry over bumps and bruises. She grabbed hold of whatever was wrong and did everything in her power to make it right. With effort. With force of will. She was the middle sister, the one who took care of everyone. And now look at her. Broken. Barely able to stand. Empty.

The sound of the radio program's theme song signaling the end of the show pulled Kate away from her thoughts. She had paid scant attention to the singers who came on after Lorena.

Jay switched off the radio. "Birdie was best."

"Birdie?" Miss Myrtle sounded puzzled. "I thought the child's name was Lorena."

"A nickname," Jay explained.

"But her name is Lorena Birdsong," Kate said softly, thinking of all the times she'd heard Lorena say that name before she went to sleep. A promise to the mother who'd left her in Rosey Corner. She looked at Jay. "Do you think her mother heard her?"

"I don't know." Jay took Kate's hand and held it against his cheek. He looked so tired. "Does it matter?"

"To her, it does."

"But does it matter to you?"

"I don't want to lose her too." Kate could almost feel Miss Myrtle's ears perking up at that, but when she looked over at her, the woman's eyes were closed. She nodded toward her and Jay pulled the curtain between the beds.

"You could never lose Birdie." He sat back down and stroked Kate's cheek. "She loves you. You know what she had us do in the waiting room last night?"

Kate shook her head, but she did know even before Jay told her.

"She had us say your name. Katherine Reece Merritt Tanner. But before we did, your father called me son." A few tears edged out of Jay's eye and traced a path down his cheek. "I wanted to be a father like your father."

She reached up to brush away his tears, but when she started to speak, he held up a hand to stop her.

"Wait, hear me out. While I was overseas, I would sometimes say your name and mine out loud before I went to sleep. If that night turned out to be my last, I wanted my final waking thought to be of you. But somehow saying our names helped me believe I would have another day and that one of those days I'd finally make it home to you."

"I'm glad you did, Jay Tanner." Kate laid her hand on his cheek.

"So am I." He took her hand and brought it around to his lips. "Very glad. But as glad as I was to come home, I didn't think about having children. I just wanted to be back with you. Then when you said you were going to have a baby, I got scared. What if I was like my father? A man who would throw away his son when things got hard." Jay's face tightened.

"Didn't you ever go back home after he sent you to live with your aunt and uncle?"

"A few times, but I never belonged after that. I was extra. Unwanted extra."

"But you had brothers and sisters, didn't you?" Kate felt ashamed she didn't already know that.

"One sister. Three or four half brothers. Maybe more after I quit going to see them." Jay seemed to look inward then. "I didn't want to like them, so I didn't give them much reason to like me."

"Why?" Kate couldn't imagine life without her sisters. "Why didn't you want to like them?"

"I don't know. Maybe I was mad because I had to go back to live with my aunt and uncle."

"Were they that bad? Your aunt and uncle."

"Yes," Jay said flatly. Then he sighed. "I guess I was that bad too."

"No, you were just a kid." Kate caressed his cheek. He needed a shave, but her mother hadn't thought to bring a razor when she brought his clean clothes that morning.

"A kid who was always in trouble. Then a man who chased after trouble before I met you." His eyes looked watery again. "Anyway, when I was afraid I might lose you along with our baby, I thought maybe the Lord was punishing me."

"No, no." Kate put her hand behind his neck and pulled his head down closer to her. "Why would you think that?"

"That maybe the Lord was punishing me for not trusting him enough. Or that he might have taken our baby because he knew I couldn't be the good father you would want for our child."

"You would have been a wonderful father." Kate swallowed and changed her words. "You will be a wonderful father." Hope. She needed hope. They both did. Then the sweet welcome sound of Aunt Hattie's words whispered through her mind. "Aunt Hattie would tell us storms of life come on us all. It's what we do in the storms that matter."

"What would she tell us to do then in this storm?" His eyes looked so sad and yet brimming with love for her.

Kate searched her mind for the words Aunt Hattie would give her. Words they both needed. At last she said, "That nothing's wrong with shedding tears when bad things happen, but that there's no use wallowing in whatever misery comes our way. The Lord is always with us to help us through the hard times."

He grasped both of her hands. "I can hear her saying that."

"I don't want her to be gone." Kate felt a yawning hole inside her. "I don't want our baby to be gone."

They were silent a minute, sharing more than could be shared with words. Finally Jay said, "I'm going to miss Aunt Hattie."

"Mama said she must have died while Fern was with me."

Kate's unshed tears made a knot in her throat. She pushed her words out around it. "She knew. I think she knew when I was with her on Sunday that I was going to lose the baby. It was just a matter of when. So that's why she sent Fern to see about me. And then she died. Both of them gone at the same time."

"That Aunt Hattie." Jay squeezed her hands and actually smiled. "You know what happened, don't you?"

Kate frowned a little. "About what?"

"I've been hearing Aunt Hattie talk about being ready to head on up to heaven ever since I got home. She couldn't figure out why the Lord kept her here, but now we know. It was so she could come by the house on her way to heaven and pick up our little boy. He didn't have to go alone."

Tears flowed down Kate's cheeks then but a smile edged out through them to match Jay's. "She would do that."

"Give him a name." His smile slid away as he stared into Kate's eyes. "We don't ever have to tell anyone else if you don't want to, but he needs a name in our hearts."

"What about Miss Myrtle?" Kate glanced toward the curtain between the beds.

"She's been asleep for a while now. Don't you hear her snoring?" He turned an ear toward the other woman's bed.

"I thought that was her oxygen machine."

"Nope. She's sawing logs. So what should we name him?" When she didn't say anything right away, he went on. "Unless that's too hard for you to think about."

"I want to think about him. His life barely flickered, but he was real."

"So give him a real name."

"All right. The names have to mean something special.

Do you have someone you want to remember with one of the names?"

"Graham?"

She shook her head. "No, I want Graham to get to tell stories to the baby we name after him."

"Right." Jay thought a moment. "I had this Sergeant in the Army. I never called him anything but Sarge. Sarge Crane. But his given name was Marion."

"Marion." Kate tried out the name on her tongue. Something wasn't quite right about it. Then she knew. "Marion Bo," she said.

Jay smiled. "After Aunt Hattie's boy."

"I only knew him through Aunt Hattie's stories, but she never forgot him."

"And we won't forget our baby either," Jay said.

They locked eyes and tightened their hold on each other's hands as they spoke in unison. "His name is Marion Bo Tanner."

And a smile curled up in Kate's heart where her baby would always live.

30

For a moment, Kate hovered in the shadowy world of some dream she couldn't quite remember, but then the whisper of silky cloth brought her fully awake as Glenda, the night nurse, stepped around the curtain. Looking greatly relieved to see Kate alone in the bed, she stuck a thermometer under Kate's tongue.

"You should have told him to go home." She glanced at Jay, asleep in the chair, as she felt for Kate's pulse.

"I did," Kate said when the nurse took the thermometer. Jay had looked so tired, but he refused to leave.

"It's sweet the way he stays right with you." The nurse kept her voice low.

"We were apart a long time during the war."

"He told me he got home in December." The nurse pumped up the blood pressure cuff and listened through her stethoscope before she went on. "A man comes home from war, he expects things to go better. Now here he is, the both of you, having to face this." She clucked her tongue as she rolled up the blood pressure cuff. "Everything's looking good, sweetie."

"Good," Kate echoed. "I'm going home in the morning."

"You'll have to talk to the doctor about that." The nurse patted Kate's hand and looked at Jay again. "I want you to know I've been a nurse a long time and I think that was the sweetest thing I've ever seen. Him holding you like that last night."

"Thank you for not making him move. He was right. I did need him to hold me."

"I know." The nurse smoothed down Kate's covers. "Sometimes the most powerful medicine is love and prayers. You're a lucky woman."

After the nurse left, Kate smiled over at Jay, still sound asleep. "You've charmed another one," she whispered.

From the first day she met Jay, she knew he was a charmer. Mike had even warned her not to fall for Jay because he had a way of leaving broken hearts in his wake. She didn't doubt that was true, but he'd come home to love when he found Rosey Corner. She was so glad she'd let him charm her.

She reached toward him, wanting to feel his skin under her fingers, but his chair was too far from the bed. Then almost as if he sensed her need even in his sleep, his eyes opened.

"Are you all right?" He leaned forward and caught her hand in both of his.

"I'm all right." And she was. Sad and feeling empty, but somehow all right in spite of that.

He scooted his chair closer to the bed. "Do you need me to stay awake?"

"No. I'm not afraid of the dark, and even if I was, it's not dark in here."

"So many ways for it to be dark," Jay said softly.

"And so many ways to reach for the light." Kate looked up toward the ceiling. "Aunt Hattie would tell me the best light to reach for is Jesus."

"Don't you know she's doing some shouting and dancing tonight up in heaven?"

"With her Bo."

"And our Marion Bo." Jay leaned closer to gently touch her face. "Now go to sleep."

"You first."

He was asleep again almost before the words were out of her mouth. She held his hand and the night passed. The darkness of grief was there inside her, but the light was too. The Lord would help her through. Jay would help her through. The whole family would be ready to love them both through. And sooner or later, the emptiness would fade away. Perhaps even be filled with a new hope.

The next morning, the room didn't spin when she stood up. After Jay helped her dress, Kate insisted he go get breakfast in the cafeteria while they waited for her to be released. She missed him as soon as he walked out of the room, but she didn't call him back. He had to eat.

"He's such a nice young man," Miss Myrtle said.

"Yes, he is," Kate agreed with a smile. Smiling was easier with the morning sun. Sadness sat heavy on her heart, but she was trying to do as Aunt Hattie would tell her and not wallow in her misery.

Before the day was over, she'd have to say goodbye to Aunt Hattie's earthly remains, but her spirit was already in paradise with Bo and Kate's baby boy, fully formed now. Marion Bo Tanner. She let the name circle in her mind as she imagined a little boy running through a field of daisies in heaven.

Miss Myrtle broke in on her thoughts. "I finally remembered why your name sounded so familiar. It was just there in my head this morning when I woke up. Isn't that the way it is? We think and think on something and then we stop thinking and the answer pops right up to the top of our minds."

"My name?"

"Well, I suppose your maiden name. Birdsong."

"Oh no, my name isn't Birdsong."

"But I thought that sweet child was your sister." Miss Myrtle frowned a little.

"She is. We sort of adopted her when she was five. Her family couldn't take care of her." Kate hoped that would be enough of an explanation for Miss Myrtle. It was too long a story to tell before the nurse came to let her go home.

"Is that so? I suppose that happened often enough during the Depression when things were so hard for everybody. Things were hard for the Birdsong man I knew too."

Kate stared over at Miss Myrtle. "You knew someone named Birdsong?"

The woman bobbed her head and pushed herself up higher in her bed. "It's such an unusual name, I don't know why it didn't come right to me. I used to be able to remember things without a whit of trouble. I knew everybody's name at the home and their grandchildren's names too." She let out a long sigh. "Age has a way of catching up with a person."

Kate clamped down on her impatience. "But you remember now. The man named Birdsong."

"Indeed I do. My cousin lives up in Cincinnati and one of her daughters, guess that would be my second cousin once removed or something like that, anyway she married a Birdsong. Juanita, I think was her name. Yes, I'm pretty sure that's it. Juanita Birdsong. Well, Juanita Hastings Birdsong. She was a Hastings before she married."

Kate jumped in when Miss Myrtle paused for breath. "Do

you know if she had children?" Kate went still listening for her answer.

"I couldn't say for certain. I haven't heard from Mattie for some time now. She probably thinks I've passed on or maybe she did. She wasn't much younger than me. I'd say it's been seven or eight years since Mattie wrote me about Juanita getting married. At last. Those were her very words. She'd about given up on Juanita finding anybody. The girl was getting a little long in the tooth, you know."

"Oh." Kate let out her breath. Juanita couldn't be Lorena's mother.

"I sent her a present. Some pretty glasses. Never did get a thank-you note."

"Did you go to their wedding?"

"Goodness no. Not all the way up there in Cincinnati. Mattie just wrote me about it all. Said the Birdsong fellow was a widower but didn't have any children. At least none they knew about. He came from out west somewhere and wasn't much of a talker. That bothered Mattie some." Miss Myrtle smoothed down the covers over her middle.

"Why's that?" Kate readjusted her thinking again. Lorena's father perhaps, but that would mean the mother Lorena hoped to find had died long ago.

"She was sure he was hiding something. Maybe something bad. He told Mattie straight out that it was better talking about the now than what was. But a body loses a lot if he doesn't remember all the times of his life. The hard ones and the easy ones." Miss Myrtle wiped her eyes with an edge of the sheet as though her words put her in mind of some of her own hard memories.

That might be the way Kate would be when she was Miss

Myrtle's age and thinking back on losing her baby. And it could be what the Birdsong man didn't want to remember was deserting his daughter in Rosey Corner.

"Do they still live in Cincinnati?" Kate asked.

"Oh, honey, I just don't know. Like I said, I haven't heard from Mattie in ages. Juanita could have moved down here next door to the home and I'd never know it these days. That's how living in the home is. We're stuck in that private little world. It can be lonely there, but now I'll have you sweet people to think about when I go back. And I can brag about knowing Lorena Birdsong. Somebody who sings on the radio. Imagine that." Miss Myrtle smiled.

"When you go back to the home, I'll bring Lorena to see you. She can sing a song for you there."

"Oh, wouldn't that be wonderful?" Miss Myrtle held her hands up against her cheek.

A nurse's aide rolled a wheelchair into the room to take Kate down to the door. Another nurse bustled around Miss Myrtle. Jay followed them in. He interrupted the nurse taking Miss Myrtle's blood pressure to give the old woman a hug.

"Fun meeting you, Miss Myrtle."

"That's Auntie Myrt to you children." Miss Myrtle raised her eyebrows at him. "That sweet Lorena, she said I could be an aunt."

"Welcome to the family, Auntie Myrt." Jay grinned over at Kate. "Can't have too many aunts, now can we, Kate?"

In the car on the way home, Jay said, "Birdie knows how to collect family."

"She does." It would have been the perfect time to tell him about Miss Myrtle remembering the man named Birdsong, but she didn't. She needed to think about it first. Maybe talk to her mother. But all that could wait until after Aunt Hattie's funeral.

"I'm glad Birdie took a liking to me and wanted me in her family." He reached a hand across the seat to grasp hers. "I'm glad you took a liking to me too."

"Everybody likes you, Jay. You're a charmer."

"You're the only girl I ever wanted to charm." He squeezed her hand. "We're going to be all right."

She looked out at the road, stretching away from them, taking them home. "Yes," she said. "Yes, we are."

31

Clay came in from the field before noon. The sun was shining and the ground was in perfect shape for planting, but some things were more important than getting the corn seeds tucked in their rows. For days, he'd jabbed the corn planter tip into the freshly worked ground and released the seed over and over until at night that's all he could see when he closed his eyes. Long rows waiting for the seed as the sound of the handles of the planter chug-chunking open and closed echoed in his ears.

He didn't mind the job, tedious as it was. The sun was in his face and the good smell of dirt in his nose. He was connected to the earth in the same way his father and his father's father and countless generations before them had been. Tilling the ground, planting the seeds with hope for a harvest, praying for rain in season. A time to plant. A time to reap.

A spring day like this first day of May begged a man to be in the fields. Especially with rain in the forecast. Not that those radio weathermen always got it right. Clay could pay attention to the turn of a maple leaf in the wind, the dew on the grass, or the call of the rain crow and be right as often.

If the weather held, he'd get the corn in before the end of the week. But planting was through for the day. His mother wanted to pay her respects to Hattie Johnson. All of Rosey Corner would pack the church for a last goodbye to the little black woman who had helped so many Rosey Corner babies into the world.

The minute Aunt Hattie walked into a house, she brought calm with her. Clay's mother said Aunt Hattie had healing hands, but Clay wondered if it wasn't her healing prayers that mattered more. The first time he heard her pray was a revelation to Clay. He didn't know a person could just look up and start talking to the Lord. His mother prayed, but she did it in her quiet corner. And he never heard his father pray out loud, although he was a churchgoing man. But when Aunt Hattie prayed, it was like she pulled up a chair to the Lord's kitchen table to ask him for a few helpings of mercy. Helpings she had full confidence of getting.

Clay had tried to pray that way while he was planting corn. He needed answers. Paulette thought she had his answers. She brought sugar cookies by the house on Monday evening. They sat out on the bench in the yard near the dogwood tree he'd dug up out of the woods for his mother after his father died. It was in full bloom, a burst of white that shouted spring.

The evening had been pleasantly cool to Clay after the day in the fields, but Paulette pulled her sweater tight around her and leaned toward Clay. He hadn't taken the hint to put his arm around her. He supposed he should have. But hugging a girl shouldn't have anything to do with should-haves, but more to do with want-tos.

They'd talked about church, about the movie, about the cookies, about the tree frogs coming out early. And all Clay really wanted to do was go in the house, eat the supper he hoped his mother was keeping warm for him, and fall into his bed. He liked Paulette. He did. But he didn't love her. He wasn't ever going to love her.

The next day, as he walked the long rows planting corn, he decided he had to tell her that. It wasn't fair to let her think she could capture his heart. He'd given his heart away already and whether, in time, he ever managed to reclaim enough of it to fall in love again, he didn't know. But it wasn't apt to happen anytime soon.

He wouldn't bother Victoria anymore. She'd been plain with him. She told him to go away. Until she told him different, that's what he would do.

But that didn't keep him from thinking about her. She'd be at Aunt Hattie's funeral. While the whole community had called the little woman Aunt Hattie, the Merritts had claimed her as part of the family. She cooked and cleaned for old Mr. Merritt, who ran the store before he left Rosey Corner some years back. Folks said he went to Oregon and married a woman half his age. Aunt Hattie stayed on in his house, keeping it for him in case he decided to come back to Rosey Corner. Folks gossiped some about that. They'd gossip even more now if that crazy Lindell woman kept living there.

People liked to talk. Plenty of them were talking about Mr. Merritt digging Aunt Hattie's grave at the church. Mr. Merritt didn't care that folks said the graveyard there was for white people only. He went to a called meeting of the church deacons and told them straight out Aunt Hattie had a right to six feet of ground at the church she had attended faithfully for more than sixty years. A couple of the deacons said that didn't change the fact she was colored and they thought it would be more fitting for her to be buried in the colored cemetery just this side of Edgeville.

Clay's mother had heard all the talk when Aaron took her to the store the day before, where they found Graham Lindell behind the counter trying to take care of customers. Victoria's sister, the one married to Pastor Mike, was there too, but Clay's mother said she was useless as a flyswatter in a swarm of bees.

"Guess she has reason, being so far along with her baby, but she might as well stayed home on the porch swing for all the help she was," his mother had said last night at supper. "If Victoria hadn't come in, I might still be there trying to pay for my groceries. But I shouldn't be fussing. Not with the hard times that family is seeing this week. Poor Kate, they say she nigh on died when she lost her baby. That would have been a bitter pill for Nadine and Victor. Can you believe it was that Fern Lindell that helped her?"

"Hard to imagine," Clay said, just to let his mother know he was listening. Or at least pretending to listen. At the first mention of Victoria, his mind had flown off, chasing after her.

"They say Fern went to the church and helped the men dig Aunt Hattie's grave. It's just a good thing Pastor Mike came in and set Willis Combes and Marvin Best straight on where Aunt Hattie was to be buried. The very idea that she couldn't lay in our graveyard when she's lived among us all these years, catching our babies and healing the sick. Reverend Winston's too new to the church to know how to handle things like this."

"Who's preaching the funeral?" Clay reached for the last piece of chicken, but Aaron snagged it first. The boy was never full these days.

"Pastor Mike. He's finally looking better. That boy came home from that German prison camp naught but skin and bones."

"At least he came home," Clay said.

"True enough." His mother looked across the table at him. "There's not the first reason for you to feel guilty because you're breathing and Victoria's Sammy is not. Folks die and those who are left go on. I did and she will too."

"You haven't remarried." Clay had never given thought to his mother remarrying, but maybe he should have. The other kids around the table suddenly got quiet as they waited for their mother to say something.

"The good Lord sends me another good man like your father, I might think on it." She poured Mary some water and buttered Willie's bread. "You children don't need to look so worried. I doubt there's a man out there willing to take on this crew. So eat your potatoes before they get cold."

Beside Clay, Mary leaned over to kiss his arm. "We've got Clay."

"Yes, indeed, a good brother to you." Clay's mother looked around the table at her children. "We've made out since your daddy passed on. The good Lord has provided our needs, and if he were to send a new husband my way, it would take some considering before I'd take him up on the offer, as old as I am." She laughed, but then her eyes settled back on Clay. "But your Victoria is in the spring of life. It would be good for the Lord to supply her with a husband for all the years lying ahead of her."

Your Victoria. He'd liked the sound of that even if there wasn't any truth to it. Now as he cleaned up for the funeral, he should be thinking about Aunt Hattie and how Rosey

Corner was going to miss her, but all he could think of was how he'd see Victoria in less than an hour. A man shouldn't think about courting when he was getting ready for a funeral.

That's what he wanted to tell Paulette when she caught him before he went in the church. She said a friend was saving them a place. But instead he told her he had to sit with his mother to help with the children.

"Willie gets restless when the services go on too long." Clay kept his eyes on Paulette, but it took effort not to look around for Victoria.

"Your mother doesn't need help." Paulette hooked her hand under Clay's elbow and tugged him toward the church door.

Clay glanced around, relieved most of the people were already inside. He didn't want to embarrass Paulette. "I'd better sit with my family today." He eased his arm away from her hand.

Red raced across Paulette's cheek bones. "You'd sit with Victoria if she asked you."

"She won't ask me." Clay kept his voice low.

"You're right about that. She's never going to ask you to do anything." Paulette's voice rose with each word.

He held his hand palm out toward her the way he might try to quiet Lillie or Mary. "Listen, Paulette, this isn't the time or place for this. I'll come by later."

"Don't bother." Paulette spun on her heel and headed toward the church door.

"I'm sorry."

"You're right there." She looked over her shoulder at him. "You're as sorry as they come and you'll end up an old bachelor living in your mother's house all your livelong days."

He stood where he was and felt as sorry as she thought

he was. An old bachelor. If that's how it turned out, so be it. Could be there were worse things than being a bachelor. Like marrying the wrong woman.

He didn't realize Victoria's sister and her husband were behind him on the walk until the man spoke. "Afternoon, Clay."

It was obvious they'd both heard Paulette's parting shot, but they looked too deep in their own troubles to give his problems much thought. Kate was pale as dandelion fluff and leaning heavily on her husband's arm.

"I'm sorry about the baby," he said, and then worried he shouldn't have mentioned the baby. Maybe they didn't want to talk about it. "And about Aunt Hattie too," he added awkwardly.

Kate lightly touched his arm. Even her fingers looked too white. "Thank you, Clay."

He moved aside to let them go into the church first. She looked in need of a seat. But just as Paulette had stopped and looked back, so did she. "Don't give up on her, Clay. Please."

"On who?" Clay said.

But music started up inside and she turned back toward the church without answering. She didn't have to answer anyway. He knew. His Victoria.

He followed them up the steps and through the doors. The church was full, but his eyes sought and found Victoria on the front row. Dare he let hope spread its wings in his heart yet another time?

32

Tori saw Paulette come back in the church. Alone. She didn't watch her all the way down the church aisle, but it was plain to see she wasn't happy. Even after Tori turned her eyes back toward the front of the church where Aunt Hattie's casket sat, she could hear Paulette and her friend whispering. She couldn't hear what they were saying. She didn't want to hear what they were saying.

The older ladies in the church would be frowning at them if they didn't hush. Some of them were probably already frowning at Tori for letting Samantha stand on the pew and look behind her. Graham was seated toward the back, and she kept holding out her arms to him and saying her baby-talk word for Chaucer. Graham thought it was funny that Samantha called him by his dog's name.

Tori should have stuck some crackers or a sucker in her purse to distract her. A funeral wasn't the best place for a two-year-old, but she wasn't the only child there. Nearly everybody in Rosey Corner was squeezed into the church. A few parents had let their children stay outside. Tori could hear them through the windows, pushed up to let in air. With every pew packed, it was a blessing the spring day wasn't any warmer than it was. Even so, fans waved all around the church and some of the men yanked at their starched collars.

Tori didn't blame those mothers who let their children run outside. She'd considered asking one of the older girls to keep an eye on Samantha, but the road was so close. The other kids might get distracted playing together and Samantha could get away quick. Just the other day she had crawled under the fence and headed across the field without a backward glance. Going fishing, she said. So it was better to keep her in her lap whether she was restless or not.

Besides, Aunt Hattie wouldn't be bothered by Samantha smiling at the people behind her. She'd be smiling and saying the last thing she wanted from any of them was solemn tears. Happy tears. That would have been her order for them. *Set your hands to clappin' and your feet to dancing 'cause that's what I'm a-doin' up in heaven.* Aunt Hattie's words had a way of showing up in a person's head.

Mrs. Weber didn't let her children stay outside either as she ushered them into a pew toward the back. Clay didn't come in with them. When Samantha saw Mary and Lillie, she squealed with excitement. Tori shushed her, and Samantha let out a wail. Tori's mother produced a small box of cookies from her purse. Mama was always prepared. Samantha happily settled down in her lap.

Lorena leaned forward from her spot sandwiched between Mama and Daddy to whisper, "They're here." Tori twisted around to see Kate and Jay coming in the church. Lorena would have popped up to go meet them, but Mama put a hand on her leg to stop her.

A hush fell over the church as Jay ushered Kate down the

aisle. The news that she'd lost her baby had already swept through Rosey Corner.

Kate looked so feeble that Tori hurt for her. When she was a kid, Tori had caught every bug going around and even now she kept a cold in the winter time, but she couldn't remember Kate ever being very sick. She was the strong one. The one who made sure everybody was all right. But now she wasn't all right. She leaned heavily on Jay, her face white with the effort of coming into the church. Jay looked sad and tired too. At the same time, they looked so connected by their love that tears welled up in Tori's eyes. Kate had Jay to love her through this.

They walked to the front to gaze down at Aunt Hattie. Tori had viewed her earlier, but had no feeling that any part of Aunt Hattie's spirit remained in that shell of a body. That didn't keep the sight of her from bringing to mind a thousand memories, and Kate had to be feeling the same. Even more so, since she and Aunt Hattie were so close.

After a minute, Mama took her hand off Lorena's leg to let her go stand with Kate. It still somehow surprised Tori to see Lorena so tall, almost an adult now, and with such a big heart. That morning Lorena lay facedown on her bed, crying with abandon because she wanted to get all the tears out so she could sing at the services. But she must not have spilled all the tears. There with her arm around Kate, she reached her free hand up to swipe away tears. How often Tori had done the same, but rarely had she seen Kate do so.

Tori couldn't tell if Kate had tears in her eyes now or not as she stared down into the casket for long moment. Then she put her hand on top of Aunt Hattie's hand and leaned down to whisper something to her, even though Aunt Hattie's ears were past hearing.

Purses all over the church clicked open as women pulled out handkerchiefs they hadn't expected to need to say goodbye to dear Aunt Hattie who they knew was so ready to make the flight to heaven. But they shared Kate's double grief with damp eyes and sympathetic hearts.

Mama handed Samantha back to Tori so she could go to Kate. Jay moved to make room beside Kate, but he hovered behind them.

Samantha pushed away the cookie Tori offered her and scrambled out of Tori's lap to stand on the pew looking behind her again. "Cay," she cried and reached out her arms.

Clay was standing just inside the door. His broad shoulders and suntanned face were a stark contrast to Kate's pale face. Tori pulled Samantha into her lap and turned back toward the front, but not before Clay's eyes swept over her. She suddenly felt too still inside, as though waiting for something to happen.

But nothing did. Another quick look over her shoulder showed Lillie scooting over and Clay lifting Mary up to perch on his knee so he had room in the pew beside his family. Tori's heart began pounding up in her ears. What in the world was wrong with her? She was at a funeral. A person wasn't supposed to think about anything but the person she was grieving. Certainly she shouldn't be noticing how Clay looked so strong. Or remembering how safe she'd felt those few seconds in his arms after he'd kept her from falling at Graham's pond. If she was thinking about anything besides Aunt Hattie or Kate, it should be Sammy.

His funeral had been in this church. The telegram said he was dead, but there'd been no body. Perhaps that was why she had such a hard time giving up Sammy. Because she hadn't seen him with the life gone from him the way she could see Aunt Hattie. If she'd had that last view of Sammy, she might have been convinced he was gone the way she could be sure Aunt Hattie had moved on up to paradise. Her head knew Sammy had moved on up to heaven too, but something in her heart refused to accept what her eyes hadn't actually seen.

Aunt Hattie's son died in the First World War. He too never came home. His grave was in France. Aunt Hattie knew how it was, and yet, she had given her beloved son over to the Lord. That was what she told Tori to do. It was futile to try to hold on to what was already gone.

The Lord gives and the Lord takes away. Tori had heard that from her more times than she could count. Then Aunt Hattie would go on. *He took away from us, Victoria, but he didn't never desert my Bo or your Sammy, and he won't never desert me and you. That you can count on. Forever more.*

And now Kate had lost the child she so wanted. Tori bounced Samantha on her knees and offered her another cookie. She hoped the child would get sleepy when Mike started talking about Aunt Hattie. At last one of the deacons pulled the bell rope to toll the three o'clock hour. Mike stood up from beside Evie at the other end of the pew. He held Evie's hand and whispered to her a minute. Whatever he said didn't work. Evie shifted uneasily in the pew. Sitting was not easy for her, but then neither was standing. Her face was a confusion of emotions as she watched Mike step up to the casket to speak to Kate.

Evie was worried about seeing Kate today or about Kate seeing her, so fully in the family way. That was all she'd talked about while they were getting ready for the funeral. That and how hard it was to find a black maternity dress.

Tori had pulled the black dress she'd worn to Sammy's funeral out of the back of the wardrobe. She had never wanted to wear it again and she hadn't until today. A funeral dress.

"Here I am about to pop with a baby and she's lost hers." Evie held her hands over her extended stomach as if to protect the baby inside her. "What in the world will I say to her?"

Their mother came in the room in time to hear Evie. "You're not about to pop, Evangeline. You've got weeks to go," she told her with a touch of irritation.

Evie let out a little breath, as though surprised by their mother's words. "Only a few weeks." She sounded close to tears.

Mama wasn't often cross with anyone, especially not Evie, but the last two days had worn her down. She'd even been short with a customer who had dallied over finishing her shopping at closing time. She apologized to the woman and added a bunch of bananas to her order without charging for them, but her smile had been forced. As they walked home, she'd confided in Tori as she never had before.

"I know Aunt Hattie was ready, even anxious to go." She spoke in little more than a whisper with her eyes straight ahead. "But I just don't know what I'll do without her."

Sometimes there were no right words to say. Tori took Mama's hand the way she might have held Samantha's hand as tears slid down her mother's cheeks.

But earlier that day, Mama's eyes were dry as she set Evie straight. "Your sister won't begrudge you a healthy baby when it's time for your confinement."

"But it might make her sad," Evie said.

"She will be sad. She's already sad, but that won't have anything to do with you, Evangeline. And I guarantee you she'll feel much worse if you back away from her because you feel a little uncomfortable. She's hurting." Mama took Evie's hand and gave it a little shake. Then she reached for Tori's hand too. "She needs her sisters. Both of you and Lorena too."

Now Mrs. Taylor moved to the piano and began softly playing a hymn. A signal of the time to begin. Beginnings and endings. Were they simply different sides of the same door?

33

The piano music meant it was time to begin the service, but Kate didn't move toward her seat. Dear Aunt Hattie. She needed her to sit up and start talking to her. She needed her prayers and her wisdom in her ears.

Almost as though she had an answer from heaven, Aunt Hattie's words were in her head. *Now, Katherine Reece, I ain't wantin' to listen to none of your nonsense. Any wisdom you ever got from me came straight from the Good Book. I'm knowin' you has a copy of that Book. All the answers you might ever be wantin' are between them covers if'n you read it with a prayerful heart. You's on a bumpy road right now, but ain't nary a one of us promised an easy road. Just ask your sweet sister Victoria about that. Sorrows come. With the good Lord's help, we keep on going till the day comes, like it has for me, o glory, when troubles are over forever more. Your little baby child what only knew a flicker of life in your womb won't never know a trouble one. Naught but love then and now.*

Kate's mother circled her arm around Kate's waist to turn her away from the casket. Kate kept her eyes on the little woman's wrinkled face, but she wasn't seeing her there. Instead Kate saw her out in the middle of the yard, her hands raised toward the heavens, talking to the Lord about whatever burden was on her mind.

Kate thought about doing the same. Just lifting up her hands there in front of the church to surrender it all to the Lord. Then she realized she'd already done that. Maybe not the way Aunt Hattie would have, but in the way she, Kate, needed to. She and Jay had given their baby to the Lord the night before.

Now it was time to tell Aunt Hattie goodbye. Not that Aunt Hattie needed any kind of send-off. She was already with the Lord she loved so much, but the words and songs might ease the hearts of those who would miss her. Kate took one last look at Aunt Hattie's peaceful face and knew without a doubt that Aunt Hattie would always be with her. Her words would echo in her head. Her prayers would sneak into her heart. But oh, how she was going to miss her voice in her ears and her hand on her cheek.

Kate reached for Jay's arm and Mama moved to let him step back beside her. Kate had hardly been aware of the full church as she'd walked down the aisle. All her attention was on the casket, but now she saw the packed church. Some of the women had hankies out, wiping away tears in between waving their fans.

Evie worked her fan too and looked miserable as she watched Kate with worried eyes. She mouthed the words, *I love you*. Kate managed a smile and relief raced across Evie's face.

Mama sat down by Tori and lifted Samantha into her lap, but Lorena stayed beside Kate. Tomorrow Kate would tell Lorena about Miss Myrtle's cousin and the man in

Cincinnati named Birdsong. But not today. Today was Aunt Hattie's. Today Kate couldn't bear the thought of perhaps losing Lorena too. Some things were better put off until tomorrow.

The church door opened and closed and people turned in their pews to see the latecomer. When they saw Fern, whispers circled around the church.

"Oh good." Lorena kept her voice low. "I was afraid she wasn't coming."

Fern stopped just inside the door as though unable to move a step farther down the aisle without Aunt Hattie urging her toward one of the pews. She wore a print dress faded by too many washings, but it looked freshly pressed. Her gray hair was combed and tied back from her face with a strip of black cloth.

Graham got to his feet, but Fern didn't pay him the first bit of attention. Her eyes bore into Kate. Kate stared back, thinking of all the years she'd known her. Strange Fern who had no interest in being like other people. Scary Fern who stepped out of the nightmares of kids in Rosey Corner—the bogeyman behind the bushes. Brokenhearted Fern who shut away the world for fear of being hurt again until Lorena pushed her way into Fern's heart. Because of Lorena's easy acceptance of Fern's oddities, Kate had begun to see Fern as more than the weird woman who lurked in the shadows of the woods. And now she was seeing her as Aunt Hattie saw her. A woman in need of a friend.

Kate smiled as much as she was able with the sadness weighing down on her and held a hand out toward Fern. "Come, sit with us." Kate's voice sounded loud in the quiet church.

Fern didn't smile back, but her face softened the barest bit.

Lorena hurried up the aisle to lead Fern down to their pew. Fern's rubber boots squeaked on the wood floor.

When they got almost to the front of the church, Lorena whispered something to Fern. Fern didn't bother whispering but spoke out loud. "I don't need to see Hattie dead. I saw that already. Better to wait and see her next in heaven."

An uneasy murmur traveled around the church, as though some doubted Fern would have that chance. She was too different. She hadn't spent enough time in church. She wasn't like they thought she should be. Kate wanted to tell the whisperers the Lord didn't care about rubber boots and shapeless dresses. He didn't care about combed hair and washed faces. He cared about hearts, and he could see into hearts that nobody else could.

But Fern didn't need Kate to defend her. She didn't care what other people thought. She was who she was, and she had come to say goodbye to a friend. That was why Kate was there too. Nothing else mattered right now. Later, other worries could horn in. Where would Fern stay with Aunt Hattie gone? Would Lorena want to go live with her birth family? Would Daddy's cough ever get better? Would she and Jay have more babies? So many worries.

It took the good Lord six days to make the world. Ain't no way you're gonna be fixin' everythin' about it in one day, Katherine Reece.

Kate's smile felt a little more at home on her face then as Tori scooted over to make room for Kate and Jay. Then they moved even closer together so Fern could push in the pew with them. She smelled of the woods, but it wasn't a bad smell. Instead it was fresh and somehow right for Aunt Hattie's funeral. The aroma of nature enduring through the ages. Storms and fires came. Branches and leaves fell, but the trunk of life continued putting out new growth.

Kate was empty now, but she wouldn't always be empty.

As Mrs. Taylor played the last chords of the hymn, Kate reached across Jay to touch Fern's hand. Fern seemed surprised for a second, but then she turned her hand over and tightened her fingers around Kate's.

"I'm glad you didn't die, Kate Merritt." Again she didn't bother whispering, and her words were plain in the quiet of the church as Mrs. Taylor turned to a new page in her hymnbook.

Kate spoke aloud too. "I am too, Fern Lindell. Thank you."

Fern let go of her hand and Kate sat back, surrounded on all sides by those who loved her. A hush fell over the church as Lorena stood to sing "Amazing Grace." Her voice was so pure and sweet that chills ran up Kate's back.

Then Mike stood up and grasped the pulpit behind Aunt Hattie's coffin. He opened his Bible and began to read. "'The Lord is my Shepherd . . .'"

He sounded like the old Mike, the Mike from before the war who knew he was meant to preach. Kate imagined Aunt Hattie smiling down on him with joy at the confident belief in his voice as he continued to read the psalm.

"'Yea, though I walk through the valley of the shadow of death, I will fear no evil . . .'"

The familiar words fell gently on Kate's ears. A laying to rest of not only Aunt Hattie, but Kate's lost baby too.

"'Surely goodness and mercy shall follow me all the days of my life: and I will dwell in the house of the Lord for ever.'"

Kate waited until Saturday to tell Lorena about the man named Birdsong. Lorena was planting the iris bulbs Mrs. Alvers next door gave Kate. Other neighbors brought food, and of course, her mother made Jay a brown sugar pie. Kate hated feeling so weak she couldn't sweep the kitchen floor without sitting down twice, but time would heal her body and soften the pain in her heart.

The morning air carried the fresh, sweet smell of lilacs, and the sun felt especially good on Kate's shoulders as she sat on the porch steps watching Lorena. It seemed the perfect time to tell her what Miss Myrtle had said.

"Do you think he's my father?" Lorena sat back on her heels to look at Kate, her face a mixture of sadness and hope.

"I don't know, Lorena. Maybe. Maybe not." The peaceful beauty of the day faded as Kate berated herself for not thinking through how the news of a man named Birdsong remarrying might upset Lorena. She should have waited for Jay to be home, but the words were out now. There was no taking them back. "But Birdsong is not a very common name. He might know your family."

Lorena stuck her trowel in the ground and turned over some of the dirt. "Poor little worm," she murmured as she picked up a fishing worm she accidently sliced in two.

"He'll be all right. He'll grow on a new end."

"I know." Lorena gently put the worm over in the part of the flowerbed already planted. Then she looked at Kate. "I'll be all right too. Whatever we find out."

Kate held out her arms and Lorena dropped the trowel to come lean against Kate the way she used to when she was little. Now Lorena was taller than Kate, but she would always be her little sister.

"Do you feel sliced in two?" Kate asked her. "Divided?"

"Not in a bad way." Lorena raised her head to look directly at Kate. "I want to know about my family. My first family. But the Lord took care of me the way he does the fishing worms. He sent you to find me that day my mommy left me at the church and gave me a new family."

"I'm glad he did." Kate tightened her arm around Lorena, who rested her head against Kate's shoulder again.

They sat like that for a few minutes before Lorena asked, "Do you think we can find this man with the same name as mine?"

"I don't know, but we'll try."

When Lorena didn't say anything, Kate pushed her back where she could see her face. She looked the way she did sometimes before she sang at a church. Eager and scared at the same time. Kate touched Lorena's cheek. "But only if you want to."

That was what she always told her about singing. Her voice was a gift, but she didn't have to sing in front of people unless she wanted to. She always wanted to. Kate knew she wanted to do this too, but Jay's warning from the night before when she told him about Miss Myrtle's cousin played through Kate's head.

"Birdie might find out things she'd rather not know."

"Like what?"

"Think about it, Kate. They deserted her and never came back. They couldn't know she found a good family to take care of her. For all they ever knew, she could have starved on that church step. That doesn't sound like a very loving family."

"It was hard times." Kate felt compelled to defend Lorena's unknown mother.

"Could times ever get so hard that you would have given up our baby?" He pushed the question at her.

Her hands had gone instinctively to her abdomen to protect what was already lost. "I don't know."

"Well, I know. It wouldn't happen. You would have found another way." He grabbed her hand and kissed it. "We would have found another way."

"But she wants to know."

"She thinks she does." Jay sighed a little. "She's still not much more than a little girl. She wants a fairy-tale ending, but there aren't many of those out there in the real world."

Kate had tried to lighten his mood. "You're my prince. My knight in shining armor."

It had worked. He laughed and pulled her into his arms. "I'm not much of a prince or knight either. But if you'd been a damsel in distress, I'd have fought the dragon for you without a moment's hesitation. What do you say we just skip the fighting dragon part and go straight to the kiss?"

Now Kate watched the emotions race across Lorena's face. Doubt, worry, hope. Kate did so want a fairy-tale ending for her, but Jay was right. Life didn't offer many perfect endings, not without pain mixed in.

"I have to know, Kate." Determination chased the other emotions away. "Even if it's bad. I have to know."

"Then if Jay can get off next Saturday, we'll go."

Lorena was right. Sometimes it was better to know than to wonder.

34

The next Saturday, Jay drove Kate and Birdie to Cincinnati. He wasn't sure he was doing either of them a favor. Kate had her hands clutched so tightly in her lap, her knuckles were white. Birdie looked every bit as nervous when he peeked in the rearview mirror at her.

The drive up was very quiet. No singing. No laughing at his silly jokes. A few pathetic smiles were all he could get out of Kate, and Birdie acted like she didn't even hear him. Maybe she didn't, in the backseat with the windows down.

Smiles hadn't been coming easy for Kate or Jay either the last couple of weeks. The sadness had settled in their hearts like silt at the bottom of a mud puddle. The puddle cleared when the water was left alone and regular life went along, but with every thought of the baby, the mud got stirred up again.

Nobody talked about it. People acted like losing a baby so early in the pregnancy was either of no importance or something too embarrassing to mention. Not that everybody hadn't been great. The church people had loaded them down with food. Kate's mother and Tori cleaned their house top to bottom, even the windows. Mike came to pray with them.

Preaching Aunt Hattie's funeral helped restore Mike's confidence in his calling to preach, and he was ready to serve a new church. He said the Lord let him know he wasn't chairman of the results committee. His job was to deliver the messages the Lord gave him and believe in the power of his Word to change lives.

If anybody knew that was true, Jay did. For years, Mike had preached at him with no visible results, but seed was sown and eventually took root in Jay's heart to change his life. That didn't mean he had this whole faith thing down pat. So it felt right having Mike back praying for him and prodding him to be a better man.

Jay wished he'd asked Mike to say a special prayer about this trip. The closer they got to Cincinnati, the more he thought they needed prayers. Lots of prayers. Jay didn't want either of the girls he loved most in the world to be hurt by whatever they might find out.

With an extra week to think on it, Miss Myrtle had remembered her Cincinnati cousin's address. When they visited her at the nursing home, she had it already written out in her shaky handwriting.

"I wrote it down, because I knew you'd come." Miss Myrtle had looked at Birdie. "A person needs to know about her family."

But what if that person found out something she'd rather not know?

When they got to Cincinnati, they stopped at the first phone booth they saw. Kate found a listing for Miss Myrtle's cousin and rang her number. Kate had to tell the woman all about Miss Myrtle before she got answers to her questions.

But she did get the answers. She hung up the phone and

looked at Birdie. "The man's name is Andy. Andy Birdsong. Does that ring a bell?"

Birdie shut her eyes. Jay could almost see her combing through long-buried memories. Finally she opened her eyes, pressed her lips together, and shook her head. "No."

"They don't have a phone, but she gave me their address," Kate said.

After a few wrong turns, they found the right street where Kate spotted a mailbox with A. Birdsong painted on it in black letters.

Pots of flowers and a green metal yard chair filled up the little porch that was not much more than a stoop. Like chairs leaned against the side of the neat white house. The front door was open to the breeze, but a screen door kept out flies. A shiny black sedan was parked in the driveway.

Jay drove past the house. At the corner, he pulled into an empty church parking lot and turned off the motor. Everything sounded too quiet then.

He twisted around to look at Birdie behind him. "Okay, Birdie. What next?"

Kate reached over the seat to touch Birdie's knee. "Whatever you want to do is what we'll do."

"It was a long drive up here." Birdie sounded hesitant.

"The drive home is the same distance whether we go back to the house or not," Jay said. "We can stop at that ice cream place we saw down the road. I bet they have fudge ripple."

Birdie smiled then the way he intended, but the smile didn't last. She slipped her eyes from him to Kate. "I'm afraid."

"I know." Kate grabbed her hand. "It's okay."

Birdie stared at Kate for a minute. "Miss Myrtle's relative can't be my mother."

"No, she can't," Kate said gently.

Birdie blinked a couple of times. "He might not want to see me."

"If that happens, then we'll go get that ice cream." Kate squeezed Birdie's hand. "But I think if we don't go back to the house, you'll end up wishing you had."

"It could not go well," Jay said.

Kate shot a frown toward him, but a person needed to be prepared.

"I know that, Tanner." Birdie blew out a long sigh. "But Kate's right. I want to know. If he slams the door in my face, that can't be any worse than leaving me on the church steps when I was five."

"He won't slam the door in your face. You'll stay in the car while I go to the door to check the lay of the land." Jay started up the car. "If any door slamming happens, it'll be in my face."

He didn't know whether to hope the man would slam the door in his face or open it wide to let them in. Maybe Jay would just knock on the door and punch the man right in the nose and get it over with. Then maybe he'd drive on down to Gaffney on the Tennessee border and knock on his father's door and punch him in the nose too. Surely the Lord didn't mean a kid had to always turn the other cheek.

At the house, Jay knocked on the screen door. After a minute, he knocked again, harder this time, rattling the door.

"Hold your horses." A woman shuffled up the hallway, drying her hands on the apron tied around her ample middle. Gray perm-set curls circled the plump face that peered through the screen at him. She shifted on her feet as though they were hurting and with reason. Her fleshy ankles lapped over the edges of well-worn house shoes.

"Mrs. Birdsong?" Jay did his best to sound nonthreatening.

"Who wants to know?" The skin around the woman's eyes tightened.

"My name's Jay Tanner. I'm looking for Andy Birdsong. Does he live here?"

"You the police?"

That surprised Jay. "Police? Why would you think that? Is your husband wanted for something?"

She lowered her voice. "I don't know. But the man hasn't ever told me one thing about what he did before we got married."

"How long ago was that?" Jay decided it wasn't all bad to be suspected of being the law.

"Eight years this August."

Jay did quick math in his head. Birdie had been with the Merritts since she was five and she would be fifteen in June. That was all she knew for sure from her past. Her name and her birth date. "Happily, I hope." Jay gave the woman his most convincing smile.

"Happy enough, if it's any of your business. But I want you to know that if he done anything illegal before we married, I didn't know nothing about it. Nothing at all."

"Ma'am, I assure you I'm not the police."

"You look like some kind of police." Her hand was on the doorknob. "But I listen to radio programs. I know you can't come in if I don't let you."

Jay shot her another smile and moved to the side so she could see past him to the car. "I'm not police. See, my wife and her sister are out there in my car. We just need to speak to Mr. Birdsong about a family matter. If he's here."

"Family matter?" Her frown grew fiercer. "The man don't have no family."

A door slammed somewhere inside the house and then a man's voice called out. "Who's at the door, Juanita?"

"Just some salesman." The woman stepped back to close the door.

Jay was tempted to turn back toward the car. He could say the woman let him know this Birdsong man was not Birdie's father. But instead he opened the screen and put his hand against the door to keep it open. She shrieked and jumped back.

"Mr. Birdsong?" Jay called. "I'm not selling anything. We just need a little information."

"Information about what?" The man came up the hallway.

The woman shrank away from the door. "Make him go away, Andy."

Jay took his hand off the door, but kept the screen door open. The man was tall and thin, but his scoop-neck undershirt revealed the muscles of a working man. His hair was streaked with gray, but it was easy to see it had once been as black as Jay's. As Birdie's.

"She's worried I'm the police," Jay said. "But I'm not."

"So not police and not a salesman. What are you then?"

"Just a friend and brother to a girl called Lorena Birdsong."

The man recoiled as though Jay had actually given him that punch in the nose.

"You told me your wife died," the woman said.

The man didn't take his eyes off Jay as he told the woman, "She did, Juanita. You go on out to the kitchen and let me handle this."

When she didn't move, he gave her a hard look. "Go on. Do as I say. None of this has anything to do with you."

The woman huffed out a breath and muttered as she shuffled

back down the hallway. Birdsong stepped through the screen door and pulled the inside door firmly shut behind him. "I never saw any need telling the woman about Lorena. Still don't."

"She's here." Jay nodded toward the car. He couldn't see anything except the very top of Birdie's black curls.

"Here?" Birdsong looked like Jay had punched him again.

"She wants to know if you're her father."

"Where is she? I don't see her." There was a timbre of longing in his voice as he stared out at the car. "That girl in the front can't be Lorena."

"She's in the back. Feeling a little unsure, I guess."

The man sank down on the porch step. "You're thinking I'm some kind of scoundrel and you're right. But I did what I thought best for the girl. It was best. I went back there once after Iris died. Poor Iris. The woman grieved herself to death after we lost the kids. She couldn't even bring herself back for the baby. A sweet little girl, but every time she looked at her she saw Lorena. She died before the baby was six months old."

The man looked up at Jay with fierce eyes. "What was I going to do with a baby? A man without a wife and no family. I had to work. There were doctor bills to pay. So I gave her up for adoption. Tried to get her back after I married Juanita in there, but it was too late. They wouldn't even tell me where she was, so I could go see her."

The man stared down at his hands hanging loose from his wrists, propped on his knees. Jay didn't say anything, but the man needed no encouragement to keep talking. The words must have been building inside him all these years and now they had to come out.

"Guess that was best too. Juanita never had any desire to be a mother. Told me that before we married. But I would have still brought my baby home if they'd let me. We named her Melanie. Iris had a fondness for fancy names." He looked back out toward the car. "Is she going to get out?"

"Do you want her to?" Jay asked.

The man's face was set, frown lines deep between his eyes, his jaw clenched. He slid his eyes across Jay's face and then out to the car where more of Birdie's head was visible now. "You can't imagine how much." The man's voice was barely above a whisper.

"Then why didn't you ever come back for her?"

The man shot Jay a hard look. "I already told you. I did go back. After Iris died." He dropped his head down and was silent a few seconds. "I didn't have anything then. Nothing except a baby I couldn't take care of. I'd found a job sweeping floors at a warehouse, but they fired me when I missed too many days while Iris was dying. I begged enough money to get the gas to drive back down there to Kentucky. I loaded up the baby and took to the road. It was the summer after we left her there at that church. The day was hot and the baby cried the whole way. I shouldn't have took her, but I didn't have anybody to leave her with."

"Couldn't find any church steps?"

The man pushed up off the step and balled up his fists. "You think I wanted to leave her there? Is that what you think?"

Jay took a step back from him. "I don't know what to think."

The fight drained out of the man and he sank back down on the step. When he started talking again, his voice was devoid of feeling. "You're right. You don't know nothing about it. I doubt you know a thing about going hungry. About watching your wife go down to skin and bones because you couldn't find work. Or hearing your babies cry because you can't get them any food."

"I'm sorry." Jay sat down beside the man. He didn't look at the car.

"I didn't want to leave her, but I couldn't watch her starve. That little town had gardens and fruit trees. Food. And I did go back. Not soon enough for Iris, but I went back."

"Couldn't you find her?" Jay asked.

"No, I found her." Birdsong looked up at the sky. "I drove down the road and there she was. In this yard, swinging high in the air. A girl was pushing her and they were laughing. I think that was the most beautiful sound I'd ever heard. Her laughing." A smile touched the man's face. "She looked so happy. I wanted to stop the car in the middle of the road and just listen. I drove by real slow and parked down at the church where we'd left her and carried the baby up toward where I'd seen her. There wasn't much traffic that day and Melanie stopped crying while I was walking with her. I stayed back in the shadows and watched Lorena while I tried to think about how I could tell her about her mother being gone."

"But you never told her that."

"No." The man looked out toward the car. "Not yet."

"What happened?"

Birdsong dropped his eyes back to the ground. "A man came down the road from the other direction. I stepped back behind some bushes. I don't know why. I just wasn't ready for anybody to see me. My little girl jumped out of the swing and ran to him. He lifted her up in his arms and he was smiling to beat the band." A tear slid out of the man's left eye and traced a path through the hard lines of his face. "And then she called him Daddy."

The man stopped talking and stared down at the concrete step. Jay waited for him to say more, but when he didn't, Jay asked, "So what did you do?"

"The right thing. I turned around and left her there." The man looked at Jay with eyes that had seen too many troubles. "It's what Iris would have told me to do. Let her keep swinging high. She'd found a new daddy. One who could feed her and make her laugh."

In spite of himself, Jay felt sorry for the man. "You never went back to Rosey Corner again?"

"Wasn't no use. I figured she'd forget all about me anyway. And that would be for the best."

"But she didn't. Every night she says her name. Lorena Birdsong."

"Her mother used to do that too before she died. She'd whisper Lorena's name like a prayer and then she'd cry. She wanted me to say it and the boy's name too, but I wouldn't. I couldn't. Just so much pain a man can bear."

"The boy. Birdie said she had a brother."

"Birdie?" The man frowned at Jay.

"A nickname I gave her," Jay explained. "But where's the boy? Is he here?"

"No." The man blew out a long breath. "We left him in Rosey Corner too. Buried him in the woods there after we left Lorena at the church." The man rubbed his hand across his eyes. "She did evermore love her big brother. It about broke my heart the way she cried when the boy wouldn't wake up to tell her goodbye. But the boy couldn't wake up. He'd gone on."

"You didn't tell her?"

"No need heaping sadness on the little thing. She was barely five years old."

They were silent for a minute, both of them thinking about things that couldn't be changed. Finally Jay looked out at the car where Birdie was waiting and then back at her father who was sitting like stone. "Are you ready to see her?"

"I never thought about her coming to find me." The man raised his head and stared toward the car. "I've never been afraid of much, but I got to admit I'm scared now."

"Of what?" Jay asked.

"What if she hates me?" His voice was low. "She's got every right."

"True, but she won't. Not Birdie." Jay got to his feet and motioned for Kate and Birdie to get out. He wondered if he should go tell them the man's story first, but then it wasn't his story to tell.

The man stood up beside him, straight and stiff. His hands trembled as he waited for Birdie to get out of the car.

35

It was hard to stay in the car while Jay talked to the man. She wanted to know what was being said, but at the same time, she had to stay with Lorena, who was so nervous she slid practically down into the floorboard.

"I can't look." Lorena hid her eyes. "Tell me what's happening."

"They're just talking."

"Does he look mad?" Lorena kept her hands over her eyes.

Kate peered out at the man as he sank down on the porch steps. She couldn't see his face well. She was about to say that nothing about his posture suggested anger, when suddenly he was on his feet glaring at Jay. But then he sank back down on the step. "No. More sad."

"That we've found him?" Lorena peeked through her fingers.

"I don't know, Lorena. We'll have to wait until Jay tells us to get out. Then we might find out the answers. If he's your father."

At last Jay motioned to them to get out. Kate held Lorena's hand as they walked toward the man whose eyes fastened on

Lorena the moment she got out of the car as though drinking in the sight of her.

Lorena stopped a few feet away from the man. "Are you my father?"

The man shifted on his feet, but he didn't step toward Lorena. They were like two boxers sizing each other up before they tried to land any blows. Kate whispered a prayer that there wouldn't be blows, only gentle words, but words could pack a punch at times too.

"I am." His voice quavered a little and he cleared his throat. "You've grown up pretty, Lorena."

"I'm too skinny, and my hair always looks like some kind of bramble bush." Lorena pushed her hair back from her face.

"You got hair like mine." A smile touched the man's lips. "I just keep my curls all whacked off, but your mama did love your hair. She was forever fussing with it. Tying ribbons in it. She thought it was beautiful. She thought you were beautiful."

"Where is she?" Lorena stared straight at the man's face, needing this answer most of all.

"She died, Lorena." The man spoke the necessary words straight out, but Kate could see the truth of them still hurt him. Being married again and years gone by hadn't changed that. "After the baby came, she never got her strength back."

Kate slipped her arm around Lorena, who seemed to have to push out the next question. "And the baby?"

"A girl." A ghost of a smile slid across the man's face. "Your mother named her Melanie. She looked like you."

"Did she die too?"

All trace of smile disappeared as the lines of the man's face deepened. He looked at Jay and then Kate as though for help before he settled his eyes back on Lorena's face. "No. I turned her over to the county and some agency found a couple to adopt her. I don't know who. They wouldn't tell me." He looked up and away from Lorena then. "She was just sitting up, trying to crawl a little."

"Why'd you give her away?" Lorena stiffened, hardly seeming to notice Kate's arm around her. She was asking about more than the baby.

"She was hungry, and I didn't even have enough money to buy her a banana. I had to get a job, but what then? I couldn't leave a baby in the car while I worked and that's all I had. My old car. A car's no place for a baby. You can understand that, can't you?"

When Lorena looked at him without answering, he went on. "That's why we left you there at that church too. So you could have a better place."

"But what about Kenton? You kept him." Lorena blinked to keep back the tears, but she wasn't completely successful. "Was it because he was a boy?"

The question seemed to stagger the man and he grabbed the porch post beside him. Grief deepened every line in his face as he swallowed hard before he answered. "I guess we should have told you. You remember how you couldn't wake Kenton up that morning?"

Lorena nodded, tears streaming down her cheeks. Kate tightened her arm around her.

"Kenton died in his sleep the night before we left you at the church. That's why we left you there. Hoping you would find somebody to take care of you. Keep you from maybe dying like he did. Your mother loved you so much. I loved you so much. Can you believe that?" He peered over at her.

"I want to," Lorena whispered through her tears. "I've always wanted to."

"We parked the car down the road and I walked back to watch from some trees on the other side of the church. I saw the girl get you. I saw her pick you up and carry you away. Like you were some kind of treasure." The man's eyes flicked over to Kate. "That was you, wasn't it?"

Kate could barely speak past the lump in her throat. "The Lord had me take that raspberry jam to Grandfather Reece at just the right time. I'll always believe that."

"I stole the jam you left there. To give Iris, but it was days before she would eat it."

Jay handed Lorena his handkerchief to mop up her tears. Then he stepped over behind them to put his arms around both her and Kate. That seemed to help Lorena pull herself together. "But what about Kenton? You didn't leave him where the rats could get him, did you?"

"You were always afraid of the rats." The man smiled sadly. "But no, we'd have never done that. We gave him a proper burial. We turned on an old road up to a barn. Found a digger and a shovel there, like it had been left for me. Took me the rest of the day, but at nightfall we laid Kenton to rest. Your mama read from her Bible. We picked daisies to put on his grave and your mama looked around in the woods until she found four good-sized rocks to lay on the grave. One for each of us and the baby she was carrying. Then I carved his name in the bark of the nearest tree."

In the silence that fell over them, a bird singing in the yard next door sounded almost too loud. A few cars passed by on the street and still they didn't say anything. It was as if they were there at the boy's grave even now, grieving over him along with his father.

At last the man said, "Maybe we were wrong, but we did what we thought we had to do. For you. Can you forgive us? Forgive me?"

Out of the corner of her eye, Kate caught the movement of the curtain in the front window. The man's wife peeked out through the window screen. She jerked back out of sight when Lorena moved away from Jay and Kate to go to her father. He held out his arms to her and she stepped into them.

Kate's heart lurched inside her chest. She wanted to pull her back. Back to Rosey Corner. Jay must have known what she was thinking, because he held her close against him and whispered in her ear. "She will always be our sister. Nothing can change that."

"I know," Kate said softly. And she did know, but she also knew she wanted her sister in Rosey Corner, not Cincinnati.

She shut her eyes and remembered catching a butterfly when she was a little girl. Her father had warned her not to hold it too tightly. "But it will get away," Kate had said.

"That's what you want. Part of the beauty of the butterfly is in the flutter of its wings. You don't want to steal that from it. Open your hand and let it be free." He had held his hand out flat.

Reluctantly she had done what he said. For a few seconds, the butterfly had stayed on her palm, its wings still. But then it had lifted up into the air as light as a downy feather. Free to follow the wind.

Now she slowly opened up her hands. As much as she wanted to clutch Lorena to her, she had to let her choose her own way.

When Lorena pulled back from the man, he said, "You can stay with us." He nodded toward the window his wife had been peeking out. "She'll be glad for the company. But whether she is or not, my home is your home if you want it to be."

Kate held her breath waiting for Lorena to answer, but she kept her hands open. Jay tightened his arms even more around her.

Lorena didn't look back at them. She kept her eyes on her father's face. "I have a home."

Kate let out her breath and relaxed in Jay's embrace.

"I'm glad," Lorena's father was saying. "Your mama prayed for you every night. She never laid her head down on the pillow without saying your name and asking the Lord to send angels to watch over you."

"And now she's up there with those angels." Lorena looked up.

Kate did too, at a sky that was suddenly bluer than it had been a moment before. She sent up a thankful prayer as Lorena asked, "Do you have a picture of her?"

He pulled his wallet from his back pocket and took a picture out to hand Lorena.

She studied it a long moment and then closed her eyes. "I can see her now."

When she started to hand the picture back, her father waved her hand away. "Keep it. I've got her picture up here." He touched his forehead.

But he wasn't as much help when Lorena asked him exactly where her brother was buried.

"I came back there once. After your mother died."

"Why didn't you tell me?" Lorena asked.

"You had a new daddy by then and I didn't have two nickels to rub together. It was best to leave you where you were happy and all. You were happy, weren't you?"

"I was. I am."

"That's what I thought." He touched her hand. "So I left. I tried to find Kenton's grave before I headed out, but the woods didn't look the same. I couldn't even find the barn or the lane through the field up to it. If I hadn't seen her pushing you in that swing." The man nodded toward Kate. "If I hadn't seen that, I would have thought I wasn't in the right place. So maybe it can be enough for both of us to know it was a peaceful spot. He's not there anyway. He's up in heaven with your mama."

They left him standing on the walk in front of his house after Lorena told him to come see her in Rosey Corner. Before they went around the corner and lost sight of the house, the man's wife stepped out on the porch behind him. Kate wondered what he would tell her about Lorena or if he'd ever come to Rosey Corner.

They were leaving Cincinnati when, almost as if she were talking to herself, Lorena said, "He was glad to see me."

"Yes, yes, he was," Jay said. "He loves you."

She was quiet again for a minute. "It's okay to love two daddies, isn't it?"

"Absolutely," Kate said. "There's no limit on love."

Jay reached across the seat and took Kate's hand. Then Lorena was scooting up to lean her arms on the back of the front seat. "Do you think Fern saw them?"

"You mean saw your parents when they left you at the church?" Kate asked.

"No, later. When they were in the woods. Fern always

knows everything that happens in the woods. Remember, she knew about the fire that night before we did."

"She could smell the smoke," Kate said.

"But she might have seen them."

"She might have," Kate agreed. Fern did know every inch of the woods. "But we can't be sure they were even in Lindell Woods. They might have driven a ways before they stopped, and that's why your father couldn't find the place when he came back. I can't think of what barn he could have been talking about."

"But Fern might remember a barn you don't."

"True, but surely if she saw a grave she would have told somebody," Kate said.

"Fern wouldn't."

"She's right, you know." Jay glanced over at Kate. "Fern wouldn't. Not unless you asked. Even then she might not tell you if she didn't want to."

"She'd tell me," Lorena said.

"Probably," Kate said.

"She would," Lorena insisted.

"Okay, but I don't want you to be disappointed if she doesn't know."

"I won't be. Sad, but not disappointed."

"Are you sad now?" Kate studied Lorena's face.

"Of course she is," Jay answered for her. "She lost her mother."

"You know about that, don't you, Tanner?" Lorena said. "But you were there when it happened to you. It's all sort of faraway for me. She still feels alive in my head the way she's been since she drove away that day. I can see her leaning out the car window waving at me. Her face had gotten fuzzy, but now I have her picture. So I can just keep her alive in my head like Tori does Sammy."

"Tori is beginning to let go," Kate said.

"Yeah. She told me she had this dream where Sammy told her goodbye and walked right across Graham's pond and up into heaven. She said he didn't look back. Not once. That he told her to keep the fish, before he walked out on the water. That was a funny thing to dream him saying, wasn't it?"

"Maybe he was telling her to let go and find a new person to love," Jay said.

"I hope she picks Clay. He's so nice," Lorena said.

"And it's obvious he loves Tori," Kate added.

"But does Tori love him?" Jay asked.

"Maybe the better question is, can she love him." Kate remembered Tori's tears the day she found her at Graham's pond. So much had happened since then, she hadn't thought about talking to Tori. Maybe she should.

"Uh-oh, I feel some matchmaking about to happen," Jay said.

"I think it's already been happening. Not by me, but Graham. He told Clay to go fishing over at his pond a couple of weeks ago when Tori was there."

"Then Tori doesn't have a chance." Jay laughed. "Just like you didn't have a chance after Graham decided I was the one for you."

"I'm glad, Tanner," Lorena said.

"I'm glad too." Kate leaned over and kissed first his cheek, then Lorena's. "And I'm glad you didn't want to stay in Cincinnati."

"I couldn't stay in Cincinnati." Lorena frowned and shook her head. "I've got to sing at church tomorrow." She put her chin down on her arms folded on the back of the seat. "Besides, we've got things we have to do."

"What things?" Kate gave her a puzzled look.

"Lots of things. We've got more flowers to plant. Then you've got to take me back to the radio station in a couple of weeks. But first we've got to do something about Fern."

"Fern?" Kate frowned a little. "I don't think Fern wants us to do anything about her."

"I don't mean try to change her or anything. But she's got to have a place to live. She says she can't stay in Aunt Hattie's house."

"She could if she wanted to. At least for a while," Kate said.

"She doesn't want to. She's been staying out in the woods, but she'll freeze when winter comes."

"Don't worry. Kate will think of something," Jay said.

"Me?" Kate hit her chest with her fingers.

"Sure. Aren't you the one always fixing things up in Rosey Corner?" He grinned over at her. "Our Rosey Corner angel."

"We've got a couch." Kate grinned at Jay.

Jay gave her a look. "Fern in our living room is not the greatest idea you've ever had."

"Fern wouldn't like that anyway," Lorena said. "We'll have to think of something else."

"How about we build her a house?" Jay said. "We do owe her."

"Do you know how to build a house, Tanner?"

"No, but I painted one once," Jay said.

"You two are crazy. How can we build a house?" Kate said.

"First, we get everybody in Rosey Corner to help." Lorena laughed. A good sound after all the tears.

Kate shook her head in mock despair at Lorena. But at the

same time her mind was racing, thinking about how it could be done. A little house on the edge of the woods. Maybe there was one they could move there piece by piece. Or they could fix up Aunt Hattie's old house where she'd lived before she moved into Grandfather Merritt's house. It was just over the hill from Lindell Woods. Aunt Hattie would like that.

It felt good to think about fixing something. And she did owe Fern.

Silence fell over them then as they headed home to Rosey Corner. A comfortable silence. A good silence. Lorena broke it by asking, "Did you really think I was a treasure?"

"Oh yes, the very best treasure I could have ever found on the church steps." Kate leaned her head over to touch Lorena's. "And that treasure's name is Lorena Birdsong."

36

Clay needed to be plowing the cornfields. The weeds were about to get ahead of him. Plus he had to work up the the garden patch so his mother could plant beans and some more sweet corn. He didn't have a day to give to working on a crazy old woman's house

When he told his mother that, she gave him a hard look. "A man needs to tithe his time the same as his money. Reverend Winston laid that out for us in his sermon Sunday. A good sermon. You should have been there to hear it."

"I guess I'm going to hear it now." Clay didn't quite hide his sigh and got another fierce frown from his mother as a result.

Clay hadn't gone to church Sunday, instead claiming an ox in the ditch. He'd been almost glad when one of the cows hadn't come up with the rest of the herd. He had to go make sure she wasn't having trouble calving. They couldn't afford to lose a cow. But hunting the cow could have waited until after church.

The truth was, he didn't have the courage to go to church. He wasn't afraid of hearing the gospel or the Lord speaking to him. What he was afraid of at church were the people. Two people in particular. Victoria and Paulette.

He hated that Paulette was so angry at him. He couldn't pretend to be in love with her to make that better, but he did like her. He hadn't wanted to hurt her. The day after Aunt Hattie's funeral, he went to her house to tell her that and explain why it was better if they didn't keep company anymore. She wouldn't talk to him. Her father came to the door and sent him on his way with a few choice words.

All the way home, Clay had wondered what he might have said or done differently to keep everybody from thinking he'd led Paulette on. First off, not be so stupid as to keep loving Victoria when loving her was hopeless. That might be what he should have been praying while he tramped through the dew-heavy fields looking for that cow. But instead he'd prayed the Lord would open a new door for him to talk to Victoria, to convince her that even if she couldn't love him, he could love her enough to make a happy life for her and her little girl.

Yet, he hadn't gone to church where that chance to talk to Victoria might happen. He hadn't seen her since the funeral. That day, he'd looked forward to seeing Victoria. Even if it was a funeral, he imagined her smiling at him, inviting him to at least be a friend again. He'd hoped she might decide to erase her words telling him to go away. Instead her eyes had landed on him when he walked in the church and skittered away like a sparrow startled by a hawk's shadow.

The idea that Victoria might actually be frightened of him had been worse, way worse, than the angry words Paulette had slung at him. Had he been so pushy at the pond that she was afraid to look at him? He remembered how she'd felt in his arms when he caught her to keep her from falling. For a moment, he'd felt her relax in his embrace. Perhaps he'd only dreamed that very brief moment, but real or imagined, he'd been dreaming about it ever since.

At the church, after she looked afraid of him, he hadn't tried to get close to her. It was better to keep his distance and simply let his eyes feast on her, loving her from afar as he had for so many years. She'd told him to leave her alone. He would do what she wanted, no matter how much it hurt.

Besides, his heart was too sore to take another pummeling if she were to refuse to speak to him. It was better to stay out on the farm where he could put seed in the ground and pray the Lord would send rain and sun to make the crop grow. Where he could find the cow and be thankful for the calf on its feet suckling its first meal. Where things kept going, day in and day out, to keep him busy. Not too busy to think, but too busy to dwell on his sorrows. Too busy to worry every livelong minute about wishing for a way to talk to Victoria again.

But his mother said they had to go help fix up Aunt Hattie's old house for Fern Lindell. She wouldn't listen to his reasons he couldn't go. She didn't think Victoria being there would be a problem for Clay. Quite the contrary. She thought it an opportunity for him. She didn't know about Victoria telling him to leave her alone. Even if she did, she wouldn't think it the obstacle that his heart felt it was. She'd say Victoria couldn't expect him to stay completely away from her. They lived in Rosey Corner. They had to see one another.

He had no doubt he'd see her at Aunt Hattie's old house. The Merritts were the only family in Rosey Corner who had much truck with Fern. Her brother, Graham, was practically an uncle to Victoria, even if he wasn't blood kin. Graham was a little different, but he was nice enough. He'd tried to help Clay out with Victoria. It wasn't Graham's fault the fishing thing went sour.

But Fern didn't care if anybody liked her. She appeared to enjoy keeping people on edge. While Clay had never been exactly afraid of the woman the way most of the kids back in school were, he did give her a wide berth. He couldn't see reason one to spend a day fixing up an old house for her that had probably been home to raccoons for years.

The Fern he saw at church, sitting stiff and straight in the pew beside Aunt Hattie without paying any mind to those around her, probably didn't even want these do-gooders to help her.

In no uncertain words, his mother let him know his thinking was all wrong when he told her that on Wednesday morning. "I would have never thought one of my own children would be so uncharitable." Her voice carried a heavy load of disappointment at his words. "What's come over you, Clay Weber? A person needs help here in Rose County, we give them help without toting up a tally sheet to see if they deserve it."

"Yes, ma'am," Clay said meekly. When his mother took that tone, he might as well gather up his tools and climb in the truck. Maybe the rain would hold off and the weeds wouldn't get too tall for his plow. And he would just have to find a way to stay away from Victoria.

The whole family piled into the truck except Aaron, who'd gotten a job with the Edgeville electric company for the summer. The girls and Joseph crawled in the bed of the truck. Clay made the girls sit on the wooden toolbox up next to the cab and told Joseph to make sure they stayed there while the truck was rolling. Willie cried to ride in the back too, but his mother made him sit in the cab with her. The boy pouted in the seat beside Clay, while their mother squeezed her feet in beside the basket holding a chocolate cake and ham sandwiches.

When they got there, the yard around the old house was already crawling with people. It was going to be a carnival. Men were sorting through lumber on a wagon up next to the house. Others were propping ladders up to the roof. Women were carrying brooms and mop buckets. The woman they were fixing the house for was nowhere in sight, but Clay spotted Victoria before he even turned off the key.

"There's Victoria." His mother looked over toward Clay before she opened the truck door. "Have you talked to her lately?"

"Not for a while." Clay kept his voice flat. He didn't know why he just didn't tell his mother Victoria didn't want him to talk to her. But then she'd want to know why and he wouldn't have anything to tell her. He didn't know why. Except that he was a country boy with nothing to offer her but love and a truck full of family obligations.

Tori saw Clay's truck as soon as it pulled off the road. Mary and Lillie waved at Samantha, who wanted to run to them. Tori held her back, even though she had the strange desire to do the same. Just run to Clay like a carefree child and tell him she was wrong. She didn't want him to go away. And how about they try fishing at Graham's pond again?

But she wasn't a carefree child. She was a widow who had desperately loved her husband. Who thought she'd be with him until she died. *But he died first.* The words whispered through her head. A forever marriage took two people. Two living people.

She'd dreamed about Sammy again. The same dream where Sammy told her goodbye and walked away across Graham's pond. When she woke up, moonlight was drifting in the window. She felt so very alone. But then Samantha stirred in her little trundle bed, and Tori reached down to lay her hand on the child's back. Her life.

In her sleep, the little girl shifted away from Tori's hand. She had turned three last Sunday. She was talking so much more, growing into her own person who was ready to explore the world on her own.

Now here in front of Aunt Hattie's old house, Samantha jerked her hand loose from Tori and ran toward Clay's little sisters, who were climbing over the tailgate of his truck. "Mary. Lil Lil."

"Stop, Samantha!" Tori chased after her. Cars and trucks were pulling into the field to park.

Clay grabbed up the little girl. "Whoa, kiddo."

She laughed and settled happily in Clay's arms, as happy to see him as she was his sisters. Tori stopped in her tracks. She wanted to change what she'd said at Graham's pond, but words deserted her.

Clay stopped too. There seemed to be a mile between them instead of only a few steps. Why did she feel so frozen?

"Hello, Victoria."

"Clay." Her throat felt tight. "Thank you." Even to her ears, her voice sounded stiff.

His face stiffened to match her voice. "Sure." He gave Samantha a hug and handed her off to Lillie, who was reaching for her. Without another look toward Tori, he turned back to his truck.

Mary was right behind Lillie. Almost in unison, they said, "We'll take care of her, Mrs. Harper. Please."

Samantha echoed them. "Pwease." Her freckles danced with eagerness.

"Okay. But you have to stay with Lillie and Mary here close to the house where I can see you. Do you understand, Samantha?"

"We won't let her get around the road. We promise." Lillie set Samantha down on the ground.

Tori watched them run off together and made herself not trail after them. She sighed. She wouldn't be much help fixing up Fern's place if all she did was follow Samantha around. Lillie was almost nine. Plenty old enough to watch Samantha.

She looked around. Cedars and brambles were pushing in on every side of the little house that backed up to the woods. Some of the men were already hacking at them, although it seemed a shame to clear away the blooming blackberry bushes. Fern wouldn't mind the brambles anyway. She liked wild. She'd probably even like that tree growing up through the porch, but no way would it survive the men's saws today.

They were like a swarm of bees on the property, finding places to fix. The house was in better shape than anyone had imagined. Jay and Kate had checked it out on Saturday after they came back from Cincinnati. They'd dropped Lorena off at the store to tell about finding her father. Her birth father.

"Kate says it's okay to love two daddies," Lorena had said at the end of her story.

The words echoed in Tori's head now. Two daddies. Would that be the way it was someday for Samantha? Loving her birth father through the stories they told her about Sammy. And loving another father. One who could swing her up in the air. One who could keep her safe and let her ride on his shoulders. Tori's eyes went to Clay, on his knees hammering new boards into the porch floor.

While she watched, he stood up to get more nails or a new board. Whatever the reason, he paused by a rosebush beside the porch that had survived years of neglect to keep bravely blooming.

Clay seemed to be admiring the rose as he ran his finger across the petals. Almost a caress. He must have felt her eyes on him because he looked up, straight toward her. A flush warmed her cheeks as she flashed her eyes away and back to the business at hand. She and some others were clearing off a wagon to spread out the lunch the women had brought.

She knew he was still watching her, but she didn't look back toward him. Instead she wished she could just walk into the woods and hide out like Fern. Nobody had seen Fern since early that morning. Lorena said Fern was happy they were fixing up the house for her and that she'd probably take up residence in it at least some of the time. That didn't mean she was going to stand around in the middle of a boatload of people.

At least Fern knew what she wanted. Or didn't want.

Tori looked toward the trees and wondered if Fern was watching from the shadows. Then she let her eyes go back to the house. Clay was hammering on the porch again. She didn't allow her eyes to dwell on him this time, but before the day was over, she'd find a way to tell him she was sorry about what she'd said at the pond. Then it would be up to him if he wanted to talk to her.

Her hands felt suddenly sweaty and her heart fluttered a little. It had never been like this with Sammy. They'd never had to wonder about whether they belonged together. They just did. But now she was wondering if she could belong with someone else. With Clay. She rubbed her hands down her skirt and looked around until she spotted Samantha rubbing Chaucer's head. Lillie and Mary were right beside her. Graham looked to be telling them a story.

It was so like Graham to stay on the fringes of the activity. He wasn't like Fern. He liked people, but he also stood just a little apart. Such a funny man. Never married, but he had played matchmaker with Kate and Jay. Now he was doing the same for Tori. It had worked for Kate.

Jay was putting new tin on the roof. Daddy watched from the ground, calling up instructions from time to time. Tori was relieved Daddy wasn't crawling around up there. Her mother had to keep the store open, but she'd charged Tori with making sure Daddy and Kate didn't overdo.

Tori smiled. She had plenty to do. Keep an eye on Samantha. Keep Daddy and Kate from working too hard. Find a way to tell Clay she wanted to take back her words telling him to go away. Wave the flies away from the pies and cakes she was setting out on the wagon.

By the middle of the afternoon, Samantha ran out of steam. Tori settled her down for a nap on a quilt under a tree. Mary and Lillie sat down beside her, making clover necklaces. The men had the roof fixed and glass back in the windows. Some people headed home to attend to their own chores. It wouldn't be long until Clay would have to gather up his family and go home to milk. Tori still hadn't found an opportunity to talk to him.

The women were inside now scrubbing every surface and painting. The men painted on the outside. The siding had never been painted, and the white planks looked almost out of place. A few people wondered aloud if they might be getting the place too fancy for Fern. Nobody could be sure, since Fern hadn't made an appearance. So they kept painting.

Every few minutes, Tori peered out the window at Samantha, asleep in the shade. She smiled when Mary stretched out beside her and went to sleep too.

She was up on a chair painting the narrow planks of the kitchen ceiling when Lillie burst through the door. "Mrs. Harper! She's gone, Mrs. Harper!"

Tori dropped her brush, spattering paint on the just scrubbed floor, and jumped down to run outside. Mary was still there on the quilt, sound asleep, but Samantha was gone.

37

"Samantha!"

The panic in Victoria's voice shot through Clay. He looked up from packing his tools back in the truck. At the edge of the clearing, Victoria screamed her little girl's name again. Beside her, Lillie was wringing her hands and weeping. On a quilt in the shade, Mary rubbed her eyes and wailed too.

Clay ran toward them, not sure what tragedy had struck. He just knew that no matter what Victoria had told him at the pond, he couldn't stay away from her now. Her father and sisters beat him to her. He was left to comfort his little sisters. That needed doing too, but he wanted to put his arms around Victoria and calm her panic by promising to fix whatever was wrong.

"I was supposed to watch Samantha, but she was asleep." Lillie could hardly choke out the words. "I had to go to the outhouse. I went fast, but when I got back, she was gone."

He pulled her close to his chest. "Shh, Lillie. We'll find her." He looked over at Victoria, who frantically searched the shadows under the trees with her eyes.

"But I already looked everywhere," Lillie said. "I didn't want to scare Mrs. Harper."

"How long did you look?" Clay asked.

"I don't know." Lillie sounded pitiful. "I ran everywhere."

The people clustered around them had grown quiet to listen. Even Victoria stopped screaming Samantha's name.

"She can't have gone far," Kate said.

"She can move faster than you think," Lorena spoke up.

"She must have gone into the woods," someone said.

All the color drained out of Victoria's face as she stared behind her toward the trees that covered acres and acres around the little house. Clay handed Lillie off to his mother and stepped closer to Victoria. He wanted to push his way through her family to put his arms around her, but he had no right to do that.

"Did somebody look in the rain barrels?" somebody else said.

Victoria looked faint.

"She's not in a rain barrel." Clay spoke the words firmly, the way he sometimes talked to little Willie to get his attention. He kept his eyes on Victoria. "Everybody calm down. We'll find her."

"Clay's right," Graham moved up beside him. "Don't matter how fast she can move, she's still just a little bit of a girl."

"You think Chaucer could track her?" Victoria looked at Graham with hope. "The quilt would have her scent."

"I'm sorry, Victoria. He ain't a bad dog, but he's no Poe." Graham shook his head sadly. "He don't do tracking, but don't you worry. We'll spread out and have this whole area covered in no time and find her for you."

Kate spoke up. "Let's be quiet to see if we can hear her. If she realizes she's lost, she might be crying."

Everybody went silent. Clay held his breath and shut his eyes, listening with every bit of his senses. A blue jay squawked nearby, while in the distance crows cawed. Way back on the main road a car went by. But he couldn't hear anybody crying except for Lillie and Mary, who were snuffling back their tears as quietly as they could.

Then the silence seemed to beg a prayer. He'd felt those times when he was alone out in the field, seeing the dirt turn over under his plow or when the sun pushed red up into the sky as he headed out to the barn. At times like that, a prayer would rise up in his heart. He never had a bit of trouble talking that prayer out loud then with the feeling the Lord was right beside him seeing the same things he was seeing. But he'd never prayed aloud in front of people. He wasn't a preacher. Or even Aunt Hattie, who everybody knew could pray down the Spirit. But he was in her yard and somebody needed to pray.

So he looked up at the sky the way he'd seen Aunt Hattie do and, without thinking about whether they were the best words or not, just opened his mouth and said what was on his heart. "Dear Lord, keep little Samantha safe and help us find her fast."

He paused before he said amen, and Lorena spoke up. "Until we find her, please send angels to watch over her."

Mr. Merritt finished off the prayer. "We beg of you, O Lord. Amen."

Amens echoed all around them. Then Graham and Mr. Merritt started organizing the searchers. Victoria stood in the middle of them, looking as lost as her little girl. Clay moved up beside her. "The Lord will answer Lorena's prayer and send angels to watch over Samantha until we find her. You have to believe."

"I prayed for Sammy. I believed then."

She sounded so sad Clay thought his heart might break. "This is different. Samantha's not in a war."

"Bad things happen everywhere."

Clay put his hands on her shoulders and stared into her eyes. "They do. But not this time. This time she's going to come running back to you and be very sorry she wandered away and you're going to hug her until she tries to squirm out of your arms. But you'll hug her one more time anyway."

She almost smiled. Then she looked at the woods behind her. "I've got to go look for her."

"No. You have to wait here so that whoever finds her can bring her straight to you."

"I can't just stand here and do nothing while my baby's lost in the woods."

"You won't be doing nothing. You'll call to her every few minutes. They say people who get lost walk in circles, so she might wander back close enough to hear you." He leaned down and brushed his lips across her forehead the way he might kiss away a hurt for Mary or Lillie. For just a second, she leaned against him. He wanted to put his arms around her, but it wasn't the right time. Instead he said, "And believe. Pray and believe." He looked around at Lorena hovering behind him. "Lorena will help you. She can keep praying down those angels."

"She summoned angels once," Victoria whispered the words.

He forced himself to lift his hands away from her shoulders and let Lorena take his place.

"Clay's right," Lorena said. "We'll pray hard and believe with every bit of us, the way Aunt Hattie always did."

When Clay turned away from Victoria, Graham was waiting for him.

"We split up in teams. The two of us are to look over that way." Graham pointed to the west. "No time to waste. The sun will be going down soon." He kept his voice low so Victoria wouldn't hear him. "It won't be easy to find the girl once dark falls."

Graham's dog barked a couple of times as it followed them into the trees.

"Do you know the woods around here well?" Clay asked.

"Not like Lindell Woods, but these trees hook up to them and I've hunted raccoons through here back when I had Poe. Those coons can take a man and his dog on a chase. Now, Fern, she probably knows these trees. She's traipsed through every woods in the county, I'm thinking, at one time or another."

"We need her helping hunt then."

Graham glanced around. "She's liable to show up. Might even have the girl with her. Or not. You never can tell about Fern."

They split apart to cover more ground. Every few minutes, Graham called Samantha's name and his dog barked. If Samantha was anywhere close, she had to hear that. Clay didn't call to her. Instead he stopped occasionally to listen. And every time he prayed too. Silently now so he could keep listening for crying or some rustle in the brush. Any noise that might mean Samantha was close by.

The last time he stopped, Graham and his dog sounded farther away, and Clay wondered if he should edge back toward them. But it seemed better to cover more ground. Light was fading under the trees. Briefly, he thought of his cows at home, but he couldn't worry about that now. Not until he heard the signal that the child was found. Somebody was to fire a shot in the air if that happened.

Not if. When. He told Victoria to believe. He had to believe too.

"Over here." The words were a whisper. A whisper he'd heard before. He stopped and listened. Nothing. Then Graham's dog barked. They'd gotten even farther apart, but the whispered words had come from the other direction. If there had actually been any whispered words. He shook his head. He was imagining things just like he did that day in Lindell Woods when he thought somebody told him to go back. Sometimes a man could want something so much his mind played tricks on him.

He moved on through the trees, but more warily now, putting his feet down slowly and listening each step. Just in case.

"Over here." The voice was louder this time. It sounded the same as that day in Lindell Woods, but this was definitely not his imagination. He moved toward the sound, not bothering to be quiet now, but moving as fast as the trees and brush allowed. If the Lord was beckoning him to the child, he was ready to listen.

But it wasn't the Lord. Without warning, Fern Lindell stepped out from behind a tree in front of him. Her purple print blouse contrasted oddly with the men's overalls she wore.

"'Bout time." A scowl stiffened her face. "The little girl is scared."

He frowned back at her. "If you found her, why didn't you bring her back?"

"Didn't want to scare her more. Kids think I'm the boogeyman. The little girl's mama did. I gave her the terrors."

"She's not afraid of you now."

"Maybe not. But she's afraid of plenty of things."

"What do you mean?" Clay asked.

Instead of answering, the woman narrowed her eyes on him. "Thought you wanted to find the girl."

"I do." The woman was strange, but she was right. "Where is she?"

The woman pointed. "You'll hear her. If you listen." She made a disgusted sound. "Sometimes you don't listen."

He did hear whimpers then. Pitiful, sorrowful whimpers. "Is she hurt?" he asked the woman as he pushed past her toward Samantha.

"Not bad. Tripped on some briars." She followed him. "She was wailing for a while, but I started singing to her till I heard you coming."

"You sing?" Clay couldn't hide his surprise at the idea of the woman behind him singing.

"Like a bird."

With her gravelly voice, he couldn't imagine her singing like any kind of bird except perhaps a crow, but it didn't matter how she sang. What mattered was getting Samantha back to her mother as fast as he could.

The little girl cried louder and pointed at the scratches on her legs when she saw Clay. "Hurt." Then she lifted her hands toward Clay.

"It's okay, baby. We'll fix those scratches." Clay scooped

her up and held her close. With his heart extra full, he looked up toward the treetops. "Thank you, Lord."

She cuddled against him with her head on his shoulder. Her sobs turned to sniffles. "I want Mommy."

"And she wants you." He wiped her face off with his shirt-tail.

"Better go." Fern stepped out of the trees behind them. "Dark comes fast in the trees."

Samantha peeked over at Fern and then hid her face against Clay's shirt. At least she didn't cry again. He headed back the way he'd come, but Fern stopped him.

"Not that way. Quicker this way."

"But what about Graham?"

"He won't get lost." Fern turned and started back through the trees. "Baby wants her mama."

Clay followed her. With the shadows deepening, Clay wasn't sure he could retrace his steps without getting lost. Graham might be the same. "Maybe I should holler at him."

"Worry, worry." She stopped and whistled like a hawk alerting the world it was on the hunt. "There. Now we'll see who gets there first."

It took Clay a minute to realize the odd sound rumbling out of her was a laugh. She took off so fast Clay almost tripped over some prickly vines in the rush to keep up.

Samantha actually giggled as she bounced against his shoulder. Kids could go from tears to happy in a minute's time. It wasn't until people piled on more years that they started hanging on to things, even things that hurt.

When they got close to the edge of the woods, Clay asked the woman, "That was you in the woods the day I went to the pond, wasn't it?"

Fern looked over her shoulder at him without slowing down. "You wouldn't listen. Girl was crying like the baby there." She nodded toward Samantha.

"What makes you think I could have made her stop?"

"Couldn't if you didn't try."

"I'll try now."

She stopped walking so suddenly Clay almost ran into her. She pointed ahead. "She's right over there. Waiting."

"For Samantha."

Her lips curled up a little. "And you." She moved off the faint path to let him pass.

"Aren't you coming?"

"Not waiting for me."

"The house is," Clay said.

"They put a bed in it?"

"I think so."

"Then I might sleep there."

"Everybody worked hard on it."

"That girl, the one who's not afraid of me, she did it." Her face softened for a moment, but then her frown came back. "You shouldn't have cut all the bushes out of the yard."

Clay almost laughed. "They'll grow back."

"Samantha," Victoria called. She sounded like she was losing hope.

Samantha's head jerked up off Clay's shoulder. "Mommy!"

Fern gave Clay's shoulder a shove. "Baby wants her mama."

With tears streaming down her cheeks, Victoria ran to meet them when they came out of the trees. She did just what Clay told her she would and grabbed Samantha away from him to hug her close. What he hadn't told her, what he wasn't expecting, was her stepping closer to him, needing his arms around them too. He didn't know how he knew that, but he did.

It was like Fern was whispering in his head. "Hold her." This time he listened.

38

Please, Tori. You have to come." Lorena caught a corner of the sheet Tori flipped across the bed and tucked it under the mattress. The sheets carried the fresh smell of May sunshine.

Tori did the same on her side. "Why? You don't need me to go walking with Fern."

A week had passed since Samantha got lost, and Tori had absolutely no desire to be in the woods. With Fern or anybody else. Even now, thinking about those long terrible minutes that seemed like hours before Clay came out of the trees with Samantha made Tori's throat so tight she could barely swallow.

Clay. He'd been so strong that day. Lending her his strength. Praying for them all. Finding Samantha. He said Fern found her, that Fern called to him in the woods to lead him to Samantha. But Clay carried her out. Clay brought her daughter back to her.

Tori held the pillowcase against her face to breathe in the outdoors. Clay smelled of the outdoors. Of sweat and soap too. A thrill went through her at the memory of his arms around her. A guilty little thrill. She kept her eyes away from

Sammy's picture on top of the bureau. Instead she handed the pillowcase to Lorena and watched her scoot it over the pillow.

Try as she might, Tori couldn't stop thinking about Clay. After services Sunday, he asked to come see her. He had to plow all week and wouldn't be able to get off the farm until Saturday unless it rained. It hadn't rained, but now it was Saturday afternoon. She was home from the store, and Samantha was at Mrs. Harper's. That made Tori's throat feel tight again.

Chores went faster without Samantha underfoot, but Tori missed her sitting on the pillows to turn making the beds into a game. Tori had wanted to say no when Mrs. Harper came by the store to see if Samantha could go home with her. Both her mother and Mrs. Harper settled their eyes on her, waiting for her answer. Her mother's eyes were troubled because of how Tori hadn't let Samantha out of her sight since she wandered off in the woods, and Mrs. Harper's hopeful because she loved Samantha so much. So she'd said yes.

Now Lorena wanted her to say yes to a walk. They hadn't finished the beds and they still needed to sweep the floors and dust. Tori sighed and plumped the pillows as the clock chimed two in the front room. She didn't have time to let Fern get her lost in the woods. Clay promised to be there around six. Only four hours from now. Her heart did a funny lurch at the thought of him stepping up on the porch, sitting with her in the swing, offering her his heart.

An argument had gone on inside Tori's head ever since Sunday. She should have said no. She couldn't do this. Not yet. But what could it hurt to talk to him? They were friends. But it wasn't a just-friends feeling that tickled awake inside her every time she thought about him. That's what scared her. She didn't know why, but it did.

Lorena smoothed the bedspread down until every wrinkle was gone. "This isn't just going walking. This is different."

"Different how?"

"She knows where Kenton's buried."

Tori reached across the bed to grasp Lorena's hand. "I'm sorry, Lorena. I've been so busy thinking about myself I haven't been listening to you."

"That's okay." Lorena gave the bedspread another tug with her free hand.

"No, it's not okay. I'm not being a very good sister." Tori pulled Lorena around to sit beside her on the bed. "I should have listened. But I can't imagine why Fern says I have to go with you. Kate and Jay maybe, but not me."

"I don't know why. But please, you have to come. She won't show me where it is unless you do."

"She would." Tori rubbed her hand up and down Lorena's back. "Fern would do anything for you. You're the only person in the world she cares anything about."

"She likes all of us. She just thinks you don't like her. She says you're afraid of her."

"I used to be. She was different before she started staying with Aunt Hattie." Tori shivered a little. "When I was a kid, I was terrified of her. I think she tried to scare us kids back then."

"Maybe, but not now. She helped Kate and then she watched Samantha when she got lost in the woods to make sure she didn't get hurt," Lorena said.

"She could have brought her back."

"Clay told you why she didn't. She thought Samantha would be scared like you used to be." Lorena leaned over in front of Tori. "Please, say you'll go."

Tori sighed. "I guess I do owe her."

"It's not for her. It's for me."

"All right. I'll go." It wasn't like Samantha would be with them. She could do this for Lorena.

"Thank you. Thank you." Lorena bounced up and grabbed Tori in a hug that almost knocked her off the bed. "I love you. You're the best sister ever."

"Better than Kate?" Tori laughed as she stood and smoothed down the bedspread again.

"It's okay to have more than one best sister." Lorena's smile wavered a bit. "I've got another sister too, you know. Her name was Melanie Birdsong, but now it's probably something different. Kate says that when people adopt a baby they usually pick a new name. I'm glad Mama and Daddy didn't want to change my name."

"You liked your name."

"I did." Lorena's smile completely disappeared then. "You remember what that Mrs. Baxter tried to name me, don't you? Pansy. Can you imagine me named Pansy?"

"No, no, I can't." Tori smiled and touched Lorena's cheek. "That was just wrong, but you're with us now. As long as you want to be."

"That's forever." Lorena's smile spread across her face. "But that doesn't mean I don't want to remember my first family. And know where Kenton is buried. I know he's not there now, but I still have to see it. I have to."

"Okay. When?"

"Now." Lorena made a face and hunched up her shoulders as she answered.

"Now?" Tori stared at her.

"Kate will be here any minute and Fern's waiting over in the woods." Lorena pushed the words out fast.

"I can't go now."

"Please," Lorena begged. "I know Clay's coming, but that's not for hours and you'll be back way before then."

"Sweaty with spiderwebs in my hair."

Lorena laughed. "Clay won't care. Kate says he loves you."

"Kate knows everything, huh." Tori turned away from Lorena to hide the color crawling up her neck.

"She does, but it's not much of a secret that Clay likes you." Lorena slid around in front of Tori to peer up in her face. "You like him too, don't you?"

"I've known him forever. Of course I like him." She hoped Lorena would let it drop, but that wasn't Lorena. She was too much like Kate. She had to know everything.

"Do you think you can love him?"

"I don't know." Tori looked up then, straight at Sammy's picture.

"Do you want to?" Lorena's eyes went to Sammy's picture too. "You said Sammy had been telling you goodbye in your dreams."

"But I can't tell him goodbye. That wouldn't be right."

"Liking Clay doesn't mean you've forgotten Sammy. I'll never forget Kenton and my mother. But see, I have this second family here now. You could have a second family with Clay."

"Let's not get carried away. He's coming to see me, not propose."

Lorena raised her eyebrows. "Are you sure?"

Tori gave her a little push. "Go put your shoes on. You can't go in the woods barefoot."

Fern barely nodded at them when they found her at the edge of the woods before she took off down a faint path. They made a funny procession with Fern leading the way in her overalls and a man's T-shirt she'd probably snatched off somebody's clothesline. Behind her, Lorena was practically walking on her toes with nervous excitement. Kate and Tori brought up the rear. Fern set a pace that had Tori breathing hard and Kate looking pale.

After they'd walked a ways, Tori put a hand on Kate's arm. "You need to rest a minute."

Kate leaned against a tree to catch her breath. "I hate feeling so weak. The doctor said it might take a couple of months to get my strength back."

"You shouldn't have come." Tori waved away a fly. "I shouldn't have come."

"We had to. For Lorena."

"Well, they can just go the rest of the way without us or wait."

Kate looked around. The color was coming back into her cheeks. "I've never been in this woods, have you? We left Lindell Woods when we climbed that fence a little ways back."

"I stick to walking to ponds with fish in them and I haven't seen the first pond. Just trees and bugs." Tori smacked at a mosquito.

Up ahead, Lorena stopped Fern, who glared at them, but then trailed Lorena back down the faint path.

"Fern says it's not much farther." Lorena motioned toward Fern, who had stopped and folded her arms across her chest. "She says you can rest when we get there."

"Kate's resting here." Tori looked straight at Fern. "This was too much for her."

"I'm all right, Tori," Kate insisted. "If we can keep up with Fern a little longer, we can take our time coming back."

"Not Tori." Lorena went on in a singsong voice. "She's got a date."

"Clay?" Kate smiled.

"It's not a date," Tori said. "He's just coming over to the house."

"To maybe propose." Lorena whirled around, her skirt flying out around her.

"He's not going to propose." Tori frowned at Lorena.

Kate pushed away from the tree and put her arm around Tori. "I'm glad, Tori."

"'Bout time," Fern muttered.

Tori didn't know whether Fern meant Clay coming to see her or Kate starting up the path again.

"He's not going to propose." But the more Tori said it, the more it didn't sound so bad.

"But he wants to," Lorena said.

Up ahead of them, Fern made an odd sound like a rusty gate hinge.

Tori looked over toward Kate. "Is she all right?"

Kate laughed. "Haven't you ever heard Fern laugh?"

Lorena looked back at them and laughed too.

Here they were, following the oddest woman in Rosey Corner, maybe in the state, through a strange woods to look for a grave. On top of that, they were talking about a man Tori had never dated once, proposing marriage to her. And they were laughing. Out loud. Even Fern.

"We're all crazy." A laugh bubbled up inside Tori. Sometimes it felt good to be a little crazy.

39

Kate leaned on Tori as she stared at the grave Fern finally pointed out to them. Bushes and brambles edged into the little clearing from the woods, but the grave was covered with soft grass and the four stones Lorena's father had put there. A good-sized tree grew up from the head of the grave. Fern planted that tree to mark the grave when she found it years ago.

"How did you know it was a grave?" Kate stared at the little plot that was as neat as any in the church graveyard.

Lorena knelt beside it and ran her hands over the rocks.

"Fresh-dug dirt. Not full-size, but child-sized. The rocks," Fern said. "Didn't take a genius."

"Why didn't you tell someone?" Tori asked. "The sheriff, maybe."

"Rosey Corner doesn't have a sheriff," Fern said.

"Rose County does," Tori insisted.

"Wouldn't have brought the child back to life. It was peaceful for him here." Fern gave Tori a hard look. "They'd have brought trucks and saws and shovels. Wouldn't nobody have had peace then."

Kate thought about Lorena's parents laying their son to rest here with such love, and she was glad Fern hadn't reported it. "So you took care of it all these years, not knowing whose grave it might be?"

"Found it after the girl came." Fern nodded toward Lorena. "We took care of her. You and me. Somebody needed to take care of him too."

"But you didn't know it was my brother." Lorena looked up at Fern. "Did you?"

"Not right away. Not till I found the tree."

"The one you planted?" Lorena asked.

"The other one." Fern nodded toward one of the bigger trees. "The one with his name."

Lorena stood up and went to the tree. Kate and Tori followed to peer around her at the letters and numbers carved in the trunk. *Kenton Birdsong. 1929–1936.*

"It must have taken my father awhile to carve this." Lorena spread her hand overtop the name. "He did love us."

Kate didn't say anything. What was there to say to the tragedy of losing one child to death and abandoning the other child even if it was for her own good? With the loss of her baby still so fresh, Kate could too easily imagine the grief Lorena's parents must have felt.

"Why didn't you tell me?" Lorena turned to Fern.

"Too many bad things happening already. Would have made you sad and Victor would have thought the trucks and shovels had to come." Fern looked from Lorena to the trees around them.

"Why did you tell me now then?" Lorena frowned a little.

"You asked," Fern said bluntly. "You never asked before."

"I couldn't ask what I didn't know."

"What you didn't know couldn't hurt you either. Didn't want you to hurt. Figured someday you'd find out and then you'd ask." Fern peered at Lorena with a worried look. "You mad?"

Lorena stepped across the space between them to hug the woman. "No, Fern. I'm glad you took care of Kenton's grave. Thank you."

"I have a question. Why did you want Tori and me to come? Why not just bring Lorena?"

"You always ask too many questions." Fern narrowed her eyes on Kate. "Always trying to explain everything. Hattie said everything can't be thought out. Some things just are."

"What things?" Kate asked.

"Always a question," Fern said.

"So how about an answer?" Kate couldn't keep from smiling when she heard herself asking another question. Fern surprised her by smiling back, at least as much as Fern ever smiled.

"Sisters help. When sad times happen. I never had a sister."

"You can be our sister too." Lorena grabbed Fern's hand.

"Too old." But she didn't pull her hand away from Lorena. "Maybe an aunt like Hattie."

"Aunt Fern," Lorena said.

Fern blinked her eyes shut and shuddered as if the sound of her name with aunt in front of it hurt her ears.

"How about Aunt Maia?" Kate said softly. Years ago, Fern had told her that her one true love had called her Maia.

"Once that might have been, but now Fern like the plant fits."

"Thank you, Fern, for bringing us here," Kate said.

"That one's not thanking me." Fern pointed at Tori. "She don't want to turn loose."

"Turn loose of what, Fern?" Tori asked.

"Sorrow. Like me. I held it too long. You hold it too long, you'll be an old woman fishing alone on a pond bank."

"I've got Samantha," Tori said.

"Samantha needs sisters." Fern looked from Tori to the grave. "Here's a good place to let go of sorrow."

"How?" Tori asked.

"Hattie would say to pray and turn them loose." Fern flung her hands out like she was flinging something away.

"You want me to pray?" Kate remembered another time Fern had asked her to pray.

"Let that one say the out-loud prayer." Fern nodded toward Tori as she grabbed Lorena's hand and reached toward Tori.

Fern's hand felt rough as sandpaper when Tori gingerly took hold of it. Kate held Tori's other hand and they stood in a circle, silent and waiting. Waiting for her to pray. But the Lord didn't listen to her prayers and it was surely wrong to pretend to pray just to please the ears around her. Then Clay's simple prayer before he'd gone into the woods to search for Samantha echoed in her head. Prayers had risen unbidden from her heart that day. Prayers the Lord answered when Clay carried Samantha out of the woods to her waiting arms.

"Dear Lord, thank you for those we loved but lost to heaven." Tori whispered. She'd bent her head to pray, but now she looked up at the blue sky peeping through the treetops and spoke in a louder voice. "And thank you for those we love who are still with us and those who love us."

When she paused to think of what to say next, Fern ended the prayer. "Amen."

It was enough. Yet, they stayed where they were, continuing to hold hands, as though waiting for something more to happen.

All at once, Lorena reached toward the sky, pulling Fern's and Kate's hands up with hers. "His name was Kenton Birdsong," she shouted.

They all lifted their hands then. A circle of love and prayer. After a moment of silence, Kate said, "His name was Marion Bo Tanner and I loved him."

"Her name was Hattie Johnson and she loved me," Fern said.

Lorena spoke up again. "Her name was Iris Birdsong and she knew my name."

Then it was Tori's turn. The others kept their eyes on the sky, but they were listening for her words next. She pulled those words straight out of her heart. "His name was Samuel Ray Harper and I will always love him."

Fern gave her hand a hard shake. "Let him go."

A tear slid out of Tori's eye and trickled down her cheek. Her voice shook a little as she added, "And I turn him loose."

Fern released her hand then, and Tori pulled her other hand free from Kate to hold them both open toward the sky. She shut her eyes and remembered her last sight of Sammy before he left on the train to go overseas. After he kissed her, he had studied her face as if memorizing every inch of it. She'd tried not to cry, but tears had traced paths down her cheeks.

"Don't cry. Be happy." He gently wiped away her tears with his fingertips. "I want to remember you happy."

That was what he would still want.

"That's that," Fern dropped her hands back to her sides. "Better head back. Be near dark before we get there. That man will be waiting for that one." She pointed at Tori. "'Bout time."

And this time Tori knew she was talking about her and Clay.

They followed Fern away from the grave, each wrapped in her own thoughts. None of them said much, as though they needed the silence. Tori wondered if the names were running through the others' heads the way they were hers. Sammy, Hattie, Kenton, Iris, and even a name for Kate's lost baby, Marion Bo. Tori embraced them all, feeling the sorrow of their loss but at the same time knowing the joy of the love they'd known for them.

Fern set a slower pace back through the woods. Now and again, she glanced back at Kate and slowed her steps even more. When they reached the old-growth trees, Fern stopped. "You won't get lost from here."

"Come eat supper with us." Lorena grabbed Fern's hand. "Mama won't mind."

"Can't." She pulled her hand away from Lorena. "Got to feed my cat."

"Cat? You got a cat?" Lorena sounded surprised.

They all stared at Fern, not sure they'd heard her right.

A corner of Fern's mouth turned up in an almost smile. "House needed a cat."

Then without waiting for them to say more, she headed on through the woods toward that house, picking up her pace now that she didn't have them to worry about.

"Bye, Fern," Lorena called after her.

Fern threw up a hand and called over her shoulder. "Best get on home. That man will be waiting. 'Bout time."

Tori watched her disappear into the trees. "Fern's full of surprises."

"Always," Kate agreed.

When they came out of the trees, Clay was waiting at the fence beside Jay. The two men swung over the fence to come across the field. Clay hung back a little, not as sure of his welcome as Jay.

"Are you okay?" Jay pulled Kate to him and then reached a hand toward Lorena too. "We were ready to call out the search party."

"No need. We were with Fern. She never gets lost in the woods." Kate told Jay, then smiled over at Tori. "I think that man is waiting for you."

Tori felt suddenly shy as she looked at Clay. "Hello, Clay. I'm sorry I wasn't here when you got here. That wasn't very polite of me. To tell you to come over and not be here." She sounded like a nervous teenager.

"You're here now." He stepped closer to her.

He didn't seem to know what to do with his hands, so she reached out and took them both in hers. Such strong hands. She stared straight into his surprised eyes and smiled without a bit of guilt rising inside her. Sammy wanted her to be happy.

"He's not worried about polite." Lorena giggled. "He wants to propose."

Clay's face flashed red.

"Birdie, you're embarrassing the man." Jay laughed.

"Well, he does, Tanner."

"Lorena!" Kate called her down, but she was smiling. "Maybe you'd better let him decide what he wants to do."

Jay put one arm around Kate and the other around Lorena to turn them toward the fence. "I think five's a crowd.

We'll just stroll on ahead of you two." He looked back over his shoulder at them. "Take your time. We'll leave the swing open for you on the porch. Great place for proposals, I'm told. Not where Kate proposed to me, but . . ."

Tori looked down at her feet, a blush rising in her cheeks to match Clay's. "I'm sorry, Clay. Pay no attention to them."

"They're right, you know." Clay pulled her hand up to kiss her knuckles. "I'd go down on one knee right here and now if I thought you wouldn't tell me to get lost."

"I won't tell you that ever again." She raised her eyes to his. Nice eyes. Eyes that had been begging her to notice him for months.

A smile flooded his face. "So should I propose now or wait until we're on the swing?"

"You can't propose to a woman you haven't kissed." Her cheeks burned redder. She let go of his hands and covered her face. "I can't believe I said that." How could she be so forward?

Clay gently pulled her hands away from her face. "I want to kiss you, Victoria. I want to marry you and love you forever. If you want me to."

"Maybe we should start with the kiss," she whispered.

He put his hands on her shoulders and stared into her eyes. "You are the most beautiful girl in the world, and I do love you, Victoria." He bent down to cover her lips with his.

She stepped into his embrace then, and knew at once she was home. *Your heart can hold many loves.* She didn't know where the words came from that whispered through her mind, but she did know she was finally ready to believe they were true.

It was so good to come home to love.

A Parting Note from Ann

Thank you so much for visiting Rosey Corner with me once again. The Merritt family came to life for me in my book *Angel Sister.* They lived on in my imagination after that story ended and kept prodding me to tell more of their stories. Love came to call on the Merritt sisters in *Small Town Girl*, and now love has come home in this story. I owe a debt of gratitude to my mother and her sisters for their wonderful stories about growing up in the small community of Alton, Kentucky. Those stories were the inspiration for my Rosey Corner books.

Once a story is written, many other people help it along its path to a book that you, the reader, can hold in your hands. So I thank all the wonderful people at Revell Books who make that happen. My editor, Lonnie Hull DuPont, is always ready with encouragement and advice on how to make my story better. Barb Barnes and the other copyeditors go over every line to make the reading easy. Cheryl Van Andel and her team design covers to fit my story and grab a reader's eye. It's been great to work with Lindsay Davis on so many details of my books. I can always count on her to be helpful and available. Many other people have a hand in getting an author's book out to readers. I don't know all their names, but I see and appreciate the result of their work.

I would be remiss not to thank my wonderful agent, Wendy Lawton, who is generous with her help and prayers. Wendy has often mentioned how she lifts me up in prayer as I help care for my mother, who has dementia. Writing this book was a struggle with the hours I've needed to spend with my mother. Wendy's prayers, the prayers of the people at Revell Books, and the prayers of my readers and friends have made such a difference in my life and often meant a more peaceful day for my mother. There's no way I can thank you all enough.

Nor can I thank the one who answers those prayers enough. Long ago the Lord heard a little girl's desire to be a writer, and he smiled down on that little girl. Over the years, he has given me words and let me share stories with you.

Last of all, I thank my husband, Darrell, and the rest of my family for their understanding and unfailing support.

I am blessed.

As an extra bonus here's a recipe for that brown sugar pie Jay loved so much:

Brown Sugar Pie

6 tablespoons	butter
6 teaspoons	all-purpose flour
1½ cups	brown sugar, packed
2 cups	milk
¼ teaspoon	salt
3 large	egg yolks, beaten (save whites for meringue)
1 teaspoon	vanilla extract
1	9″ pastry shell, baked

In a saucepan, melt the butter. Remove from heat; add flour and stir until smooth. Stir in brown sugar. Return to heat; stir in milk and salt until blended. Cook and stir over medium-high heat in a heavy pan or skillet until thickened and bubbly. Reduce heat; cook and stir 2 minutes longer. Remove from the heat. Stir about 2 tablespoons of the hot pie filling into the egg yolks and add mixture to the pie filling in the pan, stirring constantly. Bring to a gentle boil; cook and stir for 2 minutes longer. Remove from the heat. Gently stir in vanilla. Pour into pastry shell. Cover with meringue and bake (recipe below).

Meringue:

3	egg whites, room temperature
¼ teaspoon	cream of tartar
6 tablespoons	sugar

Beat egg whites with cream of tartar until soft peaks form. Gradually add sugar and continue to beat until stiff and glossy. Spread evenly over pie filling, sealing meringue to pie crust. Bake at 350 degrees for 10–12 minutes or until golden brown.

Ann H. Gabhart is the bestselling author of more than twenty novels for adults and young adults. *Angel Sister*, Ann's first Rosey Corner book, was a nominee for inspirational novel of 2011 by *RT Book Reviews* magazine. Her Shaker novel, *The Outsider*, was a Christian Book Awards finalist in the fiction category. She lives on a farm not far from where she was born in rural Kentucky. She and her husband are blessed with three children, three in-law children, and nine grandchildren. Ann loves reading books, watching her grandkids grow up, and walking with her dog, Oscar.

Ann enjoys connecting with readers on her Facebook page, www.facebook.com/anngabhart, where you can peek over her shoulder for her "Sunday mornings coming down" or walk along to see what she might spot on her walks or laugh with her on Friday smiles day. Then, come visit Ann at One Writer's Journal, www.annhgabhart.blogspot.com. You never know what might show up there. Find out more at www.annhgabhart.com.

Meet ANN H. GABHART at
WWW.ANNHGABHART.COM

Be the First to Learn about New Releases,
Read Her Blog, and Sign Up for Her Newsletter

CONNECT WITH ANN AT

 Ann H Gabhart

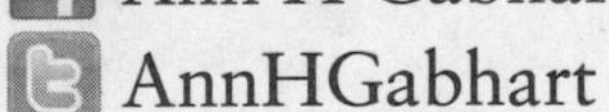 AnnHGabhart